Great Britain Foreign Office, Richard Bickerton P. Lyons

Papers Relating to the Blockade of the Ports of the

Confederate States

Great Britain Foreign Office, Richard Bickerton P. Lyons

Papers Relating to the Blockade of the Ports of the Confederate States

ISBN/EAN: 9783337382070

Printed in Europe, USA, Canada, Australia, Japan

Cover: Foto ©Andreas Hilbeck / pixelio.de

More available books at **www.hansebooks.com**

NORTH AMERICA.

No. 8.

PAPERS

RELATING TO

THE BLOCKADE OF THE PORTS

OF THE

CONFEDERATE STATES.

Presented to both Houses of Parliament by Command of Her Majesty.
1862.

LONDON:
PRINTED BY HARRISON AND SONS.

TABLE OF CONTENTS.

a 2

Papers relating to the Blockade of the Ports of the Confederate States.

No. 1.

Consul Lousada to Lord J. Russell.—(Received May 17.)

(Extract.)   *Boston, May 3*, 1861.

YESTERDAY I learnt from a high naval authority at Charleston Navy Yard that the blockading of the ports of Virginia will be effected on Monday next by a fleet between Cape Charles and Cape Henry, and that Commodore Stringham's general blockading force will consist of, at least, fifty vessels, accompanied by a sufficient number of steam-transports for the accommodation of a land force of 20,000 men. It is supposed that this will prove ample to make an efficient blockade of every inlet on the Southern coast into which a vessel drawing six feet of water might otherwise enter.

No. 2.

Consul Bunch to Lord J. Russell.—(Received June 3.)

(Extract.)   *Charleston, May 15*, 1861.

I HAVE the honour to inform your Lordship that this port and the adjacent coast were blockaded by the United States' steam-frigate "Niagara" on Saturday the 11th instant, in conformity with the Proclamation of the President of the United States dated the 19th of April last.

No vessels have been permitted to enter the port since Saturday. One British ship, however, the ———, succeeded in effecting an entrance without having been warned off, and will procure in consequence an excellent freight.

In connection with the case of this ship, and with other matters relating to the blockade, I take leave to refer your Lordship to the inclosed copy of a despatch of the 13th instant, and of its inclosures, which I addressed to Lord Lyons on that day.

There are five British and one Bremen vessels in port which will have taken their departure before the expiration of the fifteen days allowed to neutrals by the Government of the United States.

The people of this city are very indignant at the blockade. It puts them, however, to but little practical inconvenience, as the business season is entirely over. But its pressure will be greatly felt towards the autumn, when the importations for the winter are made, and the new crop of cotton is in the market. It is to be hoped that some favourable change may have occurred before that period. The detriment to British trade, both export and import, will be very considerable should the blockade be prolonged.

Inclosure 1 in No. 2.

Consul Bunch to Lord Lyons.

(Extract.)   *Charleston, May 13*, 1861.

I HAVE the honour to acquaint your Lordship that on the morning of Saturday, the 11th instant, a blockade of this port was instituted by the United States' steam-frigate "Niagara," Captain McKean, and it was currently reported that several vessels, both English and others, had been warned off by the Commander during that day.

This morning the British ship ——— came into the harbour and anchored off the city. Upon her master presenting himself at this office, I required of him an explanation of his reasons for breaking the blockade, when he informed me that he had received no warning or intimation from the blockading ship of the condition of affairs, and knew nothing whatever concerning it. I took his affidavit of the facts, and have the honour to transmit herewith to your Lordship a certified copy of it. The reasons given appear to me to be entirely satisfactory.

But as I was not aware of the view which might be entertained of his conduct by the Commander of the "Niagara," I deemed it advisable, in order to prevent subsequent complications, and the possible seizure of the ———— on her departure from the port, to visit the frigate and hear Captain McKean's version of the occurrence. I therefore hoisted the union jack on a steam-boat, and proceeded in search of the "Niagara," which I found at about fifteen miles from the city, and seven from the mouth of the harbour. I was received with the customary honours, and had a satisfactory interview with Captain McKean, who concurred in the correctness of the statement made by the master of the ————. He remarked that when the merchant-vessel anchored, the "Niagara" was engaged in supplying water to another British ship, and also that he thought the ———— seemed to be aground, for which reason he left her alone. I inquired whether the vessel would be allowed to come out with her cargo, to which he replied that she would.

I next asked Captain McKean if he would allow the masters of British vessels arriving off the port to come up to the city in their boats to receive orders from their consignee, which he declined to do; but stated that if unsealed letters were sent to him for them, they should be delivered if they contained nothing improper. I also secured his promise to supply British vessels with water and provisions should they stand in need of them.

Captain McKean informed me that he expected eight or ten vessels to arrive in a very few days as a blockading squadron, and added that the flag-officer was also expected. This was said in reply to a suggestion on my part that a single ship like the "Niagara" could hardly be considered as adequate to the blockade of so extended a coast as that between Charleston and Savannah.

I should add that Captain McKean allows twenty days for the departure of neutral vessels, counting from the evening of Friday the 10th instant.

Inclosure 2 in No. 2.

Deposition of ————.

Her Britannic Majesty's Consulate, North and South Carolina.

ON this day appeared before me ————, who, being by me duly sworn, did depose and say that he is the master of the British ship ————; that he sailed in and with the said ship from the port of Belfast, in Ireland, on the 1st day of April last, in ballast, and bound to this port of Charleston; that at the time of his so sailing he had no knowledge whatever of any blockade of this port being intended; that he arrived off the bar of Charleston at about 6 P.M. of Sunday the 12th instant; that he had seen about 4 P.M. a large steam-ship under the flag of the United States, but did not know whether she was a ship of war or not; that at about 6·30 P.M. he anchored in four fathoms water with Charleston lighthouse bearing west by south, distant about four miles; that he remained at anchor during the whole night, and at daylight hoisted a jack, the usual signal for a pilot; that at about 7 A.M. a pilot came on board, when he weighed anchor; that at 7·30 a steam-tug came to him, and brought him into port; that at no time and in no manner, either by signal, or gun, or visit was any intimation conveyed to him, the deponent, that the port of Charleston was blockaded, and that he had no knowledge whatever of the fact; that at the time of his so anchoring as aforesaid, and also when he again got under weigh, the large steam-ship previously alluded to was in sight.

(Signed)   ·————

Sworn at the British Consulate, Charleston, this 13th day of May, 1861.
    Before me,
    (Signed)   ROBERT BUNCH, *Consul.*

Inclosure 3 in No. 2.

Extract from the "Charleston Courier" of May 14, 1861.

SCENES OFF CHARLESTON BAR.—The British ship ———, which was reported in our last issue as having anchored near the outer buoy of North Channel, after having been chased by the "Niagara," escaped being boarded by the man-of-war on Sunday night, and was successfully towed into port yesterday morning. The officers of the "Niagara" supposed the ——— to have been ashore when she anchored, she was so close in, but in this supposition they were mistaken, and the ship has got into a port where she will make a most superior freight, say about 1¼d. for upland and 1½d. for sea island cotton.

The British ship ——— went to sea yesterday for Liverpool, and it was rumoured that she was boarded by a boat from the "Niagara" and her papers strictly examined; but the pilot who took her to sea informs us that he watched her closely after she got outside until she had almost disappeared, and that no such event took place. She was when last seen, going off finely, with all her canvas set. So far as we can ascertain, no outward-bound vessel has yet been stopped.

The "Niagara" was about ten miles south-east from the ship bar yesterday, and was there visited during the afternoon by Robert Bunch, Esq., Her Britannic Majesty's Consul at this port, who left the city about 2 P.M., in the steamer "Charleston," and proceeded on board the "Niagara," where he was received with the usual salute, and had every courtesy extended to him, and every matter in relation to the blockade satisfactorily explained. All neutral vessels now in this port would be allowed a reasonable time to depart, but nothing further would be allowed to come in. The ———, which got in yesterday, and whose manner of getting into port rather disturbed the nerves of some cotton-shippers, will be allowed to go unmolested. All open letters for masters of foreign vessels expected here will be received on board the "Niagara" and given to the parties when they come off the bar, but no sealed communications will be received. A fleet of eight or ten sail, with Commodore Stringham, is expected off here shortly, when the blockade will be rigidly enforced all along the coast. They expressed a willingness to have supplied the ——— with water, but the captain sailed off in such haste that it could not be done.

The commander of the "Niagara" was pained at the position he had to occupy in reference to the Seceded States, but he intended to carry out his orders. Mr. Bunch says the "Niagara" is a formidable-looking ship, has a noble crew of about 600 men, is loaded down with provisions and war materials, decks piled up with shot and guns of the most formidable size. The only Charleston ships ordered off have been those reported; say, the ———, ———, and ———. The ———, ———, &c., have not yet been seen. Several other British vessels have been ordered off, two of which it is said were bound to Savannah, but their names we did not learn. No vessels appeared off this harbour on Monday, so far as we could see or learn, and the "Niagara" had a quiet day, but she keeps steam on all the time and moves rapidly when under way.

No. 3.

Lord Lyons to Lord J. Russell.—(Received June 3.)

(Extract.) *Washington, May 20, 1861.*

MR. CONSUL BUNCH'S despatch of the 15th instant will have informed your Lordship that on the 11th instant the United States' steam-frigate "Niagara" appeared off the port of Charleston, and that the effective blockade of that port and the adjacent coast was declared to commence on that day. The inclosed copy of a despatch which I have received to-day from Mr. Bunch will show your Lordship that the "Niagara" disappeared from Charleston after the 15th instant.

By a telegram I learn that the effective blockade of Charleston had not been resumed this morning.

I am very apprehensive that the blockade is not being carried out with a due regard to the established principles of international law, or to the rights and interests of neutrals. No sufficiently public and official notice appears to be given of the precise date of the beginning of the effective blockade in each locality, or of the exact limits to which it extends. If the statement in the inclosed newspaper extract is correct, the terms of the warning given by the "Niagara" to a British vessel off Charleston were, "Ordered off the whole Southern Coast of the United States of America, it being blockaded." These terms are not only vague and indefinite, but plainly inaccurate: at the time the warning was given the greater part of the coast was not blockaded, and (so far as I know), up to the present moment, nothing like an effective blockade of the greater part of the Southern Coast exists.

Consul Bunch to Lord Lyons.

(Extract.)   *Charleston, May* 17, 1861.

I HAVE the honour to inform your Lordship that the United States' steam-ship "Niagara," by which the port of Charleston was blockaded on the 11th, 12th, 13th, 14th, and 15th instant, has entirely disappeared since the latter date, leaving free access to the harbour. In consequence, the ——, with pig-iron and coal, arrived here yesterday, whilst the ——, with, it is believed, another vessel, is now coming up to the city.

In addition to these arrivals, there have been several of coasting-steamers and other vessels, and one of an American brig from Cuba with molasses.

I beg leave to represent these facts to your Lordship. I would be permitted also to remark that the blockade is utterly ineffective.

Inclosure 2 in No. 3.

Newspaper Extract.

THE CHARLESTON BLOCKADE: BRITISH SHIPS TURNED AWAY.—The movements of the steam-ship "Niagara," the first vessel of the blockading fleet which has arrived off Charleston harbour, are thus noticed in the Charleston "Courier" of the 13th and 14th instant :—

"This steam-frigate, which it was reported some days since was coming off this port to blockade the harbour, was first noticed off here at an early hour on Saturday, by pilot-boat No. 4, then outside the bar, and also from the steeple of the Custom-house.

"The pilot-boat had observed in the offing on Friday evening what appeared to be a merchant-ship bound in, and which, not being in sight on Saturday, was no doubt ordered off. Towards mid-day the 'Niagara' disappeared, but returned off the port in the afternoon.

"On Saturday Captain Robert Lockwood, pilot in boat No. 2 (the 'W. Y. Leitch '), took to sea the schooner ———, soon after leaving which vessel outside, he made a square-rigger standing in for the bar. Being anxious to board, but not liking the 'Niagara,' then in sight, he concluded to send his large boat into port, and take to his skiff with a trusty hand.

"He reached the vessel about 7 P.M., and found her to be the British barque ——. The tide being too late to get her into port, he remained on board during Saturday night, his skiff being taken on deck and carefully placed away. On Sunday morning, it being calm, he was unable to get her under way, and about 8¼ A.M. she was boarded by a boat from the 'Niagara,' commanded by Lieutenant R. L. May, who informed the captain of the —— that the port was blockaded, the rebels inside having fired on Fort Sumter, with a garrison of less than 100 men; gave him a Yankee paper containing the latest news, and mentioned that an army of 100,000 men had landed in Louisiana. The captain of the —— informed the boarding officer that he was short of water, and requested a supply from the 'Niagara,' but he was informed that the frigate had less of that article than was necessary for her. The following is a copy of the indorsement of Lieutenant R. L. May on the papers of the —— :—

"'Boarded May 12th, and ordered off the whole Southern Coast of the United States of America, it being blockaded.

(Signed)   "R. L. MAY, *Lieutenant, U.S. steam-ship* "*Niagara.*"

"The officer remained by the —— for about twenty minutes, when he left. The boat's crew had a revolver each in a belt attached to the waist. Mr. Lockwood left the —— about 10 A.M., and reached the city in his skiff, accompanied by a valuable boat-hand, who remained faithful, although appearances indicated that the boy had only to open his mouth when he might have had a passage to some other place than 'Dixie's Land.'

"The —— went off during the day, and will proceed to the British provinces. The British ship ——, and the ship ——, from the same place, were seen off the bar yesterday, and were ordered off; and we understand that the 'Niagara' had previously sent off three other square-rigged vessels. During Sunday the 'Niagara' went well off-shore, accompanied by two of the above vessels, and while she was absent the British ship —— stood in from the eastward, when the 'Niagara' made after her; but the ship, having much the start, was run into shoal water, where the frigate could not well approach her, when the 'Niagara' put about and stood south. If the boats of the 'Niagara' fail to board her before this morning, she may get into port, with the aid of steam, in the morning. The race was anxiously watched from the wharves, and also by a party of gentlemen who were out in the pilot-boat ———. They went alongside and spoke the ship."

No. 4.

Lord Lyons to Lord J. Russell.—(Received June 4.)

(Extract.)   *Washington, May 23, 1861.*
WITH reference to my despatch of the 20th instant, I have the honour to inclose a copy of a note which I have felt it to be my duty to write to Mr. Seward relative to the cessation of the blockade at Charleston.

I understand that the cause of the departure of the blockading ship from Charleston was an order from Washington to proceed without delay to intercept, if possible, a vessel laden with arms from Belgium, which was believed to be on its way to another Southern port.

Inclosure in No. 4.

Lord Lyons to Mr. Seward.

Sir,   *Washington, May 22, 1861.*
I HAVE the honour to inform you that it appears from reports which I have received from Her Majesty's Consul at Charleston, that a blockade of that port was declared by the United States' ship "Niagara" to have commenced on the 11th instant; that the "Niagara" remained off Charleston until the 15th instant; but that subsequently she quitted the neighbourhood, and that no United States' vessel had appeared there up to the 20th instant, the date of the latest account which has reached me.

I take it for granted that if a blockade of the port of Charleston be again intended, due notice of the actual commencement thereof will be given, and that the period during which neutral vessels will be allowed to depart with their cargoes will be reckoned from the day of such actual commencement.

Trusting that you will favour me with an early acknowledgment of this note, I have, &c.
(Signed)   LYONS.

No. 5.

Lord Lyons to Lord J. Russell.—(Received June 4.)

(Extract.)   *Washington, May 23, 1861.*
I HAVE the honour to transmit to your Lordship copies of a despatch from Mr. Consul Bunch, and of its inclosure, a letter addressed to him by one of the principal British mercantile firms established at Charleston.

These gentlemen state their reasons for considering that indemnity is due from the United States' Government for losses sustained in consequence of the British ships ——— and ——— having been warned off by the United States' frigate "Niagara" during the short time that ship was off Charleston.

Inclosure 1 in No. 5.

Consul Bunch to Lord Lyons.

(Extract.)   *Charleston, May 18, 1861.*
I HAVE the honour to transmit herewith to your Lordship the copy of a letter which I have received from one of the largest English firms in this city, with reference to the warning off by the United States' steam-frigate "Niagara" on Saturday and Sunday last, of two British ships, the ——— and the ———, bound to this port and consigned to them.

Messrs. ——— consider that under the circumstances detailed in this letter these ships have been treated with injustice, and seek to establish a claim for indemnity with the United States.

I have to add that no blockading ship is in sight to-day. A large American ship is coming up the harbour.

Inclosure 2 in No. 5.

Messrs. ——— to Consul Bunch.

Sir,   *Charleston, May 16, 1861.*

AS the agents in this city of certain British subjects dwelling and doing business in Liverpool, we deem it our duty to submit to you, as the official Representative of Her Britannic Majesty, a statement of the proceedings of the commanding officer of the United States' steam-frigate "Niagara," blockade ship, against two British vessels, which have been seriously detrimental to the interests of the owners, and we would respectfully request that you communicate it to your Government should you consider our grounds of complaint sufficient to justify such a course.

We learn that your Government will only recognize a blockade of our ports when it is effective. To prove that the one instituted by the United States' Government against the Confederate States is not effective, and, therefore, not recognizable by Great Britain, we have only to state the fact that three vessels have entered this port since its investment by the blockading party, namely, the British barque ——— on 13th instant, and the British brig ——— and schooner ——— this morning, the former from Glasgow, the from Cardenas. Neither of these vessels was molested by the blockade fleet, and the two last-named saw nothing like a war-vessel off our bar.

Previous to the arrival of the ——— two British vessels, bound from Liverpool to this port and to our address, viz., the barque ——— in ballast, and the ship ——— with 4,000 sacks of salt on ship's account, arrived off our bar, and were boarded by an officer from the "Niagara," who ordered them off the Southern Coast, stating verbally and in writing that our whole coast was blockaded. With this statement of the officer we have nothing to do further than to characterize it as a palpable and deliberate falsehood, the fact being notorious that neither Savannah, Mobile, nor New Orleans was so invested.

The ——— which arrived without hindrance, has secured a full cargo of cotton on freight at the unprecedented rate of $1\frac{1}{4}d.$ per lb., whilst the ——— has a prospect of obtaining even higher rates, having been offered $2\frac{1}{2}d.$ for Sea Island cotton, which is fully equal to $2d.$ for upland.

We affirm that the ——— and the ——— had the same right to enter our port as the vessels alluded to, and had they been able to do so, would have done equally well in the way of homeward freight. The salt per ——— would likewise have realized a handsome profit. The vessels having been denied entrance into our port have been forced to proceed to British America, where they will at best procure an indifferent freight, and thus a serious loss has been sustained by their owners, for which, in our humble opinion, they should receive full indemnity.

We solemnly protest in the name of justice against this high-handed proceeding on the part of the United States' Government against a friendly and neutral Power, and have taken this method to bring it the notice of the British Government.

We remain, &c.

(Signed)   ——— & Co.

P.S. May 17th.—In further evidence of the inefficiency of the blockade of this port, we have to report the safe arrival this morning of the British ship ———.

No. 6.

Lord Lyons to Lord J. Russell.—(Received June 4.)

My Lord,   *Washington, May 23, 1861.*

I HAVE received a despatch from Mr. Magee, Acting Consul at Mobile, dated the 16th instant, informing me that the British barque ——— had arrived at that place from Grimsby, in ballast, on the previous day, having been warned off the harbour of Pensacola by United States' cruizers.

Mr. Magee states that the following indorsement was made on the register of the —— :—"Boarded by the United States' squadron, May 13, 1861, and warned not to enter the harbour of Pensacola."

It would appear, therefore, that on the 13th instant an effective blockade existed at Pensacola, and that up to the 16th instant there was no blockade of Mobile.

I have, &c
(Signed)   LYONS.

No. 7.

Lord Lyons to Lord J. Russell.—(Received June 10.)

My Lord,   *Washington, May 25, 1861.*

I HAVE the honour to inclose a notice published unofficially this morning in the "National Republican," a Washington newspaper, which is regarded as the organ of the Government.

The rule laid down by the notice appears to be a harsh one. It requires that vessels departing from blockading ports shall appear at the station of the blockading squadron within fifteen days from the notice of the date of the blockade given by the commander of the blockading force.

The distance between the ports at which merchant-vessels take in their cargoes and the stations of the blockading squadrons is in many cases very considerable. For the squadrons are naturally posted at the mouths of estuaries or rivers, in which position a small force suffices to blockade effectually all the ports above; nor do any pains appear to be taken by the blockading squadrons to give the notice of the commencement of the blockades in a formal official manner, or to make it public in the places affected by it.

The period of fifteen days is in itself but a short time to allow, and it would seem equitable to permit vessels which have cleared from the ports above within the fifteen days, a reasonable time to make the voyage down to the station of the blockading squadron.

I fear that some British vessels have been already seized, in consequence of the stringency with which the rule is applied, and that others may also suffer, in spite of any effort which I can make in their favour.

I have, &c.
(Signed)   LYONS.

Inclosure in No. 7.

Extract from the "National Republican" of May 25, 1861.

TO prevent misapprehension in regard to the blockade of the ports ordered by the Proclamation of the President, it is proper to make known that the fifteen days allowed for the departure of vessels from ports the blockade of which may have begun, will count from the date of notice of the blockade from the commander of the blockading force. If, therefore, a departing vessel shall appear at the station of the blockading force before the expiration of the fifteen days, she will be allowed to proceed to her destination ; otherwise, she will be warned to return, and will be captured if she again attempts to leave. Several captures having been made in Hampton Roads before the expiration of the fifteen days referred to, restitution in such cases has been ordered.

No. 8.

Consul Bunch to Lord J. Russell.—(Received June 11.)

(Extract.)   *Charleston, May 22, 1861.*

WITH reference to my despatch to your Lordship of the 15th instant, on the subject of the blockade of this port and coast which was instituted on the 11th instant by the United States' steam-ship " Niagara," I have the honour to state that the man-of-war in question has disappeared since Wednesday last, and that no other vessel has arrived to take her place. The port is consequently entirely open.

The British vessels —— and —— have come in without impediment, and have procured enormous freights. Other vessels are expected ; but we have every reason to suppose that the blockade will soon be resumed.

No. 9.

Mr. Murray to Her Majesty's Consuls in North America.

Sir, Foreign Office, June 13, 1861.

AS it is of the utmost importance that Her Majesty's Government should receive early and accurate information in regard to ports blockaded, and the manner in which blockades are maintained, Lord John Russell directs me to desire that you will forward to this office by every opportunity the most accurate information you can obtain as to the actual existence of any blockade, but more particularly of the port at which you reside, together with a statement of all facts bearing on the same, especially as to the date of its establishment and of its interruption, if it should be interrupted, and the cause of its being so, the date of its removal, and the manner in which it may be kept up.

You will send home in quadruplicate any public notices touching blockade or the enforcement of other belligerent rights in as authentic a shape as they can be procured.

I am, &c.
(Signed) JAMES MURRAY.

No. 10.

Lord J. Russell to Lord Lyons.

My Lord, Foreign Office, June 13, 1861.

AS it is of the utmost importance that Her Majesty's Government should receive accurate information in regard to the manner in which belligerent rights, and more especially that of blockade, are exercised by the respective parties in the civil war now prevailing in North America, I have directed a circular, of which I inclose a copy,* to be addressed to Her Majesty's Consuls, and the copies thereof intended for the Consuls in the Seceding States will be sent to your Lordship, to be forwarded as you may have opportunity.

I have at the same time to instruct your Lordship, as far as possible, to keep this office supplied in quadruplicate with copies of all authentic documents, in the form in which they are issued, and not merely in the shape of extracts from newspapers, which may emanate from the respective parties, such as the various Proclamations issued by Mr. Lincoln and Mr. Davis, the Confederate Act declaring war to exist, and so forth, together with all material State Papers having reference to the present state of things.

If there is any newspaper acknowledged as official, like the "London Gazette," you should transmit copies of it regularly to this office.

I am, &c.
(Signed) J. RUSSELL.

No. 11.

Lord Lyons to Lord J. Russell.—(Received June 13.)

My Lord, Washington, May 31, 1861.

THE following announcement appeared in the New York newspapers of yesterday :—

" Mr. Robert Mackie, Lloyd's agent at this port, received this morning the following telegraphic despatch from New Orleans :

" '*New Orleans, May 28, 1861.*

" ' Our port is blockaded. Report to London.'

" The information may be relied upon, coming from credible authority in New Orleans."

I am not in possession of any other information on the subject.

I have, &c.
(Signed) LYONS.

No. 12.

Lord Lyons to Lord J. Russell.—(Received June 17.)

(Extract.) *Washington, June 3, 1861.*

I HAVE the honour to inclose a copy of the answer which Mr. Seward has made to the note which I addressed to him on the 22nd May, respecting the discontinuance of the blockade of Charleston, and of which a copy was inclosed in my despatch to your Lordship of the 23rd ultimo.

Your Lordship will see that Mr. Seward holds that the withdrawal of the blockading vessel does not amount to a discontinuance of the blockade; and that the blockade will be continually in effect until notice of its relinquishment shall be given by Proclamation of the President of the United States.

Your Lordship will learn from Mr. Consul Bunch's despatch of the 28th ultimo that no ship had been present off Charleston to enforce the blockade from the 16th instant down to that date. I have no more recent intelligence.

Mr. Bunch informs your Lordship in the same despatch, that all the British vessels which were in the port when the effective blockade was set on foot, as well as those which arrived after it was discontinued, had sailed, and that no British vessel was in the harbour when he wrote.

Inclosure in No. 12.

Mr. Seward to Lord Lyons.

My Lord, *Department of State, Washington, May 27, 1861.*

I HAVE the honour to acknowledge the receipt of your Lordship's note of the 22nd instant. Having first submitted the same to the Secretary of the Navy for the purpose of obtaining information concerning the facts which it presents, I proceed to answer it.

The intention of the Government of the United States is to exclude all commerce, as well its own as that of foreign nations from the ports of certain States which are in an insurrectionary condition, with a view to suppress the insurrection and establish the authority of the Federal Government.

The equitable form of a blockade was adopted for that purpose: one notice of this purpose was given by the Proclamation of the President. The blockade as to the port of Charleston was carried into effect on the 11th day of this month, the United States' ship of war "Niagara" having taken her position there and enforced the blockade.

The blockade of the port of Charleston has been neither abandoned, relinquished, nor remitted, as the letter of Her Britannic Majesty's Consul would lead you to infer. We are informed that the "Niagara" was replaced by the steamer "Harriet Lane," but that, owing to some accident, the latter vessel failed to reach the station as ordered until a day or two after the "Niagara" had left.

I forbear from discussing the effect of the absence of the blockading force upon any vessel that might have entered or departed from the port of Charleston during that brief time. Your note does not submit any such case as having actually occurred.

I hasten, however, to express the dissent of this Government from the position which seems to be assumed in your note, that that temporary absence impairs the blockade and renders necessary a new notice of its existence. This Government holds that the blockade took effect at Charleston on the 11th day of this month, and that it will continually be in effect until notice of its relinquishment shall be given by Proclamation of the President of the United States. It is intended and expected that the blockade will be constantly and vigorously maintained. If any failure in that respect shall occur to the prejudice of any party or nation, its representations to that effect will be promptly considered.

I avail, &c.

(Signed) WILLIAM H. SEWARD.

No. 13.

Consul Bunch to Lord J. Russell.—(Received June 25.)

(Extract.) *Charleston, May 28, 1861.*

WITH reference to my despatch to your Lordship of the 22nd instant, in which I had the honour to inform you that the blockade of this port instituted by the United States' steam-ship "Niagara," on the 11th instant, had been raised by her disappearance on the 16th, I beg leave now to state that since that date she has neither

C

returned nor been replaced by any other vessel. The port, therefore, continues open to this day.

No British vessels, however, have arrived since the ———, already reported, and as all those in port when the blockade was instituted, as well as those which have arrived subsequently to its discontinuance, have now sailed, we are without a British vessel in Charleston.

No. 14.

Lord Lyons to Lord J. Russell.—(Received June 28.)

(Extract.)   *Washington, June 11, 1861.*

WITH reference to my despatches of the 23rd ultimo and of the 3rd instant, I have the honour to inclose copies of a further correspondence between Mr. Consul Bunch and me respecting the blockade of Charleston.

It appears from Mr. Bunch's despatches, that the blockade of that port was raised, in fact, by the departure of the United States' steam-ship "Niagara" on the 15th of May, and was resumed by the appearance on the 28th or 29th of the same month of the frigate "Minnesota."

Inclosure 1 in No. 14.

Lord Lyons to Consul Bunch.

Sir,   *Washington, May 28, 1861.*

ON the receipt of your despatch of the 17th instant, I addressed a note to the United States' Secretary of State, referring to the discontinuance of the blockade of the port of Charleston, and stating that I took it for granted that if a blockade of that port was again intended, due notice of the actual commencement thereof would be given, and that the period during which neutral vessels would be allowed to depart with their cargoes would be reckoned from the day of such actual commencement.

I inclose for your information, a copy of an answer which I received last evening from the Secretary of State.* You will see that the Government of the United States hold that the blockade took effect at Charleston on the 11th day of this month, and that it will continually be in effect untill notice of its relinquishment shall be given by Proclamation of the President of the United States. According to this doctrine, the time allowed for the departure of vessels from Charleston expired one or two days before the Secretary of State's answer reached me.

I have, &c.
(Signed)   LYONS.

Inclosure 2 in No. 14.

Consul Bunch to Lord Lyons.

(Extract.)   *Charleston, June 4, 1861.*

I HAVE the honour to report to your Lordship that the blockade of this port, which was raised by the departure of the United States' steam-ship "Niagara" on the 15th ultimo, was resumed by the appearance, on the 28th or 29th, of the frigate "Minnesota."

Inclosure 3 in No. 14.

Consul Bunch to Lord Lyons.

My Lord,   *Charleston, June 5, 1861.*

I HAVE the honour to acknowledge the receipt of your Lordship's despatch of the 28th ultimo, with which you are so good as to transmit to me a copy of a note addressed to your Lordship by the Secretary of State of the United States, under date of the 27th ultimo, with reference to the blockade of the port of Charleston.

It is not, of course, my province to discuss the views respecting blockades in general entertained by Mr. Seward; with these your Lordship may deal as you may deem expedient. But as regards the matters of fact connected with this blockade in particular, I venture to claim a right to be heard, especially as the Secretary of State implies that my report to

* Inclosure in No. 12.

your Lordship of its discontinuance by the departure of the "Niagara," and the absence of any other vessel in her place, is not warranted by the actual state of the case.

I beg leave to transmit to your Lordship a statement of the movements of shipping within this port between the dates of the departure of the "Niagara" and arrival of the "Minnesota," which has been furnished to me from the books of the Custom-house, and I appeal to it for my justification. If a blockade which suffers the arrival and egress of so many vessels is to be considered effective, and as "neither abandoned, relinquished, nor remitted," I have indeed been in grievous error, and have led your Lordship astray.

I will only add, that neither the "Harriet Lane" nor any other vessel of war has been seen or heard of in this vicinity up to this day. The "Niagara" and "Minnesota" have been, so far as we know, the only blockading ships. One, or perhaps two smaller vessels have shown themselves off the bar, but have gone away again after a very short stay, not exceeding, as I believe, six or eight hours.

I have, &c.
(Signed)   ROBERT BUNCH.

Inclosure 4 in No. 14.

List of Arrivals from Foreign Ports at Charleston.

MAY 13, 1861.—British ship ———.
May 17.—British brig ———.
May 17.—United States' schooner ———.
May 18.—British ship ———.
May 27.—Norwegian barque ———.
May 28.—British schooner ———.

These vessels all arrived after the blockade is stated to have been made effective, and have all gone out with cargoes excepting the Norwegian barque.

In addition to this, steamers and sailing vessels have been constantly, and are up to this date, arriving at and sailing from Charleston from and to ports in this State, as well as other Southern States, such as Georgetown, Darien, Jacksonville, Savannah, &c. Within the last two days five schooners have arrived here with cotton from a British ship, the ——— which has been wrecked on the coast between this and Savannah. The "Minnesota" is utterly unable to stop this owing to her draught of water, so that there is really at this moment no effective blockade of this port. Even two privateers are going out in a day or two in the very teeth of the flag-ship.

Charleston, June 5, 1861.
(Signed)   ROBERT BUNCH, *Her Britannic Majesty's Consul.*

No. 15.

Lord Lyons to Lord J. Russell.—(Received June 28.)

(Extract.)   *Washington, June 11, 1861.*
WITH reference to my despatch of the 31st ultimo, I have the honour to transmit to your Lordship a copy of a despatch from Mr. Consul Mure, from which it would appear that the commencement of a blockade of the mouth of the Mississippi was announced by Captain Poore, of the United States' steam-ship "Brooklyn," on the 27th ultimo.

Inclosure in No. 15.

Consul Mure to Lord Lyons.

My Lord,   *New Orleans, May 29, 1861.*
THOUGH I have received no official notice on the subject, I beg to inform your Lordship that it has been reported to me that the United States' ship "Brooklyn" arrived off the Balize for the purpose of enforcing the threatened blockade.

On the 27th instant Captain Poore sent out a number of boats strongly armed, with the object of boarding the vessels lying on the bar, and acquainting the masters with the terms of the blockade. The time allowed for vessels to leave is fourteen days. As the water is very low on the bar at Pass à l'Outre, it is doubtful whether all will be able to get to sea within the stipulated time.

C 2

I have not been informed whether any other vessels have arrived to assist the "Brooklyn" in maintaining the blockade, but it is said that there is a small steamer along with her.

It is singular that Captain Poore should have omitted to apprize the Consul here of his arrival at the Balize, especially as it is distant over 100 miles from the city. I have, however, considered it official by urging the masters of British vessels to get to sea within the stipulated time.

I have, &c.
(Signed)   WM. MURE.

No. 16.

Lord Lyons to Lord J. Russell.—(Received June 28.)

My Lord,   *Washington, June 11, 1861.*
I HAVE the honour to inclose a copy of a despatch from Mr. Acting Consul Fullarton, acquainting me that an effective blockade of Savannah was announced to have commenced on the 28th ultimo.

I have, &c.
(Signed)   LYONS.

Inclosure in No. 16.

Acting Consul Fullarton to Lord Lyons.

My Lord,   *Savannah, June 1, 1861.*
I HAVE the honour to report to your Lordship that the blockade of this port was commenced on the 28th ultimo, by the arrival off the bar of the United States' steamer "Union," of about 600 tons, and mounting five guns, one of a squadron of four men-of-war stationed off the coast for the purpose of blockading this port and Charleston.

I boarded the "Union" on the 29th, and ascertained from Captain Goldsboro, her Commander, that the effective blockade began on the 28th of May, and that his orders from his Government were to allow neutral vessels fifteen days from that date (or until the 12th of June), but not a day longer, to leave port, with or without cargoes, thus corresponding with the terms of your Lordship's despatch to me on the 11th of May. One British ship has since departed with a full cargo of cotton. She was boarded by an officer from the "Union," who endorsed her papers and allowed her to proceed without further hindrance.

I have, &c.
(Signed)   A. FULLARTON.

No. 17.

Lord Lyons to Lord J. Russell.—(Received June 28.)

My Lord,   *Washington, June 11, 1861.*
I HAVE the honour to inclose a copy of a despatch dated the 27th ultimo, from Mr. Acting Consul Magee, informing me that the port of Mobile was stated to be effectively blockaded by the United States' steamer "Powhatan."

I have also the honour to transmit to your Lordship copies of a further despatch from Mr. Magee, and its inclosure, from which it appears that the Commander of the blockading squadron had permitted the Mobile tow-boats to tow out British vessels.

Your Lordship will perceive that Mr. Magee states that the "Powhatan" had sailed to the eastward.

I have, &c.
(Signed)   LYONS.

Inclosure 1 in No. 17.

Acting Consul Magee to Lord Lyons.

My Lord,   *Mobile, May 29, 1861.*
CONFIRMING the tenor of my despatch to you of the 27th instant, I have the honour to inclose copy of a reply from Captain Porter, of the United States' steamer

" Powhatan," to my request as to permitting the tow-boats to tow to sea the British vessels here. All have gone to sea but two, and I learn all have sailed from Pensacola.

No official notice of blockade has yet been received here, and the " Powhatan " has sailed for the eastward.

I have, &c.

(Signed)   JAMES MAGEE.

Inclosure 2 in No. 17.

Acting Consul Magee to Lord Lyons.

(Extract.)   *Mobile, May* 27, 1861.

I BEG leave to inform your Lordship that the report here is, that this port is blockaded by the United States' steam-frigate " Powhatan," and that Colonel Hardee, in command of Fort Morgan at the entrance of this harbour, has been officially notified of the same.

As no official notice of this blockade has been received in town, I deem it well to send you the above.

All the British vessels in Pensacola, I learn, have timely gone to sea, and within this week the four now here, I expect, will follow.

I have sent a request to the officer in command of the United States' squadron off this port, desiring to know if he will allow the tow-boats to tow to sea the few British ships now here, and I presume he will offer no impediment as the blockade has not its final effect before 10th proximo.

Inclosure 3 in No. 17.

Captain Porter, U.S.N., to Acting Consul Magee.

Sir,   *" Powhatan," May* 28, 1861.

IN answer to your communication of May 27, 1861, I beg leave to inform you that British ships will be permitted to use tow-boats or any other means to get to sea, and that the tow-boats will not be molested by us in discharge of their duty, in so towing British ships.

I beg leave to add that the 28th is, I believe, the day fixed for rigid blockade, but as I am only here temporarily, and with special instructions, I will give the most liberal construction to the order : it would be better, if it could be done without injury to British interest, to get the ships to sea as soon as practicable.

Very respectfully, &c.

(Signed)   DAVID D. PORTER.

No. 18.

Lord Lyons to Lord J. Russell.—(Received June 28.)

(Extract.)   *Washington, June* 13, 1861.

THE "Hiawatha " was captured by the blockading squadron on the 20th ultimo, for an alleged violation of the blockade of Charleston, and sent as a prize to New York.

No. 19.

Lord Lyons to Lord J. Russell.—(Received June 28.)

My Lord,   *Washington, June* 13, 1861.

WITH reference to my despatch of the day before yesterday,* I have the honour to submit to your Lordship the following extract from a despatch, dated Savannah, 5th June, which I have received this evening from Mr. Acting Consul Fullarton :—

" I advised your Lordship on the 1st instant that the blockade of this port commenced on the 28th May. The war-steamer employed remained off the port until about the 1st June, when she left and has not yet been seen or heard of since, leaving the entrance entirely unobstructed."

I have, &c.

(Signed)   LYONS.

---

* No. 16.

No. 20.

Consul Bunch to Lord J. Russell.—(Received July 1.)

(Extract.)   *Charleston, June 7*, 1861.
I HAVE the honour to transmit herewith to your Lordship, for your information, the copy of a despatch, with its inclosure, which I addressed on the 4th instant to Lord Lyons.

Inclosure in No. 20.

Consul Bunch to Lord Lyons.

(Extract.)   *Charleston, June 4*, 1861.
I HAVE the honour to report to your Lordship that the blockade of this port, which was raised by the departure of the United States' steam-ship "Niagara," on the 15th ultimo, was resumed by the appearance on the 28th or 29th of the frigate "Minnesota."

No. 21.

Consul Mure to Lord J. Russell.—(Received July 4.)

(Extract.)   *New Orleans, June 6*, 1861.
I HAVE the honour to lay before your Lordship a statement of the proceedings which I have been obliged to adopt for the purpose of protecting the interests of British merchants and ships since the announcement that the threatened blockade was established at the passes of the Mississippi river.

No official notice had been given of the blockade; but as the report was current, and announced in the newspapers, that two vessels of war were off the passes, I immediately apprized the masters of the British vessels in port to lose no time in completing their cargoes, as I had been informed by Her Majesty's Minister at Washington that, after the blockade was established, the time for vessels to leave, with or without cargo, was limited to fifteen days.

In consequence of the low stage of the water on the bar nearly thirty vessels were at this time detained, being unable to get to sea. The greater number were bound for Liverpool, and the aggregate value of their cargoes could not be less than 1,000,000*l.* sterling. It therefore became a matter of great importance to know the course which the blockading squadron would pursue towards those vessels, some of whom had left port six weeks before the blockade.

On the 1st current, I was informed that the Tow-Boat Company had that day ordered all their tow-boats to withdraw from the bar, and return to the city, in consequence of apprehensions being entertained by them that their boats might be captured while engaged in tugging the vessels to sea. Although it appeared to me that their apprehensions were groundless, as the tow-boats ought to be considered in the light of neutrals, and identified with the vessels that employed them, yet the Directors refused to permit their boats to resume operations at the bar until they received the assurance from the foreign Consuls that no attack should be made on their boats while engaged in the service of transporting vessels to sea.

As no time was to be lost in endeavouring to remove this obstacle, it was resolved by myself and the Consuls of France and Spain to proceed at once to the Balize, and confer with the Commanders of the blockading vessels. Accordingly on the 2nd current we proceeded down the river in a boat, accompanied by the Consul for Bremen and one of the Managers of the Tow-Boat Company. We directed our course to the Pass à l'Outre, where the United States' steam-ship "Brooklyn" was at anchor, blockading that pass. Having exhibited the flags of our respective nations, we were immediately received on board, with the usual formalities. We had a long conversation with Captain Poore, who expressed a desire to take as liberal a view of his instructions as he could, consistently with the duty entrusted to him. He recommended us to visit the United States' steam-ship "Powhatan," stationed at the south-west pass, about twenty-eight miles distant. We arrived there late in the afternoon of the 3rd, and were received very courteously by Captain Porter, the Commander of the "Powhatan."

In order not to trespass on your Lordship's time, I shall merely give a résumé of the points discussed connected with the blockade, and the result of our conversation:—

1. The day on which the blockade was established had been officially announced by Captain Poore, of the "Brooklyn," on the 26th of May, in a letter to Major Duncan, commanding one of the forts near the mouth of the Mississippi river. Major Duncan omitted to communicate this intelligence publicly. The time when vessels could leave was therefore limited to the 10th of June. I urged that this date should be considered as applicable to vessels clearing from the port, and that some time should be allowed for them to be towed down the river and over the bar. To this suggestion both captains gave their consent, and designated the 14th current as the final day.

2. Regarding the immunity of tow-boats from molestation while engaged in taking vessels to sea, both captains assented to my view that they were to be regarded in the light of the sails of the vessel, or as pilots; in fact, to be treated as neutrals. The Commanders stated, however, that they were well aware that some of the old tow-boats carried guns, and had become privateers, and that to them no privileges could be accorded. In order to prevent any misunderstanding upon this point, I handed them a list of the names of the boats employed by the Association.

3. The next and last point discussed was the position of those vessels which had been detained for several weeks by the low state of water on the bar. The Commanders of the blockading vessels stated that their instructions from the Secretary of the United States' Navy did not allow them discretion to extend the time, but, under the peculiar circumstances of the case, they would take the responsibility, and give some latitude to those vessels, provided efforts were made to get them off, and no partiality was shown by the Tow-Boat Company in taking over certain vessels owned in the South.

I have thus given to your Lordship an abstract of the conversation we had with the Commanders of the blockading vessels, who readily assented to our requests. Before we left the bar to return to the city, we had the satisfaction of knowing that all the tow-boats were ordered to resume operations. Since our arrival I have been informed that twelve vessels have been towed to sea, and I hope that very few will be detained at the bar on the 14th current. I deemed it my duty to visit the squadron, in order to prevent, as far as possible, a large amount of property belonging to British subjects from being locked up for an indefinite period, and I feel assured that your Lordship will approve of the steps which I adopted to accomplish this end.

No. 22.

Lord Wodehouse to Consul Mure.

Sir,   *Foreign Office, July 6, 1861.*

I AM directed by Lord John Russell to express to you his Lordship's approval of the proceeding adopted by you, as reported in your despatch of the 6th ultimo, for the purpose of protecting the interests of British merchants and ships since the establishment of a blockade at the passes of the Mississippi river.

I am, &c.
(Signed)   WODEHOUSE.

No. 23.

Consul Mure to Lord J. Russell.—(Received July 8.)

My Lord,   *New Orleans, June 18, 1861.*

IN reference to the despatch which I had the honour to transmit to your Lordship on the 6th instant regarding the blockade of this port at the passes of the Mississippi river by United States' vessels of war, and the course which I adopted to facilitate the departure of the outward-bound vessels, I have now the satisfaction of reporting to your Lordship that all the British vessels, and others bound for ports in the United Kingdom, have been towed over the bar, and safely gone to sea. There are only two vessels at the bar, one bound for ——— and the other for ———, and these are so deeply laden that they will be obliged to return to the city, and be discharged.

The blockade is rigidly enforced, several vessels from foreign ports having been ordered off. Business of all kinds, except a few retail sales, is at an end. The stock of cotton is reduced to 7,000 bales, being smaller than it has been at any time during the last twenty years. Almost all the British merchants here have closed their offices and have left the city.

I have, &c.
(Signed)   WM. MURE.

No. 24.

Consul Molyneux to Lord J. Russell.—(Received July 9.)

(Extract.) London, June 27, 1861.

I INCLOSE a slip from a Savannah newspaper, giving an account of the visit of the Russian Consul and the Acting British Consul to the United States' steamer "Union," off the bar of the Savannah river. It appears that the United States' steamer, not observing that the small steamer "Resolute," on board of which were the Consuls, bore a flag of truce, fired two shots, for which breach of etiquette Captain Goldsboro subsequently apologized.

Your Lordship will perceive that the blockade of the port of Savannah commenced on the 28th of May, but that fifteen days from that date would be allowed for neutral vessels to depart.

Inclosure in No. 24.

Extract from the " Savannah Republican " of May 30, 1861

BLOCKADE OF SAVANNAH.—It having been reported that a Federal blockading-squadron was off our bar, the Russian Consul and the British Acting-Consul, for this port, chartered the steamer "Resolute" yesterday, and went down to inquire into the exact status of affairs. One vessel, the " Union," was observed at anchor off the bar, and as they approached her, when about a mile off, she fired two shots in their direction, both of which fell short. The "Resolute" had the British flag flying at her masthead, and a small white flag at her stern, which appear not to have been discovered, as she was heading directly for the "Union." She tacked so as to display her colours, when the firing immediately ceased.

Upon reaching the "Union," which is a small propeller of some 600 tons, armed with four 8-inch Columbiads and one 6-pounder cannon, with about 100 men aboard under command of Captain Goldsboro, the Consuls were invited aboard and handsome apologies were offered for having ignorantly fired on a neutral flag.

Upon inquiry as to the purpose of the "Union," the Consuls were informed that the blockade of Charleston and the Savannah, and the intermediate coast, commenced on Tuesday, the 28th instant; that neutral vessels would be allowed fifteen days from that date to leave the port; and that vessels of no nation would be allowed to enter hereafter, nor Confederate vessels to depart. The blockading squadron, he stated, consisted of the "Minnesota," the "Wabash," the "Union," and a fourth, the name of which was not recollected.

The party were treated with every consideration while on board by Captain Goldsboro, who, by the way, is a Marylander, as well as by the other officers of the crew.

As the Consuls were returning to the city they were approached by parties in a boat from the camp on Tybee, who informed them that on Tuesday night a row-boat containing officers and marines came in from sea, and when a short distance from the shore fired on the sentinels. The latter returned the compliment with interest, when the boat immediately tacked about and retired; their object, doubtless, was to discover whether or not the island was guarded, a fact of which they were informed to their entire satisfaction. It would be well to keep a sharp look-out for these fellows, for there is no telling how many troops the "Minnesota" has on board, and what they will attempt to do when they get here.

We omitted to state above that the "Union" is the only vessel of the blockading-squadron now in sight.

No. 25.

Consul Bunch to Lord J. Russell.—(Received July 11.)

(Extract.) Charleston, June 12, 1861.

I THINK that it may not be inexpedient that your Lordship should be informed of the real nature of the blockade and the manner in which it has been conducted. I am the more anxious that this should be the case in consequence of the ground which has been assumed by the Secretary of State of the United States in his correspondence with Lord Lyons, viz., that the blockade of Charleston has been " neither abandoned, relinquished, nor remitted" since the first appearance of the United States' ship "Niagara" off the port on the 11th of last month.

It is true that the "Niagara" did take up her position in front of this harbour on the above day, being Saturday. On that and the two following days she warned off several vessels, British and other, bound to this port and to Savannah, which latter port was not then blockaded, but remained open until the 28th of May. It appears to me, therefore, that the endorsement made by the commander of the "Niagara" upon the papers of the vessels bound to Savannah, viz., that the whole coast was blockaded, was improper and not warranted by the fact. On the 13th of May, the British ship ——— entered this port in the very face of the "Niagara." as reported in my despatch to your Lordship of the 15th of May. On the 15th of May the "Niagara" was no longer to be seen, and the port remained, for all practical purposes, open from that day until the 28th or 29th of May, when the "Minnesota" appeared and resumed the blockade. This fact is so perfectly notorious that not the slightest question can be raised respecting it, but I can furnish to your Lordship no more unequivocal proof of it than the following list of vessels which arrived from foreign ports in the interval between the departure of the "Niagara" and the arrival of the "Minnesota":—

May 17. British brig ———.
May 17. American schooner ———.
May 18. British ship ———.
May 27. Norwegian barque ———.
May 28. British schooner ———.

I should also remark that this number of arrivals at this advanced season of the year would have been multiplied by four had the blockade been instituted a month earlier.

In addition to these arrivals from foreign and distant ports, steamers and sailing vessels have been and still are, at this date, sailing from Charleston for Southern ports, such as Georgetown, Darien, Fernandina, and Savannah, and arriving here from those ports. Five or six schooners have also arrived with cotton from the wreck of a British ship without the interposition of any blockading force.

After these statements it seems to me unnecessary to furnish further particulars of the manner in which this blockade has, thus far, been conducted.

The Secretary of State for the United States is under the impression that the place of the "Niagara" was supplied by the "Harriet Lane," after, at the furthest, the delay of a day or two. Without desiring to impugn the correctness of Mr. Seward's statement to a greater degree than may be necessary to establish the truth, I will only remark that neither the "Harriet Lane" nor any other vessel was ever in a position to maintain the blockade, as the foregoing facts will clearly prove. But, whatever may have been the intention of the Government of the United States, it is perfectly clear that the blockade was utterly and entirely ineffective and null for nearly fifteen days. My colleagues of France and Spain have so reported it to their respective Governments, so that I am not alone in my opinion.

No. 26.

Lord Lyons to Lord J. Russell.—(Received July 13.)

My Lord,   *Washington, June 27, 1861.*

I HAVE the honour to transmit to your Lordship herewith an extract from the "New York Herald" of the 25th instant, containing a statement to the effect that Flag Officer Mervine, of the United States' frigate "Mississippi," announced on the 8th June a strict blockade of the port of Key West, Florida, but that on the following day the order for the enforcement of the blockade was partially rescinded.

This proceeding has caused some surprise, from the fact that Key West is entirely in the hands of the United States' authorities.

I am, &c.
(Signed)   LYONS.

Inclosure in No. 26.

Extract from the "New York Herald" of June 25, 1861.

OUR KEY WEST CORRESPONDENCE.

Key West, June 25, 1861.

EVERYTHING here is quiet. The United States' flag-ship "Mississippi" sails to-morrow. Flag-Officer Mervine will touch at Fort Pickens, and thence visit all the ports blockaded by his squadron. A few days since much anxiety was created by the publication by Commodore Mervine of the following Proclamation :—

"To all whom it may concern,—I, William Mervine, Flag-Officer, commanding the United States' naval forces composing the Gulf squadron, give notice that, by virtue of the power and authority in me vested, and in pursuance of the Proclamations of his Excellency the President of the United States, promulgated under date of April 19 and April 27, respectively, an effective blockade of the port of Key West, Florida, has been established, and will be rigidly enforced and maintained against any and all vessels (public armed vessels of foreign Powers alone excepted) which shall attempt to enter or depart from said port of Key West, Florida.

"Given at Key West, June 8, 1861.

(Signed)   "WILLIAM MERVINE.

"Flag Officer ' Mississippi,' Gulf Blockading Squadron."

The order of blockade took the town by surprise, and the question was on every tongue, How are we to feed ourselves and our families? We grow nothing, our island is almost a barren, rock-bound desert ; and if vessels now on their way from New York with supplies for our merchants are ordered off, and the opportunity of leaving the island taken from us, we must starve. But brighter prospects beamed upon us the day following the promulgation of this uncalled-for and extraordinary order, when there appeared upon the street corners this modified appendage to the above :—

"The declaration of blockade of this port, made by me the 18th instant, is so far relaxed in its terms as to allow legitimate trading between this port and the ports of the loyal States. Trading between Key West and the Island of Cuba, and any of the West India Islands, so long as it is confined to lawful objects of commerce, may be carried on under such restrictions as may be imposed by the Naval Commander stationed off this port.

(Signed)   "WM. MERVINE, &c."

This, to the inhabitants who had starvation staring them in the face the day before, was good news, and the Union men, who felt that they were in prison and must fare as badly as the rebels themselves, breathed more freely.

A few days after the above publications the Collector of the port, Charles Howe, Esq., issued the following notice :—

"By order of Commodore William Mervine, commanding the Gulf blockading squadron, the masters and owners of all vessels and boats are required to renew their registers or emoluments and licences on and after this date, as they arrive in port, and take the oath of ownership, according to law.

"And before any vessel or boat will be permitted to leave the harbour of Key West, they must obtain a clearance and permit from the Custom-house, setting forth the object of their voyage, excepting pilot boats on their regular daily cruising-grounds, which clearance and permit to be approved by the officer in command of the port. And if any such vessel or boat is found without such clearance, &c., they will be dealt with as violating the blockade. By order as above.

(Signed)   "CHAS. HOWE, Collector."

The "Mississippi" yesterday left port, bound to Pickens, but in clearing the harbour she grounded on Triangle Shoal, and was got off with some difficulty, and returned to the naval anchorage this morning.

No. 27.

Lord Lyons to Lord J. Russell.—(Received July 15.)

My Lord,   *Washington, July* 1, 1861.

I HAVE the honour to inclose an extract from a despatch from Her Majesty's Consul at Galveston, from which it appears that the ports of Texas were free from blockade on the 6th ultimo.

I have, &c.

(Signed)   LYONS.

Inclosure in No. 27.

Consul Lynn to Lord Lyons.

(Extract.)   *Galveston, June 6, 1861.*
I HAVE the honour to report to your Lordship that the ports of Texas are yet free from blockade, and that I have not learned that any vessels of war have appeared off the coast.

No. 28.

Lord Lyons to Lord J. Russell.—(Received July 15.)

(Extract.)   *Washington, July 1, 1861.*
THE "Tropic Wind," a British vessel, was captured by the United States' blockading squadron off the mouth of the James river, and has been released after judicial proceedings before a Prize Court at this place.

No. 29.

The Secretary to the Admiralty to Mr. Hammond.—(Received July 24.)

Sir,   *Admiralty, July 23, 1861.*
I AM commanded by my Lords Commissioners of the Admiralty to send you herewith, for the information of Her Majesty's Secretary of State for Foreign Affairs, a copy of a letter dated the 12th instant, from Rear-Admiral Sir Alexander Milne, and of its inclosure from Commander Hickley, of the "Gladiator," reporting his proceedings on the coasts of the United States of America, and that he was of opinion that no blockade existed between Cape Hatteras and Cape Fear.
I have, &c.
(Signed)   C. H. PENNELL.

Inclosure 1 in No. 29.

Rear-Admiral Sir A. Milne to the Secretary to the Admiralty.

Sir,   *"Nile," at Halifax, July 12, 1861.*
THE mail, which has this moment arrived from Boston, has brought me despatches from Her Majesty's ship "Gladiator," upon which I can do no more than forward to their Lordships a copy of Commander Hickley's letter of proceedings of the 8th instant, unless I detain the mail, which I am unwilling to do, as she is already behind time.
I have, &c.
(Signed)   ALEX. W. MILNE.

Inclosure 2 in No. 29.

Commander Hickley to Rear-Admiral Sir A. Milne.

Sir,   *"Gladiator," New York, July 8, 1861.*
I HAVE the honour to inform you, that having left New York in Her Majesty's ship "Gladiator," on the afternoon of June 21, I proceeded under sail and arrived within thirty miles north of Cape Hatteras, on the 28th, when, on the forenoon of that day, I fell in with an open boat at sea, in which I found a crew of seven men short of provisions, bound to Hampden Roads, my impression being that they were Northern men attempting to return north; but, seeing they were in want of provisions, I supplied them with what I considered sufficient to take them to where they were going, and I have since heard that they arrived safely in Hampden Roads. The quantity supplied being small, viz., thirty lbs. of bread, twenty lbs. of pork, and half a gallon of spirits, and the recipients ill-clothed, I did not ask payment for it, but logged the supply as an extra issue, and have given the Paymaster an order for the same.
Proceeding round Cape Hatteras, I came-to in the evening off the shoals to insure
D 2

position for starting the next morning, and weighing on the morning of the 29th, I sighted Ocracoke Inlet, when at the entrance I observed a small steamer with the Secession flag, which on our approach steamed in under the protection of a small fort on the right bank, both vessels and fort firing blank cartridges.

Steaming past out of range I followed the coast along, and came to again in the evening to insure position for rounding the shoals off Cape Lookout.

Weighing anchor on the morning of the 30th, I hauled in to observe another steamer inside the sandbank forming the lagoon running from cape to cape, which appeared the same as the one seen off Ocracoke the day previously; if not she was precisely similar, and I understand these vessels lie in wait at the mouths of these inlets and seize on any vessels passing, making prizes of them if under the United States' flag.

Rounding Cape Lookout, I steamed past Beaufort, where there is a considerable fort with the Secession flag flying, and observed a brig of about 200 tons and other smaller merchant-vessels lying inside, the fort being garrisoned, and every gun manned and ready. Following the coast of the bay along, I came-to off Bogue Inlet for the night, and weighing on the following morning, I pursued the same course as on the 30th to the east entrance of Cape Gear river, where a red flag was hoisted and a shotted gun fired, three or four more following the "Gladiator." Being far out of range, I accordingly hoisted the three ensigns at the mast-heads, thinking they must have mistaken our large blue ensigns, which must have been the case either from not knowing the flag, or the misty weather making its certainty doubtful, as on the flags being broken all firing ceased. Getting well into the offing, I came-to for the night; and I have to report a steamer, similar to the vessel reported off Ocracoke, lying off this fort also.

On the morning of July 2 I again weighed; and not as yet having seen anything of the blockading squadron, and only having heard of the steamer "Ancon" as having boarded the American barque —— and the English schooner ——, of Halifax, on the 27th of June, which vessel I myself boarded on the 26th, I have the honour to report that to ascertain for a certainty that no vessel was actually employed on the blockade between Capes Hatteras and Fear, I rounded the shoals off the latter; and steaming in, I made the westward entrance of Cape Fear river, and there ascertained that there was no blockade. I made out a large vessel inside the river, of 500 tons, with a small steamer ahead of her; and seeing her smoke as I was in the offing, I have little doubt but that she was taking advantage of the absence of cruizers to be towed either in or out of the port; the former I should suppose, having been already outside previous to seeing the "Gladiator." At this entrance also was a considerable fort with a red flag flying.

I have the honour to state, Sir, that, with the decided certainty of the blockade being merely nominal, I now proceeded on my way back, calling off Cape Henry on the 6th of July to communicate my views to the American Flag Officer, when the United States' steamer "Quaker City," coming to speak us, and the Captain of that vessel informing me that the Flag Officer expressed a wish to see me if it was convenient and I was coming that way, I was glad to avail myself of the opportunity of taking a passage in the vessel to Hampton Roads, and went in her accordingly; and paying my respects to Flag Officer Stringham, whose flag was flying in the "Minnesota," I begged to represent to him most respectfully the open state of the blockade between Capes Hatteras and Fear. Answering which, he said, "Yes, I know there is no blockade there, but there will be one in a day or so; the 'Roanoke' goes there shortly."

I found lying in Hampton Roads the following vessels, viz. :—

	Horse-power.	Guns.	Men.	
Minnesota (screw) ..	800	46	640	40 9-inch, 10 ft. 6 in. 2 9-inch, 10 ft.
Roanoke ,, ..	800	46	640	Ditto.
Susquehanna (paddle) ..	500	16	350	9-inch.
Cumberland (sailing ship) ..	..	32	350	5 9-inch, 10 ft. 6 in. 1 9-inch, 10 ft.
Santee ,, ..	..	50	500	
Peregrine (screw) ..	..	6	60	
Anticosta ,, ..	..	6	60	
Dawn ,, ..	..	6	60	
Daylight ,, ..	..	6	60	

Having done the duty I had come upon, I have the honour to report arriving on board the "Gladiator" at 9·45 P.M., and proceeding forthwith to sea *en route* for New

York. I have the honour to report my arrival here this day. During the cruize I have met with no suspicious vessels whatever, and with very few vessels of any sort south of Cape Henry, from which place South trade seems quite stagnant as far as I have had the opportunity of judging.

> I have, &c.
> (Signed)   H. D. HICKLEY.

No. 30.

Lord J. Russell to Lord Lyons.

(Extract.)   *Foreign Office, July* 27, 1861.

I HAVE to call your attention, and, through you, the attention of Her Majesty's Consuls in the United States, to the extreme importance of obtaining all the particulars possible respecting the blockade.

It will be desirable that you should address an instruction to all Her Majesty's Consuls at the Southern ports, pointing out the importance of accurate and complete information being furnished by them on this subject.

No. 31.

Consul Archibald to Lord J. Russell.—(Received July 29.)

My Lord,   *New York, July* 17, 1861.

I HAVE the honour to report to your Lordship that the imperfect manner in which the blockade of the Southern ports is maintained, especially at the mouth of the Mississippi, has been the subject of much and general complaint in the public newspapers. I inclose, in duplicate, a printed slip taken from the "New York Times" newspaper of the 16th instant, headed "Privateering and Pickens," which gives expression to this complaint.

I learnt unofficially from Commander Hickley, on his arrival last week from his second cruize between this port and Cape Fear, that there was no blockade whatever of the ports between Capes Hatteras and Fear; and that on his representing this to Commodore Stringham, the latter admitted it to be the case, but stated that the "Roanoke" was going to that part of the coast.

I inclose an extract, in two parts, from the "New York Evening Post" newspaper, which furnishes, so far as I am enabled to judge, a full and correct statement of the force of the blockading fleet. I regret that I am unable this morning to transmit more than one copy, but will procure and forward others by the next mail.

> I have, &c.
> (Signed)   E. M. ARCHIBALD.

Inclosure 1 in No. 31.

Extract from the "New York Times" of July 15, 1861.

PRIVATEERING AND PICKENS.—Our correspondent at Havana announces the arrival at Çienfuegos of the "Sumter," a steamer of the rebel navy, bringing six prizes, the result of a short predatory cruize. A seventh has been burnt at sea. This "Sumter" was in other times a mail-steamer plying between Havana and New Orleans, with the title "Habana;" but seized by the Rebel Government, she was converted into a man-of-war, and well-armed and manned put to sea the other day from New Orleans, in saucy defiance of what the journals of that city properly describe as the paper blockade. The news of her departure has barely reached us, when it is hotly pursued by this later news of her success. It is true the insular authorities have reclaimed the six prizes, because they had been captured within Spanish waters; but the fact of seizure shows the power for mischief possessed by the cruizer in question, and renders it almost certain that if any of these released vessels hereafter depart for their ports of destination in the United States, they will be exposed to serious danger of recapture and condemnation. Moreover, the "Sumter" sailing from Cienfuegos has doubtless placed herself in the path of the Aspinwall steamers, with their millions of California treasure. Much pains have been taken by the Steam-ship Company to put their packets in a thoroughly defensible condition, and it is possible they may be able to contend successfully against privateers. But the " Sumter," according to the New Orleans papers, is far more perfectly armed and equipped than any privateer ; and if the treasure-ship crosses its track, the odds are fearfully against an escape. These facts and dangers are the first-fruits of the laxity with which the blockade is enforced at the mouth of the Mississippi.

Another result, though indirect, is no less undesirable. The cruize of the " Sumter" furnishes the cotton-craving Governments of Europe with the best evidence that our blockade is not such as international law demands, and that they are released from all obligations to respect it. We have no right to demand of England and France, who consent to suffer while we, within legal warrant, proceed to the repression of the Southern insurrection, that they shall connive at the deficiencies of our measures, or decline to take cotton when the way to get it is thus shown to be open. If England were now to declare the blockade of New Orleans merely formal, and therefore without claim to recognition, and if her squadron were to protect British merchantmen in carrying away cargoes of cotton, we should have no right to complain. She would act strictly in pursuance of an equitable principle announced at the commencement of this contest, and which we, at that time, cordially accepted.

Our duty, therefore, is evidently to do what should have been done three months ago—make the blockade impenetrable. There has been no moment since the blockade was proclaimed, when it was not practicable to perfect it at a week's notice. It was only necessary for Government to charter, arm, and dispatch some of the many unemployed coastwise steamers, which the fishermen of New England would have hastened to man, to close every Southern port effectually, and establish such a thorough patrol of the entire coast as would prohibit the egress of armed vessels, and the ingress of vessels bearing munitions and supplies. It was only a few days since a vessel with 100,000 stand of the most approved European arms reached New Orleans, in spite of our blockade. But if reluctant to take this course, there is another which there is no apology for omitting. To the amazement of mankind, the rebels have now, for a third of a year, surrounded Fort Pickens without the garrison of the fortress taking any step to disperse them. At their leisure, they have girdled the place with every conceivable means of reducing it. Not a shot or shell has disturbed their labours ; the stranger could only suppose the garrison to be in firm and friendly league with the assailant. For some time an excuse for inactivity was found in the weakness of the force and the deficiency of the supplies. But this has been remedied. Men to the fullest extent demanded, and food and munitions, have been furnished ; and a fleet of war vessels has, since the middle of April, been anchored under the shadow of the fort. And yet shipping, and fortress, and rebel intrenchments, remain as if the object of all three was the strict preservation of peace, and the indefinite postponement of that conflict, for which the entire nation impatiently waits. One result of this culpable inactivity, and that immediately to our purpose, is that seven war-vessels, whose services in perfecting the blockade, or in cruizing after privateers, are urgently wanted, are permitted to lie idle and rotting in those tepid waters, with no more efficiency or promise of active service than if they were in the Black Sea. We are entitled to know what sinister, and it would seem treasonable, influence perpetuates this mischievous *status in quo*. It has been in the power of Colonel Brown and his auxiliaries, any time these two months, to destroy General Bragg's defences, disperse his army, and occupy Pensacola. Why has it not been done? By whose counsel is it that the fleet at Santa Rosa is anchored there for ever, while the sea within sight of their decks is swarming with insolent privateers, and bogus men-of-war? The matter demands inquiry.

Inclosure 2 in No. 31.

Extract from the " New York Evening Post."

THE BLOCKADING FLEET: STRENGTH OF OUR NAVAL FORCE.—The blockading fleet now employed on our Southern coast has assumed a magnitude which will surprise persons who have been in the habit of underrating the naval resources of the United States.

Thirty-seven regular men-of-war, thirty-nine converted steam gun-boats, and upwards of one hundred transports are now actively engaged in the service of the Government. Of course, a large number of these naval vessels and chartered transports are not calculated for offensive operations at sea, but a rough selection of the worst among them would furnish a fleet sufficiently powerful to combat successfully with the best craft in the possession of the rebels.

Ports to be Blockaded.—The following ports in the Southern States must be shut out from all commercial intercourse, if the blockade is made as efficient as the recognized law of nations requires:—

Virginia.—Norfolk, Portsmouth, Alexandria, Petersburg, Richmond.
North Carolina.—Albemarle and Pamlico Sound, Beaufort, Wilmington.
South Carolina.—Georgetown, Charleston.
Georgia.—Savannah, Brunswick.
Florida.—St. Mary's, Key West, Fort Jefferson, Cedar Keys, St. Marks, Pensacola.
Alabama.—Mobile.
Louisiana.—The mouths of the Mississippi river.
Texas.—Galveston, Matagorda Bay, Brazos Santiago, mouth of the Rio Grande.

The regular Men-of-War.—The following Table shows the number of regular men-of-war now employed in the blockading service, with the number of guns and men on board each vessel, and the tonnage:—

Vessel.	Guns.	Officers and Men.	Tons.
1. Steam frigate " Minnesota "	60	500	3,200
2. Steam frigate " Niagara "	12	540	4,580
3. Steam frigate " Wabash "	44	500	3,200
4. Steam frigate " Roanoke "	44	500	3,200
5. Steam frigate " Colorado "	44	500	3,200
6. Steam frigate " Powhatan ".	10	350	2,415
7. Steam frigate " Mississippi "	11	380	1,692
8. Steam frigate " Susquehanna "	16	340	2,450
9. Steam corvette " Richmond "	14	325	1,920
10. Steam corvette " Brooklyn "	14	325	2,075
11. Steam gun-boat " Pawnee "	6	100	1,289
12. Steam gun-boat " Water Witch "	5	94	378
13. Steam gun-boat " Mohawk "	6	110	464
14. Steam gun-boat " Wyandotte "	6	110	380
15. Steam gun-boat " Crusader "	8	110	549
16. Steam gun-boat " Pocahontas "	4	94	320
17. Steam gun-boat " Iroquois "	6	100	1,016
18. Sailing frigate " Constitution "	50	240	1,726
19. Sailing frigate " St. Lawrence "	50	500	1,726
20. Sailing frigate " Santee "	50	500	1,726
21. Sailing frigate " Sabine "	50	300	1,726
22. Sailing corvette " Cumberland "	24	300	1,726
23. Sailing corvette " Savannah "	26	300	1,726
24. Sailing corvette " Macedonian "	24	300	1,341
25. Sailing corvette " Jamestown "	22	300	986
26. Sailing corvette " Vincennes "	20	300	700
27. Sailing corvette " Vandalia "	16	300	783
28. Sailing corvette " St. Louis "	20	300	700
29. Sailing corvette " Preble "	16	300	566
30. Sailing corvette " Dale "	16	200	566
31. Sailing corvette " Marion "	16	200	566
32. Steam gun-boat " Seminole "	3	220	800
33. Sailing brig " Bainbridge "	6	100	259
34. Sailing brig " Perry "	6	100	280
Three store-ships (armed)	3	170	..
Total	726	10,113	50,229

The Flag-ship.—The " Minnesota " is the " flag-in-chief " of the blockading fleet, and flies the wide flag of Commodore Stringham, of New York. She was hauled in to the wharf at Boston, to be fitted out for the " ready " state on the 4th of June, 1859, before her present occupation was thought of. She left Boston a few weeks since, touched at Hampton Roads, and seized 300,000 dollars worth of ships and tobacco to begin with. The " Minnesota " is one of our largest screw steam-frigates, 3,200 tons burthen, rates 40 guns, and was built at Washington in 1855. She is an auxiliary propeller—that is, steam propulsion is only used by her in calm weather, or when the winds are adverse. She carries 600 tons of coal, and when under regular steam consumes 31 tons per day. Her propeller is moved by engines of 450 horse-power, which, in case of an emergency, may be increased to 800 ; and the machinery for hoisting and lowering the propeller is remarkably simple but of great force. She has made but one regular cruize, in the East Indies, from which she returned perfectly rotten, in 1858. Although rated for only 40 guns, she now carries between 50 and 70. Two of 11-inch calibre, all mounted at the stern, capable of throwing balls of 160 lbs. weight. The same number of guns, of equal size, are placed in position at the bow of the vessel.

The following is a correct list of the "Minnesota's" officers :—

Flag Officers : Silas H. Stringham, Flag Officer and Commander-in-chief; A. Ludlow Case, Commander and Flag-Captain ; Ed. C. Crafton, Flag-Lieutenant; George B. Halstead, Flag-Officer's Secretary ; Elias W. Hale, Jr., Flag-Officer's Clerk. Officers of the ship, Captain G. J. Van Brunt ; First Lieutenant and Executive Officer, Reed Werden ; Second Lieutenant, John W. Wainwright ; Third Lieutenant, Oscar C. Badger ; Fourth Lieutenant, John Watters ; Fifth Lieutenant, James P. Foster; Sixth Lieutenant, John P. Mitchell ; Paymaster, Robert Pettit ; Fleet Surgeon, Ed. Gilchrist ; Assistant-Surgeon, Samuel J. Jones ; Chaplain, George Jones ; Chief Engineer, Charles H. Loring ; Second Lieutenant Marines, George W. Collier ; Master, C. L. Franklin ; Midshipman, Roderick S. McCook ; First Assistant Engineers, W. W. Dugan and George W. City ; Second Assistant Engineers, C. H. Sevey and George S. Bright ; Third Assistant Engineers, E. J. Whitaker, George Leusner, William Musgrave, and R. S. Tablot ; Master's Mates, W. B. Cushing, C. Blanchard, G. W. Graves, and C. F. Loring ; Boatswain, T. G. Bell ; Gunner, C. W. Homer ; Carpenter, H. J. Thomas ; Sailmaker, A. A. Warren ; Paymaster's Clerk, J. F. Ferguson ; Captain's Clerk, H. G. B. Fisher ; Pilot, William Jones ; N. C. Blount, Lieutenant ; (passengers) Carpenter, George E. Anderson, Massachusetts ; Sailmaker, J. C. Bradford, Maine ; Acting Midshipman, T. Steele, Ohio ; Y. R. Smith, Maine ; N. W. Thomas, Massachusetts ; M. Forrest, Maryland ; Y. J. Hugginson, Massachusetts ; George W. Sumner, Kentucky ; H. J. Blake, Massachusetts ; Master's Mates, N. Hobbs, U. J. Hunt, M. W. Stone, George B. Carter. Massachusetts ; First Assistant Engineer, F. A. Williams, District of Columbia ; Second Assistant Engineer, J. Cox Hull, New York ; Third Assistant Engineer, A. Murray, Maryland ; L. L. Olmstead, New York ; W. L. Smith, Maryland ; George H. White, New York ; Webster Lane, Massachusetts ; J. R. McMary, New York.

The "Niagara."—The "Niagara" (attached to the Florida division of the blockading squadron) is the largest man-of-war in America, probably in the world. Her first and second cruizes were made in company with the English frigate "Agamemnon," in the Atlantic telegraph expedition, when she was commanded by Captain William H. Hudson, the present commandant of the navy-yard at Boston. She was next employed in carrying a large number of captured Africans from Charleston, South Carolina, to Liberia. On this cruize she was commanded by Captain John S. Chauncey.

After her return from Monrovia the "Niagara" laid idle at New York for six or eight months, when she was fitted up for the express purpose of carrying home the Japanese Ambassadors. A temporary house was built on the spar-deck, running forward to the mainmast, which it has been found necessary to remove, that her full armament can be worked.

The "Niagara" is a screw frigate of 4,500 tons, and the first vessel of her class in United States' Navy. She was built at Brooklyn, New York, in 1855, from models designed by the late George Steers. The vessel is 345 feet long, 56 feet beam, 33 feet hold, and is propelled by three engines, which can be worked singly or together up to 2,300 horse-power. Her greatest speed, under steam, has been thirteen knots per hour, and under sail alone seventeen knots. She carries 500 men, exclusive of officers. Her armament is the most formidable and effective of any ship in the navy. It consists of 11-inch guns for throwing shells weighing 180 lbs., and shot weighing 270 lbs. a distance of four miles. The guns are all on the spar-deck, and, working on traverse plates, can be discharged from either side of the ship. Since the appointment of her new staff of officers —many of the old ones having resigned—no proper list has been prepared.

The "Wabash."—The "Wabash" (Gulf division) was put in commission at the Brooklyn Navy-yard the first week in June, and sailed for Charleston a few days afterwards. She is without exception the handsomest and most useful man-of-war in the service. Every particle of her composition is in perfect order. Her armament, machinery, hull and rigging, are examples of neatness. Her former batteries, which could throw a broadside of 1,414 lbs., cost 86,139 dollars. The present one will throw 200 lbs. more, and will amount to about 87,000 dollars.

The "Wabash" is one of the five splendid steam-frigates constructed in 1855. She is 3,200 tons burden, carries 500 men and forty-four guns. Captain Mercer, of Maryland, commands her. When the flag was last hoisted, her officers mustered on the quarter-deck as follows :—

Captain, Samuel Mercer ; Lieutenants, J. Corbin, John Irwin, John H. Upshur, E. O. Mathews, S. B. Luce ; Surgeon, S. Jackson ; Assistant Surgeon, John J. Magee ; Paymaster, John G. Gulick ; Lieutenant of Marines, James Wiley ; Midshipmen, John F.

McGlensey, C. E. McKay, L. Phenel, J. R. Carothers, S. W. Mithols, R. H. Sampson, J. P. Robertson, J. H. Rowland; Gunner, Charles Moran; Boatswain, M. Hall; Sailmaker, W. W. Maub; Carpenter, C. Boardman; Chief Engineer, J. W. King; First Engineer, J. B. E. Stump; Third Engineers, P. R. Voorbees, H. Missiner, II. H. Maloney, W. C. Williamson.

The "Roanoke."—The "Roanoke" (Norfolk division) left this port for the Gulf on Sunday. She was built at Norfolk, and nearly broke her back in launching in 1855, and has made only one cruize, which was not by any means a successful one. Having done about a year's important service on the Home station, she returned to Boston and was refitted at a cost of 300,000 dollars. Her repairs here, on the present occasion, must have cost 110,000 dollars; so that about three years' duty have made her wear and tear, exclusive of all other matters, a tax of 410,000 dollars, or nearly 1,300 dollars a week. The "Roanoke" is 317 feet long, 54½ feet beam, 40 feet hold, and 3,400 tons burden. Her engines occupy only sixty feet of the hold. The shafting of the propeller is 148 feet long. Her armament, which was put on board some days since, consists of two 10-inch pivot guns, weighing over 10,000 lbs. each, twenty-eight 9-inch guns, 63 cwt.; two 12-pounder heavy howitzers for the launches, and two 12-pounder light howitzers for the cutters. The 9-inch and pivots are on the spar-deck; there are also 9-inch on the gun-deck. The "Roanoke's" officers are:—

Captain Nicholson; First Lieutenant, D. Ammen; Second, W. N. Jeffers; Third, J. Scott Fittebrown; Fourth, R. A. Scott; Fifth, Ed. P. Lull; Sixth, R. J. Renshaw; Captain E. Cavendy, Master; Surgeon, George Clymer; Assistant-Surgeon, J. C. Spear; Paymaster, B. J. Cahine; Chaplain, R. Given. Warrant Officers: H. G. Thomas, Carpenter; H. Payton, Sailmaker; William Senerallc, Gunner; William Bennett, Boatswain; Chief Engineer, A. C. Stimers; Assistants, H. B. Norris, R. A. Copeland, T. J. Griffen, A. Jackson, H. West, G. J. Bunap, A. Hendrick.

The "Colorado."—The steam-frigate "Colorado" (Gulf division) went in commission on the 3rd of June, at Boston, in compliance with orders from the Navy Department. The "Colorado" is 4,300 tons burden, carries forty-four guns, 509 sailors, a marine guard of fifty rank and file, and a brass band. One of her guns weighs 15,000 and another 12,000 lbs. She was built in 1855, and never made a cruize but one, namely, as flag-ship of the Home Squadron. She can throw a broadside of 1,414 lbs., and her armament cost 81,240 dollars. On the 18th she sailed, and on the 20th her machinery broke down, owing to the treachery of Mr. Quinn, who fitted out her engines. She got away, after a temporary stoppage, however. The "Colorado's" armament consists of forty Paixhan broadside guns, two Dahlgren pivot-guns and two howitzers. She carries 76,000 lbs. of powder, and about 2,000 shells, and a full complement of small arms and ammunition. Commodore Mervine, now of the "Mississippi," will soon transfer his wide flag to the "Colorado." The ollowing is a list of her officers :—

Captain, Theodosius Baily, New York; First Lieutenant and Executive officer, A. Clay, Massachusetts; Second Lieutenant, J. H. Russell, Maryland; Third Lieutenant, John G. Sproston, Ohio; Fourth Lieutenant, B. B. Taylor, Indiana; Fifth Lieutenant, E. A. Selden, Vermont; Flag Lieutenant, Francis B. Blake, Massachusetts. Fleet Surgeon, G. R. B. Horner, Virginia. Paymaster, H. Etting, Pennsylvania. Assistant Surgeon, S. D. Kennedy, Maryland. Acting-Masters, James Taylor, Massachusetts; John Shinell, New York. Captain Marines, E. Mc D. Reynolds, New York; Lieutenant Marines, Mc Lean Tilton, Maryland. Chief Engineer, George Gideon, Pennsylvania. Captain's Clerk, Thurber Baily, New Jersey; Paymaster's Clerk, H. H. Hill, New York. Boatswain, Z. Whitmarsh, Massachusetts. Gunner, J. D. Boston, Ohio.

The "Powhatan."—The "Powhatan" (Florida division) is a side-wheel steam-frigate, 2,415 tons burden, was built at Gosport in 1850, and returned from the East last year, bringing the Japanese to San Francisco; she was about to be overhauled on her return, when Spanish movements in Central America, and subsequently the Southern insurrection, necessitated her remaining in commission, but with a new crew. She carries a heavy battery, consisting of ten 9-inch guns and one 11-inch gun, mounted on the forecastle; thus armed, she is a very formidable vessel of war. The following is a list of her officers :—

Lieutenant Commanding, Porter; Lieutenants, John Rutledge, Edgar Thompson, F. C. Harris, N. N. Queen, George Brown, Philip Porcher; Surgeon, J. Wilcox; Paymaster, George M. Clarke; Passed Assistant-Surgeon, J. Laws; Marine Officer, First Lieutenant, James Riley; Chief Engineer, H. Newell; First Assistant Engineers, H. Ilvain, H. Gladding, J. Laws; Midshipman, C. W. Read; Captain's Clerk, J. H. Buckley; Paymaster's Clerk, F. G. Beal; Boatswain, F. McLoud; Gunner, B. Dyeker; Carpenter, J. G. Conley; Sailmaker, J. Stevens. The "Powhatan" is rendering good service in the Gulf.

The "Mississippi."—This is the first American man-of-war ever commissioned exclu-

[100]   E

sively with Northern officers. She was despatched to the Gulf division from Boston not many days since, Commodore Mervine taking his quarters temporarily in her. She returned from China last year, having made two cruizes in succession on that station. The " Mississippi " was attached to the famous Japan expedition, and previously to the Pacific and Mediterranean squadrons. While on the latter the famous Kossuth took passage from Constantinople to England. It cost 90,000 dollars to fit her out lately. She is a steam-frigate, rating 1,692 tons burden, carrying eleven guns and 340 men. The officers of the " Mississippi " are :—

Flag Officer of the Gulf division of the blockading squadron, William Mervine, of New York ; Commander, Captain Thomas O. Selfridge, of Massachusetts ; Second Lieutenant, A. K. Hughes, of New York ; First Lieutenant and executive officer, Francis Winslow, of Massachusetts ; Third Lieutenant, John Madgau, junior, of Maine ; Fourth Lieutenant, E. P. Williams, of New Jersey ; Surgeon, R. T. Maccoun, of New Jersey ; Assistant-Surgeon, J. W. Shivly, of Indiana ; Chief Engineer, E. Lawton, of Massachusetts ; First Assistant Engineers, R. W. Berthman, of Pennsylvania, and William Henry Hunt, of New York ; Third Assistant Engineers, S. R. Brooks, William H. Gladding, of Pennsylvania, James J. Noble and Frederick S. McKean ; Gunner, William Cope, of Pennsylvania ; Sail-maker, George F. Lozier, of New York ; Boatswain, Joseph Lewis ; Captain's Clerk, Francis O. Selfridge ; Paymaster's Clerk, David F. Powers ; Pilot, Benjamin F. Clifford ; Acting Midshipmen, Edward E. Preble, H. L. Johnson, A. C. Alexander, E. T. Woodward, Albert S. Barker, J. R. Bartlett, and Walter Abbott.

The " Susquehanna."—The " Susquehanna " (Gulf division) like the " Powhatan," is a side-wheel steamer. She is 2,450 tons burden, carries fifteen guns and about 340 officers, sailors, and marines. She was ordered into commission for service in the Mediterranean squadron last year, but remained some time in the Gulf before leaving for the East. She returned on June 4 last, was quickly renovated and sailed a short time ago for the Gulf. Her late Commander, Captain Hollins (of Greytown notoriety) having resigned, Captain Chauncy of New York replaced him. Her other chief officers are :—

Lieutenants, J. Young, Wm. Gwin, A. H. Weaver, and J. G. Walker ; Chief Engineer, Geo. Sewell ; Surgeon, J. Beale ; Paymaster, Washington Irvin ; Acting Master, Geo. B. Livingston ; Marine Officer, P. R. Tendall, jun.

The " Susquehanna" was in the first Cable expedition, in the Japan expedition, and served not long since in the Mediterranean. She has done more active duty than any other vessel in the navy.

The " Richmond."—This steamer has recently returned from the Mediterranean squadron, having, like the " Iroquois" and " Susquehanna" of the same station, been ordered to the United States for the blockade. She rates with the " San Jacinto," " Brooklyn," " Hartford," and " Lancaster," and was built at Norfolk the year before last. She is not a successful craft, her rolling propensities, and the difficulty of managing her hoisting propeller, seriously impairing her efficiency. The " Richmond" is 1,929 tons burden, carries 14 guns and 300 officers and men. Three of her officers resigned abroad, namely, Captain D. A. Ingraham, commanding at Pensacola (and reported to have died), Lieutenants A. F. Warley and W. G. Dozrer. Those who returned are as follows :—

Flag Officer, C. H. Bell, New York ; Captain, J. Pope, Maine ; Lieutenants, R. H. Wyman, New Hampshire, L. A. Kimberley, Illinois, A. B. Cummings, Pennsylvania, F. E. Shepherd, North Carolina, R. Boyd, Maine ; S. Magaw (passenger) ; Surgeon, Rushen-berger, New Jersey ; Passed Assistant ditto, James Luddards, Pennsylvania, M. P. Christian, Virginia ; Paymaster, G. F. Cutter, Massachusetts ; Chaplain, Charles A. Davis, District Columbia ; Captain of Marines, J. D. Lemmes ; Second Marine officer, Alan Ramsay ; Master, J. W. Alexander ; Second Master, E. Terry ; Commodore's Secretary, G. Scull, New Jersey ; Chief Engineer, J. H. Warner ; other Engineers, V. Freeman, Virginia, J. M. Moore, New York, Eben. Hoyt, Massachusetts, J. W. Butler, Pennsylvania, William Pollard, Alabama, B. F. Herning, North Carolina, H. Fagan, Florida ; Midshipmen, J. C. Watson, Kentucky, J. L. Taylor, Virginia ; Clerks, F. C. Casby, J. M. Falk, Pennsylvania ; Warrant-officers, J. T. Choate, New York, J. Thayer, Connecticut, E. W. Carpenter, Virginia, H. T. Stocker, Massachusetts.

The " Brooklyn."—The " Brooklyn" (Florida division), was built by Mr. Webb of this city, in 1858. She is 2,070 tons burden, rates with the " San Jacinto," " Lancaster," " Hartford," and " Richmond," and carries 25 guns. She has been in commission on the Home Station since she first went on active duty, and has carried Mr. McLane and Mr. McElger to and from Mexico. The " Brooklyn's" machinery is somewhat similar to that in the " Niagara," but the " Niagara" has three engines, four boilers, and the rest of the machinery in keeping with her dimensions. The " Brooklyn" arrived at this port after an absence of eight months, was overhauled, and went to sea again.

The "Pawnee."—This is a steam gun-boat constructed by Mr. Griffiths, of Philadelphia. Her machinery, which has been breaking down every week since she first left the Navy Yard, was built by contract. She cost 400,000 dollars, is 238 feet in length, and has 47 feet beam, one foot more than the frigate "Lancaster," whose draught is only 10 feet, a little more than one-half of the "Pawnee." She is about 18 feet longer than the "Wyoming," and has 14 feet more beam. In the construction of the "Pawnee" great strength has been added to her frame by iron braces between the timbers and outer planking; also, by strips of iron running diagonally across the beams, supporting the deck, as well as heavy iron bulkheads and heavy iron plates on the sides of the vessel between decks. The planking on the vessel is seven inches thick, and of the best timber. The theory of the constructor is, in reference to this matter, that thick planking strengthens a vessel much more than heavy, massive timbers. The bottom of the vessel, which, owing to her great breadth of beam, is in the centre quite flat, possesses something entirely new in vessels of this class. Near the keel the bottom is convex in its form, while the bilge-water surface of the bottom is on a level with the lower part of the keel. In short, she is "a model gun-boat" in everything but usefulness. Her officers are, Captain Hartstein (who went home with the barque "Resolute"), Lieutenants Marcy and Lowry, Lieutenant (of Marines) Reynolds. Her station is in the Norfolk division.

The "Water Witch."—The "Water Witch" (Florida division) took the first shot that opened the famous Paraguay war, at the Itapine Fort in South America. She was for years cruizing in command of Lieutenant Page, the explorer, and returned to the States in 1856. She is a third-class side-wheel steamer, 378 tons burthen, carries three guns, and is sixteen years old, having been built in Washington in 1845. She went into commission for duty on the Home squadron, at Philadelphia, a few months ago, and has been doing good service since off Florida. No late list of her officers has been published.

The "Crusader."—The "Crusader" (Florida division), once Cromwell's "Southern Star," is a steam propeller of 540 tons burthen, drawing 10 feet of water. She has two decks, a direct-acting engine, with cylinders of 32 inches and 26-inch stroke. She was built last year in Murphysboro, of oak. She sailed from Norfolk the first week of November, carrying two 11-inch guns and one howitzer, for Montevideo, and returned in comparative safety to join the Paraguay fleet. She arrived here, previously to her present service, from the West India waters, where she had, like the "Mohawk" and "Wyandotte," acted as one of the Cuban Coast fleet, whose duty it is to intercept slavers. She was not put out of commission, but underwent some needed repairs of an unimportant nature. Her armament consists of eight brass 24-pounders, of the Dahlgren pattern; one iron 6-pounder, and two boat howitzers, 12-pounders. The following is a list of her officers:—

Lieutenant Commanding, T. A. M. Craven, appointed to the "Freeborn;" Lieutenants, J. M. Dunlan, J. M. Breese and A. E. R. Benham; Master, R. R. Wallace; Surgeon, J. H. B. Greenhow; First Assistant Engineers, J. A. Greer; Third Assistant Engineers, O. H. Lackey, P. A. Rearick, and J. Waters; Captain's Clerk, T. A. Craven, jun.; Master's Mates, James L. Plunkett and O. H. Warren; Purser's Clerk, Joseph B. Turner. The "Crusader," formerly "Cromwell," arrived last month at this station.

The "Mohawk."—The "Mohawk" (Florida division) was formerly the Cromwell steamer "Caledonia," and was built in Philadelphia in 1853; she is a screw propeller, barque rigged, of 435 tons burthen, and has a vertical engine with a cylinder of thirty inches in diameter; she carries 110 men; her armament consists of eight guns, six 32-pounders, one 24-pounder, and one 12-pounder, and two boat guns. She was purchased in 1858, and was attached to the Paraguay expedition. The following is a list of her officers:—

Lieutenant Commanding, J. H. Strong; Lieutenants, J. M. Arnold, C. C. Carpenter, C. Hatfield; Master, not yet on board; Surgeon, Delavan Bloodgood; Acting Chief Engineer, J. S. Albert; Third Assistant Engineers, E. L. Dick, G. D. Emmons, H. Brown; Captain's Clerk, T. H. Hoadley; Master's Mates, George Van Duser, J. H. Humphrey.

The "Wyandotte."—This vessel, belonging to the Florida division, was formerly the Cromwell steamer "Westernport," and was converted into a United States' gun-boat after the Paraguay expedition; she was built at Philadelphia, and is about 400 tons burthen. Her officers, when she went into Commission, were:—

Commander, Berryman; Lieutenants, Read, Eggleston, and Stribling; Surgeon, Garnett; Engineers, Cushman, Plunkett, Wilson, Pierce, and Brooks.

The "Pocahontas."—This is a little despatch-boat, formerly employed in carrying miscellaneous matters between the Navy Yards of Washington and Norfolk. Latterly, however, she has assisted in the blockading service; at present the "Pocahontas" is guarding the Potomac, opposite Alexandria, and is in readiness to land field-artillery at a moment's notice, to co-operate against the Secessionists in case of an attack. Steam is kept up ready to sail at ten minutes' warning. Almost an entire change has recently been made in her officers; at present they are as follows:—

Commander, Benjamin M. Dove; Executive officers, Lieutenant J. W. A. Nicholson; Lieutenant, Semmes Harrison; Acting-Paymaster, Theo. Kitchen; Surgeon, J. S. Kitchen. The "Pocahontas" is 695 tons burthen, carries five guns, and was purchased by the Navy Department in 1855.

The "Iroquois."—This steam gun-boat (Gulf division) is now at the Brooklyn Navy-yard taking in coal. She lately returned from the Mediterranean fleet, having been recalled for blockading purposes. It has not been decided as yet to what part of the fleet she will be added. The "Iroquois" was the first gun-boat ever built for the navy in New York, and third put in commission, the "Wyoming" and "Narragansett" having preceded her. The dimensions of the "Iroquois" are: length, 225 feet; breadth 33 feet; burden 1,010 tons. Her armament consists of seven guns—four medium-sized 32-pounders, two 11-inch and one 9-inch bore. She has two back-action engines, with cylinders 54 inches in diameter and 28 inches stroke, and a composition propeller 12 feet 3 inches in diameter and 19 feet pitch. She was six months on the stocks, from September 1858 to April 1859, on the 10th of which month she was launched.

The "Constitution."—"Old Ironsides" (Norfolk division), although not ordered to leave Annapolis, can do some blockading even there. It is a remarkable and interesting fact that the "Constellation" and "Constitution," two of the first vessels built for our navy, after sixty-two years of unremitted, faithful, exposed, and successful service, are still existing, and in active and efficient employment. The first days of the "Constitution" were not her best days. Her glory was acquired, as all true glory is, by gradual and solid steps. She was at first a subject of reproach and slander with the opponents of the navy, because she returned from a long cruize without having made any captures. The French ships of war were at that time depredating on American commerce, and the Decrees of the French Directory subjected to seizure all American vessels which had on board British goods or products, or which had sailed from British ports. The good ship was judged unfairly, however, and her gallant Commander (Nicholson) unduly reproached, as her subsequent history proved. Her present officers are not recorded.

The "Seminole."—This vessel has just arrived from the coast of Brazil at Philadelphia, having been specially ordered home for blockading services. The "Seminole" is one of the gun-boats ordered in 1857, was built at Pensacola, and got her machinery at Norfolk. She was launched on the 26th of June, 1859. She is a barque-rigged steam propeller, 800 tons burthen; has three large guns, one of which weighs 25,000 lbs. Her machinery was got up at the Morgan Iron Works, in this city, and consists of two horizontal back-action engines, of 750 horse-power, with cylinders 50 inches in diameter and 30 inches stroke. The "Seminole" was reported lost going out, and great consternation was caused by the announcement. She left the United States on the 25th of September, 1860, and has been, consequently, over ten months in commission. Her officers are:—

Captain E. R. Thompson; Lieutenants J. C. Howell, Samuel P. Carter, W. Campbell, C. S. Norton; Passed Assistant-Surgeon, George Peck; Paymaster, W. H. Morris; Midshipmen, A. D. Wharton, A. R. McNair, Wm. H. Barton and G. A. Walker; Carpenter, Thomas Robinson; Sailmaker, Luther Anderson; Engineers—First Assistant, J. B. Kimball; Second Assistant, W. B. Sultan; Third Assistants, R. L. Harris, Wm. C. Starr, and J. S. Kelcher.

The "St. Lawrence."—The "St. Lawrence" went into commission at Philadelphia a few weeks ago. She has not been as yet detailed for any definite station on the blockade. The "St. Lawrence" is a 50-gun frigate, 1,726 tons burthen, and carries 500 sailors and marines. She was the last flag-ship of the Brazil squadron. Annexed is a list of her officers:—

Captain, H. G. Purviance; First Lieutenant, John Downs; Second Lieutenant, J. H. Gills; Acting-Master, H. F. Picking; Surgeon, R. Woodworth; Assistant-Surgeon, J. Quinn; Lieutenant Marines, J. Dewis; Acting Midshipmen, C. S. Cotton, F. J. Naile, F. Pearson, G. W. Wood, C. N. Tracy, P. W. Lowry, H. F. French, H. B. Ramsey; Pay Clerk, Benjamin Duffield; Boatswain, John A. Briscoe; Acting Gunner, L. R. Ellis; Sailmaker, Lewis Rogers; Captain's Clerk, P. E. Chappale; Lieutenant, W. C. West; Acting Masters, G. L. Allyer, Hardy.

The "Santee."—The sailing frigate "Santee" (Gulf Division), 50 guns, went to sea from Portsmouth (New Hampshire) Navy Yard on the 19th. She has on board 500 sailors, 50 marines, and a heavy armament. She was fifty years on the stocks, and is about commencing her first cruize. Her tonnage, like that of all our sailing frigates, is 1,726. Her commander, Captain Engle, is a native of Pennsylvania, a full rank Commodore, who entered the service during the last war with England. Annexed is a complete list of her officers :—

Captain, Henry Engle ; First Lieutenant, A. D. Howell ; Second Lieutenant B. N. Westcott ; Third Lieutenant, J. N. Jewitt ; Acting Masters, J. Madison Williams and F. Roges ; Surgeon, J. Foltz ; Paymaster, Lewis Warrington ; First Lieutenant Marines, C. D. Hobb ; Assistant-Surgeon, — Burbank ; Midshipmen, Symmes M. Hunt and George M. Brown ; Captain's Clerk, H. Shriven ; Paymaster's Clerk, J. W. Ritchie ; Boatswain, William Black ; Master's Mates, Henry S. Lambert, Charles Adams, Charles Riker, Hartley W. Sewall, Alfred O. Childs ; Sailmaker, — Howell ; Gunner, Wm. Carter ; Carpenter, William H. Edgar.

The " Sabine."—The " Sabine " (Florida division), a 50-gun frigate, 1,726 tons burthen, was built here, having been half a century on the stocks. Her first cruise was made on the Paraguay expedition. She was near being wrecked going out, and had to put into Bermuda for repairs. She has been temporarily recalled, but will soon sail again for Portsmouth, where she is ordered to repair. Her officers are :—

Captain, Adams ; Lieutenants, Lewis, Newman, McCunn, Maxwell, and Hopkins ; Doctor, Delany ; Lieutenant, Cash (Marines) ; Doctor, Freeman ; Paymaster, C. Upham.

The " Cumberland."—The corvette " Cumberland " (formerly a 50-gun frigate), is the flag-ship of the southern division of the blockading fleet. She carries 22 guns, and is 1,726 tons burthen. The following is a list of her officers :—

Flag-officer, G. J. Pendergrast ; Captain, John Marston ; Lieutenants, Alexander Murray (executive officer), Nathaniel C. Bryant, Pierce, Chosly, George W. Morris, Chas. H. Greene, Thomas O. Selfridge ; Acting-Lieutenant, Henry D. Todd ; Master, James B. Gordon ; Acting Masters, John E. Rickwell, Thomas H. Gifford, John McDiarmed, John W. Bentley, Henry W. Greene ; Chaplain, John L. Lenhart ; Captain of Marines, Matthew R. Kentzing ; Lieutenant of Marines, Charles Heywood ; Surgeon, Edward Gilchrist ; Assistant Surgeon, William M. King ; Flag Officer's Secretary, E. N. Schen, Jun. ; Boatswain, Edward B. Bell ; Gunner, Eugene Mack ; Carpenter, Wm. McLaighton ; Sailmaker, David Bruce ; Captain's Clerk, William H. Innis ; Paymaster's Clerk, Hugh Nott ; Master's Mates, J. M. Harrington, Charles H. Brundage, John B. Van Duzer, Victor E. Tyson, Thomas Chisholm.

The " Savannah."—This vessel went into commission last week at the Brooklyn Navy Yard, but her exact destination is not yet announced. She was formerly a frigate, and has made one cruize since razeeing. Her present crew of 150 men is about half her proper complement. She will probably be attached to the blockading fleet. Her commander is Captain J. B. Hull.

The " Macedonia."—The " Macedonia " can hardly be said to belong to the blockade fleet, as she attends almost exclusively to matters in Vera Cruz, and other Mexican ports. She is a first-class corvette, 1,341 tons burthen, and was built at Norfolk in 1836. Her last cruize was with the " Wabash," in the Mediterranean. She went into commission on last Christmas-day, at Portsmouth, New Hampshire.

The " Jamestown."—The " Jamestown " was built at the Gosport Navy Yard in 1844. When recently overhauled on her return from the Coast of Africa, no labour or expense was spared to make her equal to new, and she is believed to be as good now as she was when she made her first cruize. Her battery is a pretty formidable one, consisting of fourteen 32-pounders and six 64-pounders. She has a crew of 200 men and boys, all shipped for three years. The sloop is provisioned for one year. She is commanded by C. Green.

The " Vincennes."—The " Vincennes's " last duty was on the African station, from which she returned last year. She captured several slavers on the coast. She is not worth much for hostile purposes, but went into commission a few days ago at Boston, and is now outward bound.

The officers of the " Vincennes " are all natives of Northern States. Three-fourths of them are New-Englanders. The armament of the vessel consists of eighteen pieces of ordnance.

Other War Vessels.—The " Vandalia " is a second-class sloop-of-war, built at Philadelphia in 1828. The " St. Louis " is a sloop-of-war, built at Washington in 1828, and carries twenty guns. The " Marion " and " Dale " are second-class corvettes. The " Preble," " Bainbridge," and " Perry " are now employed in the blockading service.

The Purchased and Chartered Fleet.—The following is a list of the thirty-nine vessels which have recently been purchased or chartered by the Government and transformed into gun-boats :—

Vessels.	Guns.	Men.	Vessels.	Guns.	Men.
1. Monticello	5	60	20. A. O. Tyler	11	100
2. Quaker City	5	70	21. Lexington	11	100
3. Huntsville	3	40	22. Conestoga	11	100
4. Keystone State..	3	35	23. Penguin	5	61
5. S. R. Spalding..	4	40	24. Albatross	5	61
6. Dawn	3	30	25. Mount Vernon..	5	100
7. R. R. Cuyler	9	130	26. Harriet Lane ..	6	80
8. Montgomery	6	30	27. Mr. Stevens' gunboat*	3	40
9. Daylight	3	40	28. Union	4	80
10. South Carolina..	4	40	29. Flag ..	3	32
11. Resolute	2	20	30. Wandérer	2	26
12. Reliance	2	20	31. Montgomery	3	25
13. Yankee	2	30	Three others	6	48
14. Massachusetts ..	3	100	35. Rhode Island	4	30
15. Freeborn	4	30	36. Connecticut	3	28
16. Young America	3	35	37. Illinois	1	18
17. Uncle Ben	2	15	38. Stars and Stripes	1	20
18. Varina	1	20	39. Adriatic	1	20
19. Vixen	5	70			
			Total ..	158	1,936

* Promised, but not yet " on guard."

The " T. B. Heartt " and two Fulton Ferry boats are about to be added to this fleet, but it is not known yet whether as gun-boats or transports.

The " Chesapeake " flotilla (consisting of the steamers " Freeborn," " Reliance," and two schooners) was organized by the late Captain Ward to blockade the mouth of the " Chesapeake." It was to be a sort of " independent volunteer naval expedition," not exactly subject to the orders of the Commander-in-chief of the Southern division of the blockade fleet, Commodore Pendergrast, who is on board the sailing corvette " Cumberland." Captain Ward was not satisfied with merely stopping vessels, but commenced dislodging batteries.

The " Harriet Lane."—This little vessel, now repairing at Brooklyn, will soon leave again for the Chesapeake, where she has already rendered efficient service. She carries two medium 32-pounders, four 24-pounders, and one 32-pounder on the forecastle. The large guns are placed in the ports about the paddle-boxes ; the 24-pounders are fixed aft. She will have a larger armament however. Her complement of small arms is very strong and of the best kind. It consists of Minić rifle-muskets, Sharps' improved pistols, Colt's navy revolvers, navy boarding-pistols, and the improved navy cutlass. The following is a list of her officers :—

John Faunce, Commander ; D. B. Constable, First Lieutenant ; D. D. Tompkins, Second Lieutenant ; H. O. Porter, Second Lieutenant ; Thomas Dugan, Third Lieutenant ; J. M. Thatcher, Third Lieutenant ; Horace Gramble, Third Lieutenant ; J. R. Dryberg, Chief Engineer ; Walter Scott, First Engineer ; C. Dale, Engineer ; F. F. Pulsifer, Engineer ; seamen, firemen, coal passers, stewards, &c. ; in all ninety-four persons.

The Surveying and Revenue Vessels.—The following surveying craft would need only orders to be invaluable blockading ships :—

Surveying steamer " Bibb," 320 tons burthen, 3 guns ; surveying steamer " Corwin," 300 tons burthen, 4 guns : total 2 vessels, 7 guns, and 148 men.

There is a rumour—and only a rumour—that the revenue vessels have been ordered to the blockade. We print their names, which will be useful, whether they are or not. The " Harriet Lane " has been transferred to the navy, and is blockading, as already stated. The others are :—

" James Campbell," Captain Clark, stationed at New London, Connecticut, nearly new, carries one 32-pounder pivot-gun, and is pierced for four side-guns.

" Morris," Captain Whitcomb, stationed at Boston, is an old vessel, and carries two 12-pounder guns.

" Caleb Cushing," Captain Walden, stationed at Portland, Maine, hull in good condition ; is pierced for four side-guns, and could carry a pivot-gun, but has only one 12-pounder on board.

" Jackson," Captain Carson, stationed at Eastport, Maine, hull good ; carries two 12-pounder guns, and has a good name.

" Duane," Captain Evans, stationed at Norfolk, Virginia, and almost a new vessel.

" Philip Allen," Captain Sands, stationed at Baltimore, Maryland, and almost a new vessel.

" Forward," Captain Nones, stationed at Wilmington, Delaware, an old vessel, and carries two guns.

These are nearly all sailing-vessels, schooner-rigged.

Transport Vessels.—The following transport vessels, although in the service of the Government, are not actually attached to the blockading fleet, but will probably be detailed for that service if required :—

Baltic.	Nashua.	Fanny.	Benton.
Columbia.	Philadelphia.	Ironsides.	Farmer.
Maryland.	Herschell.	Matanzas.	Eureka.
George Peabody.	Kedar.	Valley City.	Chesapeake.
Vanderbilt.	Atlantic.	W. Whitden.	Joseph Sparks.
De Soto.	Empire City.	Alabama.	Black Diamond.
Alabama.	Jersey Blue.	Coatzacoalcos.	New York.
Roanoke.	Star of the West.	Boston.	Baltimore.
Patapsco.	Augusta.	Daniel Webster.	Cahawba.
Trenton.	Marion.	Locust Point.	Woodward.
Patroon.	Woodhull.	Kill von Kull.	Ocean Queen.
Phelps.	W. Woodworth.	Florida.	*Brigs.*
City of New York.	Roman.	James Adger.	Floyd.
Matanzas.	F. W. Bruno.	Thomas Swan.	Georgia.
Columbia.	Franklin.	F. Cadwalader.	Mississippi.
Nashville.	Elizabeth.	Badger.	Sophia.
Anthracite.	Fanny Gardiner.		

Twenty-five altered vessels are now in Government employment, but none of them can carry the smallest armament.

General Summary.—The following recapitulation shows the available naval force now at the disposal of the Government :—

	Vessels.	Guns.	Crew.	Tons.
Regular men-of-war	37	726	10,113	50,229
Gun-boats	39	158	1,936	
Total armed vessels ..	76	884	12,049	

If we add to this number the revenue, surveying and other craft, which, in case of necessity, could be used for blockading purposes, the aggregate will be increased to 150 vessels and 18,000 men.

Twenty-five new gun-boats are to be built for use on the western rivers, in addition to the large force already in service, but they will not be employed in enforcing the blockade.

No. 32.

Lord Lyons to Lord J. Russell.—(Received August 4.)

My Lord,   *Washington, July 18, 1861.*

I HAVE the honour to transmit to your Lordship a copy of a despatch addressed by me to the Acting Consul at Savannah respecting the blockade of that port, and also a copy of a report which I received yesterday from the Acting Consul in reply.

I have, &c.
(Signed)   LYONS.

Inclosure 1 in No. 32.

Lord Lyons to Acting Consul Fullarton.

Sir,   *Washington, June 27, 1861.*

I HAVE to instruct you to report to me with scrupulous precision (so far as you are able to do so), whether any United States' force was actually blockading Savannah on the 12th May last, or shortly afterwards ; and if so, of what vessels such force was composed, where it was stationed, and whether it was of such amount and so placed as to be able to enforce an effective blockade. You will also report whether any notice of a blockade of Savannah was given on or before the 12th May, or shortly afterwards.

I am aware that this information may be considered as having been in effect given by your despatch of the 1st instant. I nevertheless beg you to make a special report on the points mentioned.

I am, &c.
(Signed)   LYONS.

Inclosure 2 in No. 32.

Acting Consul Fullarton to Lord Lyons.

My Lord,   *Savannah, July* 6, 1861.

I BEG to acknowledge the receipt of your Lordship's despatch of the 27th ultimo, requesting me to report whether any United States' force was actually blockading Savannah on the 12th May last, or shortly afterwards.

In reply, I have the honour to assure your Lordship that no United States' force was blockading Savannah on the 12th May last; in fact, no blockade whatever of this port existed previously to the 28th of that month, on which day the vessels composing the United States' squadron at present blockading Savannah made their appearance for the first time.   On the 29th May I visited one of those vessels, and was distinctly informed by her commander that the blockade of Savannah did not commence until the 28th May. No other notice of blockade has ever been given, and I gathered in the course of conversation that the commander of the squadron did not deem it to be his duty to give any such notice either to the local authorities of this city or to the Consular Representatives of foreign Governments resident here.

I may add, that one of the best proofs that no blockade existed previously to the 28th May lies in the fact that five British vessels arrived in this port on various days between the 12th and 28th May, the masters of which vessels reported to me that they met with no United States' force off the port.

I have, &c.
(Signed)   A. FULLARTON.

No. 33.

Lord Lyons to Lord J. Russell.—(Received August 4.)

My Lord,   *Washington, July* 18, 1861.

I HAVE the honour to transmit to your Lordship copies of a despatch and its inclosure which I received the day before yesterday from Mr. Cridland, Acting Consul at Richmond, respecting a permission having been given to a United States' citizen of the name of Atlee to pass with a vessel through the blockade of the Chesapeake.

I should hardly have thought it necessary to mention this matter to your Lordship had it not been stated in some New York papers that several similar cases had been reported by Mr. Cridland to me, and been made by me subjects of remonstrance to the United States' Government.

No other case has been reported to me either by Mr. Cridland or by any one else, and no communication on the subject, verbal or written, has passed between the United States' Government and me.

I have, &c.
(Signed)   LYONS.

Inclosure 1 in No. 33.

Acting Consul Cridland to Lord Lyons.

My Lord,   *Richmond, July* 11, 1861.

A CASE of somewhat peculiar character has been brought up at the Mayor's Court here within the last week, which may interest your Lordship.

A merchant, named Jacob S. Atlee, a Northern man, who has been a resident of Virginia for twenty-one years past, having been offered a contract to supply the Telegraph Company here with isolators, and being unable to procure a peculiar kind of clay and potash to manufacture the same, he went to Washington, applied and obtained from Mr. Secretary Chase a permit to bring such materials into Virginia viâ Harper's Ferry. He also obtained a like permit from Mr. Secretary Cameron. Finding, however, that the route viâ Harper's Ferry was impracticable, Mr. Atlee proceeded to Old Point Comfort, and in an interview with General Butler, exhibited to that officer the above-named permits, asking him whether it would make any difference if he carried said clay and potash by water through the blockading squadron. General Butler unhesitatingly gave him a passport for his vessel, but retained his former passes.

I have the honour to inclose herewith a copy of that permit, which Mr. Atlee permitted me to take. Mr. Atlee called on me without any request on my part, and related. the above facts. He was arrested in Richmond on suspicion of disloyalty to Virginia; but as nothing but the foregoing facts were proved against him in Court, he was acquitted. He had come home with a view of raising the necessary funds to purchase the cargo, but up to that time had failed.

I have, &c.
(Signed)   F. J. CRIDLAND.

Inclosure 2 in No. 33.

Pass.

Head-Quarters, Department of Virginia,
Fortress Monroe, June 19, 1861.

PASS the bearer, Mr. Jacob S. Atlee, with his vessel, through the blockading squadron.

To the Officers of the United States' Atlantic Home Squadron.

Mr. Atlee is also furnished with my engraved card as a further voucher to the authenticity of this pass.

(Signed)   BENJ. F. BUTLER,
Copy of Card: Major-General Commanding.
BENJ. F. BUTLER,
Mass.

No. 34.

Consul Bernal to Lord J. Russell.—(Received August 5.)

(Extract.)   Baltimore, June 20, 1861.
MR. ———— has informed me confidentially that he left this city, about a month since, in a schooner of 140 tons, laden with provisions and groceries, and entering the Potomac, and finding the coast clear, sailed up the Rappahannock to Fredericksburg, where he sold his cargo.

No. 35.

Lord Lyons to Lord J. Russell.—(Received August 5.)

My Lord,   Washington, July 20, 1861.
I HAVE this morning received the following telegram from Her Majesty's Acting Consul at Mobile :—

" Mobile, July 19.
" Blockade of Galveston established 2nd instant.
(Signed)   " JAMES MAGEE, Acting Consul."

I have, &c.
(Signed)   LYONS.

No. 36.

Consul Lynn to Lord J. Russell.—(Received August 9.)

My Lord,   Galveston, July 3, 1861.
I HAVE to report to your Lordship that a blockade of the port of Galveston was established yesterday, about noon, by the United States' armed steam-ship "South Carolina."

The "South Carolina" is a propeller of 1,150 tons burthen, and of 600 horse-power. Her armament consists of six 42-pounders, one large swivel-gun, and two brass 6-pounders; the latter mounted as flying artillery.

I have, &c.
(Signed)   ARTHUR T. LYNN.

No. 37.

Earl Russell to Lord Lyons.

My Lord,   *Foreign Office, August 9,* 1861.

WITH reference to the rumours which have reached Her Majesty's Government from various sources as to the inefficiency of the blockade of the Southern ports, I have to instruct your Lordship to make every inquiry with the view of ascertaining the manner in which the blockade is conducted.

I am, &c.
(Signed)   RUSSELL.

No. 38.

Lord Lyons to Lord J. Russell.—(Received August 12.)

My Lord,   *Washington, July 29,* 1861.

I HAVE the honour to transmit to your Lordship copies of a despatch and its inclosures, which I have received from Mr. Consul Archibald, relative to the "Herald," a British vessel which appears to have been captured at sea by the United States' frigate "St. Lawrence," on account of an alleged breach of a blockade of the port of Beaufort, in North Carolina.

I have also the honour to transmit to you a copy of a note which I have addressed to Mr. Seward on the subject.

It appears that there was no actual blockade at all of the port of Beaufort when the "Herald" entered or when she left. Indeed, the case seems to be so clear that I cannot but suppose that the Government of the United States will at once comply with my request that measures be taken to remedy the error committed by the captor.

I have, &c.
(Signed)   LYONS.

Inclosure 1 in No. 38.

Consul Archibald to Lord Lyons.

My Lord,   *New York, July* 26, 1861.

I HAVE the honour to transmit, herewith inclosed, to your Lordship, affidavits made before me to-day by one of the owners and by Mr. Parmelee, a passenger on board of the British brig "Herald," taken possession of at sea on the 16th instant by the Commander of the United States' frigate "St. Lawrence," for an alleged violation of the blockade of the port of Beaufort, North Carolina.

The Master of the "Herald" is on board his vessel at Hampton Roads; and I am, of course, unable to obtain his affidavit of the facts of the case. Mr. Parmelee arrived here last night.

I am not aware that this case has been brought to the notice of your Lordship by the Master, or by any one on behalf of the owners, of the "Herald," but upon the statement of facts contained in the affidavit of Mr. Parmelee, who is a disinterested witness, and appears to be a highly intelligent and respectable gentleman, I feel confident that the United States' Government will at once permit this vessel to proceed to her destination.

Your Lordship is already aware, and Commodore Stringham will himself, I apprehend, have reported to the Government of the United States, that from the time the "Herald" arrived at, until she left, Beaufort, there was no effective blockade, if, indeed, any blockade whatever, of that port.

I have, &c.
(Signed)   E. M. ARCHIBALD.

Inclosure 2 in No. 38.

Affidavit of Messrs. De Wolf and Parmelee.

British Consulate, New York.

PERSONALLY appeared before me, E. M. Archibald, Her Britannic Majesty's Consul for the State of New York, at the British Consulate, New York, this 26th day of July, A.D. 1861, David Rowland de Wolf, of the city of New York, merchant, a native of Nova Scotia and subject of Her Britannic Majesty, and Nelson Dane Parmelee, of Gould-borough, North Carolina, merchant, a citizen of the United States, who, being severally sworn before me and the Holy Evangelists to declare the truth, deposed and stated as follows: And first the deponent, D. R. De Wolf, for himself, states that he is part owner of the brig "Herald," of Windsor, United States, of the burden of 234 tons; that the remaining interest in the said vessel is owned by British subjects resident in the United States.

And this deponent, Nelson Dane Parmelee, for himself, states that the said brig "Herald," William Folker, Master, arrived at the port of Beaufort, North Carolina, on the 10th day of June last, in ballast; that she there loaded with a cargo of naval stores and tobacco for Liverpool, in Great Britain, on freight, and sailed from Beaufort on Sunday, the 14th instant, for Liverpool; that this deponent proceeded in the said vessel as passenger to Liverpool; that on Tuesday evening, the 16th instant, the said brig was fallen in with by the United States' frigate "St. Lawrence;" that the "Herald" was at that time about 200 miles distant from Beaufort, north of Cape Hatteras, and, as the captain judged, in the outer edge of the Gulf Stream; that an officer from the frigate boarded the brig and examined the ship's papers, and, on ascertaining where she was from, he remarked to Captain Folker that "it was well she was not bound in, as he would then have been warned off, and if afterwards met with would have been captured," or words to that effect, and then left the brig and went on board the frigate. A short time afterwards the officer came back again, and said he was obliged to take charge of the brig, and that a prize crew was coming on board. After this the captain of the frigate sent another boat with an officer, who told Captain Folker to go on board the frigate, with his log-book and papers; whereupon Captain Folker went on board the frigate with such officer, taking his log-book and papers. He soon afterwards returned, and a prize crew being put on board, the brig proceeded under their charge to Hampton Roads, at which place she arrived on the 21st instant, and the prize-master reported to Commodore Stringham, taking with him the brig's papers and log-book.

And this deponent further says that he was at Beaufort for seven or eight days immediately preceding the departure from thence of the "Herald;" that during that period the said port was not blockaded in any manner; that no vessel of the United States' Government, nor any armed vessel of any kind, was off or near to the port during that period, nor had any notice of blockade been promulgated or made known to any parties here. And this deponent also saith, that from the time of the departure of the "Herald," at nine o'clock in the morning of Sunday, the 14th, until the time she was fallen in with by the "St. Lawrence," no vessel of any kind was met with by or seen from on board the "Herald." And this deponent also saith that the master of the "Herald" sailed from the said port of Beaufort confident that there was no blockade of the said port, and that there was no legal hindrance whatever to his departure from thence.

And, lastly, this deponent saith that he has no interest whatever in the said vessel or her cargo; that he has been for three years past a resident of Gouldsborough, an inland town about ninety miles distant from Beaufort, and was merely a passenger on board the said vessel.

Sworn by the said David Rowland de Wolf and Nelson Dane Parmelee, at the British Consulate, this 26th day of July.

(Signed)   D. R. DE WOLF.
        N. D. PARMELEE.

Before me,
(Signed) E. M. ARCHIBALD, *Her Britannic Majesty's Consul.*

Inclosure 3 in No. 38.

Lord Lyons to Mr. Seward.

Sir,   *Washington, July 29, 1861.*
  I HAVE the honour to transmit to you a copy of a despatch which I received yesterday from Her Majesty's Consul at New York, and an original affidavit which was inclosed in it.

These papers relate to a British brig, the "Herald," which was taken possession of at sea on the 16th instant by the Commander of the United States' frigate "St. Lawrence," for an alleged violation of a blockade of the port of Beaufort in North Carolina.

The case appears to be so clear that I am confident the Government of the United States will at once take measures to repair the error of the Commander of the "St. Lawrence."

I have, &c.
(Signed) LYONS.

No. 39.

Lord Lyons to Lord J. Russell.—(Received August 12.)

My Lord,   *Washington, July* 29, 1861.

I HAVE the honour to transmit to your Lordship a copy of a postscript which was added by Mr. Consul Lynn on the 3rd instant to a despatch dated two days previously, and which announces that a blockade of the port of Galveston was established on the 2nd instant.

I inclose, also, two printed copies of the notification of the blockade which were sent to me by Mr. Lynn. The last date in them, " 2nd June," is, I presume, a misprint for " 2nd July."

In a letter dated the 6th instant, Mr. Lynn has informed me that up to that day he had not learned that the blockade had been extended to any other port of the State of Texas.

I acquainted Rear-Admiral Sir Alexander Milne by telegraph on the 27th instant of the blockade of Galveston, and on the same day I sent him by post copies of the inclosures in this despatch, and informed him that no blockade of the other Texan ports had, to Mr. Lynn's knowledge, been established up to the 6th instant.

I have, &c.
(Signed)   LYONS.

Inclosure 1 in No. 39.

Postscript to Consul Lynn's Despatch to Lord Lyons, dated Galveston, July 1, 1861.

July 3, 1861.

THE detention to the mail-packet enables me to report to your Lordship that the blockade of this port was established yesterday, about noon, by the armed steamer " South Carolina," James Alden commanding.

The " South Carolina " is a propeller, 1,150 tons burthen, 3 decks, 600 horse-power, with an armament of six 42-pounders, one large swivel gun and two brass 6-pounders, the latter mounted as flying artillery. Her crew is estimated at 150 men.

I inclose herewith copies of the declaration of blockade.
(Signed)   ARTHUR T. LYNN.

Inclosure 2 in No. 39.

Notification of the Blockade of Galveston.

THE following is the reply of Captain Alden to Captain Moore's note :—

" *U.S. Steamer ' South Carolina,' off Galveston,*
" Captain John C. Moore, C.S.A., &c.   " *July* 2, 1861.

" In answer to your communication of this date, I take the liberty of inclosing a declaration of blockade which I am sent here to enforce, and am, &c.
(Signed)   " JAMES ALDEN,
" *Commander, U.S. Steamer ' South Carolina.' *"

" *Declaration of Blockade.*

" To all whom it may concern :—

" I, William Mervine, Flag Officer, commanding the United States' naval forces composing the Gulf Squadron, give notice that, by virtue of the authority and power in me vested, and in pursuance of the Proclamation of his Excellency the President of the United States, promulgated under date of April 19th and 27th, 1861, respectively, that an effective blockade of the port of Galveston, Texas, has been established, and will be rigidly enforced and maintained against all vessels (public armed vessels of foreign Powers alone excepted) which attempt to enter or depart from said port.
(Signed)   " WILLIAM MERVINE,
" *Flag Officer, U.S. Flag-ship ' Mississippi,' June* 8, 1861.

" I certify that the above is a true copy,
(Signed)   " JAMES ALDEN, *Commander, U.S. Navy.*

" Neutral vessels will be allowed fifteen days to depart from this date, viz., June 2, 1861.
(Signed)   " JAMES ALDEN, *Commanding.*"

[*Note by Lord Lyons.*—June 2nd is apparently a misprint for July 2nd.]

No. 40.

Lord Lyons to Lord J. Russell.—(Received August 16.)

My Lord,   *Washington, August 1, 1861.*
  WITH reference to my despatch of the 29th ultimo, I have the honour to
inclose a copy of the note from the Secretary of State of the United States, informing me
that directions have been given for the release of the "Herald," which was captured at sea
by the United States' frigate "St. Lawrence" for an alleged violation of a blockade of the
port of Beaufort, in North Carolina.
  I did not receive the note until half-an-hour after the departure of my messenger for
New York the day before yesterday, but I directed Mr. Consul Archibald by telegraph to
write to inform your Lordship of the release of the "Herald."
                                                          I have, &c.
                                      (Signed)   LYONS.

Inclosure in No. 40.

Mr. Seward to Lord Lyons.

My Lord,   *Department of State, Washington, July 30, 1861.*
  I HAVE the honour to acknowledge the receipt of your communication of yesterday
relative to the case of the British brig "Herald," which vessel was taken possession of
at sea on the 16th instant by the Commander of the United States' frigate "St. Lawrence,"
for an alleged blockade of the port of Beaufort in North Carolina.
  It gives me pleasure to be able to state in reply that the Secretary of the Navy has
directed the "Herald's" release.
                                                          I avail, &c.
                                      (Signed)   WILLIAM H. SEWARD.

No. 41.

Lord Lyons to Lord J. Russell.—(Received August 18.)

My Lord,   *Washington, August 3, 1861.*
  I HAVE the honour to inclose a copy of a despatch from Mr. Acting Consul Fullarton,
stating that a British schooner has succeeded in running the blockade of the port of
Savannah.
                                                          I have, &c.
                                      (Signed)   LYONS.

Inclosure in No. 41.

Acting Consul Fullarton to Lord Lyons.

(Extract.)   *Savannah, July 22, 1861.*
  I BEG to acknowledge receipt of your Lordship's despatch of the 3rd July, instructing
me to keep the Foreign Office supplied, in quadruplicate, with copies in authentic form
of all documents which may emanate from authorities in the Southern States.
  Your Lordship's instructions shall be complied with.
  I have now to report to your Lordship the only instance in which a vessel has succeeded
in running the blockade of this port since its establishment. It occurred recently in the
case of a British schooner; on the 1st July this vessel managed to pass through the
squadron in the night, but was, next morning, chased and fired into by one of the
squadron; being small she escaped into shallow water, where she could not be reached,
and finally slipped into this port. She departed for Havana on the 19th instant, and I have
not heard whether she again made good her escape.
  Two United States' men-of-war are reported to be constantly off this port, occasionally
a third is to be seen. The last is supposed to be the flag-ship passing at intervals from
port to port.

No. 42.

Acting Consul Fullarton to Lord J. Russell.—(Received August 19.)

My Lord,   *Savannah, July 22, 1861.*

I HAVE the honour to acknowledge the receipt of Mr. Murray's despatch of June 13, requesting me to forward to your Lordship, when opportunity offers, the most accurate information that can be obtained respecting the existence of any blockade, and the manner in which it is maintained, more especially of the blockade of this port; also requesting me to forward in quadruplicate any public notices touching blockade, or the enforcement of other belligerent rights, in as authentic a shape as they can be procured. All of which shall be carefully complied with.

The port of Savannah was blockaded for the first time on the 28th May last, by the arrival off the bar of a United States' steamer of about 600 tons, and mounting five guns. The next day, the 29th, I visited this steamer, and was notified by her Commander of the above fact, and that she formed one of a squadron of four United States' men-of-war, stationed off the coast for the purpose of blockading this port and Charleston.

The steamer remained off this port until about June 1, when she departed, leaving the entrance entirely unobstructed. About the 10th of that month she again made her appearance, and I have never been able to ascertain the cause of her departure, or where she went. During her absence no vessels arrived but many departed, having the right to do so, however, their departure being within the fifteen days allowed by the United States' Government to neutral vessels to depart from a blockaded port.

From that time to the present this port has been strictly blockaded. Two men-of-war are reported to be constantly off the port; at intervals three are to be seen. So far as I can ascertain, the other ports in this State are also strictly blockaded.

The only instance in which a vessel has succeeded in running the blockade since its establishment occurred recently in the case of a British schooner. On July 1, this vessel managed to pass the squadron in the night. She was, however, next morning, chased and fired into by one of the squadron, but, being small, she escaped into shallow water where she could not be reached, and finally slipped into this port. She departed for Havana on the 19th of this month, and I have not heard whether she again succeeded in making good her escape.

I may remark that this city is about twenty miles distant from the sea, and I have to rely altogether upon report as to the movements of the blockading fleet.

I have, &c.
(Signed)   A. FULLARTON.

No. 43.

The Secretary to the Admiralty to Mr. Hammond.—(Received August 22.)

Sir,   *Admiralty, August 19, 1861.*

I AM commanded by my Lords Commissioners of the Admiralty to send you herewith, for the information of Her Majesty's Secretary of State for Foreign Affairs, a copy of a letter dated the 8th instant from Rear-Admiral Sir Alexander Milne, and of its inclosure from Commander Hickley of the "Gladiator," reporting his further proceedings upon the coasts of the United States, between Cape Fear and New York, and reporting as to the efficiency of the blockade between those points.

I am, &c.
(Signed)   W. G. ROMAINE.

Inclosure 1 in No. 43.

Rear-Admiral Sir A. Milne to the Secretary to the Admiralty.

Sir,   *" Nile," at Halifax, August 8, 1861.*

REFERRING to my letter of the 12th ultimo, I have now the honour to inclose a copy of Commander Hickley's further proceedings in Her Majesty's ship " Gladiator " to the 29th ultimo; and I beg you will acquaint their Lordships that I have communicated to Lord Lyons that portion of Commander Hickley's letter which relates to the efficiency of the blockade of the several ports named, deeming it advisable that his Excellency should be put in immediate possession of information of that nature.

I have, &c.
(Signed)   ALEXR. MILNE.

Inclosure 2 in No. 43.

Commander Hickley to Rear-Admiral Sir A. Milne.

Sir,   *" Gladiator," at New York, July* 29, 1861.

I HAVE the honour to report that having left New York at noon of the 13th of July, I proceeded under sail to the southward of Cape Henry, and tacked off the coast at noon on the 26th, in latitude 36° 37′ north, longitude 75° 39′ west, to look into the offing, intending if the wind continued foul to steam round Cape Hatteras, and so continue my cruize in-shore; and previous to tacking I met here a United States' revenue schooner, firing shotted guns at a wreck on shore, and exchanged colours with her, the schooner working close up in-shore.

Meeting bad weather and a strong current on the 18th, I steamed in-shore, but failing rounding Cape Hatteras on the 19th, on account of the wind and set, I anchored to the northward of it in the evening, to insure position and in hope of the wind and sea abating, and here found the fore-stay carried away.

At daylight on the morning of the 20th, the wind and sea having increased considerably, I weighed with the intention of rounding the Cape, but was not successful, not being able to get sufficiently round by sunset to peep into the other bay with safety, and thus placed I had no alternative but to put to sea, and with easy steam and fore and aft sails endeavour to keep our ground as well as possible.

On the morning of the 21st, the weather became moderate, when sighting a frigate to leeward I closed with and spoke the United States' frigate " Roanoke," bearing the flag of Commander Pendergast, on a cruize, and in getting sights at noon found the longitude by observation 74° 43′ west (76° 19′ west being that by dead reckoning from good sights the day previous), having experienced a current of 98 miles north, 52 east. I now steamed in for the land, and rounding Cape Hatteras came to an anchor off Ocracoke Inlet at 12 o'clock P.M., having fallen in with and spoken at sunset the United States' gun-boat " Albatross " on a cruize.

On the 23rd, I stood in and sighted the anchorage inside the land behind Cape Hatteras, where were two steamers at anchor, also Ocracoke Inlet, finding there a steamer cruizing outside on the look-out and wearing the Secession flag, which vessel steamed in under the fort on our approach; and when off Ocracoke I have the honour to report the " Albatross," hull down, boarding a barque in the offing.

I now proceeded to visit Beaufort and the east entrance to Wilmington, and rounding the shoals off Cape Lookout, I sighted the former town at 5 P.M., but the weather threatening again, and fearing its continuance, with no anchorage ground, I steamed full speed across the bay to get more shelter, and made the east entrance of Cape Fear river the following morning, having experienced a strong gale during the night; and after this made sail along the weather-edge of Cape Fear shoal (the wind having now shifted strong to the northward) in the hope of seeing a cruizer, but have the honour to report that I was as unsuccessful here as at Beaufort. Having run our distance to the south end of the shoals I stood out to sea under sail to take advantage of the current to get north again, the weather still continuing very bad, with a very cross sea.

On the 24th I fell in with and spoke the sailing-frigate " St. Lawrence," 46 guns, bound on a cruize off Charleston, and tacking that evening in shore, sighted Beaufort the following evening, and Ocracoke on the morning of the 26th, wishing to do so a second time, as it being very bad weather on my making the former on the 22nd, I thought the vessel blockading there might possibly be blown off, and also to ascertain if the " Albatross " was guarding the latter; but there was no vessel at either place, and as the weather was very fine and clear, and from the masthead at both places a good range of coast could be seen, and on a clear look-out to seaward, I am convinced that there was no blockade, and that at that time the ports were entirely open.

I regret to have to report the breaking down of the starboard engine on the morning of the 26th, through the fracture of the trap of the air-pump rod, and damage to the connecting rod itself, and I have desired the chief engineer, who was on watch at the time, to give me the reason, by letter, of the accident happening, and have the honour to state that I am now taking steps for the necessary repairs.

At noon of this day, when rounding Cape Hatteras, I observed a schooner towing a brigantine in-shore, which proved to be one of the two steamers previously reported inside Cape Hatteras; the vessel was evidently a prize, and the steamer was taking her unmolested towards Ocracoke Inlet, neither vessel having any colours flying, and no United States' cruizer in sight. At sunset I fell in with, and communicated with the United States' frigate " Savannah," cruizing between Capes Henry and Hatteras, having previously made out a brig in-shore off New Inlet, with royal yards across, which proved to be a United

States' merchant-brig which had been taken as a prize by the Southern steamers, and with a prize crew on board had been run there on being chased by the "Savannah," to prevent capture.

On the 27th I sighted Cape Henry and the entrance to the Chesapeake, where, seeing a small steamer, I showed our colours, and proceeded at once *en route* to New York, to ensure making progress whilst the weather admitted it with one engine, and after passing the entrance fell in with three gun-boats standing into Hampton Roads, with which vessels I exchanged colours.

I have the honour to state, that as to the blockade, in my opinion, the Chesapeake is strictly blockaded.

The port of Wilmington, at the east entrance, is not blockaded.

Ocaroke Inlet, the chief inlet to Painters Sound, is not blockaded, there being no vessels stationed off these places for that purpose especially, and that I consider the coast between Cape Henry and Cape Fear to be so far under blockade from the vessels I have met, that, without doubt, vessels trying to enter any of the ports above-named risk capture.

I have the honour to report that I arrived at New York this day at 10 P.M.

I have, &c.
(Signed)   H. D. HICKLEY.

No. 44.

Lord Lyons to Lord J. Russell.—(Received August 26.)

My Lord,   *Washington, August 12, 1861.*
WITH reference to your Lordship's despatch of the 13th June last, I have the honour to inclose a copy of a despatch dated the 29th ultimo, which I have received from the Acting Consul at Mobile, relative to the blockade of that port.

I have, &c.
(Signed)   LYONS.

Inclosure in No. 44.

Acting Consul Magee to Lord Lyons.

My Lord,   *Mobile, July 29, 1861.*
I HAVE to acknowledge the receipt of your Lordship's despatch of 3rd current, inclosing a despatch from the Foreign Office regarding the course of blockade, &c., of this port.

I have replied to Lord John Russell that I have never seen or heard of any official notice of this port being blockaded; that we are aware a blockading-squadron is off Pensacola, and off this port, which has ordered off British and other vessels bound to Pensacola and Mobile; that sometimes the navigation between this port and New Orleans is interrupted by a United States' cruizer, and again the said cruizer is not to be seen, and the steam-boats and schooners then make good their voyage.

I shall hereafter keep Lord John Russell advised in quadruplicate of any documents emanating from the Confederate Government regarding the present state of affairs.

I have, &c.
(Signed)   JAMES MAGEE.

No. 45.

Earl Russell to Lord Lyons.

My Lord,   *Foreign Office, August 26, 1861.*
I LEARN from the Admiralty that Rear-Admiral Milne has communicated to your Lordship the result of Commander Hickley's observations up to the 29th of July, with regard to the efficiency of the blockade of the Southern ports; it is no doubt desirable to have this information, but your Lordship should not make any use of it unless in cases of British vessels illegally detained.

I am, &c.
(Signed)   RUSSELL.

No. 46.

Consul Mure to Lord J. Russell.—(Received August 29.)

My Lord,   *New Orleans, July 30, 1861.*

I HAVE the honour to acknowledge receipt of a despatch from Mr. Murray, dated the 13th of June, instructing me to forward, by every opportunity, the most accurate information on the subject of the blockade, and particularly of the port of this Consulate, with a statement of all facts bearing on the same, as to the date of its establishment, interruption, or renewal.

I beg to refer your Lordship to a despatch which I had the honour to address to your Lordship on the 6th of June, in which I detailed at length the particulars of my visit to the blockading vessels at the mouth of the Mississippi river, the date of its establishment, and the manner in which it was enforced.

It is very difficult to procure any accurate information regarding the events transpiring at the mouth of the river, as all communications have been interdicted by the Military Commander of this district; but I have reason to believe that since the 10th of June the blockading vessels "Brooklyn" and "Powhatan" have been joined by three or four gunboats, which are employed in cruizing between the mouth of the river and Mobile Bay. There has been no interruption to the blockade. No ship or vessel from the Gulf has been permitted to enter the river. The only vessel which has succeeded in eluding the vigilance of the blockading squadron was the steam-sloop "Sumter," in the service of the Confederate States, which got to sea when the " Brooklyn " was in pursuit of a vessel.

I ought to inform your Lordship that some small schooners are still arriving at and departing from a small port in this State called Berwick's Bay. This port is about sixty miles to the south-west of this city, and is situated on one of those numerous bayous which are partially fed by the lakes in the interior, and flow into the Gulf of Mexico. Between this city and Berwick's Bay there is a railroad, and articles from Havana and Texas are by these means imported into this city.

No public or official notice touching this blockade has been made in this city, and I am therefore unable to transmit to your Lordship copies of any documents relating to that subject.

I have, &c.
(Signed)   WM. MURE.

No. 47.

The Secretary to the Admiralty to Mr. Layard.—(Received August 31.)

Sir,   *Admiralty, August 29, 1861.*

I AM commanded by my Lords Commissioners of the Admiralty to send you herewith, for the information of Her Majesty's Secretary of State for Foreign Affairs, a copy o a letter from Commodore Dunlop, dated the 23rd July, inclosing a list of United States vessels employed on blockade of the Southern ports in Gulf of Mexico, and stating that the blockade is considered to be effectively maintained.

I am, &c.
(Signed)   W. G. ROMAINE.

Inclosure 1 in No. 47.

Commodore Dunlop to the Secretary to the Admiralty.

Sir,   *" Spiteful," Havana, July 23, 1861.*

I HAVE the honour to transmit herewith, for the information of the Lords Commissioners of the Admiralty, a list of American vessels employed on the blockade of the Southern ports in the Gulf of Mexico, fallen in with by Her Majesty's ship " Jason," and to state that Captain Von Donop is of opinion the blockade of those ports is effectively maintained.

The " Jason " did not visit Galveston, so that I am unable to state what force is employed there; but I have directed Her Majesty's ship " Desperate " to proceed off that place during her cruize in the Gulf of Mexico.

I am, &c.
(Signed)   HUGH DUNLOP.

Inclosure 2 in No. 47.

A RETURN of Foreign Ships of War boarded between the 21st June and 13th July, 1861.

Names.	No. of Men.	No. of Guns.	Captain.	Of what Nation.	When and Where fallen in with.	Remarks.
Powhatan ...	300	11	Acting Commander Porter ...	American ...	June 21st, off the south-west Pass of the Mississippi.	This vessel hailed us in the night station off Pass à l'Outre.
Brooklyn ...	260	22	Not known	Ditto ...		
Huntsville ...	50	3	Commander Price	Ditto ...	June 23rd, cruizing off Mobile	A hired vessel.
Waterwitch ...	50	3	Commander Prlmer	Ditto ...	June 23rd, at anchor off Pensacola.	
San Louis ...	200	22	Not known	Ditto ...	June 23rd, off Mobile	A sailing corvette.
Niagara ...	500	11	Captain McKean	Ditto ...	June 23rd, off Peusacola.	
Mississippi ...	350	12	Flag Officer Mervine	Ditto ...	Ditto.	
Montgomery ...	65	5	Commander Shaw	Ditto ...	July 13th, in Appalachea Bay	A hired steam-vessel, mounting one 10-inch and four 32-pounders, 33 cwt.; 120 horse-power; 180 tons.
R. R. Cuyler ...	120	9	Commander Ellison	Ditto ...	July 13th, off Tampa Bay ...	A hired screw vessel, mounting one rifle 12-pounder, two 32-pounders, 57 cwt., and six 32-pounders, 33 cwt.; about 100 tons, horse-power.
Two gunboats ...	...	...	Not known	Ditto ...	July 13th, off Pass à l'Outre.	

(Signed)   ED. P. VON DONOP, *Captain.*
Her Majesty's Ship "Jason," at Havana, July 22, 1861.

No. 48.

Lord Lyons to Earl Russell.—(Received August 30.)

My Lord,   *Washington, August* 15, 1861.
WITH reference to my despatch of the 1st instant, I have the honour to inclose a copy of a note from Mr. Seward, stating that there appears to be such probable cause to doubt the fact that the "Herald" is British property that justice to all parties requires a judicial examination of the case.

I inclose also a copy of an instruction which I have addressed to Mr. Consul Kortright on the subject.

I shall judge by Mr. Kortright's answer whether or no it will be advisable for me to make an effort to induce the United States' Government to give effect to their order for the immediate release of the vessel.

I have, &c.
(Signed)   LYONS.

Inclosure 1 in No. 48.

Mr. Seward to Lord Lyons.

My Lord,   *Department of State, Washington, August* 13, 1861.
IN a note from this Department of the 6th instant, you were informed that the Attorney of the United States for the Eastern District of Pennsylvania had been directed to restore the brig "Herald," alleged to be a British vessel, erroneously captured by one of the United States' blockading squadron, and sent in to Philadelphia for a trial of the case.

On receipt of the communication containing the order referred to, Mr. Coffey, the Attorney, addressed a letter to this Department, representing that a preparatory examination of the case resulted in ascertaining such probable cause to doubt the fact that the "Herald" is British property, that justice to all concerned required a judicial examination of the case. This will accordingly, it is presumed, be proceeded with.

I am, &c.
(Signed)   WILLIAM H. SEWARD.

Inclosure 2 in No. 48.

Lord Lyons to Consul Kortright.

Sir,   *Washington, August* 13, 1861.
WITH reference to my despatch of the 7th instant, I inclose for your information a copy of a note which I have just received from the United States' Secretary of State, stating that the District Attorney has represented that there is such probable cause to doubt the "Herald" being British property that justice requires a judicial examination of the case.

I have to request you to obtain all the information you can upon this matter, and to make a report to me upon it without delay.

> I have, &c.
> (Signed)   LYONS.

No. 49.

Lord Lyons to Earl Russell.—(Received August 30.)

My Lord,   *Washington, August* 15, 1861.

IN pursuance of the instructions conveyed to me by your Lordship's despatch of the 27th ultimo, I have addressed an instruction, of which I have the honour to inclose a copy herewith, to Her Majesty's Consuls in this country, referring them to your Lordship's circular despatch to them of the 13th June last, and calling their attention afresh to the extreme importance of obtaining all the particulars possible respecting the blockade of the Southern ports.

I have not failed myself to forward to your Lordship by the earliest opportunities all the trustworthy information which I have been from time to time able to procure concerning this blockade.

> I have, &c.
> (Signed)   LYONS.

Inclosure in No. 49.

Circular addressed by Lord Lyons to Her Majesty's Consuls in North America.

(Extract.)   *Washington, August* 14, 1861.

WITH my despatch of the 3rd ultimo I sent a circular despatch from the Foreign Office dated the 13th June last, and directing you to forward to that office by every opportunity the most accurate information you could obtain as to the actual existence of any blockade, together with a statement of all facts bearing on the same.

I am now directed by Lord John Russell to call your attention to the extreme importance of obtaining all the particulars possible respecting the blockade of the Southern ports.

I have further to observe to you that there are some points which should, as far as practicable, be particularly kept in view, in obtaining information. For the sake of convenience these points are here stated in the form of questions :—

1. Has ingress been allowed by the blockading squadron, after the first establishment of the blockade, to any and what vessels, knowingly and wittingly ?

2. Has egress been allowed, knowingly and wilfully, by the blockading squadron, after the first establishment of the blockade, to any and what vessels, with cargo laden after the blockade, and in derogation of the fifteen days of grace ?

3. Have intermissions of the blockade been caused (A) by the blockading force being wholly and deliberately withdrawn and sent elsewhere by superior orders ? (B) by weather ? or (c) by chasing vessels endeavouring to break the blockade, or other vessels generally ?

4. Has the force on the spot, from local considerations, number and class of cruizers, and so forth, been, when actually present (and, if so, for what time and in what respect), adequate to maintain an efficient blockade, or to cause obvious danger to those attempting to break it ?

You will take every opportunity of forwarding information to the Foreign Office and to this Legation on the subject of the blockade.

No. 50.

Lord Lyons to Earl Russell.—(Received August 30.)

My Lord,   *Washington, August* 15, 1861.

IN my immediately preceding despatch of this date, I have inclosed a copy of a circular instruction concerning the blockade which I have addressed to Her Majesty's Consuls in this country, in obedience to the instruction contained in your Lordship's despatch of the 27th ultimo.

I have the honour to inclose herewith a copy of a special instruction founded on the same despatch which I have addressed to Mr. Consul Bunch, with reference to his despatch to your Lordship of the 12th June last, on the subject of the blockade of Charleston.

In the despatch mentioned, Mr. Bunch comments upon the assertion made by Mr. Seward, in a note written to me on the 27th of May last, that the blockade of Charleston had neither been abandoned, relinquished, nor remitted.

G 2

The particular fact concerning which Mr. Seward would appear from Mr. Bunch's despatch to have been mistaken, is the arrival of the "Harriet Lane" to replace the "Niagara" off Charleston.

Mr. Seward's strong assertion concerning the continuance of the blockade would appear, however, to rest on an assumed principle, regardless of the presence or absence of a blockading force. For he declares that the blockade of Charleston took effect on the 11th day of May, and that "it will continue to be in effect until notice of its relinquishment shall have been given by Proclamation of the President of the United States." He adds, however, that it is expected that the blockade will be rigorously maintained, and that "if any failure in that respect shall occur to the prejudice of any party or nation, its representations to that effect will be promptly considered."

I have, &c.
(Signed)   LYONS.

Inclosure in No. 50.

Lord Lyons to Consul Bunch.

(Extract.)   *Washington, August* 15, 1861.

WITH respect to the manner in which the blockade of Charleston has been carried on, I have, in the first place, to direct your attention to the points which I enumerated in my despatch of yesterday, marked Circular, as necessary to be kept in view in obtaining information relative to the establishment and maintenance of the blockade of the Southern ports in general.

I have further to communicate to you some observations on particular parts of your despatch to Lord John Russell of the 12th of June.

In the list which you give in that despatch of vessels which entered Charleston harbour from foreign ports in the interval between the departure of the "Niagara" and the arrival of the "Minnesota," you mention none between the 18th and 27th May. Did none enter during those nine days?

Further on you say, "In addition to these arrivals from foreign and distant ports, steamers and sailing vessels have been, and still are at this date (June 12th), sailing from Charleston for Southern ports, such as Georgetown, Darien, Fernandina, and Savannah, and arriving here from these ports. Five or six schooners have also arrived with cotton from the wreck of a British ship without the interposition of any blockading force."

It would be desirable to give any particulars tending to prove the facts stated in this paragraph.

The mere fact that the blockading squadron was not visible from the shore, or not certainly known at Charleston to be in the offing, or even that certain vessels succeeded in escaping that force by entering or leaving that port, will not, of itself, render the blockade invalid. That is, in a great degree, a question of relative numbers. Your attention should be particularly directed to obtaining evidence on the point or points on which it may be considered that the validity or invalidity of the blockade is likely to turn; as for instance, first, its general and total imperfection throughout from want of a proper and sufficient force, or second, the number of cases in which either egress, or especially ingress, has been permitted by the blockading force, or third, its partial or temporary interruption by the withdrawal or absence of the blockading force during certain definite periods.

Reference with regard to these and similar questions may be made to Kent's Commentaries on "American Law," vol. i, page 143 *et seq.*, and authorities there cited.

It is considered to be extremely important that you should employ every practicable means to clear up all doubts hanging over the facts connected with the blockade of Charleston, and especially that you should furnish evidence on those points in which your allegations differ from those made in the note addressed to me by the Secretary of State of the United States on the 27th May last.

No. 51.

Lord Lyons to Earl Russell.—(Received September 2.)

(Extract.)   *Washington, August* 19, 1861.

THE "Sarah Starr," a British brig, was captured at sea on the 3rd instant by the United States' ship of war "Wabash" for an alleged violation of blockade of the port of Wilmington in North Carolina.

No. 52.

Lord Lyons to Earl Russell.—(Received September 2.)

My Lord,   *Washington, August* 19, 1861.

WITH reference to my despatch of the 15th instant respecting the case of the "Herald," I have the honour to transmit to your Lordship herewith copies of a despatch and its inclosures which I have received from Mr. Kortright, Her Majesty's Consul at Philadelphia, and of a note which I have addressed to the United States' Secretary of State.

It appears that there is no reason to doubt that the "Herald" is *bond fide* British property, and I would fain hope that the United States' Government will enforce the execution of their order for her release.

I have, &c.
(Signed)   LYONS.

P.S.—I reopen this despatch to add to the inclosures a copy of a note which I have just received from Mr. Seward, informing me, in effect, that the case of the "Herald" will be left to the ordinary legal proceedings, notwithstanding the order for her release which was announced to me by Mr. Seward.

L.

Inclosure 1 in No. 52.

Consul Kortright to Lord Lyons.

My Lord,   *Philadelphia, August* 16, 1861.

I HAVE the honour to acknowledge the receipt of your Lordship's despatch of the 7th instant, inclosing me copy of a note from the Secretary of State of the United States, together with a private letter from the Chief Clerk of the State Department, stating to your Lordship that instructions had been transmitted to the District Attorney of the Eastern District of Pennsylvania, ordering the release of the British brig "Herald," now in the custody of the United States' Marshal of this city for supposed violation of the blockade.

I have also further to acknowledge the receipt of your Lordship's despatch of the 13th instant, inclosing the copy of a note from Mr. Secretary Seward of the same date (13th), stating that the United States' District Attorney had represented to that Department that there was such probable cause to doubt the "Herald" being a British vessel that justice required a judicial examination of the case.

In conformity with your Lordship's instructions to investigate the matter, I beg herewith to inclose two affidavits taken before me, one that of the master, who has been in charge of the vessel since May 1860, and who necessarily from his position must be cognisant of any change in the ownership of the vessel; the other from a respectable merchant of Nova Scotia resident in the city, and not in any way a party interested, who testifies that he was present and saw the "Herald" launched, and that he is personally acquainted with all the owners of the vessel.

The facts contained in both these affidavits can doubtless be duly authenticated by reference to the ship's register, which being in the hands of the District Attorney I have not had access to.

In view of these facts I cannot surmise on what grounds the District Attorney justifies his doubt as to the nationality of the British brig "Herald."

I have, &c.
(Signed)   CHARLES E. K. KORTRIGHT.

P.S.—On referring to the affidavit of the master it will be observed that all the owner's names are not endorsed upon the register, but your Lordship is aware that the register of a ship is not a title of property.

C. E. K. K.

Inclosure 2 in No. 52.

Affidavit of William Folker.

WILLIAM FOLKER, master of the brig "Herald," now in the hands of the United States' Marshal at this port, personally appeared at this Consulate, and on being duly

sworn on the Holy Evangelists of Almighty God, did depose and say, that the said brig
" Herald " was built at Hanseport, Hanse county, Nova Scotia, by J. Burton North, ship-
builder, for himself and others, about seven years ago next autumn; that he was appointed
Master of said ship in May 1860; that at the time he was appointed Master the sole owners
were J. Burton North, of Hanseport, Nova Scotia, ship-builder, Jedediah Newcomb, of
Hanseport, Nova Scotia, trader, John Toye, of Hanseport, Nova Scotia, ship-captain, David
Huntly, of Cornwallis, Nova Scotia, carpenter, Kendall Holmes, Hanseport, Nova Scotia,
ship-captain, and David R. De Wolf, of Horton, Nova Scotia, a ship-broker, now doing
business in New York; that these gentlemen are now the sole and entire owners of said
ship, and that no change of ownership has occurred since this deponent has sailed in said
ship, and that he verily believes that no change could be made without his becoming
cognisant of the same. Deponent further states that the share of Mr. Eaton, of Hanseport,
Nova Scotia, ship-caulker, was purchased by Captain Toye, aforesaid, but the name was not
changed in the register, Mr. Eaton's name is still on the register; and that David R. De Wolf
purchased his share from Captain Kendall Holmes, aforesaid, but his name was not indorsed
on the register. All the owners are British subjects, and entitled to own British ships.
(Signed)   WILLIAM FOLKER.

Sworn and subscribed before me :
(Signed)   CHARLES E. K. KORTRIGHT,
*Her Britannic Majesty's Consul for the State of Pennsylvania, at Philadelphia,
this 16th day of August, 1861.*

Inclosure 3 in No. 52.

Affidavit of Joseph E. Woodworth.

Her Britannic Majesty's Consulate.

TO all to whom these presents shall come :
I, Charles Edward Keith Kortright, Her Britannic Majesty's Consul for the State of
Pennsylvania, Esquire, do hereby certify, that Joseph E. Woodworth, of the firm of Vanhorn,
Woodworth, and Co., of this city, personally appeared at this Consulate, and on being duly
sworn on the Holy Evangelists of Almighty God, did depose that the brig "Herald," now
in the hands of the United States' Marshal of this city, is a British-built vessel, built at
Hanseport, Nova Scotia, about seven years ago, that he was present when she was launched,
and that the owners of said vessel are all British subjects.
(Signed)   JOSEPH E. WOODWORTH.

In faith and testimony whereof, I, the said Consul, do hereunto set my hand and affix
my seal of office, at the city of Philadelphia, this fifteenth day of August, in the year of our
Lord one thousand eight hundred and sixty-one.
(Signed)   CHARLES E. K. KORTRIGHT.

Inclosure 4 in No. 52.

Lord Lyons to Mr. Seward.

Sir,   *Washington, August 17, 1861.*
IN a note which you did me the honour to address to me on the 30th of last month,
you were so good as to inform me that the Secretary of the Navy had directed the release
of the "Herald," a British brig, taken possession of at sea by the United States' frigate
" St. Lawrence," for an alleged violation of a blockade of the port of Beaufort, in North
Carolina.
I was further informed, by a note from the State Department, dated the 6th instant,
that the Attorney of the United States for the Eastern District of Pennsylvania had been
requested to order the restitution of the "Herald," in conformity with the instructions of
the Navy Department.
But by a note from you, dated the 13th instant, I learned, much to my regret and
disappointment, that these orders had not been executed, in consequence of a representa-
tion from the District Attorney of Eastern Pennsylvania, that there was probable cause to
doubt the fact of the "Herald" being British property. The inclosed affidavits of
Mr. Folker, master of the "Herald," and of Mr. Woodworth, who is, I am informed, a
respectable merchant of Nova Scotia, resident at Philadelphia, and in no way interested

in the vessel, appear to show clearly that she was built in the British dominions, and that she is, and always has been, owned exclusively by British subjects.

Such being the case, I trust you will deem it right to take measures to enforce the immediate execution of the orders already given for her release.

I beg you to be so kind as to return the affidavits to me.

I have, &c.
(Signed)   LYONS.

<hr>

Inclosure 5 in No. 52.

Mr. Seward to Lord Lyons.

My Lord,   *Department of State, Washington, August* 19, 1861.

I HAVE the honour to acknowledge the receipt of your communication of the 17th instant, relative to the case of the British brig " Herald," which vessel was captured at sea on the 16th ultimo by the United States' frigate " St. Lawrence," for an alleged violation of a blockade of the port of Beaufort, in North Carolina.

In reply, I have to inform you that, as the case is now under adjudication, it is not deemed advisable for the Executive Government to accept the *ex parte* affidavits which accompanied your note as conclusive in the case. An authenticated copy of the papers has, however, been sent to the Attorney of the United States for the Eastern District of Pennsylvania, in order that they may be allowed due weight in the investigation.

The original affidavits are herewith returned.

I have, &c.
(Signed)   WILLIAM H. SEWARD.

<hr>

No. 53.

Consul Bernal to Earl Russell.—(*Received September* 2.)

(Extract.)   *Baltimore, August* 19, 1861.

I HAVE the honour to inclose herewith two extracts from the " Daily Exchange " newspaper, published in this city, respecting the inefficiency of the blockade of the Mississippi.

Inclosure in No. 53.

Extracts from the " Baltimore Daily Exchange."

[SPECIAL.]

The Paper Blockade.—Private advices from New Orleans, dated July 31, bring the intelligence that the Confederate steamer " McRae " was again at that port. It will be recollected that we noticed the fact a few days since that she had run the blockade and proceeded to Ship Island, where she attacked the steamer " North Carolina." Ship Island is off Lake Pontchartrain, and the " North Carolina " had been stationed there for the purpose of stopping the intercourse between Mobile and New Orleans. The " McRae " put two shells in the hull of the " North Carolina," who, having the heels of her, escaped. The " McRae " again returned to the mouth of the Mississippi, ran the blockade a second time without being interfered with, and reached New Orleans in safety.

Louisiana, July 23, 1861.

WE came over here on June 22, one day before the blockading steamer " Massachusetts " came inside of Ship Island and established the blockade of the Sound. An expedition from the Confederate States' war-steamer " McRae," fitting out at New Orleans, put a couple of lake-steamers in fighting trim, and came out in quest of the " Massachusetts," but she was informed of their proximity, doubtless by Spanish fishermen, and left. The steamers of the expedition repaired to her anchorage, and finding her absent took possession of Ship Island, where we had an unfinished fort just ready for the first tier of guns. In a few hours the steamers' guns were in battery at the fort, and the steamers off for New Orleans, for men to replace the marines at the fort. The "Massachusetts" returned next morning, and engaged the fort forthwith. She fired some twenty-four guns to our eighteen, but ours being longer and well directed, it is thought she was struck at least twice or three times, when she retired, and has never been within striking distance since. Our little steamers have been out firing at her several times, to persuade her to come under the guns of the fort; but she is prudent. Thus the blockade is raised, and the steamers pass to and from Mobile.

No. 54.

Consul Bunch to Lord J. Russell.—(Received September 3.)

(Extract.)   *Charleston, July* 25, 1861.

IN my despatch of the 12th ultimo I took occasion to furnish your Lordship with an account of the manner in which the blockade of this port and of the neighbouring coast had been conducted by the naval forces of the United States from the time of its institution by the frigate "Niagara," on the 11th of May, to the date of my despatch. In it I endeavoured to show the extreme laxity with which it was carried out, even at the time when it was supposed to be most stringently enforced, and to impress upon your Lordship my conviction that it was totally inoperative as against any but large vessels.

Since the period in question no change has taken place in the management of the matter, various vessels of the United States, amongst others the "Minnesota," "Wabash," "Flag," "Percy," and "Roanoke," have been at different times off the mouth of this harbour. Once I believe that there were four together; generally, however, there has been but one. At the moment at which I am writing there is none whatever, nor has there been for upwards of twenty-four hours, although no bad weather has arisen to drive a ship off the coast. In fact, I have no hesitation in stating that the blockade of this portion of the American coast is effective only as regards large vessels, the property for the most part of neutrals; whilst the coasting trade between Charleston and the ports of North Carolina, of Georgia, and of Florida, conducted in steamers of light draught, and schooners of from 100 to 300 tons burthen, goes on unmolested.

In proof of the assertions I have made, and of the opinions I have advanced, I beg leave to transmit to your Lordship certain documents which I venture to hope may be found of use in the consideration of this question.

The first, marked inclosure No. 1, is a list of the vessels which have arrived in this port since the 28th of May, when the "Minnesota" resumed the blockade, interrupted by the departure of the "Niagara." It comprises 51 vessels, every one of which has been compelled at some time or other of its voyage to emerge into the open ocean, although a portion of it may have been performed through inland creeks and rivers.

Mr. Vice-Consul Walker, by whom the Table has been prepared, has excluded every vessel which could not have been stopped by a blockading ship had one been present, so that it would be unfair to allege the impossibility of intercepting them as a reason for not interfering with their voyage.

As the newspapers do not publish a list of the vessels that have cleared outwards during the above period, I cannot furnish a detailed account of them, but your Lordship may see by the paper now sent that many of the vessels enumerated in it have arrived several times in this port.

The paper marked Inclosure No. 2 contains the affidavit of ———, respecting the arrival at South Edisto, an inlet to the southward of Charleston, of the ———, belonging to him, showing, amongst other things, that although he was warned off the coast near Savannah, he put into Edisto in stress of weather, and was becalmed off the mouth of the inlet for eleven hours and a-half, during which time no vessel of war came near him.

Inclosure No. 3 is the affidavit of ———, Master of the steamer ———, a transport in the service of the Confederate Government. It shows that the steamer in question has, on several occasions (having the Confederate colours flying), carried guns, men, engineers, and munitions of war to the northward of Charleston, in full view of the blockading squadron, which has either not chosen or been able to interfere with her.

These two affidavits, which could be almost indefinitely multiplied, conclusively establish the fact that both to the northward and southward of Charleston free access can be obtained to the harbour at all times, and in defiance of the blockading squadron.

I transmit also to your Lordship, marked Inclosure No. 4, a list of the various privateers which have left this port during the so-called blockade.

Inclosure 1 in No. 54.

LIST of the Vessels reported as having arrived at Charleston, South Carolina, since the 28th day of May, 1861 (when the Blockade was resumed by the United States' ship "Minnesota"), without interference on the part of any Blockading Vessel.

Date.	No.	Class.	Name.	Master.	Cargo.	Where from.
1861 May 30	1	Schooner.	.	.	1,600 bushels rough rice, 31 bales Sea Island cotton	Back River.
	2	Steamer .	.	.	221 barrels clean rice and sundries . .	Santee.
June 1	3	Schooner.	.	.	2,050 bushels rough rice	Combahee.
	4	Sloop .	.	.	67 bales upland cotton	Wreck of British barque "Coronet," off Hunting Islands.
" 2	5	Schooner.	.	.	1,600 bushels rough rice, 7 bales upland cotton	Chehan.
	6	Do.	.	.	100 barrels clean rice	Combahee.
" 3	7	Sloop .	.	.	61 bales upland cotton	Wreck of British barque "Coronet."
	8	Smack .	.	.	43 bales upland cotton	Ditto.
	9	Do. .	.	.	40 bales upland cotton	Ditto.
" 5	10	Schooner.	.	.	24 bales Sea Island cotton . . .	Beaufort, South Carolina.
	11	Sloop .	.	.	85 bales upland cotton	Wreck of British barque "Coronet."
" 6	12	Schooner.	.	.	3,000 bushels rough rice, 5 bales Sea Island cotton, 2 bales upland cotton	Combahee.
	13	Do. .	.	.	2,500 bushels rough rice	Ditto.
	14	Steamer .	.	.	11 bales Sea Island cotton and sundries .	Georgetown.
" 8	15	Do. .	.	.	87 bales Sea Island cotton—45 from South Carolina, 42 from Florida	Pilatka, Florida, viâ Fernandina and Savannah.
	16	Do. .	.	.	21 bales Sea Island cotton and sundries .	St. Helena and Edisto.
	17	Do. .	.	.	Confederate States' Schooner "Howell Cobb" in tow	Ditto.
" 10	18	Schooner.	.	.	1,800 bushels rough rice, 50 sacks flour .	Santee.
	19	Steamer .	.	.	8 bales upland cotton, 315 bales naval stores, and sundries	Ditto.
" 11	20	Do. .	.	.	52 bales rice straw, 43 barrels spirits of turpentine	Georgetown.
" 12	21	Do.	.	.	. . . .	Jacksonville, Florida, viâ Fernandina and Savannah.
" 14	22	Schooner.	.	.	2,800 bushels rough rice	Santee.
" 15	23	Steamer .	.	.	190 hogsheads sugar (part of cargo of prize brig "Joseph")	Georgetown.
" 18	24	Do. .	.	.	Sundries	St. Helena.
" 19	25	Schooner.	.	.	2,400 bushels rough rice	Pocotaligo.
	26	Steamer .	.	.	4 bales Sea Island cotton, 18 barrels rice, 20 hogsheads sugar, 115 head cattle	Pilatka, viâ Jacksonville, Fernandina, Savannah, and Beaufort.
" 22	27	Schooner.	.	.	1,410 bushels rough rice	Combahee.
	28	Do. .	.	.	730 bushels rough rice	Ditto.
	29	Steamer .	.	.	234 bushels rough rice and sundries . .	North Santee.
" 25	30	Schooner.	.	.	2,300 bushels rough rice	Darien, Georgia.
	31	Do. .	.	.	2,800 bushels rough rice	Ditto.
	32	Do. .	.	.	3,050 bushels rough rice	Back River.
" 26	33	Do. .	.	.	2,800 bushels rough rice	Ashepoo.
" 29	34	S. Carolina Schooner	.	.	. . . .	From a cruize to the southward.
	35	Schooner .	.	.	3,700 bushels rough rice	Combahee river.
July 1	36	Steamer .	.	.	88 head cattle, iron, and sundries . .	Pilatka, viâ Jacksonville, Fernandina, &c.
" 6	37	Schooner.	.	.	50 barrels rice	Santee river.
	38	Sloop .	.	.	2,000 bushels rough rice	Ditto.
	39	Do. .	.	.	47 barrels rice	Georgetown, S. Carolina.
" 9	40	Steamer .	.	.	2 bales Sea Island cotton, 72 barrels turpentine, 101 barrels resin, 77 head cattle, and sundries	Pilatka, viâ Jacksonville, Fernandina, Savannah, and Beaufort.
" 10	41	Schooner.	.	.	1,000 bushels rough rice	Santee.
" 15	42	Do. .	.	.	2,200 bushels rough rice	Ditto.
	43	Do. .	.	.	2,800 bushels rough rice	Ditto.
	44	Sloop .	.	.	2,070 bushels rough rice	Ditto.
" 17	45	Schooner.	.	.	71 barrels rice	Georgetown.
" 18	46	Do. .	.	.	Coal	Savannah, Georgia.
" 21	47	Steamer .	.	.	Ballast.	Georgetown, S. Carolina.
" 24	48	Schooner.	.	.	1,650 bushels corn, 103 bushels ground-nuts	Ditto.
	49	Steamer .	.	.	41 bales Sea Island cotton, 15 head sheep, 27 head beef cattle, spirits of turpentine, and sundries	Fernandina, viâ Savannah and Beaufort.
" 25	50	Schooner.	.	.	2,070 bushels rough rice	Ashepoo.
	51	Sloop .	.	.	75 barrels clean rice	Georgetown, S. Carolina.

(Signed) ROBERT BUNCH, *Consul.*

Inclosure 2 in No. 54

Affidavit of ———.

British Consulate, Charleston, South Carolina.

——— maketh oath and saith, that he is the owner of a schooner called ———;
that ——— became the master of the said schooner; that on the 12th day of May this
deponent being on board she sailed with a cargo of 225 tierces of rice for Havana; that
at that time the United States' steam-frigate "Niagara," Captain McKeon, was stationed
about ten miles from the Swash Channel of Charleston harbour; that the ——— went
out over the Ship Channel and was brought-to by a gun from the said steamer, and
boarded by an officer from the same; that such officer indorsed upon the provisional
register of the ——— as follows :—

"May 12, 1861. Boarded and warned off the whole Southern coast of the United
States from the Capes of the Delaware to Texas by United States' frigate 'Niagara.'
(Signed)   "J. C. P. DE KROFT, *Lieutenant, U.S.N.*"

Deponent further saith that he continued on his voyage without further molestation
and reached Havana on the 23rd May, and then found the said United States' frigate
"Niagara" there; that with all convenient despatch deponent took in a cargo at Havana
of 70 hogsheads of molasses and 100,000 cigars, and cleared for the port of New York,
and set sail on the 3rd of June; that he proceeded on his course and on the 10th day of
June, when off Tybee lighthouse, fell in with the United States' flag-ship "Minnesota,"
Commodore Stringham, and run under her lee; that the Captain was required to go on
board the frigate with his papers, when the following indorsement was made on the said
provisional register :—

"Schooner ——— boarded fifteen miles east from Tybee lighthouse, Georgia,
and again warned off the coast of the United States south of the Capes of Chesapeake Bay;
if found on the Coast by another United States' vessel to be taken charge of, and sent in
as a prize.
"'*Minnesota*,' *off Tybee Lighthouse, Georgia, June* 10, 1861.
(Signed)   "A. LUDLOW CASE,
"*Commander U.S.N., and Fleet Captain, Atlantic Blockading Fleet.*"

And deponent saith that before meeting with the said United States' frigate "Minnesota"
he had encountered much bad weather, and found that it would be impossible, considering
the heavy swell and adverse winds, to reach his port of destination, and he therefore
resolved to terminate his voyage at the port of Charleston.

And deponent further saith that the harbour of Charleston is capable of being entered
by various channels other than those before which have been stationed blockading vessels,
that is to say, by way of South Edisto river, North Edisto river, and Stone river to the
southward; and that believing all of the said three entrances to be free from any blockading
force, deponent resolved to enter port through one of them, and selected the South Edisto
river, which he made on the 11th day of June, after having been becalmed on that day for
eleven hours and-a-half, and reached Charleston on the following day, having found no
blockading force whatever to prevent his entering the said last-mentioned river.
(Signed)   ·———.

Sworn before me, this 22nd day of July, 1861.
(Signed)   H. P. WALKER, *Vice-Consul.*

Inclosure 3 in No. 54.

Affidavit of ———.

British Consulate, Charleston, South Carolina.

——— maketh oath and saith, that he is the Master of the steamer ———,
a transport in the service of the Confederate States of America, at the port of
Charleston. That on Saturday, the 13th instant, he left the port of Charleston, bound
for Bull's Bay; that he went over Maffitt's Channel, and all the way by sea, the distance
from Charleston bar to Bull's Bay being about twenty miles. That he had on board
officers and seventy-five men, and necessary implements and materials for the construction
of a fort at the eastern end of Bull's Island. That the blockading fleet, consisting of
three vessels, were stationed off the Bar of Charleston between what are called the Swash

Channel and the Ship Bar. That deponent went out between 7 and 8 o'clock in the morning, with the flag of the Confederate States flying from his flag-staff aft, but no notice whatever was taken of him by the said blockading fleet. That on the next day he returned to Charleston by the same route; another vessel had then been added to the blockading fleet, and deponent, notwithstanding, came in at about 1 o'clock P.M. with his flag flying as before, but no notice whatever was taken of him.

Deponent further saith that there are various channels through which the harbour of Charleston may be reached, independently of those before which the blockading fleet has been stationed; that those to the north-east of Charleston are Breach Inlet, Caper's Inlet, Price's Inlet, and Bull's Bay. That on Thursday, the 18th instant, deponent sailed on another trip to Bull's Bay, carrying artillery, munitions, and a corps of Engineers. That he proceeded with his colours flying, going out to sea at Breach Inlet, and continuing outside all the way. That on the next morning, the 19th instant, he proceeded from Bull's Island to Georgetown, going out to sea through an inlet a little north of Cape Romain, called the Horns, and continued outside until he reached Georgetown bar.

Deponent saith that during the two days last mentioned, he was closely watched by what he presumes to have been a United States' vessel which was cruizing off the coast. Deponent further saith that on his return from Georgetown with a company of troops on Sunday morning, the 21st instant, he took the same course and channels; and on leaving Bull's Island on the 23rd instant, he took the inland navigation, in consequence of the bad weather and heavy swell, until he reached the Breach Inlet, through which he went out and crossed Maffitt's Channel entrance to Charleston harbour. Deponent further saith that the capacity of the steamer under his command is 314 tons register, and she carries 1,700 bales of cotton.

Deponent further saith that the inland navigation from Bull's Bay to Charleston is much used by vessels not drawing more than eight feet of water; and that the steamer ———— has this day arrived from Bull's Island through the connecting creeks, and without going outside at all in the course of her passage.

Deponent further saith that on his return from Georgetown, he saw nothing of the cruizer before referred to; and upon arriving off Charleston bar, the blockading fleet was not in sight.

(Signed) ————.

Sworn to before me, this 23rd of July, 1861.
(Signed)   H. P. WALKER, *Vice-Consul.*

Inclosure 4 in No. 54.

List of Privateers which have left the Port of Charleston during the Blockade.

AMONG the vessels that have left the port of Charleston, South Carolina, since the 28th May, 1861 (when the blockade was resumed by the United States' ship "Minnesota"), are :—

The privateer schooner ————, which sailed on the 23rd June.
The privateer brig ————, which sailed on the 28th June.
The privateer steamer ————, which sailed on the 16th July.
The privateer schooner ————, which sailed on the 19th July.
The privateer schooner ————, which sailed on the .
(Signed)   ROBERT BUNCH, *Consul.*

No. 55.

Consul Bunch to Lord J. Russell.—(Received September 3.)

My Lord,   *Charleston, July 25,* 1861.
I HAVE the honour to transmit to your Lordship herewith four copies of a Proclamation issued on the 13th instant by Flag Officer Pendergrast, of the United States' Navy, the Commander-in-chief of the West India squadron, relative to the blockade of the ports of North Carolina, which he states that he is a condition to render effective from that date. The customary fifteen days are given to vessels in the various ports. Your Lordship will also find a letter from the Commander of the United States' steamer "Daylight" to the officer commanding the fort at the mouth of the Cape Fear river, inclosing the Proclamation of the Flag Officer for the information of the people of Wilmington.

H 2

As Commodore Pendergrast issued a similar Proclamation on the 30th of April last, which has never been carried into effect, it remains to be seen whether or no a really effective blockade will now be established. I shall not fail to keep your Lordship fully informed respecting it. But I am quite certain beforehand that only large vessels will be repelled, whilst the coasting trade and the privateers will go on as usual.

I have, &c.
(Signed) ROBERT BUNCH.

P.S.—Since this despatch was written I have received from Mr. Vice-Consul Mac Rae the accompanying list of the vessels which have entered the port of Wilmington since the date of Commodore Pendergrast's first Proclamation, ninety-three in all. We shall see whether the same result follows the second notification of blockade.

R. B.

Inclosure 1 in No. 55.

Proclamation.

U.S. Flag-ship " Roanoke," off Charleston, July 13, 1861.

To all whom it may concern.

I HEREBY call attention to the Proclamation of his Excellency Abraham Lincoln, President of the United States, under date of the 27th April, 1861, for an efficient blockade of the ports of Virginia and North Carolina, and warn all persons interested that I have a sufficient naval force here for the purpose of carrying out that Proclamation.

All vessels entering the ports of North Carolina, or hovering about the coast of the same, will subject themselves to capture. Those coming from abroad, and ignorant of the blockade, will be warned off.

All vessels bound to the Capes of Virginia will be allowed to proceed by having their papers endorsed, and will be allowed to enter any of the ports of Maryland.

Fifteen days after this date the above Proclamation will be rigidly enforced against all vessels.

(Signed) G. J. PENDERGRAST, *Flag-Officer,*
Commanding West India Squadron.

Inclosure 2 in No. 55.

Commander Lockwood, U.S.N., to the Commanding Officer of Fort Caswell, Fear River,
North Carolina.

Sir, *U.S. Steamer " Daylight," July* 20, 1861.

I HAVE the honour of forwarding herewith by a flag of truce a notification of the blockade of this port, which I request may be forwarded for the information of all whom it may concern. Bad weather has prevented an earlier delivery.

I am, &c.
(Signed) SAMUEL LOCKWOOD, *Commander.*

Inclosure 3 in No. 55.

STATEMENT of Vessels arrived at, and cleared from, the Port of Wilmington, N.C., from 1st May to 25th July, 1861.

No.	Class.	Name.	Arrived.	Where from.	Cleared.	Where for.
			1861		1861	
1	British brig	..	..	. . .	July 25	Liverpool.
2	Schooner	..	..	. . .	May 2	Baltimore.
3	„	..	..	. . .	„ 2	Hertford, N.C.
4	„	..	..	. . .	„ 3	Baltimore.
5	„	..	..	. . .	„ 3	New York.
6	Brig	..	..	. . .	„ 4	Barbadoes.
7	„	..	..	. . .	„ 4	Baltimore.
8	British brig	..	..	. . .	„ 4	Liverpool.
9	Brig	..	..	. . .	„ 4	Ditto.
10	Schooner	..	..	. . .	„ 4	New York.
11	Brig	..	..	. . .	„ 4	Rio Janeiro.
12	„	..	..	. . .	„ 4	Thomaston, Me.
13	Schooner	..	..	. . .	„ 4	New York.
14	„	..	..	. . .	„ 4	Ditto.
15	„	..	..	. . .	„ 4	Baltimore.
16	„	..	..	. . .	„ 5	New River, N.C.
17	„	..	..	. . .	„ 5	Ditto.
18	„	..	..	. . .	„ 5	Ditto.
19	„	..	May 1	Boston . . .	„ 6	Boston.
20	„	..	„ 1	Philadelphia . .	„ 10	Philadelphia.
21	„	..	„ 1	St. Barts . .	„ 20	Ditto.
22	„	..	„ 1	New Orleans .	„ 10	New York.
23	„	..	„ 1	Baltimore . .	„ 9	London.
24	„	..	„ 1	Hyde Co., N.C. .	„ 6	Hyde Co.
25	„	..	„ 1	Ditto . . .	„ 6	Ditto.
26	„	..	„ 2	Richmond, Va. .	„ 14	New York.
27	„	..	„ 2	Perquimmons Co., N.C.	„ 6	Beaufort, N.C.
28	„	..	„ 2	Ditto . . .	„ 6	Ditto.
29	„	..	„ 2	Hyde Co., N.C. .	„ 6	Hyde Co.
30	„	..	„ 2	Ditto . . .	„ 6	Ditto.
31	„	..	„ 2	Ditto . . .	„ 6	Ditto.
32	„	..	„ 3	Ditto . . .	„ 7	Ditto.
33	„	..	„ 3	Jacksonville . .	„ 5	Jacksonville.
34	„	..	„ 3	Hyde Co., N.C. .	„ 5	Hyde Co.
35	„	..	„ 3	Philadelphia .	„ 10	Philadelphia.
36	„	..	„ 3	Hyde Co., N.C. .	„ 10	Hyde Co.
37	„	..	„ 4	Charleston, S.C. .	„ 8	Baltimore.
38	„	..	„ 4	Hyde Co., N.C. .	„ 12	Hyde Co.
39	„	..	„ 6	Sloop Point, N.C .	„ 12	Still in the river.
40	„	..	„ 6	Georgetown, S.C..	„ 12	Georgetown, S.C.
41	„	..	„ 7	New Orleans .	„ 11	New York.
42	„	..	„ 8	Shallotte, N.C. .	„ 11	Shallotte.
43	„	..	„ 10	Charleston . .	„ 15	New York.
44	„	..	„ 10	Nassau . .	June 6	Nassau.
45	„	..	„ 10	Little River, S.C. .	„ 13	Little River, S.C.
46	„	..	„ 17	Hertford, N.C. .	„ 25	Beaufort, N.C.
47	Ship	..	„ 17	Campeachy . .	July 6	Liverpool.
48	Schooner	..	„ 18	Hertford, N.C. .	May 6	Hertford, N.C.
49	„	..	„ 18	Washington, N.C .	„ 21	Washington.
50	„	..	„ 18	Rockport, Me. .	June 5	London.
51	„	..	„ 18	Hertford, N.C. .	„ 1	Martinique.
52	Brig	..	„ 19	Cardenas . .	„ 10	Portland, Me.
53	British brig	..	„ 19	Cardiff, Wales .	„ 5	Liverpool.
54	Schooner	..	„ 19	Georgetown, S.C .	May 21	Washington, N.C.
55	„	..	„ 19	Ditto . . .	„ 22	Georgetown, S.C.
56	„	..	„ 19	Ditto . . .	„ 24	Hertford, N.C.
57	British brig	..	„ 26	Liverpool . .	„ 24	Liverpool.
58	„	..	„ 26	Bologne . .	June 3	Ditto.
59	„	..	„ 27	Cardiff . .	„ 12	Hull.
60	Schooner	..	„ 27	Shollotte . .	May 28	Shallotte.
61	„	..	„ 27	Georgetown, S.C. .	„ 30	Georgetown, S.C.
62	„	..	„ 27	Jacksonville . .	„ 30	Jacksonville.
63	„	..	„ 27	Ditto . . .	„ 30	Ditto.
64	„	..	„ 28	Little River, S.C. .	June 1	Little River.
65	„	..	June 1	Hertford . .	„ 6	Beaufort, N.C.
66	„	..	„ 1	Scuppernong, N.C. .	„ 8	Edenton, N.C.
67	„	..	„ 4	Little River . .	„ 8	Little River.
68	„	..	„ 10	Newbern . .	„ 26	Nevis, W.I.

Arrived previous to 1st May, 1861

Statement of Vessels, &c.—*continued.*

No.	Class.	Name.	Arrived.	Where from.	Cleared.	Where for.
			1861		1861	
69	Schooner	.. ..	June 10	Georgetown . . .	June 11	Georgetown, S C.
70	,,	.. ..	,, 10	Ditto	,, 28	West Indies.
71	,,	.. ..	,, 10	Little River . . .	,, 28	Little River.
72	,,	.. ..	,, 12	Washington, N.C. .	,, 20	Washington, N.C.
73	British schooner	.. ..	,, 15	Cardiff	July 9	Liverpool.
74	Schooner	.. ..	,, 16	Washington, N.C. .	June 18	Washington, N.C.
75	,,	.. ..	,, 19	Shollotte . . .	,, 19	Shallotte.
76	,,	.. ..	,, 19	Washington, N.C. .	,, 22	Washington, N.C.
77	,,	.. ..	,, 20	Ditto	,, 22	Ditto.
⁻8	,,	.. ..	,, 25	Hertford, N.C. . .	,, 30	Edenton. N.C.
79	,,	.. ..	,, 25	Shollotte . . .	,, 28	Shallotte.
80	,,	.. ..	,, 25	Smithville . . .	..	Still in port.
81	,,	.. ..	,, 25	Hertford . . .	,, 28	Onslow, N.C.
82	,,	.. ..	,, 25	Ditto	,, 28	Hertford, N.C.
83	,,	.. ..	July 1	Georgetown . . .	July 5	Georgetown, S.C.
84	,,	.. ..	,, 2	Smithville . . .	,, 15	Cardenas.
85	,,	.. ..	,, 2	Little River, S.C. .	,, 4	Little River.
86	,,	.. ..	,, 10	Nassau . . .	,, 25	Nassau.
87	Steamer	.. ..	,, 10	Smithville . . .	,, 15	Privateering cruise.
88	,,	.. ..	,, 17	Charleston, S.C. . .	,, 20	Ditto.
89	Schooner	.. ..	,, 20	Georgetown . . .	..	In port.
90	,,	.. ..	,, 17	Washington, N.C. .	,, 18	Washington, N.C.
91	,,	.. ..	,, 17	Ditto	,, 18	Ditto.
92	,,	.. ..	,, 24	Pasquotank, N.C. .	..	In port.
93	,,	.. ..	,, 24	Hertford, N.C. . .	..	Ditto.

Nos. 1, 39, 86, 89, 92, and 93, are still in port, or in the river.
Nos. 1, 8, 53, 57, 58, 59, 73, 80, 84, are British vessels.
Nos. 87 and 88, are armed Confederate States' privateers.
Nos. 83 and 89, were chased and fired at when coming in by a United States' steamer.
Nos. 88, 89, 90, 91, 92, and 93, came in since 13th July (date of blockade).
Nos. 84, 86, 87, 88, 90, 91, went to sea since 13th July (date of blockade).

No. 56.

Consul Bunch to Lord J. Russell.—(*Received September* 3.)

My Lord,   *Charleston, August* 6, 1861.
   WITH reference to my various despatches on the subject of the blockade of the
coasts of the States of North and South Carolina, and especially to my despatches of the
12th of June and of the 25th of July, I beg leave to inclose herewith to your Lordship a
copy of an affidavit made before Mr. Vice-Consul Walker.
   This document conclusively shows that there is in reality no blockade at all of this
coast, except so far as large vessels are concerned.
   The several privateers which have sailed from this and other Southern ports are
making captures every day, and sending their prizes into all the ports, quite unmolested by
any of the ships of the United States.
   In North Carolina the same state of affairs prevails. Even the little steamer the
" Daylight," which remained for five days off the port Wilmington, has been withdrawn,
and, so far as I believe, not a single ship of war is at present to be found on the entire
coast of the State.
                                                     I have, &c.
                                 (Signed)   ROBERT BUNCH.

Inclosure in No. 56.

Affidavit of ———

                                         British Consulate, Charleston, South Carolina.
   ——— maketh oath and saith, that he is the master of the steamer ———.
That on the 27th day of July last he left the port of Charleston for Fernandina,

taking the inland navigation; that he crossed St. Helena Sound abreast of Otter Island; that there was no blockading vessel there, either inside or outside, so far as deponent could see; that he had made a previous trip to Fernandina and back without meeting any vessel of the blockading fleet there; that a vessel stationed there would cut him off. That he proceeded from St. Helena Sound up the Coosan River to Beaufort, and down the Port Royal River to Broad River, and then across to Skull Creek; that at Broad river the blockading fleet might station vessels which would cut off vessels taking the course deponent pursues, but there are no vessels there either inside or out. From thence he proceeded across Callibogue Sound and up Tybee River to Savannah. Upon coming back through Tybee River, deponent saw two frigates of the United States' blockading fleet riding at anchor, well out to the southward, about six miles outside the bar, and about twelve miles distant from his steamer. Deponent's course after leaving Tybee passes by Thunderbolt village down to Romney Marsh, then across the mouth of the Ogeechee River, then inland to St. Katherine's, and from thence to Sapels. That at Sapels vessels might be cut off; that there is a very good bar there to come in at, but there are not, and have not been, any blockading vessels there. That from thence deponent passes inland to Doboy; that that also is a very good bar, but there is not, nor has there been, any blockading vessel there; from thence the course is inland to St. Simon's, from thence to St. Andrew's Sound, and from thence to St Mary's, and then across to Fernandina. That at each of the three last named places, viz., St. Simon's, St. Andrew's, and St. Mary's, vessels might be prevented from proceeding on their course by the presence of a blockading vessel.

That deponent arrived at Fernandina by the route described on Tuesday, the 30th July last, and left again for Charleston on Wednesday at noon, or thereabouts, and reached Charleston on Saturday the 3rd of Augnst instant, having passed through the same channels, and without meeting with any interference or obstruction from any vessel of the United States' blockading fleet, and is about to leave to-morrow on another voyage to Fernandina.

Deponent further saith, that to the best of his knowledge and belief, there are not, and have not been, any United States' blockading vessels stationed upon the coast from Charleston to Fernandina, a distance of about 200 miles, elsewhere than off Charleston Bar, and off Tybee Lighthouse.

(Signed) ------

Sworn to before me, this 5th August, 1861.
(Signed)   H. P. WALKER, *Vice-Consul.*

No. 57.

Consul Bunch to Lord J. Russell.—(*Received September 3.*)

My Lord,   *Charleston, August 7,* 1861.

JUST as my messenger is leaving for the North, I have received the affidavit which I have the honour to inclose herewith to your Lordship. It is made by Mr. Thomas J. Moore, the master of the privateer " Dixie," and contains an account of his cruize, which extends over sixteen days. Time does not permit me to analyze it, but it is of the highest importance, as showing the utter inefficiency of the blockade.

Your Lordship will observe that vessels of 287 and 330 tons have been safely brought into ports of both North and South Carolina. The " Dixie " has in her cruize captured upwards of 100,000 dollars' worth of Northern property.

I have, &c.
(Signed)   ROBERT BUNCH.

Inclosure in No. 57.

Affidavit of Thomas J. Moore.

British Consulate, Charleston, South Carolina.

THOMAS J. MOORE maketh oath and saith that he is the master of the privateer schooner " Dixie," duly commissioned by the President of the Confederate States of America; that he sailed from the port of Charleston on the 19th day of July last, and went to sea through the channel of the North Edisto river on the day following at about half-past 6 in the afternoon. That there were no blockading vessels in sight.

And deponent saith that from the time he went to sea on the 20th of July last up to the 5th instant, when he again came into North Edisto river, he saw no vessel of the United States whatever.

Deponent further saith that in the course of his cruize, that is to say, on the ——— day of July (the precise day deponent cannot state without reference to his log-book) he captured as a prize the American barque " Glen " of Portland, Maine, of 287$\frac{34}{95}$ tons register, laden with 391 tons of coal, and consigned to the commanding officer at Fort Jefferson, Tortugas, which vessel was placed in charge of Prize-master George D. Walker, the First Lieutenant of the " Dixie," to be taken into port. That the said George D. Walker has succeeded in carrying the said barque into the port of Beaufort in North Carolina, and is now in this city to report his action. That afterwards, on the 31st July or 1st of August, the American barque " Rowena," of Philadelphia, was captured as a prize. She is a vessel of 330$\frac{8}{95}$ tons, and laden with a cargo of 1,000 sacks of coffee.

The deponent says he thereupon left the " Dixie " in command of his third officer, James Benton, and himself took command of the said last-mentioned barque, and brought her into the North Edisto river in safety, where she now remains awaiting condemnation. That the said James Benton succeeded in taking the " Dixie " into Bull's Bay, where he arrived yesterday, the 5th instant, and is now in Charleston, where he has come to report his arrival.

Deponent says he cruized eastward as far as longitude 67° or thereabouts, and between latitudes 33° and 36° north.

(Signed)   THOS. J. MOORE.

Sworn before me, this 6th August, 1861.
(Signed)   H. P. WALKER, *Vice-Consul.*

No. 58.

Acting Consul Fullarton to Lord J. Russell.—(Received September 6.)

My Lord,   *Savannah, August* 12, 1861.
IN accordance with Mr. Murray's despatch of the 13th of June, requesting that information respecting the blockade be from time to time transmitted to the Foreign Office, I have the honour to report that this port continues to be strictly blockaded by the United States' squadron, and there is no doubt that it would be dangerous for a vessel to pass in or out.

From reliable information I have received since my despatch of the 22nd of July, it is otherwise with the smaller ports on the coast to the south of this. The blockade of such ports is not effective, being maintained by the United States' Government, not by vessels of war permanently stationed off the mouth of each harbour, to prevent access thereto, as is the case with this port, but merely by a few vessels cruizing up and down the coast, appearing off a port one day, and leaving the same unobstructed the next. In proof of this I beg to report that the prize of a Confederate privateer was lately taken into Brunswick, one of the most considerable ports in this State, the entrance to which was at the time quite unobstructed by the presence of any blockading vessel whatever.

On the other hand I have also to report the unsuccessful attempt of another prize of the same privateer to enter Fernandina, Florida. This prize being chased by a blockading vessel, which happened to be off the port at the time the attempt was made, was run on shore by the prize crew and afterwards burnt by the boats of the man-of-war.

The above allusion to this port refers to the main entrance, by which alone large vessels can approach. The peculiar formation of the coast south of this, indented as it is by numerous inlets and arms of the sea, forming the well-known Sea Islands, renders it very difficult for a blockading squadron, however large, to exclude effectually vessels of light draft, which entering by any of the inlets can easily be brought to this city by the many channels inside of said islands.

I have, &c.
(Signed)   A. FULLARTON.

No. 59.

Lord Lyons to Earl Russell.—(Received September 7.)

My Lord,   *Washington, August* 22, 1861.
I HAVE the honour to transmit to your Lordship a copy of a despatch from Mr. Acting Consul Fullarton, containing information with respect to the blockade of the ports of Georgia.

I have, &c.
(Signed)   LYONS.

Inclosure in No. 59.

Acting Consul Fullarton to Lord Lyons.

My Lord,   *Savannah, August* 7, 1861.

THE brig " John Welch," of Philadelphia, from Trinidad de Cuba, bound to Falmouth for orders, with a cargo of sugar, was captured on the banks of Newfoundland by the Confederate privateer " Jeff. Davis," and taken about the 30th ultimo into the port of Brunswick in this State.

The prize-master informs me that he lay becalmed off Brunswick for a considerable time, and finally got in without seeing anything whatever of a blockading vessel, showing that that port is not at all times so effectually blockaded as to prevent access thereto.

From the fact that there is no Court of Admiralty within the limits of this Consulate, no Judge having yet been appointed, the libel has been filed in Charleston, where the Court will decide the question of ownership of cargo. The result of my inquiries shows that the consignees per bill of lading are Messrs. A. E. Campbell and Co., of London. The shipper, however, a merchant named Zelente, makes affidavit on the back of the bill of lading that he is a Spaniard and sole owner of the cargo, said affidavit being certified by W. Sydney Smith, Her Majesty's Vice-Consul. I may add that A. E. Campbell and Co. are bankers in London, part of whose business consists in issuing credits for a large portion of the Spanish business in this country and the West Indies; through them, no doubt, the negotiations were made, and this may explain why they are consignees. The " John Welch " will be taken to Charleston, which can be done by the passage inside the numerous islands on this coast.

The " Jeff. Davis " (formerly, I believe, the slaver " Echo ") is owned in Charleston. She succeeded in running the blockade of that port on the 28th June last.

This port continues to be strictly blockaded. There is little doubt that it would be dangerous for any vessel to attempt to pass in or out. It is, however, otherwise with the smaller ports to the south of this. They appear to be blockaded not by vessels stationed off the mouth of each harbour, but only by a few of the United States' steamers cruizing up and down the coast. leaving frequent opportunities for vessels to pass in, as shown in the case of the " John Welch " above mentioned. On the other hand I have to report the unsuccessful attempt of another prize, lately taken by the " Jeff. Davis," to enter Fernandina, Florida. Being discovered and chased by a blockading vessel, she was run on shore and abandoned by the prize crew. Subsequently the boats from the man-of-war, finding it impossible to get her off, set fire to and destroyed her. I believe the vessel was bound to Boston from India.

I have, &c.

(Signed)   A. FULLARTON.

No. 60.

Consul Archibald to Earl Russell.—(Received September 9.)

(Extract.)   *New York, August* 27, 1861.

REFERRING to Mr. Murray's circular despatch of the 13th June, instructing me to forward to the Foreign Office information respecting the existence and maintenance of the blockade of the ports of the Seceded States, and also to a circular despatch recently received by me from Her Majesty's Minister at Washington on the same subject, and referring likewise to my despatch of the 17th July utimo, I have the honour to report that the information obtainable at this port with reference to the maintenance o the blockade is derivable almost entirely from newspaper intelligence, and is by no means reliable. Announcements are made from time to time of the " energetic efforts which are being made by the Government to render the blockade complete," but no regular official or authentic report is published of the distribution and actual movements of the vessels of the blockading force from which a judgment of the efficiency of its operations might be formed. This intelligence will be obtained with more accuracy from parties at or in the vicinity of the blockaded ports.

From Commander Hickley I learn that during his last cruize, which terminated on the 18th instant, the ports of North Carolina, or rather both entrances to Cape Fear, the ports of Wilmington and Beaufort, and Ocracoke Inlet, had not, as yet, been blockaded, and remain open. Some of the vessels of the blockading force have since been dispatched to that part of the coast, but I am unable to report by this packet any facts in reference to their movements.

I have reason to believe that several merchant-vessels have taken advantage of the open state of the ports in question, and have both entered and departed with cargoes without molestation.

Commander Hickley further informed me that there was a barque loading at Beaufort as he passed by; that there were also two schooners there, three schooners at Ocracoke, and one at New Inlet.

With regard to the blockade of other Southern ports, I beg leave to transmit herewith inclosed printed extracts from the "New York Times" newspaper of this date, giving a report of the cruise of the "Roanoke," and of the mode in which the blockade is maintained off Charleston. It will be seen from this statement that the service is performed in an exceedingly loose and inefficient manner; that several vessels passed in, and a steamer passed out of Charleston, in the presence of the whole squadron, whose feeble efforts to prevent or overhaul the latter vessel were utterly unavailing.

I transmit, likewise, printed extracts from the "New York Herald" of this date containing a similar but more detailed report of the proceedings of the blockading force off Charleston.

I have not heard of any instance (unless the absence of vigilance and activity above referred to is to be so regarded) in which in ingress to, or egress from, any port has been knowingly or wilfully allowed by the blockading squadron after the first establishment of the blockade of such port.

Inclosure 1 in No. 60.

Extract from the "New York Herald" of August 27, 1861.

"*Roanoke*," *off Charleston, August 6, 1861.*

THE BLOCKADE ON THE NORTH CAROLINA COAST.—I see by a communication in the "Herald" of the 13th ultimo, from Fall river, that the writer speaks of the reception of a letter from North Carolina, in which it is stated that the ports of Wilmington, Beaufort, Washington, &c., on the coast, have no actual blockade. As we have made two cruises in the vicinity of these places, I can speak understandingly of the subject. The writer also states that an English brig is now loaded in the port of Wilmington and will leave the first fair wind. Now, we ran into the harbour of Cape Fear river, where Fort Caswell is located, the entrance to the port of Wilmington, about three weeks ago, and since that time have passed outside the coast twice. While, with the present available force of the navy, it is impossible to station a man-of-war, or even gun-boat, at every one of the little out and inlets along the coast, nevertheless at all the large and important ports there are one or two vessels strictly guarding the blockade. Then, again, transport vessels in the employ of our Government are passing and repassing nearly every day, and sometimes oftener. There is no doubt that there are several small steamers and also some sailing vessels fitted out as privateers that are now cruizing in and out at Beaufort, Wilmington, Newbern, and Hatteras Inlet. They are of light draught of water, swift sailers and never venture far out to sea. They watch their chances, and have thus far been quite fortunate in escaping the vigilance of our fleet. No doubt some prizes have been taken of late, as we have known others to be—a sort of petit larceny affair; still it is very annoying, and will soon be remedied. With the naval force now in the hands of the Department, I am satisfied all is being done that can be to prevent these depredations being made. Commodore Pendergrast is active and vigilant along the shore, and it is only to be regretted that he has not better facilities afforded him. What we want is at least twenty gun-boats immediately—such as the "Flag," "Union," and that class, or better ones, along the coast. They could all be profitably employed. The large vessels—like our ship, the "Wabash," "Vandalia," "Jamestown," &c.—now on duty here between Key West and Fortress Monroe, could be stationed along at the more important points and occasionally move as they might deem it advisable. With such an arrangement it would be an impossibility for a craft of any magnitude to run the blockade.

Even as the operations are at present conducted I have very little fear of any English brig of any magnitude, or in fact any other, undertaking to get out of a port with a load of cotton. In the desperateness of their condition, I have no doubt the Confederate rebels would run any risk to get a small schooner, with arms and munitions of war, into their dominions, and practise the most 'cute specimens of smuggling. Even with the fleet we have now here—the "Roanoke," "Vandalia" and gun-boat "Seminole"—at present, I am satisfied small coasting vessels could, of a dark night, and I am not sure but even in the day time, come out of Charleston harbour, but I do not think they could get far at sea.

Confederate Point, which the writer speaks of, is doubtless Hatteras Inlet, where we were fired upon about three weeks ago, an account of which I sent you at the time. Since then some of our gun-boats have been quite near the shore, but were not troubled. It is, however, as being an important entrance to Pamlico and Albemarle Sounds, a point of much interest, and I am only surprised that our Government does not pay more attention to it. From there vessels can run direct to Norfolk, viâ the Dismal Swamps; and if I had my say I would occupy the Point with Union troops if possible, and keep a vessel-of-war there to protect them or carry them off if necessary. The Point is on a barren strip of sand beach, many miles from the mainland, that forms the outside of the Sound, and with a good sand battery, with long-range rifled guns, would be as impregnable as Fortress Monroe from an attack either by land or water from the Confederate troops, and by holding it would give our rebel friends a mighty sight of uneasiness. This is my programme.

Inclosure 2 in No. 60.

Extract from the " New York Times" of August 27, 1861.

THE BLOCKADE OF CHARLESTON.

" Roanoke," Flag-ship Blockading Squadron, off Charleston,
August 17, 1861.

WE arrived at Hampton Roads on the 3rd, left on the 8th, passed down the coast of North Carolina, and were fired at by a Secession battery near Cape Hatteras. The shots fell very far short (the distance being about four and a-half miles), when we hoisted colours and returned the compliment with our 10-inch pivots and a 12-pounder rifled howitzer; had the satisfaction of seeing one shell fall and explode near the rebel battery, but could not note the effects.

On July 12, we arrived at Smithfield, North Carolina, and left on the 13th; set fire to an abandoned Secession pungy; we reached Charleston Harbour on the 14th, and on the evening of the next day arrived off Savannah, where we found the sloop-of-war " Jamestown " at anchor, continuing our course as far as latitude 30°, when we went about and returned north.

Returning north, we came to anchor at Hampton Roads July 22. On the 24th, the " Albatross " brought in a prize. On the 25th, our launches came in with a schooner and three canoes, having burned nine or ten others that were aground. We weighed anchor on the 27th, and met the " Savannah " steering north, also the gun-boat " Union," which latter was chasing and firing into a Southern vessel. She afterwards reported that she destroyed the same, with a valuable cargo, being unable to save the prize, as it was run aground purposely.

On August 2, we anchored off Charleston Harbour. The " Wabash " left in the evening. We found the " Vandalia " at anchor here. The " Seminole " hove in sight with her head-gear and bowsprit carried away. She came to anchor, and reported a collision with the " Wabash."

Two fugitive slaves from Charleston came on board on the 4th. Our worthy Captain informed them that he " did not come here to pick up fugitive negroes, but to fight their masters." They will probably be made to act as coal-heavers for Uncle Sam. About half-past 8 o'clock in the evening of the next day lights were seen crawling along close inshore, in the direction of the harbour, one of which was made out to be quite a large sail, but she passed in safely. Since this event other sails have been duly reported. It is but proper to state that the blockading squadron, composed at present of the " Roanoke," the gun-boats " Seminole " and " Iroquois," and the sloop-of-war " Vandalia," lay at least twelve miles from the entrance of the harbour. It is also true that some of these sails were pronounced to be fishing-smacks by those having glasses; but, be this as it may, there was an evident desire on the part of the crew to have a "smack" at them, fish or otherwise. And although the " Roanoke " was at anchor, and the " Vandalia " and " Iroquois " on a roving cruise, yet the " Seminole " was within hail, her cables ready to slip at any moment.

But if this should occasion surprise, what will your readers think when they are told that on the 9th instant, a Secession steamer ran the blockade? She was first seen puffing away toward the coast, on our starboard bow. After expending much valuable time in staring through glasses, hoisting signals and examining signal books, the " Vandalia " was finally ordered in pursuit, but having only a quarter wind, you may judge the result. After the steamer had made good her retreat, the " Seminole " made chase. Hardly had the excitement of this event subsided, when another steamer, emboldened by the success of the former, attempted the same exploit; but pursuit in this instance could not be avoided, and, finding herself well headed off from the entrance of the harbour, she put back with redoubled speed. She was vigorously pursued by the sloop and gun-boat, our crew watching eagerly until they were out of view. They have since returned, with no trophies appended.

In the afternoon of the 14th, about half-past 3 o'clock, a steamer left the harbour bearing the English flag forward, and a flag of truce at the main. She lay-to at about good firing distance, when we sent one of our boats alongside, and brought off the British Consul. What the nature of his interview with the Commodore was, none but the initiated can tell. Of course, there was no end to rumours, surmises, &c., among the men. Some had it that he narrated with a good grace a deplorable state of things amongst the rebels—others that he came to intercede for two English vessels laden with cotton. Shortly after the Consul left us, orders were given to get up anchor, and at about half-past 9 o'clock anchored again some eight miles from our first anchorage, where we still lie.

The steamer " Harriet Lane" arrived early on the morning of the 15th. We can just see her through the thick haze. She brings a large mail.

The "Seminole" has captured a small schooner laden with coffee, sugar, tea, and liquor. She is of about forty tons burden. This mail goes by the "Seminole," the "Harriet Lane" having left on the 16th for the South.

Our crew, up to this date, have enjoyed excellent health—but one death has occurred. The heat is much subdued by a constant breeze, and our supply of water is inexhaustible, as it is procured by condensing.

TRUTH.

No. 61.

Lord Lyons to Earl Russell.—(Received September 13.)

(Extract.)   *Washington, August* 29, 1861.

THE " Prince Leopold," a schooner under the British flag. has been seized at New York for an alleged violation of a blockade of the port of Berne in North Carolina.

No. 62.

Lord Lyons to Earl Russell.—(Received September 13.)

(Extract.)   *Washington, August* 29, 1861.

I HAVE the honour to transmit to your Lordship copy of a despatch relative to the seizure at Newport of the British schooner "Adelso" for an alleged violation of a blockade of the port of Wilmington in North Carolina.

Inclosure in No. 62.

Vice-Consul Edwards to Lord Lyons.

(Extract.)   *New York, August* 17, 1861.

I HAVE the honour to report to your Lordship that the British schooner " Adelso " was seized upon the 14th instant as a prize by the authorities at Newport, Rhode Island (which port she was forced to enter under stress of weather), for an alleged violation of the blockade of the port of Wilmington, North Carolina.

No. 63.

Consul Archibald to Earl Russell.—(Received September 15.)

(Extract.)   *New York, September* 3, 1861.

REFERRING to my despatch of the 27th ultimo, I beg leave to transmit herewith inclosed, for your Lordship's information, printed extracts from the " New York Daily Tribune," containing what I believe to be a full and correct list of the ships of the blockading squadron, and of the ships purchased and chartered by the Secretary of the Navy for the purposes of the blockade.

From various sources of intelligence I have reason to believe that no great increase of vigilance has taken place in the maintenance of the blockade of the ports of North and South Carolina. Vessels with naval stores from North Carolina appear to have reached several of our colonial ports, and vessels from colonial and foreign ports are reported to have recently entered the port of Charleston.

I inclose some printed slips containing intelligence respecting blockade matters.

Inclosure 1 in No. 63.

Extract from the "New York Daily Tribune" of August 29, 1861.

THE BLOCKADING SQUADRON, &c., &c.

DISTRIBUTION OF THE NAVAL FORCES.

Atlantic and Gulf Squadrons.

Vessels.	Class.	Guns.	Men.	Vessels.	Class.	Guns.	Men.
Congress	Frigate ..	50	400	Bainbridge	Brig ..	6	72
St. Lawrence	Ditto ..	50	400	Harriet Lane	Side-wheel steamer.	5	75
Potomac	Ditto ..	50	400	Seminole	Screw sloop	5	110
Santee .	Ditto ..	48	400	Massachusetts ..	Screw steamer	5	112
Wabash	Screw frigate	44	523	South Carolina ..	Ditto ..	5	113
Colorado	Ditto ..	44	523	Montgomery	Ditto ..	5	75
Roanoke	Ditto ..	44	522	Mohawk .	Ditto ..	5	60
Minnesota	Ditto ..	43	522	Wyandotte	Ditto ..	5	60
Savannah	Sloop ..	24	290	Union..	Propeller	4	75
Cumberland	Ditto ..	23	289	Daylight	Ditto ..	4	61
Macedonian	Ditto .	22	282	Penguin	Ditto ..	4	68
Brooklyn	Screw sloop	21	259	Albatross	Ditto ..	4	68
Jamestown	Sloop ..	20	130	Supply .	Store-ship	4	75
Vandalia	Ditto ..	20	131	Connecticut	Side-wheel steamer .	4	100
St. Louis	Ditto ..	18	133	Rhode Island	Ditto ..	4	100
Vincennes	Ditto ..	17	136	National Guard..	Ship ..	4	75
Susquehana	Steam sloop	15	230	Nightingale	Ditto ..	4	75
Preble ..	Sloop ..	14	98	Huntsville	Screw steamer	3	50
Marion .	Ditto ..	14	98	Waterwitch	Side-wheel steamer.	3	56
Richmond	Steam sloop	14	98	Monticello	Propeller	3	60
Dale ..	Sloop ..	14	98	Quaker City	Ditto ..	2	30
Niagara	Screw frigate	12	387	Dawn ..	Ditto ..	2	34
Mississippi	Side-wheel steamer .	11	229	Yankee	Steam-tug	2	25
Powhatan	Ditto ..	11	217	Falmouth	Store-ship	2	30
Mount Vernon	Propeller	9	50	Roman	Ship ..	2	30
R. R. Cuyler	Screw steamer	9	101	Wm. Badger	Ditto ..	2	30
Keystone State	Side-wheel steamer	9	112	Chas. Phelps	Ditto ..	2	30
Crusader	Screw steamer	8	65	Young America..	Steam-tug	1	6
Iroquois	Screw sloop	6	118				
Flag ..	Propeller	6	116		Total ..	697	9,212
Cambridge	Steamer .	6	100				

On Potomac River.

Name.	Description.	Name.	Description.
Pawnee	Screw sloop.	Howell Cobb	Schooner.
Pocahontas	Screw steamer.	Bailey .	Ditto.
Anacostia	Screw tender.	Underwriter	Side-wheel steamer.
Ice-boat	Tug.	Jacob Bell	Tug.
Powhatan (2nd)	Steamboat.	Penguin	Propeller.
Philadelphia .	Ditto.	Union	Ditto.
Mount Vernon (2nd)	Ditto.	Leslie	Tug.
Baltimore	Ditto.	R. B. Forbes	Ditto.
Perry .	Brig.	Pembroke	Gun-boat.
Thomas Freeborn .	Side-wheel steamer.	Rescue (Philadelphia) .	Tug.
Resolute	Propeller.	Ceres .	Ditto.
Reliance	Ditto.	Philadelphia	Side-wheel steamer.
Dana .	Schooner.		

On Pacific Coast.

Name.	Class.	Guns.	Men.	Name.	Class.	Guns.	Men.
Lancaster .	Steam sloop	22	321	Cyane .	Sloop .	18	160
Saranac	Steamer .	9	190	Fredonia .	Store sloop	4	30
Wyoming .	Steam sloop	6	137	Warren .	Ditto .	2	30
Narragansett	Ditto .	5	137				
St. Mary's .	Sloop .	22	99		Total .	88	1,097

Vessels to remain Abroad.

Names.	Class.	Guns.	Men.	Where stationed.
Saratoga . .	Sloop . .	18	144	Coast of Afriaa.
Pulaski . .	Steamer . .	1	20	Coast of Brazil.
	Total . .	19	164	

Vessels ordered Home, and not yet arrived.

Name.	Class.	Guns.	Name.	Class.	Guns.
Hartford . .	Screw sloop .	16	Mohican . .	Steam sloop .	6
John Adams .	Sloop . .	18	Mystic . .	Screw steamer .	5
Dacotah . .	Steam sloop .	6	Sumter . .	Ditto . .	5
Saginaw . .	Ditto . .	3	Relief. . .	Store ship .	2
Constellation .	Itazee sloop .	20	Release . .	Ditto . .	1
San Jacinto .	Steam sloop .	15			
Portsmouth .	Sloop . .	16		Total . .	113

VESSELS BUILDING.

Steam Sloops.

Name.	Yard where building.	Name.	Yard where building.
Tuscarora . .	Philadelphia Navy Yard.	Wachusett .	Boston Navy Yard.
Juniata . .	Ditto.	Housatonic .	Ditto.
Oneida . .	New York Navy Yard.	Kearsage .	Portsmouth Navy Yard.
Adriondack .	Ditto.	Ossipee . .	Ditto.

Gun-boats.

Name.	Where building.	By whom.
Tahoma . .	Wilmington, Delaware .	W and A. Thatcher.
Wissahickon .	Philadelphia . . .	John Lynn.
Scioto . .	Ditto	John Birely.
Itasca . .	Ditto	Hillman and Streaker.
Unadilla . .	New York	John Englis.
Ottawa . .	Ditto	J. A. Westervelt.
Pombina . .	Ditto	Thomas Stack.
Seneca . .	Ditto	Jeremiah Simonson.
Chippewa . .	Ditto	Webb and Bells.
Winona . .	Ditto	C. and R. Poillon.
Owasco . .	Mystic River, Connecticut .	Maxson, Fish, and Co.
Kanawha . .	E. Haddam . . .	E. G. and W. H. Goodspeed.
Cayuga . .	Portland	Gildersleeve and Son.
Huron . .	Boston	Paul Curtis.
Chocura . .	Ditto	Curtis and Tilden.
Sagamore . .	Ditto	Messrs. Sampson.
Marblehead .	Newburyport . . .	G. W. Jackman, jun.
Kennebec . .	Thomaston, Maine . .	G. W. Lawrence.
Aroostook . .	Kennebunk, Maine . .	A. W. Thompson.
Kineo . .	Portland, Maine . .	J. W. Dyer.
Katahdin . .	Bath, Maine . . .	Larrabee and Allen.
Penobscot . .	Belfast, Maine . . .	C. P. Curtis.
Pinola . .	Baltimore	J. J. Abrahams.

The steam-sloops are of about 1,200 and 1,400 tons burden. Their construction was ordered since the commencement of the rebellion, and four of them are now nearly ready for launching.

The gun-boats are of about 500 tons burden, are of light draught, strongly built, and are calculated to carry one 150-pounder rifled gun and four 32-pounders.

Fast Side-wheel Steamers.

Twelve fast side-wheel steamers, suitable for running in shallow water, will soon be on the stocks, and their construction pushed with all possible speed. The building of five of them has been ordered in navy yards, and the remaining seven will in a few days be under contract. These steamers are to be built alike at bow and stern, and when run into narrow rivers, or unexpectedly cornered within range of a masked battery, can pass out without the delay or danger incidental to turning round.

Fast Propellers.

The Department is about contracting for the building of several fast propellers—faster than anything now afloat.

Iron-clad Vessels.

Early in September the plans for iron-clad vessels are to be decided upon, and their construction will be vigorously prosecuted.

Vessels Purchased.

Name.	Class.	Tonnage.	Price paid.	Name.	Class.	Tonnage.	Price paid.
			$				$
Flag	Propeller ..	938	90.000	Young Rover ..	Steam barque.	..	27,500
Massachusetts ..	Ditto ..	1,155	172.500	Gem of the Sea ..	Barque ..	371	15,000
South Carolina ..	Ditto ..	1,165	172,500	Mercedita ..	Steam-ship ..	1,070	100,000
Thos. Freeborn ..	Side-wheel st.	269	32,500	Arthur.. ..	Barque ..	554	20,000
Resolute ..	Propeller ..	90	15,000	Gemsbok ..	Ship ..	622	*
Reliance ..	Ditto ..	90	15.000	King Fisher ..	Clipper whaler	451	17,000
Roman.. ..	Ship ..	330	7,400	Quaker City ..	Side-wheel st.	1,600	117,500
Wm. Badger ..	Ditto ..	334	7,150	Restless ..	Barque ..	266	12,000
Penguin ..	Propeller ..	389	75,000	Mercury ..	Steam-tug ..	229	*
Albatross ..	Ditto ..	378	75.000	O. M. Petit ..	Ditto ..	165	15,000
Yankee ..	Side-wheel st.	328	19,000	Jacob Bell ..	Ditto ..	229	12,000
Keystone State ..	Ditto ..	1,364	125,000	Ceres	Ditto ..	..	12,100
Chas. Phelps ..	Ship ..	362	7,000	New boat, Mystic..	Propeller ..	1,300	135,000
Connecticut ..	Side-wheel st.	2,250	200,000	New boat, Norwich	Ditto ..	400	37,000
Rhode Island .	Ditto ..	1,517	185,000	Rescue (N. Y.) ..	Steam-tug ..	..	17,300
Pampero ..	Ship ..	1,375	29,000	R. R. Cuyler ..	Propeller ..	1,250 }	320,000
National Guard ..	Ditto ..	1,046	35.000	Huntsville ..	Ditto ..	960 }	
Nightingale ..	Ditto ..	..	13,000	Montgomery ..	Ditto ..	860 }	
J. C. Kuhn ..	Ditto ..	888	32,000	Underwriter ..	Side-wheel st.	..	18,500
Chotank ..	Schooner ..	53	1,250	R. B. Forbes ..	Tug ..	..	*
Louisiana ..	Steamer ..	235	35,000	Baltimore ..	Side-wheel st.	250	35,000
Stars and Stripes..	Propeller ..	407	55,000	Powhatan (2nd) ..	Ditto ..	..	*
Brazeliera ..	Barque ..	540	22.000	Philadelphia ..	Ditto ..	..	*
Satellite ..	Steam-tug ..	217	19.000	Rescue (Phil.) ..	Steam-tug ..	..	17,500
Gen. W. G. Putman	Ditto ..	149	14,000	Ino	..	895	40,000
James Adger ..	Side-wheel st.	1,152	85,000	De Soto. ..	Side-wheel st.	2,400	161,250
Fear Not ..	Sailing ship ..	1,012	40,000	Bienville ..	Ditto ..	2,400	161,250
Cambridge ..	Steamer ..	..	80,000	Florida.. ..	Barque ..	297	14,000
Valley City ..	Propeller ..	190	18,000	New London ..	Propeller ..	300	30,000
Augusta ..	Side-wheel st.	1,310	96,000	Racer ..	Schooner ..	252	7,500
Alabama ..	Steamer ..	1,261	93,000	Sarah Bruin ..	Ditto ..	233	7,000
Roebuck ..	Barque .	455	20,000	Shepard Knapp ..	Ship ..	838	36,872
Midnight ..	Ditto ..	387	19,000	C. P. Williams ..	Schooner ..	210	6,000
E. B. Hale ..	Propeller ..	220	23,000	Sophronia ..	Ditto ..	217	8,000
Florida (1st) ..	Steam-ship ..	1,261	87.500	O. H. Lee ..	Ditto ..	200	7,000
Fernandina ..	Barque ..	297	15,000	Morning Light ..	Ship ..	938	37,500
Lucky Star ..	Ditto ..	..	*	Pursuit . ..	Barque ..	600	22,000
Flash	Ditto ..	..	*	Island Belle ..	Steam-tug ..	123	14,000
Amanda ..	Ditto ..	368	15,000				
Zephyr .	Ditto ..	..		Total ..	..	..	3,524,572

* In a few instances the price is not given, complete Returns not having been made. In addition to the above, nineteen hulks have been purchased, and filled with stones, to sink at the mouths of rivers and inlets. Three steamers have been chartered to tow them to their destination. Other similar expeditions will follow.

Chartered Vessels.

Monticello (propeller), 8,000 dollars per month.
Mount Vernon (propeller), 8,000 dollars per month.
Dawn (propeller), 7,000 dollars per month.
Daylight (propeller), 8,000 dollars per month.
Union (propeller), 7,000 dollars per month.

Pembroke (tug).
Edwin Forrest (tug), 25 dollars per day.
Tigress (tug), 35 dollars per day.
Hebert† (tug), 40 dollars per day.
Pusey† (tug), 30 dollars per day.
† These will be attached to the fleet of the Potomac.

Vessels now Fitting-out.

Name.	Class.	Tonnage.	Name.	Class.	Tonnage.
Sabine	Frigate.. ..	1,726	New boat at Mystic..	Propeller ..	1,300
Pensacola.. ..	Steam sloop ..	2,158	New boat at Norwich.	Ditto ..	400
E. B. Hale ..	Propeller ..	220	Flag	Ditto ..	938
Fernandina ..	Barque.. ..	297	J. C. Kuhn ..	Ship ..	888
Lucky Star ..	Ditto ..		Chotank ..	Schooner ..	53
Flash	Ditto ..		Louisiana.. ..	Steamer .	295
Amanda	Ditto	368	Stars and Stripes ..	Propeller ..	107
Zephyr	Ditto ..		Brazeliera.. ..	Barque.. ..	540
Young Rover ..	Steam barque ..		Satellite ..	Steam tug ..	217
Gem of the Sea ..	Barque	371	General Putnam ..	Ditto ..	149
Mercedita ..	Steam ship ..	1,070	James Adger ..	Side-wheel ..	1,152
Arthur	Barque.. ..	554	Fearnaught ..	Ship ..	1,012
Gemsbok	Ship	622	Valley City ..	Propeller ..	190
Kingfisher ..	Clipper whaler ..	451	Augusta	Side-wheel steamer	1,310
Florida	Steam ship ..	1,261	Alabama	Ditto	1,261
Restless	Barque.. ..	266	Roebuck ..	Barque ..	455
Mercury ..	Steam tug ..	229	Midnight ..	Ditto	387
A. M. Petit ..	Ditto	165			

Vessels captured by the Squadrons.

Steam.	Hiawatha.	William and John.	Haxall.
Gipsey.	H. E. Spearing.	Belle Conway.	Geo. B. Baker.
Steam-tug.	Octavia.	Industry.	Ann Ryan.
Young American.	*Brigs.*	Arcola.	George B. Sloat.
	Amy Warwick.	Brilliante.	Venus.
Coal vessel.	Herald (English).	Trois Frères.	Louisa.
Coal vessel.	Nahum Stetson.	Olive Branch.	Coralia.
Coal vessel.	Hoellie Jackson.	Fanny.	Falcon.
Coal vessel.	*Schooners.*	Almira Ann.	*Sloops.*
Cotton vessel.	Sarah and Mary.	Basilide.	Alena.
Cotton vessel.	Mary Willis.	Volasco.	Jane Wright.
Ships.	Delaware Farmer.	Ringdove.	Leon.
Amelia.	Emily Ann.	Brunette.	*P. Boats.*
Lynchburg.	Geo. M. Smith.	Tropic Wind.	Sam. Houston.
Arago.	Union.	Winfred.	Dart.
North Carolina.	Forest King.	General Parkhill.	*C. Boat.*
Greensham.	Aid.	Iris.	Mc Camfield.
General Green.	Buena Vista.	Catharine.	*L. Boats.*
H. M. Johnson.	Mary Clinton.	Elizabeth Ann.	Morning Star.
Barques.	Sally Mears.	Enchantress.	Richard Lacey.
Sally Magee.	John Hamilton.	Shark.	*Privateers.*
Star.	J. H. Etheridge.	T. W. Johnson.	Petrel (sunk).
Pioneer.	Mary.	William Henry.	Savannah.

And a number of others, names not returned.

Privateer.—The brig "Grace Worthington," Captain Trethy, at Belize, Honduras, August 8, reports that on his passage out she was boarded by a full-rigged brig, calling himself a privateer, and belonging to the Southern Confederacy. A ter examining the papers, the " Grace Worthington" was allowed to proceed.

Inclosure 2 in No. 63.

Newspaper Extracts.

To the Associated Press.   *Washington, August* 31, 1861.

IT seems certain that the Administration at present has no intention whatever to avail itself of the permissive sanction given by Congress to the collection of duties on shipboard, or to the entire closing of ports, which on the land side are in the possession of the insurrectionary authorities. Our Government will rely on the existence and efficiency of its blockade, for a sufficient answer to any reclamation, which may be made by foreign Governments in regard to their maritime rights. The " Intelligencer " of to-day contains an article to the above effect, and this telegraphic agency has such authentic information as warrants the expression of the correctness of the statement.

Louisville, Kentucky, August 31, 1861.

SOUTHERN NEWS FROM REBEL SOURCES.—A despatch from the "Nashville American" says that it is believed in Richmond that the blockade has been effectively broken by the arrival of the ——— at Beaufort, North Carolina.

President Davis is reported as convalescent.

An engagement took place at Cross Lane, Virginia, on the 26th instant, between 3,000 Confederate soldiers and 900 Federal troops, resulting in our favour.

Commercial non-intercourse with the North, under a limitation, is to be enforced by penalties during the war. Letter correspondence is also prohibited.

Advices from Matanzas to the 25th instant state that a British schooner ran the blockade off Newbern, and has arrived at this port (Matanzas). She has sailed again for Charleston. A sloop from Charleston also ran the blockade.

(From the "New York Times" of August 30, 1861.)

RUNNING THE BLOCKADE.—The Savannah " Republican " says :—

"The schooner ——— successfully ran the blockade at Fernandina on Thursday last. The schooner was chased and fired at several times by the vessel blockading the port. The cruizer also lowered her boats and went in pursuit of the schooner, which they thought had run on a shoal, but a sudden squall coming up compelled them to return to their vessel, to better secure their own safety. The ———, however, continued on her course, and arrived safely in Fernandina on Thursday. The cargo of the ——— consists of coffee, cigars, fruit, &c., and is worth between 40,000 and 50,000 dollars. The ——— also brought as passengers ——— and several officers who had resigned from the United States' navy. They arrived here Saturday by the Gulf Road, and left the same day for Richmond, to tender their services to the Confederate Government. This is the second time the —— has encountered the blockading squadron, passing it successfully both times. We set Captain —— down as a trump."

(*From Matanzas.*)

BRITISH VESSELS VIOLATING THE EMBARGO.—The mail steam-ship "Matanzas" arrived here to-day from Matanzas, Cuba, bringing dates to August 25th. The city and harbour of Matanzas were entirely free from sickness.

Purser Huertas reports two violations of the embargo of the Southern ports, as follows :—

The British schooner —— ran the blockade off Newbern, North Carolina, and arrived at Matanzas on the 12th, and sailed again for Charleston on the 25th. The sloop —— ran the blockade off Charleston, and arrived at Matanzas on the 21st with the Secession flag.

(*From the "New York World."*)

CASE OF THE BRITISH SHIP ——: RUNNING THE BLOCKADE.—Our telegraphic despatches this morning announce by the way of Richmond and Louisville that the British ship —— has successfully run the blockade at Beaufort, North Carolina.

No. 64.

Consul Bunch to Lord J. Russell.—(Received September 15.)

My Lord,   *Charleston, August* 10, 1861.

WITH reference to my various despatches on the subject of the blockade of the coasts of North and South Carolina by the naval forces of the United States, I have the honour to transmit herewith to your Lordship two documents, which may be of use as evidence of its inefficiency.

The first, marked Inclosure No. 1, is the affidavit of ——, a highly respectable planter of Georgetown, who swears that since the 20th of May there has been no blockading vessel at or near Georgetown Harbour, but all vessels of all kinds, including a prize-brig, have entered and departed freely.

The second, marked Inclosure No. 2, is the affidavit of ——, who swears that he has lately run both up and down the coast to the southward of Charleston, in full view of the blockading ships off Charleston Harbour, without the slightest molestation. The —— had the Confederate flag always flying, and is actually engaged in transporting material for the construction of forts and batteries along the coast.

I have, &c.
(Signed)   ROBERT BUNCH.

Inclosure 1 in No. 64.

Affidavit of ——.

British Consulate, Charleston, South Carolina.

—— maketh oath and saith, that he is a planter; that his resort during the sickly months is on the sea-shore of South Island, at the mouth of Winyau Bay; that he has resided there this summer, since the 20th day of May last; that from that time to this there has been no blockading force stationed off the entrance to the said bay, which is also known as Georgetown harbour; that sailing-vessels and steamers run in and out of the said harbour without any hindrance or interruption; that in doing so they run within a quarter of a mile of deponent's said summer residence; and that among those that have entered is the prize-brig "Joseph," which was captured by the Confederate States' privateer "Savannah," and sent in there for condemnation.

(Signed)   ——,

Sworn to before me, this 7th August, 1861.
(Signed)   H. P. WALKER, *Vice-Consul.*

Inclosure 2 in No. 64.

Affidavit of ———.

British Consulate, Charleston, South Carolina.

——— maketh oath and saith, that on Thursday, the 1st instant, he sailed for Hilton Head and Bay Point; that he took the inland navigation as far as the bar of South Edisto River, which he crossed and went to sea, and then came in over the bar of St. Helena Sound, and proceeded by inland navigation to his destination; that upon his return he took the inland navigation as far as the bar of St. Helena Sound, which he crossed this morning at 6 o'clock, and came outside all the way to Charleston bar, entering the harbour through Lawford's channel, which lies between the main Ship Channel and Morris Island; that the distance from St. Helena bar to Charleston is about forty miles; that deponent passed three of the blockading vessels (two steamers and a sailing vessel), which are at the usual station between the Swash and Ship Channels, and about eight miles distant; that they took no notice whatever of deponent's steamer, although his colours, the flag of the Confederate States of America, were all the while flying from his flagstaff aft.

Deponent further saith, that for a week past there have been no United States' vessels within sight of Hilton Head; and that he went to Savannah on the 7th instant; and that but one vessel was then at the blockading station off Tybee.

(Signed)   ———.

Sworn to before me, this 9th August, 1861.
(Signed)   H. P. WALKER, *Vice-Consul.*

No. 65.

Consul Bunch to Lord J. Russell.—(Received September 15.)

(Extract.)   *Charleston, August 20, 1861.*

I HAVE the honour to report, that since the date of my despatch of the 10th instant, no change has taken place in the character of the blockade of the ports of North and South Carolina. The coasting trade continues in full force, and I feel quite assured that were larger vessels to approach the coast, they could easily enter almost any of the ports.

As an exemplification of the manner in which the blockade is conducted, I beg leave to call your Lordship's attention to the following case :—The British schooner ——— sailed from Wilmington, North Carolina (a nominally blockaded port), about the 1st of July, with a full cargo of lumber. She went to Nevis, and thence to Santa Cruz, where she sold her outward cargo, took in a return load of coffee, and arrived with it in safety at Georgetown, South Carolina, ten days ago. She saw a large frigate at a distance from the land, but was not interfered with. She has now loaded again at Georgetown with rice, and is to sail to-day for Santa Cruz, where she has already purchased her return cargo, so certain is the master of again eluding the blockading fleet.

No. 66.

Earl Russell to Lord Lyons.

(Extract.)   *Foreign Office, September 21, 1861.*

I TRANSMIT to you herewith a copy of a Memorial from the owner of the British ship " Perthshire,"* setting forth the circumstances under which that vessel was interfered with by the United States' ships of war, and asking compensation for the losses thereby occasioned to him; and I have to instruct your Lordship to ask the Government of the United States for an explanation.

---

* Compensation was made by the United States' Government to the owner of this vessel.

Inclosure in No. 66.

Memorial.

To the Right Honourable Earl Russell, Secretary of State for Foreign Affairs.

My Lord,

I TAKE the liberty of directing your Lordship's attention, in your official capacity as Secretary of State for Foreign Affairs, to the following facts connected with the seizure and detention by a United States' steam-ship of the ship " Perthshire," of the port of Hartlepool, whilst engaged in lawful commerce upon the high seas, and to request that your Lordship will, through the British Ambassador at Washington, bring the case before the Government of the United States, and demand compensation for the loss I have sustained by the detention of my ship, and which loss I estimate at the sum of 200*l.* sterling, besides rendering void all insurances effected upon the ship, her cargo and freight (of the gross value of 40,000*l.* sterling), by compelling the ship to deviate from her voyage.

The " Perthshire," a ship of 810 tons register, was chartered by a merchant in Liverpool in March last to proceed in ballast from Grimsby to Pensacola, and there load a cargo of timber for the United Kingdom; the charterer, however, having the option, through his agent at Pensacola, of ordering the ship to Mobile to load cotton for Liverpool at a lump sum of 2,300*l.*

The ship sailed from Grimsby in March last, and on the 13th of May was making for the harbour of Pensacola, when she was ordered to heave-to by the Commander of the United States' steam-ship " Niagara." She was boarded by Lieutenant Brown, boarding officer, who informed Captain Oats, of the " Perthshire," that Pensacola was blockaded, and endorsed the vessel's register as follows :—

" Boarded by the United States' squadron May 13, 1861, and warned not to enter the harbour of Pensacola.

(Signed) " GEORGE BROWN,
" *Lieutenant, U.S.N., Boarding Officer.*"

In reply to the inquiry of Captain Oats, the Lieutenant informed him that Mobile was not blockaded. The ship then proceeded to Mobile, where she arrived on the 14th May. Mobile was not blockaded until the 26th May.

At Mobile the " Perthshire " loaded a cargo of cotton for Liverpool, and proceeded to sea on the 31st May. Outside the port she was again boarded by the boarding officer of the United States' steam-ship " Niagara," who examined her clearances, expressed himself satisfied with them, and said the ship might proceed on her voyage. She proceeded with light and variable winds until the 9th of June, when she was boarded by the boarding officer of the United States' steam-ship " Massachusetts," who, after communicating with his ship, sent a prize crew of twenty-nine men and two officers on board the " Perthshire," who took possession of the ship and all the Captain's papers, hauled down the British flag, and hoisted the United States' flag; they altered the course of the ship, and took her back towards Pensacola, off which place, on the 12th June, after sailing about 200 miles back, they fell in with the United States' squadron, the Commander of which ordered the " Perthshire's " release, without, however, making any compensation for the detention to which she had been subjected, nor for the ship's stores, consisting of tea, coffee, and sugar, used by the prize crew whilst on board the " Perthshire."

On the ship being released, the Captain's papers were returned to him, and his clearance endorsed as follows :—

" Boarded June 9, 1861, by the United States' steam-ship 'Massachussetts,' detained under note 159, page 339, Vattel's ' Law of Nations.' Liberated by commanding officer of the Gulf squadron, June 12, 1861."

This endorsement was without any signature.

A paper was given to the Captain of the " Perthshire," on which was written also without signature, as follows :—

" Vattel's ' Law of Nations.' Sir William Scott's opinion, note 159, page 339, Article 3. Things to be proved—

" 1. The existence of a blockade.

" 2. The knowledge of the party supposed to have offended.

" 3. Some act of violation."

Such, my Lord, is a plain, unvarnished statement of the facts connected with this extraordinary seizure and detention. The ship having reached her destination safely,

K 2

prevents a discussion as to liability in the event of loss after the deviation in the voyage ; but which the Liverpool underwriters say they would have been exempted from had such taken place.

The ground upon which I base my claim for 200*l.* is as follows: the ship had been nine days at sea when she was seized ; she was taken back almost to the place from which she first started, and three days after that (or twelve days from leaving Mobile) she was as far from Liverpool as on the 31st May, when she sailed from Mobile ; her freight was about 550*l.* per month, and twelve days at that rate is about the sum I claim.

The case of the " Perthshire," my Lord, has been commented upon by all the leading journals in Great Britain, and, without exception, they pronounce it a case in which our Government ought to make a demand for damages. I venture to hope, therefore, that your Lordship will take such steps with regard to this matter as will prevent a repetition of improper interference with British ships, and at the same time obtain for me the reasonable and fair compensation I claim.

I have, &c.
(Signed)   WILLIAM GREY,
Hartlepool, August 28, 1861.   *Owner of the ship " Perthshire."*

No. 67.

Consul Archibald to Earl Russell.—(*Received September* 23.)

(Extract.)   *New York, September* 10, 1861.

REFERRING to my despatch of the 3rd instant, I have the honour to acquaint your Lordship that the inefficiency of the blockade of Charleston, South Carolina, and of some of the ports of North Carolina, is still the subject of complaint in the public newspapers. The United States' frigate " Wabash " has relieved the " Roanoke," off Charleston. Small craft appear to enter and leave this port without much difficulty ; and from the contents of a published letter, dated from on board the United States' ship " Vandalia," it appears that two vessels, one of them a steamer called the ——, of 400 tons, the other the schooner ——, of 100 tons, both partially armed, had got safely out of Charleston harbour, and escaped the blockade.

A schooner called the " H. Middleton " was captured by the " Vandalia " on the 21st ultimo, in attempting to escape the blockade of Charleston, which port she had just left. Her crew have been brought to this port, and on Sunday last were imprisoned in Fort Lafayette.

It is complained that the blockading ships are useless, owing to their heavy draft of water, and their consequent unfitness for in-shore operations.

The ship ——, belonging to Charleston, has arrived without molestation at Beaufort, North Carolina.

No. 68.

Acting Consul Fullarton to Lord J. Russell.—(*Received September* 23.)

My Lord,   *Savannah, August* 22, 1861.

IN my despatches of July 22 and August 12, I had the honour of reporting to your Lordship several instances in which vessels had succeeded in running the blockade off this coast, and in arriving safely in this port.

In no instance, however, has this been done by the river or main entrance. As remarked in a former despatch to your Lordship, the inlets and arms of the sea, forming the numerous islands on this coast, afford inland means of communication by water, navigable by vessels not exceeding 200 tons, between this port and the smaller ones to the south. Into some of these inlets and harbours the vessels referred to have succeeded in getting, whence they were easily brought here.

I have now the honour to report several additional instances. The British schooner which I before reported as having successfully run the blockade, has again done so. She left this port on July 19, for Havana, getting to sea on the 21st, through one of the inlets above-mentioned, without seeing anything whatever of a blockading vessel, and returned to Fernandina, Florida, on the 15th instant, having been chased off that port by a United States' man-of-war, from which she escaped in safety.

Again, on the 17th instant, the prize of a Confederate privateer was brought into

Darien, off which port she lay for thirty-six hours, during which time no blockading vessel was to be seen.

Besides being apparently too few for the establishment of an effective blockade of this coast, the vessels used by the United States' Government seem to be too large for that purpose. They cannot, as these instances prove, prevent vessels of a small size from leaving and approaching it. Some of the harbours of this State, such as Brunswick and Darien, will admit vessels of large size, but such vessels cannot come by the inland passage to this port. None of this class have, however, yet succeeded, or indeed attempted, so far as I can learn, to run the blockade.

I have, &c.
(Signed)   A. FULLARTON.

No. 69.

Lord Lyons to Earl Russell.—(Received September 27.)

My Lord,   *Washington, September* 13, 1861.

I HAVE the honour to transmit to your Lordship copies of a despatch, and its inclosures, which I have received this morning from Consul Archibald, and which will make your Lordship acquainted with the facts concerning the blockade observed by Captain Hewett, of Her Majesty's ship " Rinaldo," during his recent cruize.

I have, &c.
(Signed)   LYONS.

Inclosure 1 in No. 69.

Consul Archibald to Lord Lyons.

(Extract.)   *New York, September* 12, 1861.

I HAVE the honour to report to your Lordship that Her Majesty's ship " Rinaldo" arrived last night.

Captain Hewett has kindly furnished me with a précis of his Report to the Admiral, and a copy of his letter to Commodore Stringham, which I now beg leave to send to your Lordship herewith inclosed.

Inclosure 2 in No. 69.

Précis of a Letter of Proceedings from Commander Hewett, of Her Majesty's ship " Rinaldo," to Rear-Admiral Sir A. Milne, dated September 12, 1861.

ON the 2nd instant exchanged colours with United States' sloop of war " Dale," off Oregon Inlet. The 3rd instant communicated by boat with the United States' frigate " Cumberland," cruizing off Hatteras Inlet. Steamed into the anchorage. Communicated with the " Susquehanna." Several United States' men-of-war in the same roadstead. Was informed that the Federal naval force bombarded the Secession force on the 28th and 29th ultimo; they surrendered the second day. Many prisoners fell into the hands of this force, with whom the Flag Officer Stringham returned to Old Point. Anchored nine miles off Beaufort on the 4th, and remained there till the following day. Whilst lying there was boarded by the master of the English ship ――――, then in the harbour, accompanied by an officer of the Confederate forces. The purport of this visit was to gain information as to whether a blockade really existed, as he arrived, and also the English vessel ――――, a short time previous, without seeing any United States' cruizers during their passage or during their stay at Beaufort.

Spoke the United States' frigate " Susquehanna" on the 7th instant. Sent a boat on board us. The boarding officer reported that they boarded a British schooner from Halifax, and that it was his opinion, as the master informed him he had done it several times, she intended to run the blockade.

No. 70.

Lord Lyons to Earl Russell.—(Received September 30.)

My Lord, *Washington, September* 16, 1861.

I HAVE the honour to inclose a copy of a despatch from the Commander of the United States' ship "Pawnee" to the Secretary of the Navy, which appeared in a newspaper yesterday. It reports the capture of the British schooner ——, and of other vessels at Hatteras Inlet.

I am not in possession of any further information on the subject.

I have, &c.

(Signed)   LYONS.

Inclosure in No. 70.

Newspaper Extracts.

THE following important despatches were received last evening in the Navy Department:—

"*United States' steamer 'Pawnee,' Hatteras Inlet,*

"Sir,   "*September* 10, 1861.

" I have to state, for the information of the Department, that I have taken a valuable prize this morning, now called the 'Susan Jane,' of Nevis, West Indies.

" This schooner was called the 'Charles McCoos' when she cleared at Newbern, North Carolina, two days before the blockade went into effect on this coast.

" She took a cargo of spirits of turpentine to the West Indies, and at Charleston, Nevis' Island, obtained an English register, but without a bill of sale or endorsement of any kind on the part of the master or agent, and without any other paper required under English law.

" She sailed from Nevis to Halifax, Nova Scotia, and there took on board an assorted cargo, consisting of blankets, cloth, iron, steel, brogans, axes, &c., all of which were purchased in New York and Boston, as is shown by bills of lading from different leading houses in those cities.

" I send the prize to Philadelphia or New York, at the discretion of the prize-master, Lieutenant Crosby, so that he may be authorized to enter the port most accessible at this stormy period of the year.

" I send all the papers found on board the prize, in charge of Lieutenant Crosby, to be handed to the proper Admiralty officer; also Captain Ireland and four of the crew. I shall detain for the present two passengers, believed to be supercargoes; also the mate.

" When this duty is completed, I have to request that Lieutenant Crosby may be permitted to return to his important duties at this place, as Port Captain, under the orders of General Wool.

" I send Captain Crosby on board of the prize, because he is the important witness of what occurred after we boarded the schooner.

" This vessel, like the three already captured, stood in under the belief that the forts were still in the hands of the enemy (the 'Pawnee,' showing no colours, was taken for an English cruizer), and were not boarded until they were inside the bar.

" We are beginning to see signs of the enemy on the south-western side of the entrance, where it is believed a picket guard frequents to watch our movements.

" I inclose a letter found among the papers of the so-called 'Susan Jane,' which may give the Department some idea of the policy in Nova Scotia.

"I have, &c.

"Gideon Welles,   (Signed)   "J. C. ROWAN, *Commander, U.S.N.*

"Secretary to the Navy, Washington, D. C."

List of Vessels and Crews captured at Cape Hatteras Inlet.

" SCHOONER 'Susan Jane,' captain and crew sent home with vessel; George Shackleford, mate, sent to Fortress Monroe, per steamer 'R. S. Spaulding.'

" Schooner 'Ocean Wave,' crew sent to Fortress Monroe per steamer 'R. S. Spaulding.'

" Schooner 'Harriet Ryan,' crew sent to Fortress Monroe per steamer 'R. S. Spaulding.'

" Schooner 'Mary Ware,' crew sent to Fortress Monroe per steamer 'R. S. Spaulding.'

(Signed)   "J. C. ROWAN, *Commander United States' steamer 'Pawnee.'*

"Flag Officer S. H. Stringham,

"Commanding Atlantic Blockading Squadron."

No. 71.

Lord Lyons to Earl Russell.—(Received September 30.)

My Lord,   *Washington, September* 14, 1861.

I HAVE the honour to inclose copy of a despatch from Her Majesty's Acting Consul at Savannah, concerning the blockade, which, although written so long ago as the 27th of last month, has reached me only this evening.

The inclosed is the only copy which the Acting Consul has sent of the newspaper extract.

I have, &c.
(Signed)   LYONS.

Inclosure 1 in No. 71.

Acting Consul Fullarton to Lord Lyons.

(Extract.)   *Savannah, August* 27, 1861.

I HAVE now the honour to report several instances of vessels having run the blockade since my last despatch to your Lordship.

The British schooner ——, which I before reported as having successfully run the blockade, has again done so. She left this port on the 19th of July, getting to sea on the 21st, through one of the numerous inlets indenting this coast, without seeing anything whatever of a blockading vessel, and returned to Fernandina, Florida, on the 15th instant, having been chased by a United States' man-of-war, from which she escaped in safety.

On the 17th instant the schooner ——, bound from Porto Rico to New York, a prize of the Confederate privateer "Jeff. Davis" was brought into Darien, off which port she lay for thirty-six hours, during which time no blockading vessel was to be seen.

Again on the 25th instant the schooner ——, said to be a British vessel, ran into Fernandina, off which she was detained three days without encountering a blockading vessel.

The masters of these vessels laugh at the blockade as at present maintained. The ——, above-mentioned, is now loading here with the intention of again passing out. Several other small vessels are doing the same thing.

I inclose your Lordship a newspaper slip recounting the doings of the privateer "Jeff. Davis," on her late cruize. Her last act proves the inefficiency of the blockade, since she encountered no United States' man-of-war off St. Augustine.

In no instance has any vessel come into this port by the river or main entrance. The inlets or arms of the sea, forming the numerous islands on the coast, afford inland means of communication by water between this port and those to the South, navigable by vessels not exceeding 200 tons. Into some of these inlets the vessels above referred to have succeeded in getting, whence they were easily brought here.

Inclosure 2 in No. 71.

Newspaper Extract.

ADVENTURES, CAPTURES, AND MOVEMENTS OF THE PRIVATEER "JEFF. DAVIS."— We had the extreme pleasure yesterday of a conversation with Mr. F. C. Dutrieux, one of the gallant crew of the bold privateer, who arrived in this city by the Savannah Railroad on Saturday evening.

He kindly furnishes us with the following interesting account of the departure of the " Jeff. Davis " from that port, and her subsequent career and adventures.

On the night of the 28th of June the "Jeff. Davis " was towed through Maffit's channel out of Charleston harbour by the steamer " Gen. Clinch." They had lights stationed in the channel on both sides, and it was feared at one time that the blockading squadron would detect their movements. They fortunately got clear, however, and made their escape without any difficulty. When well outside the bar they observed the men-of-war vessels exchanging signals. They had a fair wind, and in a very short time passed out to sea, close on Rattlesnake Shoals.

In making their course northward they espied a large ship, which being of a doubtful and uncertain character, and night coming on, she was not fired at. This vessel afterwards falsely reported at New York that she had been chased three days by a privateer. The next vessel spoken was a brig from Baltimore bound to Porto Rico. Under their instructions she was not molested. The brig " Mary Worthington " was soon after boarded. She exhibited, however, a British register, and although it was evident that it was a late transfer, they felt bound to let her proceed.

Saturday, July 6.—A sail was discovered, which proved to be the brig " John Welch." The privateer hoisted the French flag, and the brig believing her to be a French vessel that had lost her way, immediately came up to give the latitude and longitude. The men on board the " Jeff. Davis " were ordered to keep below. When close enough, one of the long toms belched forth for the brig to heave-to, which was obeyed, and the officers and part of the crew of the " John Welch " were soon transferred to the " Jeff. Davis " as prisoners. A prize crew was placed on board the brig and the vessel ordered to a Southern port. This vessel and cargo arrived safely.

The same evening they fell in with the schooner " Enchantress," which also came up to the Frenchman to give the longitude and latitude. She was taken, her crew made prisoners, and a prize crew placed on board the captured vessel. The " Enchantress " was afterwards recaptured.

The following day, while the privateer was under a close press of canvas, a sail was discovered astern, which kept closing up with them. At 12 o'clock the vessel had got near enough to warn her to heave-to. She was greeted with a shot across the bows, and soon reported herself as the schooner " S. J. Waring," of New York. A prize crew was put on board, and the vessel headed for the South. This vessel was recaptured afterwards, and arrived at New York.

The next vessel spoken was the ship " Mary Goodall," of New York. She was boarded, but being of very heavy draft, and her cargo of no importance, she was let go, after having transferred to her a number of prisoners. It was found impossible to keep on board the privateer the very large number of prisoners captured, hence the necessity for the above step.

Whilst making the transfer of prisoners, a small brig hove in sight, and came up towards them, not knowing the character of the privateer. She was brought-to, and found to be loaded with lumber. Being a prize of no value, the captain at first determined to burn her. Some more prisoners, however, were put on board of her, and the vessel allowed to proceed. This was the brig " Thompson," from Westport, Maine, bound to Antigua. She afterwards returned to Newport, Rhode Island.

On Sunday the 19th they fell in with the bark " Alvarado," of Cape Cod, from the East Indies, bound to Boston, with a valuable cargo. The captain of this vessel had his wife with him. She was taken and sent off with a prize crew in a southern direction. [An account of the destruction of this vessel has already been published in the " Courier."]

The " Jeff. Davis " then sailed for Porto Rico, and arrived at that port on Friday, the 26th of July. She remained in port until Monday.

On Sunday, August 2, she espied a schooner and gave chase. The privateer, when close enough, lowered her small boats and boarded the vessel. She was found to be a vessel with a cargo of salt. As this was esteemed of no value, the proposition was made to burn and sink her. Just at that moment the " Santa Clara " hove in sight, and bore immediately down upon them. She was captured with her cargo of sugar and molasses. The prisoners were then transferred to the salt vessel, and the latter turned adrift. The " Santa Clara " has recently arrived safely at Savannah.

Another brig was espied a few days afterwards, two of the small boats lowered, armed, and well manned, and with muffled oars they succeeded in reaching her. She was discovered to be a British vessel and was allowed to proceed unmolested.

On Sunday, the 9th instant, having no more prize masters on board, and the brig proving a dull sailer, the captain determined to make sail for home.

When about 800 miles east of Cape Florida they came in contact with the ship " John Crawford," Captain Edge, from Philadelphia, bound to Key West, with arms and coal for the United States' forces. She was found to draw twenty-two feet of water, and could not possibly be brought in. The officers and crew, numbering in all twenty-two persons, were taken on board the privateer, the vessel fired and holes bored in her sides and bottom. This was about 4 o'clock in the morning, and by good daylight the ship was wrapped in flames, going down shortly afterwards. It was found impossible to procure any of the arms, as they were stowed under the coal.

They then turned their course, with a light wind, for St. Augustine, Florida. Upon nearing the coast the wind increased, until finally it blew a perfect gale. The vessel had crossed the Gulf safely, and on Friday night, the 15th, they hove-to and found themselves in sixteen fathoms water. At daylight land was discovered and a clear coast. They were then about ten miles south of Matanzas. Squared away and made for St. Augustine bar. Found the tide too low upon their arrival, and stood off,

The captain hoisted the Confederate flag at the fore topgallant mast and fired a gun as a signal for a pilot. Three attempts were made to get into the harbour, but it was found they could not weather it. The people on shore kept a light burning for them, as was afterwards discovered, but which the privateers did not observe, or were unable to see. The vessel kept working up to the windward through the night, and at daylight they discovered themselves ten miles from the bar.

The flag was again hoisted, and a pilot was observed coming towards the brig 'and giving the usual signals. In attempting to cross the bar, however, the brig grounded on the north breakers. This was about half-past 6 o'clock Sunday morning, the 17th instant. A small boat was sent ashore with Dr. Babcock and Lieutenant Baya, and the prisoners landed. The officers and crew of the privateer then went ashore, and were greeted with the most enthusiastic demonstrations by the inhabitants. About half-past 9 two light boats went off to the brig, along with Captain Coxetter and other officers. The starboard guns were thrown overboard to lighten the vessel, in order to clear her decks of water, and save as much as possible of the supplies on board the brig.

Every effort was made to save everything then on board, but it is supposed that the guns thrown overboard stove her in and caused her to bilge. The light boats, however, were filled with a large amount of provisions and baggage, and finally succeeded in saving all the small arms on board.

About 2 o'clock all hands had left and were conveyed to St. Augustine.

The ladies threw open their houses and they were received with cheers upon cheers. Cheers were given for the "Jeff. Davis," for the Southern Confederacy, and the utmost hilarity and rejoicing for the safe arrival of the privateers was manifested. While there they were sumptuously provided for, and furnished with every comfort that could possibly be devised.

They learned afterwards that there had been considerable excitement in the town on the appearance of the "Jeff. Davis," it having been suspected that she was a Yankee cruiser in disguise, and had hoisted the Confederate flag to deceive or decoy some of the vessels from the shore. The prisoners were also treated very kindly, and supplied with everything comfortable.

Before our informant left, Captain Coxetter had again returned to the wreck and succeeded in saving an additional amount of provisions and some of the sails.

Every effort was made by Captain Coxetter to secure as much as possible for the stockholders. The brig is a total loss. But a small piece of her bow was remaining on Thursday morning, when our informant left, and it was then thought that she would go to pieces before daylight. The crew of the privateer left there for this city on Monday last, but lost the connecting boat at Toccoa, and were delayed at Fernandina. It is thought they will arrive here this evening.

Our informant took the cars from Jacksonville, Florida, to Monticello, from thence to Savannah. He says that the ladies of St. Augustine were particularly warm in their reception of Captain Coxetter, and gave him a parting testimonial of their respect and esteem for his gallant exploits. They also complimented him with a serenade on their own guitars, accordions, &c.

We hope the brave captain will receive from our citizens some fitting token for the patriotic and glorious deeds that have sent such thrills of joy into every Southern bosom, and filled every Yankee heart with terror of this bold privateer.

We are glad to learn that there will soon be another "Jeff. Davis" afloat, and that the same brave crew are anxious to again go forth to avenge the death of Amiel, and make up for any shortcomings of their first adventures.

No. 72.

Consul Archibald to Earl Russell.—(Received September 30.)

(Extract.)   *New York, September* 17, 1861.

I HAVE the honour to report, with reference to the blockade, that four British vessels, the schooners "Susan Jane," "Ocean Wave," "Harriet Ryan," and "Mary Ware," were, on the 10th instant, captured at Hatteras Inlet in attempting to violate the blockade of that place. They passed in under the supposition that the forts were still in possession of the Confederate forces.

Two other British schooners have recently been brought into this port for alleged violation of blockade, and have been libelled in the Prize Court—the " Aigburth" and " Louisa Agnes."

Three other British vessels have been, within the last three days, seized here, the " Mystery," the "Fellow Craft," and " Prince Alfred." In regard to two of the latter vessels, it appearing to me from the reports of their masters that there was no good cause whatever for seizing them, on my application to the Collector they have been released. The " Mystery " is still under examination and will, probably, be released also.

By the next week's mail I will furnish a full list of all the British ships seized in or brought to this port for alleged violation of the blockade, with observations on the course of procedure in the Prize Court with reference to certain of them.

No. 73.

The Secretary to the Admiralty to Mr. Hammond.—(Received October 1.)

Sir,   *Admiralty, September 30, 1861.*

I AM commanded by my Lords Commissioners of the Admiralty to send you herewith, for the information of Her Majesty's Secretary of State for Foreign Affairs, copy of a letter dated the 18th instant, from Rear-Admiral Sir A. Milne, inclosing copy of a report from the commanding officer of the " Racer " on the actual state of the United States' blockades between Cape Fear and the southern coast of Florida.

I am, &c.
(Signed)   C. PAGET.

Inclosure 1 in No. 73.

Rear-Admiral Sir A. Milne to the Secretary to the Admiralty.

Sir,   *" Diadem," at Halifax, September 18, 1861.*

IN transmitting the accompanying letter of proceedings from Commander Lyons of Her Majesty's ship " Racer," dated 31st July last, I beg you will call their Lordships' attention to the particulars given therein as to the United States' blockades between Cape Fear and the south coast of Florida, only two of the ports within those limits, viz., Charleston and Savannah, being then blockaded.

I have communicated a copy of the inclosed, as well as of the Return transmitted in my other letter of this date, to Her Majesty's Minister in Washington.

I am, &c.
(Signed)   ALEXR. MILNE.

Inclosure 2 in No. 73.

Commander Lyons to Commodore Dunlop.

(Extract.)   *" Racer," Nassau, July 31, 1861.*

I HAVE the honour to report proceedings since leaving Havana in Her Majesty's steam-sloop under my command on the evening of the 15th instant.

Experiencing on the following day (the 16th) a fresh easterly breeze, I stood sufficiently close to Key West to observe lying at anchor in that harbour three United States' ships of war, one apparently a large frigate and two smaller vessels.

At 1 A.M. on the 17th we sighted the Carysfort Reef Light, thence with a light north-east breeze we beat up to Cape Florida, making the Light at 1·30 A.M. the next day. The wind then shifting more to the southward, I was enabled to hug the land.

We arrived off Cape Carnaveral on the afternoon of the 19th, passed close to St. Augustine the next day to St. Mary's at daylight, and at St. Andrew's at 8 A.M. on the 21st.

We arrived off Savannah on the evening of the same day (21st). Lying at anchor off the mouth of the river, blockading the port, were the United States' sailing-frigate " James Town," of 22 guns, and the chartered screw-steamer " Flag," carrying eight 8-inch guns. (This latter vessel when we appeared in sight, weighed, closed, and communicated with us.) I hove-to under the stern of the " James Town," and went on board to pay my respects to the senior officer ; Captain Green informed me that he had been on his present station two months, during which time no vessel of any sort had attempted to break the blockade.

Leaving the "James Town" I proceeded at 10 P.M. for Charleston, arriving off that place at 8 o'clock the next morning (22nd). We found blockading this port the United States' screw-frigate "Wabash," of 44 guns, which vessel on our approach weighed and closed us. I went on board to call on Captain Mercer. This officer told me that he had been stationed off Charleston forty-five days, during which time only two vessels (both American) had attempted to break the blockade, and were consequently made prizes of. On leaving the "Wabash" I continued on our course along the coast. Off Bull's Island twenty miles north-east of Charleston, we met cruizing under sail the United States' sailing-corvette "Vandalia," of 22 guns. I likewise communicated with this vessel, but did not gain any intelligence. Captain Lee informed me that he was under the orders of Captain Mercer of the "Wabash," and was cruizing within signal distance of that vessel. We passed George Town at 5 P.M., and then stood towards Cape Fear. When about twenty-five miles from that Cape the breeze, which had been strong all day from the southward and westward, freshened considerably; I therefore stood out from the land. During the night it blew a moderate gale from the same direction (south-west), shifting in the morning to the north-west, and that with very heavy rain. I therefore did not think it advisable to carry out my intention of sighting Cape Fear, and consequently stood away to the southward and westward. My purpose of looking in again off Charleston and Savannah on our return to the southward was likewise frustrated by the weather. On the 24th the wind having moderated, and the weather cleared, I again closed the land, and at 6 P.M. sighted St. Augustine lighthouse. From this time until the 27th, when we turned off towards the north-west Providence Channel, I was enabled, the wind continuing from the northward, to hug the land. Up to the date I had not during my cruize fallen in with any vessel of any description, except those mentioned in the accompanying Return.

You will have observed, Sir, that the only ports on my cruizing-ground at present blockaded by the forces of the United States are Savannah and Charleston; the blockades of both these places being in my opinion effective. I am not aware what importance may be attached to the many other harbours and inlets along the coast from the South Point of Florida to Cape Fear, such as St. Andrew, St. Mayo, St. Augustine, and George Town, off none of which places there are any United States' ships of war stationed. Captain Mercer of the "Wabash" informed me that it was the intention of his Government as soon as they had sufficient vessels at their disposal, which would probably be in October next, to station them all along the coast, and more particularly off the places I have above named. This would scarcely appear to agree with the announcement made by Commodore Pendergrast, that he had at his disposal a force sufficient to maintain effectually the blockade of the ports of the States mentioned by the President of the United States in his Proclamation of the 19th and 28th of May.

I have met with the greatest possible courtesy from all the officers of the United States' ships with whom I have come in contact.

None of the lighthouses from the south point of Florida to Cape Fear show any light, except those of Carysfort Reef and Cape Florida.

The ship continues in a most healthy state.

We have expended no coal since leaving Havana, and are consequently nearly complete.

I have the honour to report my arrival here at 2 P.M. this day; I beg to inclose the detached service Returns. I trust, Sir, my proceedings will meet with your approval.

No. 74.

The Secretary to the Admiralty to Mr. Hammond.—(Received October 1.)

Sir,   *Admiralty, September* 30, 1861.

I AM commanded by my Lords Commissioners of the Admiralty to send you herewith, for the information of Her Majesty's Secretary of State for Foreign Affairs, a copy of a letter from Rear-Admiral Sir Alexander Milne dated the 18th instant, transmitting a letter from Commander Hickley of the "Gladiator," inclosing a report on the state of blockade of the ports and inlets off the Coast of North Carolina in the months of June, July, and August last.

I am, &c.
(Signed)   C. PAGET.

Inclosure 1 in No. 74.

Rear-Admiral Sir A. Milne to the Secretary to the Admiralty.

Sir,   *"Diadem," at Halifax, September* 18, 1861.

I BEG to transmit, for the information of the Lords Commissioners of the Admiralty, the accompanying letter from Commander Hickley, of Her Majesty's ship "Gladiator," inclosing a Return showing in a tabular form the state of the blockade by United States' vessels of war of the coasts and ports between the Chesapeake and Cape Fear, by which their Lordships will observe that between the 9th of June and the 8th July no vessels of war were blockading that coast ; that between the 13th July and 18th August several ships of war were fallen in with near some of the ports, whilst others were without the presence of any ship of war.

I directed Commander Hickley to make the Return in this form, affording as it does a more easy reference to the respective localities, as also to dates, and which their Lordships will observe contains a summary of his letters of proceedings forwarded by me on the 12th July, and the 8th and 24th August last.

I am, &c.
(Signed)   ALEXR. MILNE.

Inclosure 2 in No. 74.

Commander Hickley to Rear-Admiral Sir A. Milne.

Sir,   *"Gladiator," at Halifax, September* 5, 1861.

I HAVE the honour to inclose for your information a report of the state of blockade of the ports and inlets off the coast of Carolina, during the cruize of Her Majesty's ship "Gladiator," off the American coast, in the months of June, July, and August of the present year.

I have, &c.
(Signed)   H. D. HICKLEY.

Inclosure 3 in No. 74.

REPORT on the State of the Blockade of the Ports and Inlets of the Coast of North Carolina, between Chesapeake Bay and Cape Fear, in the Months of June, July, and August, 1861.

Places.	1st Cruise. Between 9th and 19th June. South.	North.	2nd Cruise. Between 21st June and 8th July. South.	North.	3rd Cruise. Between 13th and 29th July. South.	North.	4th Cruise. Between 2nd and 13th August. South.	North.	REMARKS. 1st Cruise.	2nd Cruise.	3rd Cruise.	4th Cruise.
Cape Henry	Passed to the Eastward	Boarded by the United States' ship "Monticello," hired steamer, 569 tons, 6 guns, 62 men	Passed to the Eastward	Boarded by the "Quaker City," hired vessel, 6 guns, 60 men	Three small steamers lying in the offing	Three small steamers lying in the offing	Two gun-vessels cruising off Cape Henry to the north; one ditto anchored at the entrance to the Chesapeake; made out two gun-boats coming from the north.	Spoke the United States' gun-boat "Quaker City," off the entrance to the Chesapeake; two gun-boats coming from the north.	On the 18th June the following vessels were lying at Hampton Roads:— Cumberland ... 24 guns all 10-inch Jamestown ... 16 " Harriet Lane ... 6 " Daylight ... 4 " Anacostia ... 6 " Dawn ... 6 " Resolute ... 2 " Reliance ... 2 " Freeborn ... 6 " Pocahontas ... 5 "	On the 8th July the following vessels were lying at Hampton Roads:— Minnesota ... 40 guns Roanoke ... 46 " Cumberland ... 32 " Susquehanna ... 16 " Santee ... 50 " Penguin ... 6 " Anacostia ... 6 " Dawn ... 6 " Daylight ... 6 " Quaker City ... 6 "	No means of ascertaining the Number of vessels at Hampton Roads.	
Oregon Inlet	No vessel	No vessel	No vessel	No vessel	Lat. 35° 37' N., long. 75° 20' W., revenue schooner making a passage to the south, and looking along the coast.	Spoke the United States' sailing-frigate "Savannah," lat. 35° 30' N., long. 75° 38' W.	No vessel	Spoke the United States' sloop "Dale," blockading the Inlet of Oregon and New Inlet.				
New Inlet	Ditto	Ditto	Ditto	Ditto	None	Spoke "Savannah," cruising	Ditto					
Cape Hatteras	Ditto	Ditto	Ditto	Ditto	Spoke the United States' screw-frigate "Minnesota," 46 guns, cruising; United States' Government vessel "Albatross," 6 guns, 60 men cruising	No vessel	Ditto	Spoke the United States' paddle-steamer "Harriet Lane," 6 guns, 60 men, lat. 35° 30' N., long. 75°09' W.				
Ocracoke Inlet	Ditto	Ditto	Ditto	Ditto	No vessel	Ditto	Ditto	No vessel.				
Cape Lookout	Ditto	Ditto	Ditto	Ditto	Ditto	Ditto	Ditto	Ditto.				
Beaufort	Ditto	Ditto	Ditto	Ditto	Ditto	Spoke the United States' ship "St. Lawrence," lat. 33° 30' N., long. 75° 46' W., on passage to Charleston	Ditto	Ditto.				
Cape Fear and Wilmington East Entrance	Ditto	Ditto	Ditto	Ditto	No vessel; did not round the shoals	No vessel	Spoke the United States' gun-boat "Penguin," 6 guns, 60 men, off north entrance of Cape Fear; none at the entrance	Ditto.				
West Entrance	Did not round the shoals	Did not round the shoals	Ditto	Ditto	Did not round the shoals	Did not round the shoals	No vessels.	Ditto.				

No. 75.
Lord Lyons to Earl Russell.—(Received October 7.)
(Extract.)   *Washington, September* 23, 1861.

I HAVE the honour to transmit to your Lordship copy of a despatch which I received the day before yesterday from Mr. Consul Archibald concerning a British schooner, the "Aigburth," which was seized at sea on her way from Matanzas in Cuba to St. John's, New Brunswick, by the United States' ship "Jamestown."

Inclosure in No. 75.
Consul Archibald to Lord Lyons.
(Extract.)   *New York, September* 19, 1861.

BRITISH schooner "Aigburth" seized and sent into this port in charge of a prize crew from the United States' ship "Jamestown," on charge of intending to violate the blockade of the ports of Florida.

No. 76.
Consul Kortright to Earl Russell.—(Received October 7.)
(Extract.)   *Philadelphia, September* 20, 1861.

I HAVE the honour to report that on the 4th instant the British schooner "Albion." was brought into this port in charge of a prize crew, having been captured off the port of Charleston on the 16th ultimo, by the United States' squadron, under Commodore Pendergrast.

No. 77.
Lord Lyons to Earl Russell.—(Received October 14.)
My Lord,   *Washington, September* 30, 1861.

I HAVE the honour to inclose duplicates of two despatches addressed to your Lordship by Mr. Coppell, Acting Consul at New Orleans. The one contains information respecting the blockade; the other incloses a copy of instructions from the so-called Confederate Government, in virtue of which vessels are to be allowed to discharge cargo at any point on the coast of the Southern States.

The duplicates were sent to me for my own information; but I send them on to your Lordship lest, in the present uncertain state of the communications with the South, the originals should miscarry. I have kept copies of them.

                                         I have, &c.
                            (Signed)   LYONS.

Inclosure 1 in No. 77.
Acting Consul Coppell to Earl Russell, No. 45, *September* 16, 1861.
[See No. 78.]

Inclosure 2 in No. 77.
Acting Consul Coppell to Earl Russell, No. 46, *September* 16, 1861.
[See No. 79.]

Inclosure 3 in No. 77.
Mr. Memminger to the Collector of the Port of New Orleans, August 22, 1861.
[See Inclosure in No. 79.]

No. 78.
Acting Consul Coppell to Earl Russell.—(Received October 14.)
My Lord,   *New Orleans, September* 16, 1861.

WITH reference to the despatch of date June 13, from Mr. Assistant Under-Secretary Murray, directing the Consul to transmit accurate information regarding blockaded ports and the manner in which blockades are maintained, I have the honour to inform your Lordship that the schooner ———, of 102 tons register, sailing under a provisional certificate of registry, granted at this Consulate on the 6th of June last, was entered at this Consulate on the 11th current, as having arrived from Havana. She is lying in a small river or bayon, named Grand Caillou, about sixty-five miles distant from this city, but by means of the Opelousas Railroad, which connects New Orleans with several of these bayons, having outlets in the Gulf of Mexico, is easy of access to this port. The mouth of this bayon is ninety-five miles west of the south-west pass of the Mississippi river, and there is at this season sufficient water on the bar to admit of vessels of 150 or 200 tons to enter it. The Master reports to me that he did not see any vessels blockading that part of the coast.

The —— had on board a general cargo, comprising wines, cigars, printing-paper, coffee, camphor, &c., &c., valued at Havana at 4,600*l*. sterling.

I understand it is the Master's intention to leave port as soon as he can discharge the cargo.

As this is the first vessel in cargo of whose arrival since the establishment of the blockade I have positive information, I have deemed it my duty to lay before your Lordship these particulars.

I have, &c.
(Signed)   GEORGE COPPELL.

No. 79.
Acting Consul Coppell to Earl Russell.—(Received October 14.)
My Lord,   *New Orleans, September* 16, 1861.

IN accordance with the instructions contained in Mr. Assistant Under-Secretary Murray's despatch of date June 13, I have the honour to inform your Lordship that the Government of the Confederate States, " in view of what may appear to be the inefficiency of the blockade," has thrown open the whole Southern Coast, and has issued instructions to the Collectors of the Ports, allowing vessels to discharge their cargoes, after communicating with the nearest Collector of Customs, at any point they may "make port."

I have the honour to inclose, herewith, a copy of these instructions to the Collector of this port, which is authentic, but cannot be obtained in a more reliable form.

I have, &c.
(Signed)   GEORGE COPPELL.

Inclosure in No. 79.
Mr. Memminger to the Collector of the Port of New Orleans.

Confederate States, Treasury Department,
Sir,   *Richmond, August* 22, 1861.

VESSELS from foreign countries engaged in trade passing in the neighbourhood of the coast of the Confederate States, and deeming it advisable, in view of what may appear to be the inefficiency of the blockade, to enter any port on said coast, where there is no Collector or Custom-house, for the purpose of discharging their cargoes; and it being desirable that this should be effected without inconvenient delay to the parties concerned, the following regulation is established, to wit :—

When a vessel has thus made port, such port shall be considered the proper port of entry for such vessel, if the master or owner shall without delay despatch a messenger to the nearest Collection District, in order that a proper Revenue-officer may be sent by the Collector, or the Surveyor acting as such, to take charge of the cargo. This officer will be invested, for the time being, by the Collector or Surveyor acting as such, in writing, with power to execute the formalities required in connection with the entry of goods at a regular port.

Very respectfully,
(Signed)   C. C. MEMMINGER, *Secretary of the Treasury.*

No. 80.
Consul Archibald to Earl Russell.—(Received October 14.)
(Extract.)   *New York, October* 1, 1861:

SINCE the date of my last despatch on the subject of the blockade, I have little of importance on that subject to report to your Lordship.

The British schooner " Aigburth," bound from Matanzas to St. John's, New Brunswick, seized by the United States' ship " Jamestown," off the coast of Florida, on suspicion of intending to run into some port in that State, has been sent to New York for adjudication.

The British schooners " Louisa Agnes " and " Argonaut," of and from Nova Scotia, captured by the blockading squadron off North Carolina, on suspicion of intending to run into some one of the ports of that State, have also been sent into this port for adjudication.

No. 81.

Consul Archibald to Earl Russell.—(Received October 21.)

My Lord,   *New York, October 8,* 1861.

I HAVE the honour to transmit herewith inclosed, for your Lordship's information, a list of British vessels and of cargoes, being property of British subjects, laden on board foreign vessels, libelled in the Prize Court of the Southern District of New York, and comprising a list of other British vessels seized for alleged violation of the blockade, and still under detention.

I have, &c.
(Signed)   E. M. ARCHIBALD.

Inclosure in No. 81.

List of British Vessels or Cargoes which have been Libelled as Prize in the Southern District of New York.

British barque "Hiawatha," and her cargo consigned to British houses (the greatest part tobacco, small portion cotton).

May 27, 1861, libelled ; charge, that the vessel broke blockade (sailing from City Point, Virginia). June 18, claims and answers interposed ; Mr. Archibald, as Consul, intervening for some of the British owners. Same month, cause heard. September 27, Decree entered, confiscating vessel and cargo.

Appeal entered.

Charles Edwards, Proctor and Advocate for all the claimants.

The "Forest King," an American vessel, but the whole of her cargo (coffee from Rio) belonging to Messrs. Rostron, Dutton and Co., of Manchester, England, valued at 88,320 dollars.

June 22, 1861, libelled. Charge, that the vessel ran into Key West (alleged to have been under blockade), and enemies' property. July 16, claim and answer of owners of cargo interposed. July 19, cause heard. September 27, Decree entered releasing cargo, but without costs, and claimants having to bear their own costs ; seven-eighths of the vessel also restored as belonging to Northern owners, while one-eighth condemned as enemy's property (belonging to a resident of Georgia).

Mr. Edwards, Advocate and Proctor for owners of cargo.

The barque "Winnifred," an American vessel (belonging to Messrs. Crenshaw and Co., of Richmond), but the whole of her cargo claimed by the British house of J. L. Phipps and Co., of New York (Phipps and Co., of Liverpool), Messrs. J. L. Phipps and Co. claiming three-eighths absolutely, and the remaining five-eighths from having advanced upon it to the amount of 20,622 dollars 26 cents. Whole value of cargo 80,640 dollars.

Libelled, claiming condemnation of vessel and cargo as belonging to rebels and enemies. Claims and answers interposed. Cause heard. Decree entered ; three-eighths of cargo in favour of J. L. Phipps and Co., but without costs, and they having to bear their own costs, and condemning vessel and remaining five-eighths of cargo, with liberty, however, to J. L. Phipps and Co. to go into further proof as to the five-eighths.

Appeal taken as to the vessel and five-eighths of cargo.

Mr. Charles Edwards, Advocate and Proctor for vessel and cargo.

The British schooner "Tropic Wind" and cargo, consigned to a British house. (The vessel, with her present cargo on board, heretofore condemned in the United States' District Court at Washington, and afterwards released. Vessel seized, this second time, by General Butler of Fort Monroe, on information from the coloured crew that the Captain had run blockade by entering Rappahannock River, and there put a box of despatches on shore for the Southerners. The Captain, in a protest, states that he only put a small box containing shells, newspapers, and letter for his wife on shore.

August 5, 1861, libel filed. Mr. Archibald, Consul, intervenes for cargo (consigned to Charles Allison, Esq., of Halifax, for British subjects in Liverpool). Messrs. James T. and Theodore Farrington, of Bermuda, are owners and claimants of vessel.

General Butler was ordered to send this vessel to Washington ; instead of that, he sends her to New York, and yet forwards the ship's papers to the Department of State at Washington. All this delays the hearing.

Mr. Charles Edwards, Proctor and Advocate for vessel and cargo.

The British schooner "Aigburth" (under provisional register), owned by Mr. Cowlam Graveley, of Charleston, a British subject, as also the cargo. Vessel had left New Berne, North Carolina, reached Cuba, and was on her way to St. John's, New Brunswick, with a cargo of molasses.

August 31, seized, out of sight of land in the north course of the Gulf Stream. Cause of seizure not clearly ascertained ; probably taken on the idea she broke blockade coming out of New Berne, but this is denied by the Captain. September 11, vessel brought to New York. Monition returnable.

Answer prepared.

Mr. Charles Edwards, Proctor and Advocate for vessel and cargo.

The British brig " Sarah Starr," under provisional register, owned by Mr. Cowlam Graveley, of Charleston, British subject, and who claims an interest in the cargo (turpentine, resin, and beeswax), the greater portion of which is owned by Messrs. Munro, of Newport, Rhode Island (American citizens).

She sailed from Wilmington for Liverpool, August 3, 1861 (thirty-two miles at sea seized).

August 10, 1861, brought to New York. Libel filed. Ownership is attempted to be doubted, and it is supposed that a breaking of blockade will be claimed.

Answers prepared, and cause ready for hearing.

Mr. C. Edwards, Proctor and Advocate for vessel ; Mr. Cutting, Proctor and Advocate for cargo.

The British schooner "Prince Leopold," under full register, owned by Henry Augustus Mc Leod, of Charleston. Cargo belongs to Amos Wade, an American citizen (who is trying to get it released).

The vessel had gone from Wilmington to Bermuda, with cargo of spirits of turpentine, &c., which were not transhipped, but brought northward.

August 21, 1861, came into New York for sails and supplies, and there seized as prize. Libel filed. Supposed to be seized on an idea of breaking a blockade at starting from Wilmington.

Claims and answers prepared.

Mr. Edwards for vessel and cargo.

The "Louisa Agnes," British schooner. Owned in Nova Scotia ; cargo also owned in Nova Scotia.

September 6, 1861, seized near Cape Lookout. Cause of seizure unknown, but must have been taken on very slight grounds. Master not rightly treated while on board capturing vessel. September 12 or 13, brought into New York. September 13, libel filed.

Answer ready to be filed.

Mr. Charles Edwards appears for vessel and cargo.

The "Crenshaw," American schooner, owned in Richmond, Virginia. Cargo partly owned in Richmond, and partly in Scotland.

May 17, 1861, seized in Hampton Roads. Cause of seizure, alleged attempt to run blockade, and of being enemy's property. May 29 or 30, brought into New York. May 31, libel filed. September 28, decree made and entered condemning vessel as enemy's property, and also condemns property claimed by Ludlam and Watson, and Lear and Son. October 7, appeal taken to United States' Circuit Court.

Mr. Edwards appears for Ludlam and Watson, and Lear and Son.

The "Argonaut," British schooner, owned in Nova Scotia. Cargo also owned there.

September 13, 1861. seized about four miles distant from Cape Hatteras, wanting light and water. Seized on presumption of intention to run blockade. Prize-master drunk. Two men of the crew not well treated on board capturing vessel. September 30, brought into New York. October 7, libel filed.

Answers prepared.

Mr. Charles Edwards appears for vessel and cargo.

Other British vessels seized by the blockading squadron or in the port of New York, and still detained :—

Brig "Herald," of Hantsport, United States, sailed from Beaufort for Liverpool 26th June, seized on 28th June, 200 miles at sea, by United States' frigate "St. Lawrence," and sent to Philadelphia. Ordered to be released by United States' Government; order subsequently revoked. Vessel now under libel in Prize Court, Philadelphia.

Schooners "Harriet Ryan," "Mary Ware," "Ocean Wave," and "Susan Jane," seized in Hatteras Inlet between 7th and 10th September, bound to that place from Nova Scotia with assorted cargoes. Brig "Mystery," of St. John, New Brunswick, Wade master, seized in New York Harbour on the 13th September, on her arrival from Matanzas with cargo of molasses, on suspicion of having previously proceeded from Boston to Georgetown with a cargo of ice.

No. 82.

Consul Bunch to Earl Russell.—(Received October 21.)

My Lord, Charleston, September 4, 1861.

I HAVE the honour to report that the blockade of this port continues to be conducted with the laxity which has hitherto distinguished it. Vessels of various sizes enter and sail almost at pleasure.

On one day last week the privateer steamer " Gordon " came into port over the bar and through the principal channel, in broad daylight, and in the very face of the blockading ships.

On Sunday last, the 1st instant, a brig from Rio de Janeiro arrived with a full cargo of 1,500 sacks of coffee. She was chased by the United States' ships, but quite ineffectually, as she entered the port in defiance of them.

The British schooner ——— arrived on the same day from Cuba. She, however, ran the blockade (which is only a paper one) at Fernandina, in Florida, and came by the inland route, to Beaufort, in South Carolina. She had a full cargo of molasses.

I have, &c.
(Signed) ROBERT BUNCH.

No. 83.

Consul Bunch to Earl Russell.—(Received October 21.)

My Lord, Charleston, September 4, 1861.

THE blockade of the coast of North Carolina has, so far as I am informed, been totally ineffective since the date of my last despatches on the subject.

With reference to the port of Wilmington, I have the honour to transmit herewith a Return, prepared by Mr. Vice-Consul MacRae, of the vessels which have entered and cleared from the 15th to the 28th of August.

The port of Beaufort, in North Carolina, has also remained open, and has received two British ships, each of over 600 tons burthen, and drawing about 15 feet of water.

The first of these, the ———, sailed from ——— with a cargo of lead, pig-iron, and other articles. She was nine days on the passage, during which time she did not meet a single United States' ship-of-war. Her supercargo informs me that the schooner ———, from the West Indies, went into Beaufort on the day before he arrived.

The second British ship is the ———, 778 tons, from Liverpool, with 4,193 sacks of salt and 100 tons of iron. This vessel was for three days off Beaufort Bar, during which time she was not approached by any ship of war. She finally entered Beaufort in broad daylight.

It is possible that the blockade may now become more rigid, as several men-of-war have lately participated in an attack upon some forts in the vicinity of Beaufort.

I have, &c.
(Signed) ROBERT BUNCH.

Inclosure in No. 83.

LIST of Vessels arrived at, and cleared from, the Port of Wilmington, North Carolina, from the 10th to 31st August, 1861.

Date of Arrival.	Class.	Name.	Where from.	Cargo.	Date of Clearance.	Where for.
August 15	Schooner	.. .. ..	Beaufort, N.C. ..	Corn ..	August 16	Georgetown, S.C.
,, 15	,,	.. .. ..	Ditto	Ditto ..	,, 16	Ditto.
,, 15	,,	.. .. ..	Washington, N.C. ...	Ditto ..	,, 21	Washington, N.C.
,, 15	,,	.. .. ..	Newbern, N.C. ..	Ditto ..	,, 22	Newbern, N.C.
,, 15	,,	.. .. ..	Beaufort, N.C. ..	Ditto ..	,, 26	Beaufort, N.C.
,, 15	,,	.. .. ..	Hyde, N.C. ..	Ditto ..	,, 27	Hyde, N.C.
,, 17	Steamer	.. .. ..	Beaufort, N.C. ..	Privateer ..	..	In port.
,, 20	Schooner	.. .. ..	Shallotte, N.C. ..	Naval stores	,, 22	Shallotte, N.C.
,, 23	,,	.. .. ..	Elizabeth City, N.C.	Corn ..	,, 23	Georgetown, S.C.
,, 25	,,	.. .. ..	Hertford, N.C. ..	Ditto ..	,, 29	Hertford, N.C.
,, 26	,,	.. .. ..	Beaufort, N.C. ..	Ditto ..	,, 30	Beaufort, N.C.
,, 27	,,	.. .. ..	Havana	Ballast ..	..	In port.
,, 28	Steamer	.. .. ..	Beaufort, N.C. ..	Privateer ..	,, 29	Charleston, S.C.

No. 84.

Consul Bunch to Earl Russell.—(*Received October* 21.)

(Extract.)   *Charleston, September* 14, 1861.

THE blockade of the coast of both North and South Carolina continues to be totally ineffective. No difficulty whatever seems to be experienced by vessels either in entering or sailing from even this port of Charleston, which is supposed to be fully blockaded, there being two ships-of-war always in sight from the town. Within the last week various vessels have sailed for the West Indies ; amongst others, the British schooner ———.

As regards the numerous inlets and ports to the southward of Charleston as far as Savannah, not even the pretence of a blockade exists.

The port of Wilmington in North Carolina has received four British vessels within the last fortnight. All of these vessels are from foreign and distant ports.

The port of Beaufort in North Carolina is now carefully watched by the United States' ship " Susquehanna." It is known that two large British ships are there, and the presumption is that they will be captured as they come out.

No. 85.

Lord Lyons to Earl Russell.—(*Received October* 28.)

My Lord,   *Washington, October* 12, 1861.

I HAVE the honour to transmit to your Lordship copies of two despatches which I have received from Mr. Consul Bunch concerning the blockade ; the one in answer to the instruction of which a copy was inclosed in my despatch to your Lordship of the 15th of August last; the other in answer to the instruction of which a copy was inclosed in my other despatch to your Lordship of the same date.

I have, &c.
(Signed)   LYONS.

Inclosure 1 in No. 85.

Consul Bunch to Lord Lyons.

My Lord,   *Charleston, September* 30, 1861.

I HAVE the honour to acknowledge the receipt, yesterday, by Her Majesty's ship " Steady," of your Lordship's despatch, marked Circular, of August 14, in which you are so good as to convey me your own instructions, together with those of Earl Russell, respecting the absolute necessity of my procuring and transmitting all possible particulars respecting the blockade of this coast. Your Lordship is pleased to subjoin a list of questions bearing upon this matter, to which I beg to reply as fully as may be possible:—

1st. Ingress into the port of Charleston has certainly been allowed at all times, since the first establishment of the blockade, to steam-transports in the service of the Confederate States which have come in from the surrounding coast with the Confederate flag flying, in full sight of the blockading squadron, without even an attempt being made to capture them. Similar ingress has not been allowed to any other vessels.

2nd. With the exception of the transports mentioned above, which have been laden with guns, men, and stores, no egress has been allowed knowingly or wittingly to any vessels from this port.

3rd. As regards intermissions of blockade : (*a*.) I cannot say that the blockading ships have been withdrawn by superior orders, as I have no means of knowing. They have certainly been out of sight of the town on many occasions. (*b*.) There has been no bad weather until four days ago, when both the " Wabash " and " Vandalia " were compelled to run out to sea. (*c*.) I am not aware of any absence of ships caused by chasing vessels.

4th. It has been adequate to cause obvious danger to large vessels, but totally inadequate to prevent either the ingress or egress of smaller vessels, by which I mean vessels of from 50 to 300 tons, and drawing less than ten feet of water.

The above remarks apply to the port of Charleston. Of the ports between it and Savannah, I can safely say that there has been no blockade at all. Vessels of various sizes, amongst others the barque ———, of 330 tons, and brig ———, of 250 tons, prizes

M 2

to privateers, have been brought in in safety. Schooners and brigs have arrived from and sailed for the West Indies, with cargoes, ever since the nominal commencement of the blockade. Of the blockade of North Carolina, I can only say that it has scarcely existed at all. A reference to my numerous despatches respecting it must conclusively establish that fact. Off Wilmington, up to two or three days ago, there has been no blockading vessel except the " Daylight," on July 20, which vessel went away on the 25th. At Beaufort, the blockade did not begin until the 6th or 7th of September. I beg to inclose herewith a letter from the Collector of that port in confirmation of this fact. The arrival of the ships ———— and ————, alluded to in my despatch to the Foreign Office of the 4th instant proves that no blockade existed on August 22 and 28.

I have, &c.
(Signed)   ROBERT BUNCH.

Inclosure 2 in No. 85.

Mr. Bell to Vice-Consul Walker.

Sir,   *Custom-House, Beaufort, North Carolina, September* 25, 1861.
IN reply to your verbal inquiries made at this office under present date, I have the honour to submit the following statement:—

Schooner ——— sailed from this port on August 8, for Liverpool, loaded with tobacco and naval stores.

Schooner ——— arrived here on August 17, from the West Indies, loaded with salt, molasses, and sugar, and is still in port.

Ship ——— arrived here on the 23rd ultimo direct from St. John's, New Brunswick, with a cargo of sundry articles.

Ship ——— arrived here on the 28th ultimo from Liverpool, with a cargo of sack, salt, and pig-iron.

Since the date you have specified, to wit, the 13th of July last, the schooner ——— cleared from this port for Georgetown, South Carolina.

This port has only been blockaded since the 7th instant, when a side-wheel Federal steamer, supposed to be the " Susquehanna," anchored in close proximity to the bar.

I have, &c.
(Signed)   JOSIAH F. BELL.

Inclosure 3 in No. 85.

Consul Bunch to Lord Lyons.

My Lord,   *Charleston, September* 30, 1861.
I HAVE the honour to acknowledge the receipt of your Lordship's despatch of August 15, with reference to the blockade of Charleston; and proceed to reply as fully as the extreme shortness of the time at my disposal will permit. This consideration will, I trust, serve as my excuse for any imperfections of matter or of style.

1. There were no arrivals from foreign ports at Charleston between the 18th and 27th of May. The business season was over for the year, which fact, and not the presence of any blockading ship, accounts for the apparent cessation of traffic.

2. In my despatch to Earl Russell of July 25, of which a copy was sent to your Lordship in my despatch of July 30, full lists were given. I beg to inclose a continuation of the same in the despatch.

I venture to think that my various despatches received by your Lordship subsequently to the date of the despatch to which I am now replying, will cover all the ground of the information required.

I have, &c.
(Signed)   ROBERT BUNCH.

Inclosure 4 in No. 85.

LIST of the Vessels that have entered Charleston Harbour from places beyond Bull's Bay, north-eastwardly, and South Edisto Bar, southwardly, from July 25 to September 30, 1861.

Date.	No.	Class.	Name.	Master.	Cargo.	Where from.
1861						
July 27	1	Schooner	.	.	104 barrels clean rice - - - -	Santee.
Aug. 3	2	Steamer	.	.	65 head of cattle, 25 bales Sea Island cotton, 25 hides, 125 packages merchandize and sundries	Fernandina, viâ Savannah, Beaufort, and Edisto.
,, 8	3	Ditto	.	.	Ballast - - - - - - -	Savannah.
,, 9	4	Schooner	.	.	Coal - - - - - - -	Ditto.
,, 10	5	Ditto	.	.	Ditto - - - - - - -	Ditto.
	6	Ditto	.	.	3,000 barrels rough rice - - -	Pocotaligo.
	7	Confederate States' steamer	.	.	Cruizing - - - - - -	Savannah.
,, 11	8	Steamer	.	.	Ditto.	
,, 12	9	Ditto	.	.	17 bales Sea Island cotton, 40 head cattle, 22 bags corn, 12 turtles and sundries	Fernandina, viâ Savannah, Beaufort, and Edisto.
,, 13	10	Schooner	.	.	85 barrels clean rice - - - -	Georgetown.
	11	Steamer	.	.	Ballast - - - - - -	Savannah.
,, 16	12	Schooner	.	.	2,500 bushels rough rice - - -	Santee.
	13	Ditto	.	.	1,000 ,, ,, - - -	Ashepoo.
,, 14	14	Sloop	.	.	1,750 ,, ,, - - -	Santee.
	16	Ditto	.	.	95 barrels clean rice - - -	Georgetown, S. Carolina.
,, 19	17	Ditto	.	.	1,000 bushels rough rice - - -	Santee.
,, 21	18	Steamer	.	.	Sugar, cargo of the prize brig "John Welch"	Savannah.
,, 22	19	Schooner	.	.	65 barrels clean rice and sundries -	Georgetown, S. Carolina.
,, 23	20	Steamer	.	.	65 head cattle and sundries - -	Fernandina, Savannah, Beaufort.
	21	Ditto	.	.	Officers and crew of the prize ship "Thompson," in charge of Captain Kirk, of 9th South Carolina Volunteers	Beaufort, South Carolina.
,, 26	22	Ditto	.	.	Ballast - - - - - -	Georgetown, S. Carolina.
,, 27	23	Ditto	.	.	31 hogsheads sugar - - - -	Georgetown and Bull's Bay.
	24	Schooner	.	.	111 barrels clean rice - - -	Santee.
,, 29	25	Steamer	.	.	Merchandize - - - - - -	Fernandina, viâ Savannah.
,, 30	26	Private armed steamer	.	.	From a cruize on the coast of N. Carolina	Smithville, North Carolina.
Sept. 1	27	Steamer	.	.	With the "Prince of Wales" in tow	Fernandina, Florida.
	28	Brig schooner	.	.	Molasses, fruit, and cigars - -	Havana, viâ Fernandina.
	29	Brig	.	.	1,500 bags coffee - - - - -	Rio de Janeiro.
,, 3	30	Ditto	.	.	This vessel was sent in as a prize of the privateer "Jeff. Davis;" she had a valuable cargo of sugar, consigned to A. E. Campbell and Co., of London	Trinidad de Cuba, viâ Fernandina and Savannah.
,, 9	31	Steamer	.	.	21 bales Sea Island cotton, 50 head cattle, and sundries	Fernandina and Beaufort, South Carolina.
,, 10	32	Ditto	.	.	2,200 bushels corn - - - - -	Georgetown, S. Carolina.
	33	Sloop	.	.	Coffee, cigars, and fruit - - -	West Indies.
,, 11	34	Barque	.	.	1,000 bags coffee (ship and cargo brought in as prize for condemnation)	Puerto Cabello.
	35	Sloop	.	.	50 barrels cleaned rice - - -	Georgetown, S. Carolina.
	36	Ditto	.	.	1,900 bushels rough rice - - -	Santee.
,, 15	37	Schooner	.	.	1,800 ,, corn - - - -	Edenton, North Carolina.
,, 18	38	Ditto	.	.	1,600 ,, rough rice - - -	Combahee.
	39	Steamer	.	.	35 bales Sea Island cotton, 50 head cattle	Fernandina, viâ Savannah and Beaufort, S. Carolina.
,, 19	40	Schooner	.	.	125 barrels cleaned rice - - -	Georgetown, S. Carolina.
,, 21	41	Ditto	.	.	2,140 bushels rough rice - - - -	Santee.

The Confederate transports alluded to in my despatch of this day are not included in this Return.

Charleston, September 30, 1861.

(Signed)   ROBERT BUNCH, *Consul.*

No. 86.

Lord Lyons to Earl Russell.—(*Received October* 28.)

(Extract.)   *Washington, October* 12, 1861.

I HAVE the honour to transmit to your Lordship herewith copies of correspondence relative to the capture of the schooner "Revere," of Nova Scotia.

Inclosure 1 in No. 86.

Consul Lousada to Lord Lyons.

(Extract.)   *Boston, October* 4, 1861.

I HAVE the honour to forward copy of a letter from the owner of the British schooner "Revere."

Inclosure 2 in No. 86.

Mr. Clements to Consul Lousada.

(Extract.)   *Boston, October* 3, 1861.

THE schooner "Revere," of Yarmouth, Nova Scotia, on a voyage from Halifax to Key West, has been captured by the United States' steamer "Cambridge," the United States' steamer "Susquehanna" being in sight, near Cape Lookout, on the coast of North Carolina, and is brought to this port for adjudication, charged with an attempt to run a blockade said to exist here.

No. 87.

Consul Lynn to Mr. Murray.—(Received October 31.)

Sir,   *Galveston, August* 8, 1861.

WITH reference to your despatch of the 13th of June last, the receipt of which I have the honour to acknowledge, I have to report that the blockade of this port has been maintained by the United States' steamer "South Carolina," with one of the schooners captured by her, armed as a tender or gun-boat, since the date of my despatch of the 3rd of July last, announcing that the blockade was established on the 2nd ultimo, and also that another United States' steamer arrived to-day, and is now at anchor off the bar. Whether she is to relieve the "South Carolina," or to assist in maintaining the blockade, I have not ascertained, as no communication has been yet held with her by the Confederate States' officer commanding this post.

The report received by me from the Observatory, copies of which I have the honour to transmit herewith, shows, however, that the blockade has not hitherto been very effective.

The interruption to trade occasioned by this blockade has so far only prevented the introduction of the manufactures of the Eastern States and the articles of agricultural produce supplied by the North-Western States through the port of New Orleans.

The foreign trade of the port usually commences in the month of September, the season when vessels can return with freights of cotton. Of this article, it is estimated, the State can export, during the year from the 1st of September next, 260,000 bales, but which will be retained on the plantations so long as the blockade continues.

I have, &c.

(Signed)   ARTHUR T. LYNN.

Inclosure in No. 87.

Messrs. Hitchcock and Hendly to Consul Lynn.

Sir,   *J.O.L.O. Observatory, Hendly's Buildings, August* 7, 1861.

THE following named vessels have run the blockade at this port, as noted from this observatory since the blockade commenced on the 2nd of July, viz., viâ Main Channel :—

July 3.	Steamer ———	.. in ...	about	237	tons.
„ 8.	Schooner ———	.. in ..	„	10	„
„ 9.	Schooner ———	.. out ..	„	30	„

Viâ St. Louis Pass, a channel used by light draft coasters :—

July 4.	Schooner ———	.. out ..	„	50	„
„ 10.	Schooner ———	.. out ..	„	40	„
„ 5.	Sloop ———	.. out ..	„	18	„
„ 13.	„ „	.. in ..	„	18	„
„ 18.	Schooner ———	.. out ..	„	35	„
„ 20.	Sloop ———	.. in ..	„	50	„
„ 22.	Schooner ———	.. in ..	„	40	„
„ 22.	Sloop ———	.. out ..	„	18	„
„ 26.	Schooner ———	.. out ..	„	43	„
„ 28.	Schooner ———	.. out ..	„	61	„

In addition to the foregoing list of vessels there has been a continual communication between this port and Sabine and New Orleans, viâ Berwick's Bay, by small sail boats, from two to six or eight tons, carrying passengers, and sometimes mails and other matters. Of the twelve vessels captured by the blockading fleet (all were pilot-boats and small coasting schooners), eight were captured within three days after the arrival of the blockading squadron, and the other four within ten days from their arrival. No notice or warning was given them until they were fired upon and then taken possession of; and every vessel knowing of the blockade that has attempted to run it either out or in has been successful.

(Signed)   **L. M. HITCHCOCK,** *Secretary.*
J. J. HENDLY, *Captain of the Watch.*

No. 88.

Acting Consul Cridland to Lord J. Russell.—(Received October 31.)

(Extract.)   *Richmond, August 10, 1861.*

I HAVE had the honour of receiving your Lordship's despatch dated June 13, 1861, stating it to be of the utmost importance that Her Majesty's Government should receive early and accurate information in regard to ports blockaded and the manner in which blockades are maintained, with instructions to forward to the Foreign Office accurate information as to the actual existence of any blockade, but more particularly of the ports within this Consulate.

In reply to your Lordship's instructions, I beg to state that the blockade of the port of Virginia was established, or became effective, on the 30th of April, having been proclaimed at Washington by the Executive on the 27th of that month.

The outlet and inlet of Norfolk, Petersburg, and Richmond, being Hampton Roads, one frigate was quite sufficient to make the blockade effective, its narrowest channel being one mile and a quarter wide.

Other vessels have blockaded the coast of Virginia between Old Point Comfort and the mouth of the Potomac river.

No interruption of the blockade has taken place in Hampton roads, and no vessels have entered or left the above-named ports since the 16th of May last, the supposed date allowed by the blockading squadron for vessels loading to leave port.

The blockade has not proved so effective north of Old Point Comfort.

At the port of Fredericksburg, on the Rappahannock river, there arrived about the 30th of June a steamer called the "St. Nicholas," which had been captured on the 29th of June, near Baltimore, by an armed body of Confederates, and then used for the capture of three United States' merchant-vessels in the Chesapeake bay. The steamer and her three prizes evaded the blockading ships off the mouth of the Rappahannock, and reached port in safety.

The number of blockading ships, as reported by Mr. Vice-Consul Myers, consists of five ships of war and five armed merchant steamers.

No public notices have been issued by the Confederate Government in regard to blockade.

No. 89.

The Secretary to the Admiralty to Mr. Hammond.—(Received October 31.)

Sir,   *Admiralty, October 30, 1861.*

I AM commanded by my Lords Commissioners of the Admiralty to send you herewith, for the information of Her Majesty's Secretary of State for Foreign Affairs, a copy of a letter from Rear-Admiral Sir Alexander Milne, dated the 14th of October, with copies of its inclosures from Commodore Dunlop, and extracts from a letter of Commander Ross, of Her Majesty's ship "Desperate," relating to the blockade of the American coast from Charleston to Mexican frontier.

I am, &c.
(Signed)   W. G. ROMAINE.

Inclosure 1 in No. 89.

Rear-Admiral Sir A. Milne to the Secretary of the Admiralty.

(Extract.)

I BEG you will acquaint their Lordships that Commodore Dunlop reports to me that, after leaving Bermuda on the 6th September last, he proceeded to Cape Fear, and arrived there on the 12th of that month. From thence he proceeded along the coast towards Charleston, off which he arrived on the 14th, and then proceeded off Havana, which he found still sickly. I inclose a copy of the Commodore's Report of the state of the blockades, as well as that of Commander Ross, of the "Desperate," who in August last had made a circuit of the northern part of the Gulf of Mexico, and who, their Lordships will observe, states that the coast is effectively blockaded from Galveston to Tampa Bay.

Inclosure 2 in No. 89.

Commander Ross to Commodore Dunlop.

(Extract.)   "*Desperate,*" *Vera Cruz, September* 1, 1861.

IN compliance with your orders I left Vera Cruz, in Her Majesty's ship "Desperate," on the 1st August, and proceeded to Galveston.

We were here speedily chased and hailed by the armed steamer "South Carolina."

My conclusion is that the coast is effectively blockaded from Galveston to Tampa Bay. We have seen no merchant-vessel at sea in the whole distance from Vera Cruz to Tampa, except the American schooner "Acatala" returning from Pensacola to Key West, and employed by the United States' Government in carrying provisions. The armed steamers are almost all merchant-vessels of upwards of 1,000 tons, carrying 5 guns, and 100 men. In many instances it appeared as if on making us out to be a British cruiser no inclination to board or communicate with us was shown.

There appeared to be several other United States' schooners cruizing along that we have not fallen in with, owing, probably, to their keeping in very shallow water.

At Tampa I crossed the bay within two miles and a-half of the lighthouse, and close to the buoy, but saw no cruizer, nor could the signalman from the masthead see anything inside; but the schooner told us that she had been boarded by the United States' armed steamer "Cyla" from Tampa Bay.

This light was sighted at night, being the only lighted one we have seen. At Pensacola we passed close to the frigate in a light breeze, and ready to square our main-yard, had she shown any sign of lowering a boat.

Inclosure 3 in No. 89.

Commodore Dunlop to Rear-Admiral Sir A. Milne.

Sir,   "*Challenger,*" *at Key West, September* 26, 1861.

I HAVE the honour to inform you, that on leaving Bermuda on the 6th instant I steered for Cape Fear, and made the coast of America to the northward of that Cape on the 12th instant. We found the light-vessel removed off the Frying-pan shoals, and during our progress to the south coast of Florida no lights were visible. The lights on Cape Florida and Carysfort reef, which Commander Lyons reported as the only lights to be seen in July last, seem now to have been extinguished.

2. We met with no United States' cruizers until we arrived off Charleston, where we found the frigate "Wabash" and corvette "Vandalia."

3. Supposing the captain of the "Wabash" to be in command of the blockading squadron on the coasts of South Carolina, Georgia, and Florida, I addressed a letter to him, relative to the state of the blockade, as reported to me by Commander Lyons of the "Racer," in the latter end of July, a copy of which I have the honour to inclose, with the answer received.

4. On the evening of the 14th we were off Savannah, but saw no American cruizers; as it was near sunset when we made Savannah, it is possible a ship might have been at anchor inside Tybee lighthouse without our having seen her, but no cruizer was off the port, and no notice was taken of our approach.

5. As we passed along the coast southwards, after leaving Savannah, no American cruizers were seen, and I have reason to believe that none are stationed off any of the small harbours and inlets between Savannah and Cape Florida.

6. I am of opinion that Charleston is at present the only port between Cape Fear and Cape Florida that is effectively blockaded.

7. I was informed, as Commander Lyons mentions in his report that he was also, by the American officer who came on board from the "Wabash," that gun-boats were expected soon, for the purpose of being anchored within the mouths of the various small ports and inlets, as the only possible means of effectually blockading them; up to the present time, however, these vessels have not arrived.

8. In my communications with the American officers off Charleston and at this place, I have met with every courtesy and attention.

I am, &c.
(Signed)   H. DUNLOP.

P.S.—I shall send a copy of this letter to the Secretary of the Admiralty.

Inclosure 4 in No. 89.

LIST of American Vessels of War fallen in with by Her Majesty's ship "Challenger."

Name.	No. of Men.	No. of Guns.	Name of Captain.	When seen.	Where seen.	Remarks.
				1861		
"Wabash," screw frigate	600	44	Saml. Mercer	September 14	Off Charleston ..	Blockading.
"Vandalia," sailing corvette	250	22	— Lee ..	„ 14	Ditto	Ditto.
"Potomac," sailing frigate	460	44	— Parnell ..	„ 16	Entrance of Gulf of Florida	Making passage
				„ 22	Arrived at Key West	

(Signed)   HUGH DUNLOP, Commodore, 1st Class.
"Challenger," Key West, September 26, 1861.

Inclosure 5 in No. 89.

Commodore Dunlop to Captain Mercer, U.S.N.

Sir,   "Challenger," off Charleston, September 14, 1861.
IT having been represented to me by Commander Lyons, of Her Britannic Majesty's ship "Racer," that during his progress along the coast from Cape Florida to Cape Fear, he found only the ports of Savannah and Charleston under blockade by the United States' squadron, I have the honour to notify the same to you, and I will feel much obliged by your informing me whether, subsequently to the "Racer's" being on that part of the Coast of America in July last, any force has been stationed off the ports and inlets between Savannah and Cape Florida for the purpose of establishing the blockade of the same.

I am, &c.
(Signed)   H. DUNLOP.

Inclosure 6 in No. 89.

Captain Mercer, U.S.N., to Commodore Dunlop.

                              "Wabash," at anchor off Charleston, South Carolina ;
Sir,   September 14, 1861.
I HAVE the honour to acknowledge the receipt of your communication of this date, and in reply to your several inquiries in reference to the blockade of certain ports of the United States, I have to state that I am unable to give the information you demand, as I am specially charged with the blockade of Charleston.

I am, &c.
(Signed)   SAMUEL MERCER.

No. 90.

The Secretary to the Admiralty to Mr. Hammond.—(Received November 1.)

Sir.   Admiralty, October 30, 1861.
I AM commanded by my Lords Commissioners of the Admiralty to send you herewith, for the information of Her Majesty's Secretary of State for Foreign Affairs, copies of two letters from Rear-Admiral Sir Alexander Milne, dated the 15th and 16th instant, with copies of their inclosures from Commander Hewett, of Her Majesty's sloop "Rinaldo," relative to the blockade of the American coast between Capes Henry and Fear.

I am, &c.
(Signed)   W. G. ROMAINE.

Inclosure 1 in No. 90.

Rear-Admiral Sir A. Milne to the Secretary to the Admiralty.

Sir, "*Nile*," at Halifax, October 15, 1861.

IN continuation of the report of the state of the blockades made by Commander Hickley, of Her Majesty's ship "Gladiator," and which I forwarded in a previous communication, I have now the honour to inclose in original the report on the same subject up to the 11th ultimo, from Commander Hewett, of the "Rinaldo," who relieved Commander Hickley on the coast between New York and Cape Fear.

I have, &c.
(Signed) ALEXR. MILNE.

Inclosure 2 in No. 90.

Commander Hewett to Rear-Admiral Sir A. Milne.

(Extract.) "*Rinaldo*," New York, September 12, 1861.

I HAVE the honour to acquaint you that after leaving your flag on the 23rd ultimo, I proceeded under sail for New York, but was obliged very soon after to get up steam in consequence of light and variable winds, and continued steaming off and on till my arrival at that port. On the 28th ultimo at daylight I sighted the "Gladiator," about eight miles from New York, at anchor, awaiting my arrival ; I accordingly anchored and communicated with Commander Hickley, and at 11 A.M. weighed and proceeded for the harbour, anchoring off the quarantine ground, Staten Island.

Having delivered the various mails, &c., to Her Majesty's Consul, and purchased the necessary quantity of coal to fill up (payment for the coals and pilotage being made by the Consul at my request), I left New York on the 30th ultimo.

On the 2nd instant, having sailed along the coast and exchanged colours with several American merchant-vessels, and the United States' corvette "Dale," cruizing off Oregon Inlet, I came to an anchor off that inlet and laid there for the night.

The following morning I weighed under steam and proceeded round Cape Hatteras, and on rounding that Cape I exchanged colours with a United States' steamer wearing a pendant and steaming north, and at the same time I proceeded to close another man-of-war in sight, which proved to be the United States' frigate "Cumberland," cruizing off Hatteras Inlet. Having stopped and communicated with that vessel by boat, I steamed for the anchorage off Hatteras Inlet, and found lying here the United States' steam-frigate "Susquehanna," and two other small steamers purchased into the navy. Inside the bar the "Pawnee" and Harriet Lane" were at anchor. Shortly after coming to an anchor I visited the "Susquehanna ;" the Captain of the "Cumberland" having informed me that the senior officer of the blockade was on board her, the flag-officer having returned with most of the squadron to Old Point with the prisoners captured at the Hatteras Inlet forts.

These forts were bombarded on the 28th and 29th ultimo by the Federal naval force, and surrendered on the second day ; during the bombardment the "Harriet Lane" got on shore and received injuries to such an extent as to oblige her to leave for the north, in order to be docked.

On the morning of the 4th instant, I weighed under steam and proceeded along the land towards Cape Lookout, passing Ocracoke Inlet : having rounded the cape and cleared the shoals, I steamed in and reconnoitered Beaufort, and observed several merchant-vessels in the harbour, two of them wearing English ensigns ; there was also Secession flag flying on Fort Macon at the entrance of the harbour.

Steaming to the westward six miles, I anchored, remaining at anchor all the next day as I was anxious to see if any United States' cruizers would sight Beaufort.

While lying here on the evening of the 5th, a boat came on board from the English ship ———, then in the harbour, with the master, accompanied by an officer of the Confederate army, as the master applied to the Commandant of the fort for an officer to accompany him, in order to prove that he was a British subject, being under apprehension that the ship might be a United States' cruizer.

The purport of this visit was to gain information from me as to whether a blockade really existed, as he (the captain of the ———) stated that he arrived a fortnight previous with a general cargo, and also the English ship ———, the last-mentioned vessel having only arrived about a week ago, and that neither of them saw any United States' cruizers on their passage, or during their stay at Beaufort. I informed him that the blockade had been declared, and also read to him the Queen's Proclamation relative to the existing war between the Northern and Southern States. He informed me that he had nearly completed his return cargo, consisting of naval stores.

I learned from the officer who accompanied him that Fort Macon and the fortifications adjacent to it mounted 60 guns and was garrisoned by 2,000 men.

On the morning of the 6th, I weighed and steamed along the land to Cape Fear, sighting the many inlets between Beaufort and that cape, and at 4 P.M. that afternoon I was off Federal Point, the entrance of the River Fear, which river leads to the port of Wilmington. The Confederate flag was flying on a small battery at the entrance, and there were also several fore-and-aft-rigged vessels inside, but none ship-rigged; I then stood off the land for the night, having reached the extremity of my cruizing-ground.

The following forenoon of the 7th, Cape Lookout Lighthouse bearing north-west eighteen miles, I sighted and communicated by boat with the United States' steam-frigate "Susquehanna;" the boarding officers informed me that the day previous they boarded a British schooner from Halifax, and it was his opinion that she evidently intended to run the blockade.

On the morning of the 8th I was off Ocracoke Inlet, and at 9 A.M. sighted four vessels off Hatteras Inlet, one apparently the United States' gun-boat "Pawnee," and two others, which I left there on the 4th instant, previously mentioned.

The wind falling very light, but with the appearance of a heavy gale, I got up steam for the purpose of rounding Cape Hatteras, exchanging colours at 2 P.M. that afternoon with the United States' frigate "Cumberland," off the cape.

Towards evening, the weather still continuing to look very breezy, I stopped, and stood off the land under sail, and the latter part of that evening and the next day experienced a strong breeze from the north-east, with a heavy sea; the same day (the 9th), being under close-reefed topsails, I exchanged numbers and communicated by signal with Her Majesty's ship "Ariadne," wore, and kept company with her the rest of the evening.

In conclusion, I beg to report that I do not consider the coast from Cape Lookout to Cape Clear efficiently blockaded, having seen no United States' cruizers between those capes, either on my passage south or on my return.

I have nothing further of importance to communicate up to the 11th instant, when I have to report my arrival here on the evening of that day, having run in before a strong south-westerly breeze.

Inclosure 3 in No. 90.

Rear-Admiral Sir A. Milne to the Secretary to the Admiralty.

(Extract.) *"Nile," at Halifax, October 16, 1861.*

WITH reference to my letter of the 15th instant, I now inclose the report of Commander Hewett's further proceedings when again visiting, in Her Majesty's ship "Rinaldo," the blockaded ports between Capes Henry and Fear, of which I have expressed to him my full approval.

Inclosure 4 in No. 90.

Commander Hewett to Rear-Admiral Sir A. Milne.

(Extract.) *"Rinaldo," New York, October 1, 1861.*

I HAVE the honour to acquaint you with the arrival of Her Majesty's steam-sloop under my command, at this port, at 1 P.M. of this day, and to inform you that I left New York on the 16th ultimo, having completed coal on the 13th. I have to acknowledge the receipt of further orders from you, as well as a mail from Her Majesty's ship "Steady," and upon the receipt of those orders I telegraphed to Lord Lyons, and his answer only reached me on the evening of the 15th ultimo.

After steaming out of New York bay I proceeded to the southward, under sail, and cruized along the coast, occasionally exchanging colours with merchant-vessels, and on the 25th ultimo arrived at Hatteras inlet, and came-to in that anchorage, nothing worthy of note having occurred up to this time. I found the United States' ship "Susquehanna" anchored here, also the United States' gun-boat "Pawnee," with several smaller vessels inside the bar. The next day I communicated with the "Susquehanna."

Having remained here till the 23rd, during which time it was blowing very heavily, accompanied by much hail and fog, I got under weigh on the morning of that day, and sailed along the coast, sighting Ocracoke inlet. The battery on the point of that inlet, I learned from the Captain of the "Susquehanna," had been destroyed by him a few days previous, spiking six 32-pounder guns, without any resistance on the part of the Confederate forces, it having been evacuated at the time. I was also informed by him that the British schooner mentioned in my letter of proceedings of the 12th of September, as having been boarded by the "Susquehanna," and warned off the coast, was captured a few days afterwards, by the United States' ship "Cambridge," in the act of running in to Beaufort. Whilst rounding Cape Lookout I exchanged colours with the "Cambridge," blockading Beaufort. After clearing the shoals I sailed to the West, and came-to in sight of Beaufort, for the night, to ensure position.

Two vessels flying English colours were in the harbour of Beaufort, apparently the —— and ———, mentioned in my letter of proceedings dated the 12th of September.

Early on the morning of the 24th I weighed and proceeded to the southward, and observed the "Cambridge" giving chase, but on making out our colours she altered her course and stood back to Beaufort, running along the land. I came-to for the night off Federal Point, Cape Fear, and immediately after a United States' steamer chased, and making us out stood off the land again. I have reason to suppose that this was the United States' cruizer "Young Rover," blockading the mouth of the River Fear. On the morning of the 25th I weighed under steam and proceeded north, along the land, and at 1 P.M. spoke the United States' ship "Albatross," blockading Beaufort; kept company with her till I came to an anchor off Beaufort the same evening. I found the United States' ship "Cambridge" also anchored here. Shortly after coming to an anchor, I went on board the "Albatross," and was informed by Captain Prentiss, of that vessel, that the British ships in Beaufort had made a request through Mr. Walker, the Vice-Consul, to be permitted to put to sea, but that officer informed me that he had not the power to comply with this request. The reason for making this demand is explained hereafter.

At 2·30 A.M. on the morning of the 26th, the English Vice-Consul from Charleston, Mr. Walker, came on board to have an interview with me concerning the English vessels then in the harbour of Beaufort. It appears that Mr. Walker has been commissioned by the English Consul, Mr. Bunch, at Charleston, to claim as a right, from the United States' cruizers, that these vessels should be permitted to put to sea with their return cargoes unmolested, on the ground that at the time they entered Beaufort there was no actual blockade of the port; he therefore says that they were entitled to put to sea on the fourteenth day after the actual blockade commenced, viz., on the 6th September last, which date he proved, by certificates from the captains of these vessels and the military authorities at Beaufort quartered at Fort Macon, was the day on which the actual blockade commenced, though the United States' naval officers persist in saying that it commenced in June.

Having visited the United States' blockading vessels twice, and not receiving a favourable answer, he has, according to Mr. Bunch's orders, referred the matter to me.

The only advice I gave to Mr. Walker was to inform the captains of these vessels that they ought not to attempt to run the blockade after having claimed it as a right that they should be permitted to put to sea.

The same day, the 26th, I left Beaufort, and proceeded for Hatteras Inlet for the purpose of communicating with the "Susquehanna." Arrived and anchored there that evening.

Owing to it coming on to blow the next morning, I was forced to beat out to sea under sail and steam, being on a dead lee shore, and for eight hours it continued to blow a very heavy gale from the south and south-west, the sea running very high, washed away the jib-boom, jib, all the head-gear berthing, &c., and dingy; the weather moderating towards morning, I proceeded under sail for New York, also steaming easy, and on the 29th ultimo I sighted a United States' frigate, supposed to be the "Dale," cruizing off Oregon Inlet.

On the day of my arrival here I learned that the schooner referred to as having been captured by the United States' ship "Cambridge," was the ———; also that the battery at the entrance of Oregon Inlet has been evacuated and destroyed by the Confederate forces, who have retired on Roanoke Island, which they have strongly fortified.

I beg also to report that on my arrival at this port I dispatched the original copies of the correspondence and letters presented to me by Mr. Walker to Lord Lyons, with a letter giving him a general outline of the cases of these two vessels.

A mail containing despatches for Lord Russell from Mr. Bunch I delivered to the British Consul at this port to be forwarded.

No. 91.

Lord Lyons to Earl Russell.—(Received November 4.)

(Extract.)   *Washington, October 21, 1861.*

I HAVE the honour to transmit to your Lordship a copy of a despatch dated the 31st of July last, from Mr. Consul Lynn, relative to the state of the blockade.

Mr. Lynn's despatch reached me only on the 15th instant.

Inclosure in No. 91.

Consul Lynn to Lord Lyons.

(Extract.)   *Galveston, July 31, 1861.*

THE blockade is still maintained, though its efficiency is very questionable. Upon reference to a chart of this coast your Lordship will observe that the Pass of St. Louis, at the west end of this island, admits of the entrance of vessels having a draught of eight to nine feet. This is yet open, and schooners from this port have gone to sea by that channel. There is also a south-west pass for vessels of light draught ; this is between the east end of the island and what is designated the South Breaker, and I understand that one or more schooners have also proceeded to sea by this pass. To the above I would most respectfully add, that many of the merchants in Galveston have requested that, should I at any time consider it my duty to report to your Lordship the state of the blockade, to state also that they would regret should my information lead to more effective measures, as these means of egress have been used in the endeavour to obtain a supply of medicine, of which there is but a scant store, and other necessaries of life.

No. 92.

Consul Archibald to Earl Russell.—(Received November 11.)

(Extract.)   *New York, October 29, 1861.*

IN reference to the blockade, there are renewed complaints of its inefficiency at Charleston, from which port a small privateer, called the "Sallie," recently issued, and shortly afterwards captured an American brig, named the "Granada," laden with West India produce.

No. 93.

Consul Lynn to Lord J. Russell.—(Received November 23.)

My Lord,   *Galveston, September 23, 1861.*

I HAVE the honour, in continuation of my report on the blockade of this coast, to state that from the 8th ultimo, the United States' steam-ship "South Carolina" has been at anchor off or in the vicinity of the bar, until the 18th instant, when she departed, leaving a frigate to occupy her position.

The armament of the frigate is reported to be about 56 guns ; but, as the Commander of the Confederate forces at this point has prohibited all intercourse with the blockaders, I have been unable to learn the particulars of her equipage.

The ports to the westward of Galveston, together with the Pass of San Luis, are yet open ; and I have the honour to transmit herewith a copy of a letter received from Colonel C. G. Forshey, having reference to that part of the coast within his command.

The vessels referred to by Colonel Forshey were the schooner ———, of about thirty tons, the schooner ———, and sloop ———, each of about eighteen tons burthen.

These vessels have again departed by the way of San Luis.

I have, &c.

(Signed)   ARTHUR T. LYNN.

Inclosure in No. 93.

Colonel Forshey to Consul Lynn.

Sir,   *Rutersville, Texas, September 2, 1861.*

IN reference to effective blockade on the Coast of Texas, I have to inform you that Pass San Luis, west end Galveston island, ten feet water, has at no time been blockaded ;

and that vessels have entered and departed from the harbour of Galveston by way of this Pass continually since the pretended blockade of Galveston.

It is proper to say, in this connection, that vessels leaving Galveston, and arriving there, by way of this Pass, are visible outside from the position of the vessels of the blockade for nearly the whole length of the West Bay. In truth, the smoke of the steamer " South Carolina " can be distinctly seen from Pass San Luis, twenty-eight miles from Galveston Pass.

Further, the Brazos river, with a bar of six feet water, is entirely free from blockade, vessels passing out and in continually, and carrying on their trade with Velasco, Quintana, Brazoria, and Columbia, the heart of the wealthiest portion of Texas. Through this inlet vessels, moreover, pass by canal to West Bay, and thence to Galveston.

Within the past week no less than four vessels laden with salt have entered the canal from the river, and passed up to Galveston. You will be able to learn the names of these vessels now at your wharves.

The mouth of the San Bernard also, with four feet water, is in like manner unguarded. This leads into the plantations of Brazoria and Wharton, and is frequently entered by small trading vessels.

By application to the officers in command of the Forts San Luis, Velasco, and San Bernard, you will hereafter be able to learn the names of vessels and the dates of entry at these three inlets, as I shall direct the registry of all the vessels passing under our guns in future.

(Signed) C. G. FORSHEY,
Colonel Commanding Brazoria Coast Defence.

No. 94.

Lord Lyons to Earl Russell.—(Received November 23.)

(Extract.)   Washington, November 7, 1861.

THE case of the "Louisa Agnes " has been brought under my notice by Rear-Admiral Sir A. Milne. I have the honour to inclose a copy of his despatch, and an extract from the affidavit of the master of the vessel, which accompanied it.

Inclosure 1 in No. 94.

Rear-Admiral Sir A. Milne to Lord Lyons.

(Extract.)   "Nile," at Halifax, October 28, 1861.

I DEEM it right to forward to your Excellency the accompanying original papers relative to the capture of the British schooner "Louisa Agnes," of Lunenburg, which have been forwarded to me by the owner of her cargo, Mr. Moran, a merchant of this city.

Inclosure 2 in No. 94.

Extract from Affidavit of Robert Nickelson, Master of the British Schooner "Louisa Agnes," dated New York.

THIS appearer immediately came to, and a boat with an officer and crew came on board the "Louisa Agnes," it being the same officer who had boarded him before from the "Cambridge," and he told this appearer that his vessel was a prize.

No. 95.

Consul Archibald to Earl Russell.—(Received November 30.)

(Extract.)   New York, November 16, 1861.

IN reference to the blockade I have little to report. The ———— has sailed from Savannah with a cargo of cotton for Liverpool ; and, from the reports in the papers of this morning, it appears that a British steamer, supposed to be the " Fingal," has been seized by an United States' cruizer, and taken into Key West. The steamer is said to have on board a considerable quantity of arms and munitions of war.

No. 96.

List of Vessels which have arrived at and cleared from the ports of Charleston, Savannah, New Orleans, Pensacola, &c., since the Declaration by the United States of the Blockade of those Ports. Communicated by Messrs. Yancey, Rost, and Mann, in their letter of November 30. (See Correspondence, North America, No. 1, page 105.)

(1.)—LIST of Vessels arrived at and cleared from Wilmington, North Carolina, from May 1 to August 10, 1861.

Date of Arrival.	Class.	Name.	Port where from.	Date of Clearance.	Port bound for.
May 6	Schooner ..	..	..	Georgetown, S.C. ..	May 12	Georgetown.
„ 7	„ ..	..	..	New Orleans ..	„ 11	New York.
„ 8	„ ..	..	..	Charlotte, N.C. ..	„ 11	Charlotte.
„ 10	„ ..	..	..	Charleston . ..	„ 15	New York.
„ 10	„ ..	..	..	Nassau ..	June 6	Nassau.
„ 10	„ ..	..	..	Little River, S.C. ..	„ 13	Little River, S.C.
„ 17	„ ..	..	..	Hertford, N.C. ..	„ 25	Beaufort, N.C.
„ 17	Ship ..	..	..	Campeachy . ..	July 6	Liverpool.
„ 18	Schooner ..	..	..	Hertford, N.C. ..	„ 6	Hertford.
„ 18	„ ..	..	..	Washington, N.C. ..	May 21	Washington, N.C.
„ 18	„ ..	..	..	Rockport, Me. ..	June 5	London.
„ 18	„ ..	..	..	Hertford, N.C. ..	„ 1	Martinique.
„ 18	Brig ..	..	..	Cardenas ..	„ 10	Portland, Me.
„ 18	„ ..	..	..	Cardiff, Wales ..	„ 5	Liverpool.
„ 18	Schooner ..	..	..	Georgetown, S.C. ..	May 21	Washington.
„ 18	„ ..	..	..	Ditto ..	„ 22	Georgetown.
„ 18	„ ..	..	..	Ditto ..	„ 24	Hertford, N.C.
„ 26	Brig ..	..	..	Liverpool ..	June 10	Liverpool.
„ 26	„ ..	..	..	Boulogne ..	„ 13	Ditto.
„ 27	„ ..	..	..	Cardiff ..	„ 12	Hull.
„ 27	Schooner ..	..	..	Charlotte, N.C. ..	May 28	Charlotte, N.C.
„ 27	„ ..	..	..	Georgetown, S.C. ..	„ 30	Georgetown, S.C.
„ 27	„ ..	..	..	Jacksonville, N.C. ..	„ 30	Jacksonville, N.C.
„ 27	„ ..	..	..	Ditto ..	„ 30	Ditto.
„ 28	„ ..	..	..	Little River, S.C. ..	June 1	Little River.
June 1	„ ..	..	..	Hertford, N.C. ..	„ 6	Beaufort, N.C.
„ 1	„ ..	..	..	Scuppernong, N.C. ..	„ 8	Edenton, N.C.
„ 4	„ ..	..	..	Little River, S.C. ..	„ 8	Little River.
„ 10	„ ..	..	..	Newbern ..	„ 26	Nevis, W.I.
„ 10	„ ..	..	..	Georgetown, S.C. ..	„ 26	Georgetown, S.C.
„ 10	„ ..	..	..	Ditto ..	„ 28	West Indies.
„ 11	„ ..	..	..	Little River, S.C. ..	„ 28	Little River, S.C.
„ 12	„ ..	..	..	Washington, N.C. ..	„ 20	Washington, N.C.
„ 15	„ ..	..	..	Cardiff ..	July 9	Liverpool.
„ 16	„ ..	..	..	Washington, N.C. ..	June 18	Washington, N.C.
„ 19	„ ..	..	..	Charlotte, N C. ..	„ 19	Charlotte, N.C.
„ 19	„ ..	..	..	Washington, N.C. ..	„ 22	Washington, N.C.
„ 20	„ ..	..	..	Ditto ..	„ 30	Ditto.
„ 25	„ ..	..	.. "	Hertford, N.C. ..	„ 30	Edenton, N.C.
„ 25	„ ..	..	..	Charlotte, N.C. ..	„ 28	Charlotte, N.C.
„ 25	„ ..	..	..	Smithville, N.C. ..	July 27	Nassau.
„ 25	„ ..	..	..	Hertford, N.C. ..	June 28	Onslow County.
„ 25	„ ..	..	..	Ditto ..	„ 28	Hertford, N.C.
July 1	„ ..	..	..	Georgetown, S.C. ..	July 5	Georgetown, S.C.
„ 2	„ ..	..	..	Smithville, N.C. ..	„ 15	Cardenas.
„ 2	„ ..	..	..	Little River, S.C. ..	„ 4	Little River, S.C.
„ 10	„ ..	..	..	Nassau ..	„ 25	Nassau.
„ 10	Steamer ..	..	..	Smithville, N.C. .	„ 15	Privateering cruize.
„ 17	„ ..	..	..	Charleston, S.C. ..	„ 20	Ditto.
„ 20	Schooner ..	..	..	Georgetown, S.C. ..	Aug. 9	Georgetown, S.C.
„ 17	„ ..	..	..	Washington, N.C. ..	„ 9	Ditto.
„ 25	„ ..	..	..	Ditto ..	July 31	Washington, N.C.
„ 26	„ ..	..	..	Edenton ..	„ 31	Hertford, N.C.
„ 27	„ ..	..	..	Halifax ..	Aug. 5	Halifax, N.S.
„ 29	„ ..	..	..	Ditto ..	„ 5	Ditto.
	Brig ..	..	..	In port ..	July 24	Liverpool.

(Signed)　　　JAS. O. MILLER, *Collector.*

Collector's Office, Wilmington, August 12, 1861.

(2.)—LIST of Vessels Entered and Cleared at Port of Charleston, South Carolina, from May 11 to August 12, 1861.

Date of Entry.	Class.	Name.	Port where from.	Date of Clearance.	Port of Destination.	Flag.	Remarks.
May 13	Ship ...	...	Belfast ...	May 24	Liverpool ...		
„ 17	Brig ...	...	Glasgow ...	„ 24	Glasgow ...		
„ 17	Schooner	...	Cardenas ...	„ 24			
„ 18	Ship ...	...	Liverpool ...	„ 24	Liverpool ...		
„ 27	Barque	...	Fredestadt, Norway	June 1	New York ...		
„ 28	Schooner	...	Eleuthera, Bahama	May 30	Harbor Island ...		
„ 13	„	...	Darien, Georgia	„ 16	Darien, Georgia ...		
„ 13	Steamer	...	Fernandina, Fla	...			
„ 13	„	...	Jacksonville, Fla.	„ 24	Jacksonville, Fla. ...		
„ 17	„	...	Jacksonville, Fla.	„ 24	Ditto		
June 8	Schooner	...	Havana ...	„ 24			
„ 17	Steamer	...	Fernandina, Fla.	July 17	Fernandina, Fla. ...		
July 20	„	...	Ditto ...	„ 26			
„ 26	Schooner	...	Ditto...	August 1	Smyrna, Fla. ...		
Aug. 5	Steamer	...	Ditto...	„ 5	Fernandina, Fla. ...		
„ 5	Sloop ...	...	Ditto...	„ 6	Matanzas, Cuba ...		
„ 8	Steamer	...	Ditto...	...			
...	Schooner	...	Ditto...	„ 10	Liverpool ...		

LIST of the Vessels Entered and Cleared at the Port of Charleston, South Carolina, from August 11 to 17, 1861.

Date of Entry.	Class.	Name.	Port where from.	Date of Clearance.	Port of Destination.
August 11	Steamer ..	. .	Savannah, Georgia.		
„ 11	Schooner	. .	Ditto.		
„ 11	„	. .	Ditto.		
„ 12	„	. .	Pocotalega, South Carolina		
„ 14	Steamer ..	. .	Fernandina, Florida ..	August 16	
„ 14	Schooner	. .	Georgetown, South Carolina.		
„ 16	„	. .	Ashepoo, South Carolina.		
„ 16	„	. .	Santee, South Carolina.		
„ 16	Sloop ..	. .	Ditto.		
„ 17	„	. .	Georgetown, South Carolina.		

(Signed) W. F. COLCOCK, *Collector.*

Collector's Office, Charleston, S.C., August 17, 1861.

N.B.—This form is in compliance with the instructions of the Department, but as many vessels are not required by law to enter and clear, this is more properly a list of arrivals at this port; all these vessels must pass the blockading squadron at some point.

W. F. C.

LIST of Vessels Entered and Cleared at the Port of Charleston, South Carolina, from August 25 to September 2, 1861.

Date of Entry.	Class.	Name.	Port where from.	Date of Clearance.	Port of Destination.	Flag.	Remarks.
August 29	Steamer ...	...	Georgetown, S.C. ...	...			
„ 29	Schooner ...	...	Santee River ...	...			
„ 30	Steamer ...	...	Jacksonville, Fla. ...	August 31	Jacksonville, Fla.		
„ 30	Privateer steamer	...	From a cruise ...	...			
„ 30	Privateer ...	...	Arrived inland from Bull's Bay	...			
Sept. 1	Brig ...	...	Rio de Janeiro ...	...			
„ 1	Schooner ...	...	Havana, via Fernandina, Fla., and Beaufort, S.C. inland	...			

LIST of Vessels Entered and Cleared at the Port of Charleston, South Carolina, from September 3 to 16, 1861.

Date of Entry.	Class.	Name.	Port where from.	Date of Clearance.	Port of Destination.	Flag.	Remarks.
Sept. 10	Steamer ...	...	Fernandina, Fla. ...	Sept. 12	Fernandina, Fla.		
„ 11	„	...	Georgetown, S.C. ...	„ 12	Ditto		
„ 12	Sloop ...	...	Ditto ...	„ 12	Ditto		
„ 13	„	...	Ditto ...	„ 12	Ditto		
„ 13	Barque ...	...	Edisto—(prize to privateer "Dixie")	„ 12	Ditto		
„ 16	Sloop ...	...	Matanzas, Cuba	„ 12	Ditto		
	Schooner ...	...	Edenton, N.C...	„ 12			
	„	...	Ditto ...	„ 11	Matanzas, Cuba		
	„	...	Ditto ...	„ 16	Ditto		

(Signed) W. F. COLCOCK, *Collector.*

Collector's Office, Charleston, South Carolina, September 16, 1861.

(3.) —LIST of Vessels Entered and Cleared from the Port of Savannah, Georgia, from May 28 to August 1, 1861.

Date of Arrival.	Class.	Name.	From what Port.	Date of Clearance.	Bound to what Port.
May 1	British ship	.. ..	Liverpool, England .	May 28	Liverpool, England.
,, 31	Schooner	.. ..	Darien, Georgia .	June 1	Darien, Georgia.
,, 15	British barque	.. ..	Cape de Verde ..	,, 1	Cardiff, Wales.
,, 17	British ship	.. ..	Liverpool, England .	,, 1	Liverpool, England.
,, 22	Spanish barque	.. ..	Barcelona, Spain ..	,, 2	Barcelona, Spain.
,, 13	British ship	.. ..	Greenock, Gt. Btn..	,, 3	Liverpool, England.
,, 18	,,	.. ..	Liverpool, England .	,, 5	Ditto.
,, 20	,,	.. ..	Ditto	,, 6	Ditto.
,, 21	,,	.. ..	Ditto	,, 6	Ditto.
,, 27	Swedish barque	.. ..	Barcelona, Spain ..	,, 10	Barcelona, Spain.
June 4	Confederate States' schooner ..	.. ..	Savannah, Georgia..	Aug. 10	Fernandina, Florida.
,, 5	,,	.. ..	Ditto	June 5	Darien, Georgia.
,, 8	,,	.. ..	Ditto	,, 8	Ditto.
,, 8	,,	.. ..	Ditto	,, 8	Ditto.
,, 11	,,	.. ..	Ditto	,, 11	Ditto.
,, 24	,,	.. ..	Ditto	,, 28	Ditto.
July 1	British schooner	.. ..	Nassau, N.P. ..	July 17	Havana, Cuba.
,, 20	Confederate States' schooner..	.. ..	Savannah, Georgia..	,, 20	Darien, Georgia.
,, 27	Confederate States' steam-boat	.. ..	Pilatka, Florida ..	,, 27	Pilatka, Florida.

Vessels cleared for Foreign ports	..	..	..	10
Ditto	Home ports	..	..	.. 9
Total	..	..	..	.. 19

(Signed)   JOHN BOSTON, Collector.

Custom-House, Collector's Office, Savannah, August 14, 1861.

LIST of Vessels Arrived at and Cleared from the Port of Savannah, Georgia, from August 1 to September 1, 1861.

Date of Arrival.	Class.	Name.	Port where from.	Date of Clearance.	To what Port bound.
	Steam-boat ..	.. ..	.. ..	Aug. 2	Charleston, South Carolina.
	,,	.. ..	.. ..	,, 15	Pilatka, Florida.
	Schooner	.. ..	.. ..	,, 21	Matanzas, West Indies.
Aug. 23	,,	.. ..	Havana ..		
	,,	.. ..	.. ..	,, 27	Fernandina.

(4.)—A LIST of Vessels Arrived at and Cleared from Mobile, from June 1 to August 31, 1861.

Date of Arrival.	Class.	Name.	Port where from.	Date of Clearance.	Port where Bound.
1861				1861	
June 3	Schooner ..	.. ..	New Orleans.		
,, 3	British steamer ..	.. ..	Havana, Cuba.		
,, 3	Steamer ..	.. ..	New Orleans.		
,, 3	,, ..	.. ..	Ditto.		
,, 1	,, ..	.. ..	Ditto.		
,, 3	Schooner ..	.. ..	Ditto.		
,, 3	,, ..	.. ..	Ditto.		
,, 3	,, ..	.. ..	Ditto.		
,, 3	,, ..	.. ..	Ditto.		
,, 4	,, ..	.. ..	Ditto.		
,, 4	,, ..	.. ..	Ditto.		
,, 5	Steamer ..	.. ..	Ditto.		
,, 5	Schooner ..	.. ..	Ditto.		
,, 6	,, ..	.. ..	Ditto.		
,, 7	Steamer ..	.. ..	Ditto.		
,, 7	,, ..	.. ..	Ditto.		
,, 8	Schooner ..	.. ..	Ditto.		
,, 8	Steamer ..	.. ..	Ditto.		

List of Vessels Arrived at and Cleared from Mobile, &c.—*continued.*

Date of Arrival.	Class.	Name.	Port where from.	Date of Clearance.	Port where Bound.
1861				1861	
June 11	Schooner ..	.. ..	New Orleans.		
„ 11	Sloop ..	.. ..	Ditto.		
„ 11	Steamer ..	.. ..	Ditto	June 14	New Orleans.
„ 14	Schooner ..	.. ..	Ditto.		
„ 14	„ ..	.. ..	Ditto.		
„ 15	„ ..	.. ..	Ditto.		
„ 16	Steamer ..	.. ..	Ditto.		
„ 17	Sloop ..	.. ..	Ditto.		
„ 17	Schooner ..	.. ..	Ditto.		
„ 17	„ ..	.. ..	Ditto.		
„ 17	„ ..	.. ..	Ditto.		
„ 18	„ ..	.. ..	Ditto.		
„ 18	„ ..	.. ..	Ditto.		
„ 18	„ ..	.. ..	Ditto.		
„ 20	Steamer ..	.. ..	Ditto.		
„ 20	Schooner ..	.. ..	Ditto.		
„ 20	„ ..	.. ..	Ditto.		
„ 24	Steamer ..	.. ..	Ditto.		
„ 24	Schooner ..	.. ..	Ditto	Aug. 8	Ditto.
July 29	„ ..	.. ..	Ditto.		
Aug. 5	„ ..	.. ..	Ditto.		
„ 5	„ ..	.. ..	Ditto.		
„ 16	„ ..	.. ..	Ditto.		
„ 16	„ ..	.. ..	Ditto	„ 18	Ditto.
„ 16	„ ..	.. ..	Ditto.		
„ 3	„ ..	.. ..	Ditto	„ 6	Ditto.
„ 19	Steamer ..	.. ..			
„ 21	Schooner ..	.. ..	Ditto	„ 19	Ditto.
„ 23	„ ..	.. ..	Ditto.		
„ 23	„ ..	.. ..	Ditto.		
„ 23	„ ..	.. ..	Ditto.		
„ 23	„ ..	.. ..	Ditto.		
„ 27	„ ..	.. ..	Ditto.		
„ 28	„ ..	.. ..	Ditto.		
„ 28	Sloop ..	.. ..	Ditto.		
„ 28	Schooner ..	.. ..	Ditto.		
„ 30	„ ..	.. ..	Ditto.		
„ 30	..	.. ..	Ditto.		

Collector's Office, Mobile, August 31, 1861.

(Signed)　　H. SANDFORD, *Collector.*

(5.)—LIST of Vessels entered and cleared from the District of Fernandina, Florida, from June 1 to July 20, 1861.

Date of Arrival.	Class.	Name.	Port where from.	Date of Clearance.	Port bound for.
May 13	Schooner ..	.. ..	St. Thomas . ..	June 3	Port of Spain.
		.. ..	Fitted out here ..	„ 4	Nassau, N. P.
July 24	Steamer ..	.. ..	Charleston.. ..	July 23	Charleston.
„ 30	Ditto ..	.. ..	Ditto	„ 31	Ditto.
August 7	Ditto ..	.. ..	Ditto	Aug. 8	Ditto.
	Schooner ..	.. ..	Fitted out here ..	„ 10	Matanzas.
„ 15		.. ..	Havana	„ 15	Savannah.
„ 19	Steamer ..	.. ..	Charleston.. ..	„ 20	Charleston.

(6.)—A STATEMENT of Vessels which have entered the Port of Pensacola, and of those cleared therefrom, from May 13 to August 15, 1861, inclusive.

Date of Entry.	Class.	Name.	Whence arrived.	Date of Clearance.	Destination.
	Schooner ..	.. ..	.. ..	May 13	New Orleans.
	Barque ..	.. ..	.. ..	„ 22	Queenstown, Ireland.
	Ship ..	.. ..	.. ..	„ 23	Cork, Ireland.
		.. ..	.. ..	„ 24	Ditto.
	Barque ..	.. ..	.. ..	„ 25	Sunderland, Ireland.
	Ship ..	.. ..	.. ..	..	Liverpool, England.

(Signed)　　JOSEPH SIERRA, *Collector.*

Pensacola, August 15, 1861.

(7.)—LIST of Vessels Arrived at New Orleans, from May 15 to August 20, 1861.

Date of Arrival.	Class.				Name.			Port where from.
May 15	Schooner	..		..		..		Fort Smith, Arkansas.
	„			..		..		St. Louis, Missouri.
	„	..		..		..		Havana, Cuba.
	Flat-boat	..		..		..		Hickman, Kentucky.
	„			..		..		Obion, Tennessee.
	„	..		..		..		Ditto.
	„	..		..		..		Ditto.
	„	..		..		..		Swallow Bluff, Tennessee.
	„			..		..		Jeffersonville, Arkansas.
	„	..		..		..		Troy, Tennessee.
	„			..		..		Big Sandy, Kentucky.
	Steam-boat	..		..		..		Fort Smith, Arkansas.
„ 16	Ship	..		..		..		Calcutta, East Indies.
	„			..		..		Liverpool.
	Flat-boat	..		..		..		Patoca, Indiana.
	„	..		..		..		Pittsburg, Pennsylvania.
	„	..		..		..		Ditto.
	„			..		..		Ditto.
	Steam-boat	..		..		..		Camden, Arkansas.
	Flat-boat	..		..		..		Fairfax, Indiana.
	„	..		..		..		Obion, Tennessee.
„ 17	Steam-boat	..		..		..		St. Louis, Missouri.
	„			..		..		Ditto.
	Ship	..		..		..		Bremen.
	„	..		..		..		Havre, France.
	Flat-boat	..		..		..		Cedar Brand, Kentucky.
	„			..		..		Ditto.
	Barque	..		..		..		Malaga, Spain.
	Ship	..		..		..		Havre, France.
„ 18	Barque	..		..		..		Barcelona, Spain.
	Schooner	..		..		..		Charleston, South Carolina.
	Ship	..		..		..		Havre, France.
	Steamer	..		..		...		Havana, Cuba.
	Barque	..		..		..		New York.
	Brig	..		..		..		Ruatan, Honduras.
	Barque	..		..		..		Rio de Janeiro, Brazil.
	Flat-boat	..		..		..		Pittsburg, Pennsylvania.
	„	..		..		..		Ditto.
	„	..		..		..		Ditto.
	„	..		..		..		Ditto.
	„	..		..		..		Ditto.
	„	.		..		..		Ditto.
	„	..		..		..		Ditto.
	„	..		..		..		Ditto.
	„	..		..		..		Ditto.
	„	..		..		..		Ditto.
	„	..		..		..		Ditto.
	„	..		..		..		Ditto.
	„	..		..		..		Ditto.
	„	..		..		..		Ditto.
	„	..		..		..		Ditto.
	„	..		..		..		Ditto.
	„	..		..		..		Ditto.
	„	..		..		..		Ditto.
	„	..		..		..		Ditto.
	„	..		..		..		Ditto.
	„	..		..		..		Ditto.
	„	..		..		..		Ditto.
	„	..		..		..		Ditto.
„ 20	Schooner	..		...		..		Ruatan, Honduras.
	Flat-boat	..		..		..		Rochester, Kentucky.
	„	..		..		..		Virginia.
	Steamer	..		..		..		Galveston, Texas.
	„	..		..		..		Pittsburg Pennsylvania.
	„	..		..		..		Ditto.
	„	..		..		..		Louisville, Kentucky.
	Schooner	..		...		..		Philadelphia, Pennsylvania.
	Flat-boat	..		..		..		Pond River, Kentucky.
	„	..		..		..		Ditto
„ 21	Steam-boat	..		..		..		St. Louis, Missouri.
	Flat-boat	..		..		..		Pittsburg, Pennsylvania.

O 2

List of Vessels Arrived at New Orleans, &c.—*continued.*

Date of Arrival.	Class.	Name.	Port where from.
May 21	Flat-boat	..	Ditto.
	,,	..	Troy County, Kentucky.
	,,	..	Wigg, Kentucky.
	Schooner	..	Charleston, South Carolina.
	Ship	..	Liverpool, England.
	Barque	..	Havana, Cuba.
,, 22	Steam-boat	..	St. Louis, Missouri.
	Schooner	..	Tampa Bay, Florida.
	Flat-boat	..	Tennessee River, Tennessee.
	,,	..	Ditto.
	,,	..	Meade, Kentucky.
	,,	..	Blue River, Indiana.
,, 23	,,	..	Hickman, Kentucky.
	,,	..	Ditto.
	,,	..	Columbus, Kentucky.
	,,	..	White River, Indiana.
,, 24	,,	..	Dorum, Illinois.
	,,	..	Huntsville, Illinois.
	,,	..	Ditto.
	Steam-ship	..	Brazos, Texas.
	Steamer	..	Galveston, Texas.
	,,	..	Memphis, Tennessee.
	Schooner	..	Mobile, Alabama.
	Steamer	..	Galveston, Texas.
,, 25	Flat-boat	..	Vevay, Indiana.
	,,	..	Ditto.
	,,	..	Balard, Kentucky.
	Brig	..	Vera Cruz, Mexico.
	Flat-boat	..	Memphis, Indiana.
	Schooner	..	Galveston, Texas.
	Ship ..	..	Rio de Janeiro, Brazil.
	Flat-boat	..	Obion River, Tennessee.
,, 27	Steamer	..	Memphis, Tennessee.
	Ship ..	..	Havana, Cuba.
	Steamer	..	Peoria, Illinois.
	Ship ..	..	Liverpool, England.
	,, ..	..	Ditto.
	Steamer	..	Sabine, Texas.
	,,	..	Indianola, Texas.
,, 28	Flat-boat	..	Perryville, Tennessee.
	,,	..	Jaranora, Tennessee.
	,,	..	Ditto.
	,,	..	Harrisburg, Indiana.
	,,	..	Oil Creek, Indiana.
,, 29	,,	..	Wuhlenburg, Tennessee.
	Ship ..	..	Liverpool, England.
	Flat-boat	..	Green River, Kentucky.
	Schooner	..	Tampico, Mexico.
	Flat-boat	..	Indiana.
	,,	..	Ditto.
	,,	..	Ditto.
	,,	..	Oil Creek, Indiana.
	,,	..	St. Francis River, Arkansas.
	Barque	..	Palermo, Sicily.
,, 31	Flat-boat	..	Rockport, Tennessee.
	,,	..	Swallow Bluff, Tennessee.
	Schooner	..	Tampico viâ the Atchafalaya.
	Flat-boat	..	Cairo, Illinois.
	Steam-boat	..	Pittsburg, Pennsylvania.
June 1	Flat-boat	..	Ditto.
	,,	..	Ditto.
	,,	..	Ditto.
	,,	..	Ditto.
	,,	..	Ditto.
	,,	..	Ditto.
	,,	..	Ditto.
	,,	..	Ditto.
	,,	..	Ditto.
	,,	..	Ditto.
,, 3	,,	..	Saline City, Arkansas.
	Schooner	..	Campeachy, Mexico.
,, 4	Steamer	..	Memphis, Tennessee.

List of Vessels Arrived at New Orleans, &c.—*continued.*

Date of Arrival.	Class.				Name.			Port where from.
June 4	Flat-boat	..		..		..		Obion River, Tennessee.
	,,	..		..		..		Carrolton, Kentucky
	,,	..		..		..		Darien. Illinois.
,, 5	,,	..		..		..		Blue River, Kentucky.
	,,	..		..		..		Ditto.
	,,	..		..		..		Hickman, Kentucky.
	,,	..		..		..		Arkansas, Arkansas.
	,,	..		..		..		Sportsville, Kentucky.
,, 6	,,	..		..		..		Saltillo, Tennessee.
	,,	..		..		..		Wolf Creek, Kentucky.
	,,	..		..		..		Troy, Indiana.
	,,	..		..		..		Maxville, Indiana.
	Steam-boat	..		..		..		Memphis, Tennessee.
,, 7	,,	..		..		..		Louisville, Kentucky.
,, 8	,,	..		..		..		Memphis, Tennessee.
	,,	..		..		..		Ditto.
	Flat-boat	..		..		..		Grayson City, Kentucky.
	,,	..		..		..		Warrechoe, Indiana.
,, 10	,,	..		..		..		Tennessee, Tennessee.
,, 11	Schooner	..		..		..		Tampico, Mexico.
	Steamer	..		..		..		Memphis, Tennessee
,, 12	Schooner	..		..		..		Mobile, Alabama.
	Flat-boat	..		..		..		St. Francis' River, Arkansas.
,, 14	Steam-boat	..		..		..		Columbus, Kentucky.
,, 15	,,	..		..		..		Memphis, Tennessee.
	Flat-boat	..		..		..		Columbus, Kentucky.
	,,	..		..		..		Derby, Indiana.
	,,	..		..		..		Perryville, Tennessee.
,, 17	Steam-boat	..		..		..		Memphis, Tennessee.
,, 18	,,	..		..		..		Ditto.
,, 19	Schooner	..		..		..		Mobile, Alabama.
,, 22	Steam-boat	..		..		..		Memphis, Tennessee.
	Flat-boat	..		..		..		Ditto.
,, 25	Brig	..		..		..		Havana, Cuba.
,, 28	Steamer	..		..		..		Memphis, Tennessee.
July 1	Flat-boat	..		..		..		Green River, Kentucky.
	Steam-boat	..		..		..		Memphis, Tennessee.
,, 3	,,	..		..		..		Ditto.
,, 6	Flat-boat	..		..		..		Wolf Creek, Kentucky.
,, 12	Schooner	..		..		..		Havana, Cuba.
,, 31	,,	..		..		..		Mobile, Alabama.
Aug. 3	Ship	..		..		..		Liverpool, England.
,, 12	Schooner	..		..		..		Mobile—Alabama.

This list has been compiled from the records of the Office, showing the dates when the vessels entered at the Custom-house, which dates correspond, within a day of those of arrival, except in the case of the ————, which was brought into the port as a prize by the privateer armed steamer "V. H. Ivy," on the 28th May, and not entered until 3rd August, after the decision of the Court had been rendered in the trial for condemnation. Many of the vessels from foreign ports by sea, arrived within the waters of this Collection district, at Atchafalaya, Barrataria, and other inlets on the coast, previous to entering at this office. Since the admission of Tennessee, &c., vessels from them do not enter at the Custom-house.

(Signed)   F. H. HATCH, *Collector.*

Custom-House, New Orleans, Office of the Collector,
August 20, 1861.

(6.)—LIST of Vessels Cleared from New Orleans from May 15 to August 20, 1861.

Date of Clearance.	Class.				Name.			Port where bound.
May 15	Schooner	..		..		..		Libourne, France.
	Steamer	..		..		..		Cairo.
	,,	..		..		..		Galveston.
	,,	..		..		..		Ditto.
	Ship	..		..		..		Bath.
	Barque	..		..		..		Liverpool, England.
	Schooner	..		..		..		Mobile.
	,,	..		..		..		Ditto.
,, 16	,,	..		..		..		Ditto.
	,,	..		..		..		Ditto.
	,,	..		..		..		Ditto.

List of Vessels Cleared from New Orleans, &c.—*continued.*

Date of Clearance.	Class.	Name.	Port where bound.
May 16	Schooner ..	.. ..	Havana, Cuba.
	Steamer ..	.. ..	Camden, Arkansas.
„ 17	„ ..	.- ..	St. Louis, Missouri.
	Ship ..	.. ..	Havre, France.
	Brig ..	.. ..	Tampico, Mexico.
	Schooner ..	.. ..	Mobile, Alabama.
„ 18	„ ..	.. ..	Ditto.
	„ ..	.- ..	Ditto.
	„ ..	.. ..	Ditto.
	„ ..	.. ..	Ditto.
	„ ..	.. ..	Pensacola, Florida.
	Steamer ..	.. ..	Galveston, Texas.
	Schooner ..	.. ..	Vera Cruz, Mexico.
	„ ..	.. ..	Ditto.
	Barque ..	.. ..	Liverpool, England.
	Ship ..	.. ..	Ditto.
	„ ..	.. ..	Ditto.
	Barque ..	.. ..	St. Mark's, Hayti.
„ 20	„ ..	.. ..	Liverpool, England.
	Brig ..	.. ..	Barcelona, Spain.
	Steamer ..	.. ..	Havana, Cuba.
	„ ..	.. ..	Ditto.
	„ ..	.. ..	Pittsburg, Pennsylvania.
	„ ..	.. ..	Ditto.
	„ ..	.. ..	St. Louis, Missouri.
	Barge ..	.. ..	Mobile, Alabama.
	Schooner ..	.. ..	Apalachicola, Florida.
„ 21	„ ..	.. ..	Mobile, Alabama.
	„ ..	.. ..	Ditto.
	„ ..	.. ..	Ditto.
	„ ..	.. ..	Ditto.
	Steamer ..	.. ..	Louisville, Kentucky.
	Barque ..	.. ..	Bordeaux, France.
	„ ..	.. ..	Ditto.
	Schooner ..	.. ..	Ditto.
	„ ..	.. ..	Havana, Cuba.
„ 22	Barque ..	.. ..	Malaga, Spain.
	„ ..	.. ..	Liverpool, England.
	Brig ..	.. ..	Bordeaux, France.
	Ship ..	.. ..	Ditto.
„ 22	Schooner ..	.. ..	Mobile, Alabama.
	„ ..	.. ..	Ditto.
	„ ..	.. ..	Ditto.
	„ ..	.. ..	Ditto.
	„ ..	.. ..	Ditto.
	„ ..	.. ..	Apalachicola, Florida.
„ 23	„ ..	.. ..	Mobile, Alabama.
	Ship ..	.. ..	Havre, France.
	„ ..	.. ..	Liverpool, England.
	Steamer ..	.. ..	Memphis, Tennessee.
„ 24	Ship ..	.. ..	New York, New York.
	„ ..	.. ..	Cadiz, Spain.
	Schooner ..	.. ..	Mobile, Alabama.
	„ ..	.. ..	Ditto.
„ 25	„ ..	.. ..	Ditto.
	„ ..	.. ..	Ditto.
	Ship ..	.. ..	Bremen.
	„ ..	.. ..	Ditto.
	„ ..	.. ..	Liverpool, England.
	„ ..	.. ..	Ditto.
	Schooner ..	.. ..	Belize, Honduras.
	„ ..	.. ..	Tampico, Mexico.
	Barque ..	.. ..	Genoa, Italy.
	„ ..	.. ..	Havana, Cuba.
„ 27	„ ..	.. ..	Ditto.
	„ ..	.. ..	Barcelona, Spain.
	Ship ..	.. ..	Havre, France.
	Steamer ..	.. ..	Memphis, Tennessee.
	Schooner ..	.. ..	Mobile, Alabama.
	„ ..	.. ..	Ditto.
	„ ..	.. ..	Ditto.
„ 28	„ ..	.. ..	Ditto.
	„ ..	.. ..	Ditto.
	„ ..	.. ..	Galveston, Texas.

List of Vessels Cleared from New Orleans, &c.—*continued.*

Date of Clearance.		Class.	Name.	Port where bound.
May	28	Ship	..	Liverpool, England.
„	29	„	..	Ditto.
		„	..	Bordeaux, France.
		Brig	..	Belize, Honduras.!
		Schooner	..	Matanzas, Cuba.
		„	..	Mobile, Alabama.
		„	..	Ditto.
		Steamer	..	Memphis, Tennessee.
		„	..	Ditto.
„	30	Barque	..	Bordeaux, France.
„	31	„	..	Liverpool, England.
		Ship	..	Ditto.
		Schooner	..	Matamoros, Mexico.
		„	..	Mobile, Alabama.
June	1	Ship	..	Bremen.
		Steamer	..	Memphis, Tennessee.
		„	..	Ditto.
		Schooner	..	Mobile, Alabama.
		„	..	Ditto.
„	4	„	..	Vera Cruz, Mexico.
		Barque	..	Barcelona, Spain.
		„	..	Liverpool, England.
		„	..	Ditto.
„	5	„	..	Ditto.
		Ship	..	Ditto.
		„	..	London, England.
		Barque	..	Malaga, Spain.
		Schooner	..	Mobile, Alabama.
„	6	Brig	..	Campeachy, Mexico.
		Schooner	..	Tampico, Mexico.
		„	..	Matamoros, Mexico.
		„	..	Havana, Cuba.
„	7	„	..	Mobile, Alabama.
		Ship	..	Civita Vecchia, Italy.
		„	..	Liverpool, England.
		„	..	Ditto.
		„	..	Ditto.
		Steamer	..	Memphis, Tennessee.
		„	..	Ditto.
„	8	„	..	Ditto.
		Ship	..	Liverpool, England.
		„	..	Ditto.
		Schooner	..	Tampico, Mexico.
		„	..	Havana, Cuba.
		„	..	Mobile, Alabama.
„	10	„	..	Ditto.
		Ship	..	Liverpool, England.
„	11	Schooner	..	Mobile, Alabama.
„	12	„	..	Ditto.
		„	..	Ditto.
		Steamer	..	Memphis, Tennessece.
„	14	Schooner	..	Mobile, Alabama.
		„	..	Ditto.
		„	..	Ditto.
		„	..	Ditto.
„	16	„	..	Ditto.
		„	..	Ditto.
		Steamer	..	Memphis, Tennessee.
„	17	Schooner	..	Campeachy, Mexico.
		„	..	Fish River.
„	18	Steamer	..	Memphis, Tennessee.
„	19	„	..	Ditto.
		„	..	Ditto.
		Schooner	..	Mobile, Alabama.
„	20	„	..	Ditto.
		„	..	Ditto.
		„	..	Ditto.
		„	..	Ditto.
		Barque	..	Mobile, Alabama.
		Sloop	..	Memphis, Tennessee.
		Steamer	..	St. Louis, Missouri.
		Schooner	..	Biloxi, Missouri.
„	21	Lugger	..	Mobile, Alabama.
		Sloop	..	Ditto.
		Schooner	..	

List of Vessels Cleared from New Orleans, &c.—*continued.*

Date of Clearance.		Class.		Name.		Port where bound.
June	21	Schooner	..	..	..	Mobile, Alabama.
,,	22	,,	..	..	..	Ditto.
		,,	..	..	..	Ditto.
,,	24	,,	..	..	..	Ditto.
,,	25	Sloop	..	..	..	Ditto.
		Schooner	..	..	..	Pearl River, Mississippi.
,,	27	Steamer	..	..	..	Memphis, Tennessee.
		,,	..	..	..	Ditto.
,,	28	,,	..	..	..	Ditto.
		,,	..	..	..	Galveston, Texas.
,,	29	Schooner	..	..	..	St. Louis, Maine.
July	3	Steamer	..	..	..	Memphis, Tennessee.
		,,	..	..	..	Ditto.
,,	8	Schooner	..	..	..	Bay St. Louis, Missouri.
,,	13	,,	..	..	..	Mobile, Alabama.
		,,	..	..	..	Ditto.
,,	16	,,	..	..	..	St. Louis, Missouri.
		,,	..	..	..	Mobile, Alabama.
,,	19	Lugger	..	..	..	Ditto.
		Schooner	..	..	..	Havana, Cuba.
,,	20	,,	..	..	..	Mobile, Alabama.
,,	21	,,	..	..	..	Ditto.
		,,	..	..	..	Ditto.
,,	27	,,	..	..	..	Ditto.
,,	28	Sloop	..	..	..	Ditto.
		Schooner	..	..	..	St. Louis, Missouri.
Aug.	2	,,	..	..	..	Mobile, Alabama.
,,	5	,,	..	..	..	Ditto.
,,	9	,,	..	..	..	Ditto.
,,	10	,,	..	..	..	Ditto.
,,	14	,,	..	..	..	Ditto.
,,	15	Sloop	..	..	..	Ditto.
,,	16	Schooner	..	..	..	Ditto.
		,,	..	..	..	Ditto.
,,	17	,,	..	..	..	Ditto.
		,,	..	..	..	Ditto.
		,,	..	..	..	Ditto.
,,	19	,,	..	..	..	Ditto.
		,,	..	..	..	Havana, Cuba.
		,,	..	..	..	Mobile, Alabama.
,,	15	,,	..	..	..	St. Louis, Missouri.
,,	20	Sloop	..	..	..	Mobile, Alabama.
		,,	..	..	..	Ditto.

The foregoing list of vessels is compiled from the record of vessels cleared at this Custom-house.

Since the admission of Tennessee, &c., vessels from those States have not cleared, the vessels more recently cleared for foreign ports by sea have departed from the waters of this Collection district by the Acchafalaya, Barrataria, and other inlets on the coast.

Custom-House, New Orleans, Collector's Office, August 20, 1861.

(Signed)　　F. H. HATCH, *Collector.*

No. 97.

Acting Consul Fullarton to Earl Russell.—(Received November 30.)

My Lord,　　　　　　　　　　　　　　*Savannah, October* 11, 1861.

SINCE the beginning of September the blockade of this port has been less strictly maintained than at any period since its commencement. Intermissions of the blockade have lately been very frequent, during which the entrance to the river was left quite unobstructed; they occurred as follows: from the 8th to the 14th September, from the 15th or 16th to the 23rd September, and from the 29th September to the 4th October. Since the latter date another intermission took place of about two days' duration, and I am informed that yesterday the blockading squadron again left its post. These intermissions have not been caused by the weather, or, so far as could be observed, by chasing vessels endeavouring to break the blockade.

During one of the above-mentioned intermissions the most important instance of running the blockade which has yet taken place occurred; I refer to the arrival, on the 17th September, in the river, of the screw-steamer ——. On the 16th September this vessel coasted for about forty miles to the south without seeing any blockading vessel whatever. She lies in port at this moment.

So much for the blockade of this port. The blockade of the coast to the south of this has all along been maintained in a very ineffective manner, and at the present moment as much so as ever. The vessels employed are too few in number, and not suitable in class to prevent access to the various harbours and inlets on the coasts; they merely cruize up and down, visiting for a day or two at a time one harbour after another. The consequence has been that many vessels have run in and out, to and from various points on the coast, without seeing a blockading vessel. I proceed to give your Lordship a list of these vessels :—

The schooner —— sailed on 30th August from Sapelo inlet for Nassau, where her name was changed to the ——, a register taken out in the name of a British subject, and the vessel put under British colours. She went thence to Havana, took in a cargo, and returned to the coast of Georgia, entering on the 6th October by St. Simon's Sound, nothing being seen of a blockading vessel, either in going or returning.

The schooner —— arrived in the St. John's river from the West Indies, about the 29th September, without seeing a blockading vessel.

The schooner —— arrived at Darien, from Nassau, about the 28th September ; saw no blockading vessel.

The schooner —— sailed 10th, and the schooner —— on the 20th September, for the West Indies ; both have arrived at their destinations.

The high prices which many of the necessaries of life command in the South have stimulated the people to greater exertions in procuring a larger supply. Accordingly many parties here are fitting out a number of small vessels suitable for the West India trade and the peculiarities of this coast. Maintained as the blockade is at present, I see no reason to doubt the success of their enterprize. These vessels will not go out by the river ; they run less risk by departing by some of the inlets to the south, which they reach from this city through the channel inside the islands which form the coast of this State.

Another proof of the inefficiency of the blockade of the coast consists in the fact that, since the commencement of the blockade, the line of steamers between this city and the St. John's river, Florida, has kept up an uninterrupted communication. These steamers always go out to sea from the St. Mary's to the St. John's bars. In a very few instances they have seen a blockading vessel off the St. John and Fernandina bars, but not sufficiently near to prevent their regular ingress and egress.

I have, &c.

(Signed)   A. FULLARTON.

No. 98.

Consul Bunch to Earl Russell.—(Received November 30.)

My Lord,   *Charleston, October* 15, 1861.

THE blockade of this port and of the adjacent coast has undergone no change since the date of my last despatches. Two, three, and even four ships of the United States have been observed off the harbour, but the blockade can scarcely be considered as effective, as I shall proceed to show.

The steamer —— got successfully to sea, going over the bar and through the main channel.

The barque ——, which cleared from Liverpool under the Confederate flag, with a cargo of salt, eluded the vigilance of the squadron, and nearly succeeded in entering the port on the day before yesterday. Unfortunately, however, she got aground inside the bar, where she remains. But her failure to reach her destination is not attributable to the blockade.

The inclosed affidavit of —— of the schooner ——, shows that the vessel under his command sailed on the 8th instant from North Edisto, about twenty miles from Charleston and returned through Broad River, without having seen a blockading ship. It also establishes the fact that other vessels have prosecuted their voyages without molestation or interference.

I have, &c.

(Signed)   ROBERT BUNCH.

Inclosure in No. 98.

Affidavit of ———.

British Consulate, Charleston, South Carolina.

——— maketh oath and saith, that he lately took command of the schooner ———, and sailed from the port of Charleston by the north-east channel, on Tuesday, the 8th day of October instant, and found no blockading vessels off that outlet; that he was bound for Nassau, New Providence, and proceeded on his course, steering south-east about seventy-five miles, when his vessel sprung a leak, and deponent put back and entered Broad River, by Port Royal entrance, at about 5 P.M. of the next day, and has since been towed to Charleston; that he had a cargo of 193 tierces of rice, and sailed under the flag of the Confederate States, and met with no blockading vessels on his return.

Deponent further saith, that the privateer " Sally " also left the port of Charleston about the same time, and went to sea through the same channel, the weather being beautifully clear. Also the schooner ———, of Charleston, a large vessel, carrying perhaps 350 tierces of rice, went out through the same channel on the same day. And the Confederate States' transport-steamer " Edisto " was at the same time engaged outside of the bar taking up buoys, and the bar is about three miles and a-half from shore.

(Signed) ———.

Sworn to before me, this 15th day of October, 1861.
(Signed)   H. P. WALKER, *Vice-Consul.*

No. 99.

Lord Lyons to Earl Russell.—(Received December 2.)

My Lord,   Washington, November 18, 1861.
I HAVE the honour to transmit to your Lordship herewith, copies of three Reports which I have received from Consuls in the South concerning the state of the blockade.
I am, &c.
(Signed)   LYONS.

Inclosure 1 in No. 99.

Acting Consul Fullarton to Lord Lyons.

(Extract.)   Savannah, October 11, 1861.
I HAVE the honour to acknowledge receipt of your Lordship's circular despatch of the 14th August, calling my attention to the great importance of obtaining all possible particulars respecting the blockade of the Southern ports.
Your Lordship further observes that there are some points which should, as far as practicable, be particularly kept in view in obtaining information. These points are stated in the form of questions which I now proceed to answer :—
1. Ingress to this port has not been allowed to the blockading squadron after the first establishment of the blockade to any vessel knowingly or wittingly.
2. Egress has not been allowed knowingly and wilfully by the blockading squadron after the first establishment of the blockade to any vessel with cargo laden after the blockade in derogation to the fifteen days' grace. Numerous small vessels and transports have, almost daily, since the commencement of the blockade, and still continue to pass in and out of this port to different points on the coast. They do this through the passage which exists inside the islands forming the coast of Georgia, the blockading squadron being totally unable to prevent such communication.
3. Intermissions of the blockade have certainly taken place by the blockading force being wholly and deliberately withdrawn and sent elsewhere, but whether caused (*a*) by superior orders I am unable to say; (*b*) not caused by the weather; (*c*) not caused by chasing vessels endeavouring to break the blockade. The intermissions referred to take place frequently, more so recently than at the commencement of the blockade. The first occurred from the 29th or 30th May to about 12th June, the second from the 8th to the 14th September, the third from about the 15th or 16th to the 23rd September. During this intermission (on the 17th September) the screw-steamer ———, of about 700 tons, arrived in the river from England, having on the previous day coasted to the south for forty miles without seeing a blockading vessel. The fourth intermission occurred from the 29th September to the 4th October, since which day another took

place of about two days, and I am informed that yesterday morning the post was again deserted.

4. Sometimes the squadron consists of two vessels; at such times it is, when actually present, in my opinion, adequate to maintain an effective blockade in all respects. At other times, and most frequently, it consists of one vessel, which, when present, is adequate to guard the approaches against vessels of large tonnage; but hardly adequate, because of the position she usually occupies, to prevent ingress and egress of very small vessels, which, by reason of not being compelled to keep in the channel on account of their light draft, could possibly, particularly at night, evade the blockade. No instance of the latter kind has, however, yet taken place, vessels of that class finding it much more easy to get out by some of the inlets on the coast, which they reach, from this city, through the island channel already mentioned.

The above particulars refer exclusively to the blockade of the Savannah river according to the most reliable information within my reach. The blockade south of this is maintained in a very ineffective manner, the vessels being too few in number, and not suitable in class for the purpose of preventing access to the various harbours and inlets indenting it. The blockading vessels merely cruize up and down, visiting for a few days at a time one harbour after another. Advantage is not slow to be taken of this, as is shown by the numerous instances of vessels successfully running the blockade to and from the West Indies, in most cases without seeing the blockading vessels at all. Since the beginning of the blockade the line of steamers between this port and St. John's river, Florida, has kept up an uninterrupted communication. In a very few instances they have seen a blockading vessel off the St. John and Fernandina bars, but not sufficiently near to prevent their regular ingress and egress.

Inclosure 2 in No. 99.

Acting Consul Coppell to Lord Lyons.

My Lord,   *New Orleans, October 22, 1861.*

I HAVE the honour to acknowledge receipt of a circular despatch from your Lordship, of date 14th August, with respect to the blockade of the Southern ports, directing attention to the importance of obtaining all possible particulars respecting it, and, for convenience sake, your Lordship has placed in the form of questions some points which should be kept in view in obtaining information.

In reply, I have the honour to inform your Lordship that I have taken every means practicable to obtain information on the subject, and that, to the best of my knowledge and belief, no vessel has been allowed to enter or depart this port knowingly or willingly by the blockading squadron. Two or three small vessels, which have been loaded for some time, and waiting opportunities to elude the blockading vessels, have succeeded in leaving the neighbouring bayons within the past few days, but I am given to understand that the blockading squadron on this coast has been considerably increased, and ingress or egress is almost impossible.

With regard to the third question your Lordship propounds, I would beg respectfully to remind your Lordship of the great difficulty, in fact, almost impossibility, there is in obtaining any accurate information from the mouths of the river, in consequence of the distance from the city and the destruction of the telegraph wires below the forts.

Early in the present month some of the light draught vessels of the blockading force crossed the bar and proceeded up the river to the head of the passes, about fifteen miles distant from the mouth, took possession of the telegraph station, and commenced to build a fort, which would have commanded all the channels of the river, and the blockade could have been maintained with a much smaller force than is at present necessary. This design was frustrated on the morning of the 12th instant by an attack from the naval forces of the Confederate States, which resulted in the United States' vessels being driven out of the river, the materials for building the fort destroyed, and it is stated that one of the United States' vessels, supposed to be the " Preble," was sunk. No communication is now allowed lower than the forts, which are sixty miles below this city.

In reply to the fourth question, from the causes already stated, I beg to inform your Lordship that no reliable information of the names, armament, &c., of the vessels blockading can be obtained, nor how long each or any of them have been actually present, but it would seem there has been a force sufficient to maintain an effective blockade; for, from the time of its establishment, no vessels have entered, and since the 14th of June I have not heard of any vessels leaving this port by the river, with the exception of the Confederate States' steamer "Sumter."

Your Lordship's despatch shall at all times be before me, and I will not fail to transmit any information respecting the blockade that I may obtain.

I have, &c.

(Signed)   GEORGE COPPELL.

Inclosure 3 in No. 99.

Consul Bunch to Lord Lyons.

My Lord,   *Charleston, November 5, 1861.*

I AVAIL myself of the departure of the French Imperial corvette " Pronie," Commander de Fontagnes, to report to your Lordship that the blockade of this port and of the adjacent coast has undergone no particular change since the date of my last despatch. The remarks contained in my despatch to your Lordship of the 30th of September last apply strictly to the present condition of things. Small vessels arrive almost daily, whilst larger ships incur risk by approaching the coast.

I beg leave to inclose a list of the vessels which have entered this port of Charleston during the month of October. I also transmit a second copy of the list, in case your Lordship should desire to send it to Earl Russell.

The blockade of North Carolina has undoubtedly become more stringent. The port of Beaufort continues to be closed, and that of Wilmington has been carefully guarded. There are two British vessels in each of the above ports which entered when there was no blockade beyond a paper one, but as the questions involved in these cases are in the hands of your Lordship, I forbear from remarking upon them.

I have, &c.

(Signed)   ROBERT BUNCH.

Inclosure 4 in No. 99.

LIST of the Vessels that have entered Charleston Harbour from places beyond Bull's Bay, north-eastwardly, and South Edisto Bar south-westwardly, from September 30 to October 31, 1861.

Date.	No.	Class.	Name.	Master.	Cargo.	Where from.
October 1	1	Schooner	...	...	40 barrels rice	Georgetown, South Carolina.
1	2	Steamer	...	...	33 bags Sea Island cotton, maize, &c.	Savannah, Bluffton, Beaufort, &c.
5	3	Schooner	...	...	2,551 bushels rough rice	Santee.
8	4	Steamer	...	...	41 bales Sea Island cotton; 10 hogsheads sugar; 23 barrels molasses; 10 barrels lemons; and sundries	Fernandina, St. Mary's, Brunswick, and Savannah.
9	5	Schooner	...	...	2,900 bushels rough rice	Santee.
10	6	Sloop	...	...	2,050 bushels rough rice	Euhaw.
13	7	Steamer	...	...		Augusta, Savannah, and Beaufort.
13	8	Schooner	...	...	Merchandize	From the Gulf Stream, having sprung a leak, and put back in distress.
15	9	Ditto	...	...	2,000 bushels rough rice	Back River.
15	10	Steamer	...	...	193 bales Sea Island cotton, naval stores, pig iron, and fruit	Fernandina, St. Mary's, Savannah, Beaufort, and Edisto.
20	11	Ditto	...	...	110 tierces rice, 6 bales cotton, 110,000 shingles, and 3 yawl boats	Georgetown.
20	12	Brig-Schooner	...	...	Coffee and molasses	Nuevitas.
21	13	Schooner	...	...	8,000 bushels rough rice	Darien, Georgia.
21	14	Ditto	...	...	3,000 bushels rough rice	Darien.
21	15	Sloop	...	...	3,000 bushels rough rice	Santee.
17	16	Schooner	...	...	150 barrels rough rice	Ditto.
19	17	Ditto	...	...	2,600 bushels rough rice	Ditto.
24	18	Ditto	...	...	2,800 bushels rough rice	Combahee.
24	19	Sloop	...	...	2,050 bushels rough rice	Santee.
25	20	Steamer	...	...	101 bags Sea Island cotton, fruit, hides, iron, &c.	Fernandina, Brunswick, Savannah, and Edisto.
28	21	Schooner	...	...	2,900 bushels rough rice	Euhaw.
31	22	Ditto	...	...	2,250 bushels rough rice	Georgetown, South Carolina.
31	23	Ditto	...	...	14 bags Sea Island cotton, and 250 bushels corn	Beaufort.
31	24	Ditto	...	...	2,423 bushels rough rice	Pocotaligo.
31	25	Ditto	...	...	2,600 bushels rough rice	Combahee.

(Signed)   ROBERT BUNCH, *Consul.*

British Consulate, Charleston, October 31, 1861.

No. 100.

Acting Consul Magee to Earl Russell.—(Received December 5.)

My Lord,   *Mobile, October 14, 1861.*

I HAVE the honour to acquaint your Lordship that on the 7th instant the sloop ——, with a cargo of spirits of turpentine, forced the blockade and got safe to sea, without molestation from any of the ships-of-war at the entrance of this port.

I have, &c.

(Signed)   JAMES MAGEE.

No. 101.

Lord Lyons to Earl Russell.—(Received December 9.)

My Lord,   *Washington, November 25, 1861.*

I HAVE the honour to transmit to your Lordship a copy of a despatch and its inclosure which I have received from Commander Lyons, of Her Majesty's ship " Racer," relative to the blockade of the coast of North Carolina.

I have, &c.

(Signed)   LYONS.

Inclosure 1 in No. 101.

Commander Lyons to Lord Lyons.

(Extract.*j*   *" Racer," off Staten Island, New York, November 21, 1861.*

I HAVE the honour to annex herewith, for your Lordship's information, an extract from a letter of this day's date, addressed by me to Rear-Admiral Sir Alexander Milne, K.C.B.

Inclosure 2 in No. 101.

Commander Lyons to Rear-Admiral Sir A. Milne.

(Extract.)   *New York, November 21, 1861.*

YOU will have observed, Sir, that neither the entrance to the port of Wilmington by the New Inlet, Bogue Inlet, where, as I have already had the honour of reporting, I observed three schooners at anchor, nor the many other inlets between Cape Fear and Beaufort, are at present blockaded by the forces of the United States ; and I am of opinion that one sailing vessel, such as the " Braziliera," is not sufficient to maintain effectively the blockade of the port of Beaufort.

Several ships of the blockading squadron have recently been taken off their station to join the expedition which, I now learn, has arrived at Bull's Bay.

No. 102.

Consul-General Crawford to Earl Russell.—(Received January 1, 1862.)

(Extract.)   *Havana, December 3, 1861.*

THE British Vice-Consul at Key West informs me that the British schooner " Adeline," which cleared at this port for New York on the 9th ultimo, had been sent in there by the United States' cruizer " Connecticut," having been taken twenty miles from Carnaveral.

The Vice-Consul also reports the capture of the schooner " Zeeland " by the same United States' cruizer 140 miles north of the Tortugas.

No. 103.

Consul Molyneux to Earl Russell.—(Received January 2, 1862.)

(Extract.)   *Savannah, November 26, 1861.*

THE expected attack by the naval forces of the United States on the Southern coast has taken place, resulting in the capture, on the 7th instant, of Port Royal, in South Carolina. For several weeks previous to that event the force employed to blockade this coast seems to have been inadequate to prevent access thereto, probably in consequence of many of the vessels on that service having been required to take part in the expedition. The arrivals and departures during that time were numerous, consisting of eight Confederate and six British vessels, and I have every reason to believe that all those outward bound succeeded in running the blockade in safety.

I have now the honour to report the movements of the British vessels referred to above.

The steam-ship ——— sailed hence for Havre with a full cargo of cotton on the night of the 1st November. The night was dark and stormy, and, though the blockading squadron was observed off the port on that day, I have the strongest reasons for believing she escaped.

The schooner ———, sailing under a provisional register, dated 6th July, 1861, granted by Her Majesty's Consul in Charleston, arrived from Havana at Fernandina on 27th September, without seeing a blockading vessel, and went to Charleston by the inland passage.

The schooner ——— came into this port by Warsaw Sound, on the 1st October, unmolested, and sailed again for Havana on 27th October. I have since heard of her arrival there.

The schooner ——— arrived from the port of Halifax, Nova Scotia, on the 10th October, by Warsaw Sound, and sailed again, for the same place, on the 29th October. I have reason to believe this vessel also escaped.

The schooner ——— arrived at Doboy on the 11th November, from Kingston, Jamaica, and came to this city by the inland passage. She was chased for several hours on the 10th by a war steamer, from which she escaped. This is the first instance of a blockading vessel having been seen for some time off that port. This vessel is still in this port.

The most important arrival of all is that of the screw steamer ———. The first land made on this coast was Warsaw Island, off which she arrived at 4 o'clock on the morning of the 12th November. She steamed slowly up to the bar of the Savannah river, which she crossed at 7 o'clock, without seeing the blockading squadron. During the night a thick fog prevailed, which was gradually dispersed by the sun as the morning advanced. At the moment of crossing the bar, it had lifted sufficiently in-shore to make the land distinctly visible, while a thick bank still existed to seaward. The blockading squadron must have either gone into Port Royal during the night, or were enveloped in this fog bank, probably the latter, since two vessels of war could be seen close to the bar two hours after the ——— dropped anchor under the guns of Fort Pulaski.

Port Royal is situated about fifteen miles north of the entrance to the Savannah river. The harbour is large and commodious, and admirably adapted for a naval rendezvous. The batteries guarding the entrance were attacked on the morning of the 7th instant by the Federal fleet, and after a four hours' bombardment the Confederate troops were compelled to abandon their works, which were immediately taken possession of by the Federal forces. Beyond taking possession of a few of the adjacent islands, including Tybee Island, at the mouth of the Savannah river, they have, as yet, undertaken no other offensive operations, contenting themselves with securing the advantages already gained, by throwing up entrenchments, and landing stores and munitions from their transports. For a few days after the battle, this city was in imminent danger, and, had the Federalists followed up their advantage promptly, it would undoubtedly have fallen into their hands. The measures since adopted, however, by the military authorities, while by no means rendering its position impregnable, have vastly increased the difficulties of approach by any force, whether naval or military. Among others, obstructions in the shape of sunken vessels have been placed at various points in the river. The proximity of Port Royal, and the occupation of Tybee Island, will effectually blockade this river in future.

Several cotton planters in the neighbourhood of Port Royal set fire to and destroyed their dwellings and cotton crops, to prevent their falling into the hands of the Federalists. Should the latter obtain any further successes hereafter, I am convinced that nearly all those forced to abandon their houses will deal with their property in like manner. This will give your Lordship some idea of the bitter hostility to the United States' Government entertained by the people of the Southern States, and of their determination to achieve their independence.

No. 104.

Consul Molyneux to Earl Russell.—(*Received January 2, 1862.*)

My Lord,   *Savannah, November 30, 1861.*

WITH reference to my despatch of the 26th instant, in which I stated that the Federal forces had taken possession of Tybee island, situated at the entrance of the Savannah river, I have now to report, more particularly, that this island is at present occupied, as nearly as the Commanding Officer at Fort Pulaski can judge, by about 1,200 men.

On the morning of the 24th instant, a squadron consisting of five vessels of war and transports entered the river, and landed in the afternoon about 400 men; and, on the 27th instant, this force was increased, immediately after the arrival of two other vessels, by the landing of about 800 men.

The want of a navy rendering it impossible to prevent attacks, by Federal fleets, on the most exposed islands on the coast, induced the Confederate officer in command to withdraw his forces from many of them; the landing on Tybee was, therefore, unopposed.

The Federal occupation of Tybee will, hereafter, render the blockade of the Savannah river effective; their batteries will command the channel, and prevent any vessel coming in or going out. Warsaw entrance, which will admit vessels of considerable size, is, however, still open.

I have, &c.

(Signed)   E. MOLYNEUX.

No. 105.

Consul Molyneux to Earl Russell.—(Received January 2, 1862.)

My Lord,   *Savannah, December 7, 1861.*

I BEG to report to your Lordship four instances of vessels having successfully run the blockade of this coast since the date of my despatch of the 26th November.

The schooner —— made St. Catherine's Island on the 28th November, and entered Sapelo Sound same day without seeing a blockading vessel. Fell in with a Federal frigate on the eastern edge of the Gulf stream, which chased her for about five hours, but from which she made her escape.

The schooner —— made St. Catherine's Island at 3 o'clock in the afternoon of the 28th November, coasted south until daylight of 29th, at which time she entered Sapelo Sound without having fallen in with a blockading vessel.

The schooner —— made Ossabaw Island on the 1st December, and entered Ossabaw Sound the same day; was chased by a Federal steamer for a short time, but escaped.

The schooner —— made Warsaw Island on Friday, 30th November, coasted south to Sapelo Sound, by which she entered on the night of the 1st December, without seeing a blockading vessel. Anchored well in in the Sound, and on the morning of the 2nd December saw a Federal war steamer off the bar, not stationary, but under weigh, bound south.

All these vessels have come to this city by the inland passage.

I beg also to acquaint your Lordship with the fact that the Federal Government has adopted an unusual mode of blockading the Savannah river, namely, by sinking across the channel vessels heavily laden with stone. A few days ago, a large fleet of such vessels, accompanied by seven vessels of war, arrived off Tybee, some of which are now being sunk in such a manner as to prevent the passage of any vessel. It is reported to be the intention of the Federal Government to block up all the Southern harbours in the same manner.

I have, &c.

(Signed)   E. MOLYNEUX.

No. 106.

Consul Lynn to Lord J. Russell.—(Received January 2, 1862.)

My Lord,   *Galveston, October 19, 1861.*

WITH reference to my despatches of the 8th of August and of the 23rd ultimo, I have the honour to report that the United States' frigate mentioned in my despatch of the latter date as maintaining the blockade of this port is the "Santee," of 50 guns, Captain Frederick Engle commanding.

In accordance with the circular instructions transmitted by his Excellency Lord Lyons, under date of the 14th of August last, I have to state that,—

1st. Ingress has not been allowed by the blockading squadron after the first establishment of the blockade, to any vessels, knowingly or wittingly.

2nd. Egress has not been allowed, knowingly and wilfully, by the blockading squadron, after the first establishment of the blockade, to any vessels.

3rd. There has been no intermission of the blockade.

4th. The force on the spot has never consisted of more than one vessel, assisted by an armed schooner, one of the captures, of about 75 tons. This force has always maintained a position commanding the main entrance to the harbour, but the Pass of San Luis, at the west end of the island, has never been blockaded, though occasionally visited by the schooner. In the present position of the blockading frigate, any vessel attempting to enter by the main channel would have to pass under the guns of the frigate, but vessels of not more than six feet draught can have egress or ingress by the shore channels, east and west of the main channel, should they elect to run out, or approach these channels, during the night.

All the ports to the westward of Galveston are yet open.

I have, &c.
(Signed)   ARTHUR T. LYNN.

No. 107.

Consul Bunch to Earl Russell.—(Received January 2, 1862.)

My Lord,   *Charleston, November 20, 1861.*

WITH reference to my various despatches on the subject of the blockade of the ports of North Carolina, I have the honour to report that the British schooner ——— has again successfully entered the port of Wilmington, without any molestation or attempt at detention.

This vessel left Wilmington in September for the West Indies, with a full cargo of lumber. Her outward voyage was not interfered with, and she returned to Wilmington on the 15th instant with a cargo of 4,500 sacks of salt, seventy-one hogsheads of sugar, and other matters. This is the second round voyage which she has made without even seeing a ship of war of the United States.

It is my firm conviction that the ports of Newbern and Beaufort, in North Carolina, are blockaded only because the British ships ——— and ——— are known to be there; the other ports seem to be treated with the same disregard of "effectiveness" that has characterized the blockade of this coast since its commencement.

I have, &c.
(Signed)   ROBERT BUNCH.

No. 108.

Lord Lyons to Earl Russell.—(Received January 7, 1862.)

(Extract.)   *Washington, December 21, 1861.*

I HAVE the honour to inclose copies of despatches from Her Majesty's Consul and from the Acting British Consul at New Orleans and at Richmond, respecting the mode in which the blockade is maintained.

Inclosure 1 in No. 108.

Consul Bunch to Lord Lyons.

My Lord,   *Charleston, December 9, 1861.*

I HAVE the honour to transmit herewith to your Lordship, a list of the vessels which have entered the port of Charleston during the month of November. A second copy of the list is also inclosed for the use of the Foreign Office.

Since the commencement of November the privateer "Sallie" has returned from her first cruize in safety. Three of her prizes being vessels of 250 tons, have been brought into port for adjudication; two of them into ports of South Carolina.

Among the larger vessels which have sailed from Charleston during the same period may be enumerated the barque ——— with naval stores, and the steamers ——— and ———, laden with cotton.

The coast to the southward of Charleston is now more effectively blockaded than it ever has been, owing to the presence of the numerous vessels composing the expedition against Port Royal: but this city can still be approached by the various channels and inlets to the north-eastward.

In North Carolina the port of Wilmington has been for several days without a blockading vessel at either entrance. The British brig ———— and schooner ———— have both sailed for England with cargoes of naval stores, whilst the schooner ———— has lately arrived from Matamoros with wool, lead, and tin.

So far as I know, the port of Beaufort is still blockaded, owing to the presence of the British ships ———— and ————.

I have, &c.
(Signed)   ROBERT BUNCH.

Inclosure 2 in No. 108.

LIST of Vessels that have entered Charleston Harbour from places beyond Bull's Bay, north-eastwardly, and South Edisto Bar, south-westwardly, from October 30 to November 30, 1861.

Date.	No.	Class.	Name.	Master.	Where from.	Cargo.
Nov. 1	1	Steamer ..	..	..	..	Savannah ..	Ballast.
" 2	2	Schooner .	..	..	..	Ogeechee, Geo. .	3,900 bushels rough rice.
	3	Sloop ..	..	..	..	do. ..	2,880 bushels rough rice.
	4	do. ..	..	..	..	Santee ..	1,600 bushels rough rice.
	5	Steamer ..	..	..	..	Ogeechee, Geo. .	5,000 bushels rough rice.
" 4	6	do. ..	..	..	..	From prize brig "Grenada"	185 hhds. molasses, 71 hhds. sugar, honey, cedar, &c.
" 6	7	Schooner .	..	..	..	Combahee ..	3,800 bushels rough rice.
	8	Steamer ..	..	..	..	Fernandina, Brunswick, Savannah, Beaufort, &c.	11 bales Sea Island cotton, 256 boxes soap, 56 sacks coffee, 23 packages zinc and merchandize.
" 9	9	Schooner .	..	..	..	Combahee ..	2,200 bushels rough rice.
	10	do. ..	..	..	..	Back River ..	3,300 bushels rough rice.
	11	do. ..	..	..	..	do. ..	3,000 bushels rough rice.
	12	do. ..	..	..	..	do. ..	3,000 bushels rough rice.
	13	do. ..	..	..	..	do. ..	3,000 bushels rough rice.
	14	do. ..	..	..	..	Combahee ..	2,500 bushels rough rice.
" 10	15	do. ..	..	..	..	Santee ..	2,900 bushels rough rice.
	16	Sloop ..	..	..	..	do. ..	1,500 bushels rough rice.
	17	do. ..	..	..	..	Combahee ..	1.500 bushels rough rice.
	18	do. ..	..	..	..	do. ..	1,500 bushels rough rice.
	19	do. ..	..	..	..	Santee ..	2,030 bushels rough rice.
	20	Steamer ..	..	..	..	Georgetown, S.C.	38 tierces cleaned rice.
" 11	21	Prize brig	..	..	..	Edisto Inlet ..	Cargo previously taken out.
	22	Sloop ..	..	..	..	Combahee ..	2,000 bushels rough rice.
" 15	23	Prize brig .	..	..	..	St. Helena ..	
	24	Flat ..	..	..	..	From prize brig "Grenada"	51 hhds. sugar, 94 hhds. molasses.
	25	Schooner .	..	..	..	Euhau ..	23 bales Sea Island cotton, 33 bales upland cotton.
" 17	26	Sloop ..	..	..	..	Santee ..	1,800 bushels rough rice.
	27	Steamer ..	..	..	..	Ashepoo ..	20 bales Sea Island cotton.
" 18	28	Sloop ..	..	..	..	Santee ..	1,600 bushels rough rice.
" 19	29	Steamer ..	..	..	..	do. ..	86 barrels rice.
" 20	30	Schooner .	..	..	..	do. ..	128 barrels rice.
	31	do. ..	..	..	..	do. ..	2,900 bushels rough rice.
	32	Sloop ..	..	..	..	Georgetown ..	88 barrels rice.
" 23	33	do. ..	..	..	..	Santee ..	2,060 bushels rough rice.
" 25	34	Steamer ..	..	..	..	Hutchinson Island	22 bales Sea Island cotton, 22 bales upland cotton, 5,000 bushels rough rice, 150 bales rice straw.
" 26	35	Sloop ..	..	..	..	Santee ..	2,060 bushels rough rice.

(Signed)   ROBERT BUNCH, Consul.
British Consulate, Charleston, November 30, 1861.

Inclosure 3 in No. 108.

Acting Consul Coppell to Lord Lyons.

(Extract.)   *New Orleans, October 29, 1861.*

WITH reference to the circular despatch from your Lordship of date August 14th, respecting the blockade, I have the honour to transmit the following information, the facts of which I have but recently been in possession of.

On the morning of the 26th May last, the Italian barque ———, with a cargo of fruit for this port from Palermo, arrived at the mouth of the Mississippi River. It being low water at the time, there was not sufficient water on the bar of the Passe à l'Outre to admit her entrance. Whilst thus detained, and two or three days after her arrival, the United States' vessel "Brooklyn" came to the same place, announced the blockade, and notified the officer of the barque, who was summoned on board of the "Brooklyn," that his vessel would not be allowed to enter the river. The master remonstrated, and represented that his cargo was of a perishable nature, upon which Commander Poore held a consultation with his officers, when it was decided that the ——— should be permitted to enter, and permission was given the master to that effect, and a stated time (ten days) allowed him to take cargo and leave this port. I may state to your Lordship that Commander Poore was opposed to this, but yielded to the wishes of his officers. Accordingly the ——— crossed the bar on the 27th or 28th of May, was boarded in the river on the 28th by a custom-house officer, her manifest being endorsed to that effect; entered at the custom-house of this port on the 30th May; discharged her cargo and cleared on the 5th June for Liverpool, with a cargo of resin and staves.

The above information your Lordship may rely upon being correct.

Inclosure 4 in No. 108.

Acting Consul Cridland to Lord Lyons.

(Extract.)   *Richmond, November 12, 1861.*

ON the receipt of your Lordship's circular despatch of August 14, 1861, which arrived here from Charleston on the 7th day of October last, stating that your Lordship had been directed by Lord John Russell to call my special attention to the extreme importance of obtaining all the particulars possible concerning the blockade of the Southern ports, I at once had an interview with Mr. ———, and gave that gentleman a copy of the four questions respecting the blockade, as stated in your Lordship's despatch to me.

I have the honour to transmit herewith the answers appended to the questions.

The great distance of this port from the sea-coast makes it very difficult for me to procure any information on the subject of the blockade, unless obtained from the officials of the *de facto* Government.

Inclosure 5 in No. 108.

Memorandum.

UP to this date replies have been received only from Wilmington, North Carolina; Mobile, Charleston, St. Mark's, Florida, Savannah, Fernandina, Beaufort, North Carolina; and Brunswick, Georgia.

Question 1.—Has ingress been allowed by the blockading squadron after the first establishment of the blockade, to any and what vessels, knowingly and wittingly?

Question 2.—Has egress been knowingly and wilfully allowed by the blockading squadron after the first establishment of the blockade, to any and what vessels, with cargo laden after the blockade, and in derogation of the fifteen days' grace?

Answer.—The writers concur in stating that they do not know whether ingress or egress has been allowed to any vessels with the knowledge and consent of the blockading squadron.

Question 3.—Have intermissions of the blockade been caused (A) by the blockading force being wholly and deliberately withdrawn and sent elsewhere by superior orders? or (B) by weather? or (c) by chasing vessels endeavouring to break the blockade, or other vessels generally?

Answer.—They state that intermissions of the blockade, varying in point of duration, have frequently occurred, and that for several consecutive days no blockading ship has been in sight, but that the Collectors cannot accurately determine whether such intermissions have been caused by a deliberate withdrawal of the squadron by superior orders, by stress of weather, or being employed chasing vessels.

Question 4.—Has the force on the spot, from local considerations, number and class of cruizers, and so forth, been, when actually present (and, if so, for what time and in what respect), adequate to maintain an efficient blockade, or to cause obvious danger to those attempting to break it?

Answer.—They all affirm positively that at no time has the enemy's force been sufficient to maintain an efficient blockade, and that the best proof of this is afforded by the long lists of vessels which have entered and cleared from their respective ports from the date of the establishment of the blockade to the present time, copies of which have been communicated to Her Majesty's Government.

No. 109.

The Secretary to the Admiralty to Mr. Hammond.—(*Received January 8.*)

Sir, *Admiralty, January* 8, 1861.

I AM commanded by my Lords Commissioners of the Admiralty to transmit herewith, for the information of Earl Russell, copies of two letters, dated the 21st of November and 24th December last, from Commander Lyons of the "Racer," reporting his proceedings on the coast of the United States, and the inefficiency of the blockade of Wilmington, and other ports of the so-called Confederate States.

I am, &c.
(Signed) C. PAGET.

Inclosure 1 in No. 109.

Commander Lyons to Rear-Admiral Sir A. Milne.

Sir, "*Racer*," *off Staten Island, New York, November* 21, 1861.

I HAD the honour of informing you by telegraph on the 31st ultimo that it was my intention to leave that anchorage in Her Majesty's sloop under my command the following day.

I accordingly weighed under sail at 10·30 A.M. on the 1st instant. The wind before we got clear of New York bay entirely failed us; I therefore proceeded under steam as far as the Sandy Hook light-vessel, then put the fires out and made sail.

The next day (2nd), we experienced a fresh gale from the eastward, which gradually shifted round to the south-west, with a heavy cross swell.

On the afternoon of the 6th Cape Hatteras bearing north by south about eighty miles, it blew a violent gale from the westward, veering round on the 7th to the north-north-west. The wind during some of the puffs was eleven in force, and there was also a very heavy sea. The cutter at 5 A.M. on the 7th was washed away from the lee-quarter avits.

The weather moderated about noon of second day (7th). The ship behaved remarkably well in both the storms, and is not strained in the slightest degree.

On the morning of the 9th, Ocracoke Inlet bearing north north-west twenty miles, we exchanged colours with a United States' gun-boat standing to the south-west.

At noon of the 10th I arrived off Beaufort. Blockading this port was the United States' sailing barque "Brazalario" (lately purchased by the Government), carrying six guns. This vessel, on our approach, closed and communicated with us. I was informed that the United States' screw-steamer "Albatross" was also stationed off Beaufort, but had the previous day left for Hampton Roads, to replenish with coal. The flag of the Confederate States was flying on Fort Hampton, and inside the harbour were lying two ships with English colours flying.

A United States' steam-transport, with munitions of war, was, during the late gale, driven on shore near Beaufort, and was consequently made a prize of by the Secessionists.

Proceeding along the coast we observed, about twenty miles west of Beaufort, a wreck close in to the beach. She was a large paddle-wheel steamer, and from the number of men

Q 2

about her I imagine she was also driven on shore during the late gales. Arriving off Bogue Inlet, at 4 P.M. the same day (10th), we saw three schooners lying at anchor inside.

On the morning of the 11th I approached within about three miles of Cape Fear, thence stood close in off the entrance to the port of Wilmington. The Confederate flag was flying on rather a formidable earthwork battery, apparently recently thrown up, on Federal Point. After going a few miles along the coast I stood out to sea.

At 1 P.M. on the 12th instant, Cape Hatteras bearing north-west sixty-five miles, we fell in and communicated with Her Majesty's ship "Immortalité."

It had been my intention on my return passage to New York to have coasted along from Cape Lookout, but my purpose was frustrated by the strong northerly winds we experienced.

You will have observed, Sir, that neither the entrance to the port of Wilmington by the new inlets, Bogue Inlet, where, as I have already had the honour of reporting, I observed three schooners at anchor, nor the many other inlets between Cape Fear and Beaufort, are at present blockaded by the forces of the United States, and I am of opinion that one sailing vessel such as the "Braziliera" is not sufficient to maintain effectively the blockade of the port of Beaufort. Several ships of the blockading squadron have recently been taken off their station to join the expedition which, I now learn, has arrived at Bull's Bay.

I have the honour to report my arrival at this anchorage in Her Majesty's steam-sloop under my command, at 4 P.M. this day.

I have informed Her Majesty's Minister at Washington of my return, and have acquainted his Excellency that I shall be ready for sea on Saturday the 23rd instant.

The sanitary condition of the ship continues most satisfactory.

I beg to inclose the detached-service Returns.

I have, &c.
(Signed) ALGERNON LYONS.

Inclosure 2 in No. 109.

Commander Lyons to the Secretary to the Admiralty.

(Extract.) "*Racer*," *New York, December* 24, 1861.

THE Federal Government, with a view of closing the passages, have sunk a number of vessels laden with stones off the harbours of Charleston and Savannah.

No. 110.

Acting Consul Magee to Earl Russell.—(*Received January* 8, 1862.)

My Lord, *Mobile, October* 31, 1861.

I BEG leave to inform your Lordship that a British sloop called the ———, arrived here to-day with a cargo of coffee, cigars, &c., &c., from Havana, thus coming into port in face of any blockade.

I have, &c.
(Signed) JAMES MAGEE.

No. 111.

Acting Consul Magee to Earl Russell.—(*Received January* 8, 1862.)

My Lord, *Mobile, December* 3, 1861.

I BEG leave to apprise you that the Confederate schooner ———, bound to Havana, with a cargo of spirits of turpentine, left this port on Saturday last, 30th November, and made good her exit past the blockading fleet off Mobile Point.

She was chased by one of the Federal steamers, but outsailed her.

I have, &c.
(Signed) JAMES MAGEE.

No. 112.

Consul Lousada to Earl Russell.—(Received January 8, 1862.)

My Lord,   *Boston, December 23, 1861.*

I HAVE the honour to inclose copies of a letter which has appeared in this day's "Boston Courier," and which has made considerable sensation from its self-evident truthfulness.

The details set forth are better understood by a reference to the charts of the localities named.

It appears to me that on any question as to the efficiency of the blockade, this letter would have a very important bearing.

I have, &c.
(Signed)   FRANCIS LOUSADA.

Inclosure in No. 112.

Extract from the "Boston Courier."

THE BLOCKADE OF SOUTHERN PORTS.

To the Editor of the "Boston Courier."

I SAW the arrival of the schooner ———, with a cargo of naval stores. The report says that she ran out of the harbour during a gale, and thus eluded the blockading squadron—a most absurd idea for a vessel to leave a Southern port in a gale, that our blockading ships could not see. No vessel can leave a barred harbour in a gale, as the sea breaks constantly at the entrance ; the fact is, that our ports are not blockaded. What I shall state are facts in regard to Georgetown. I passed that port Friday, November 15, at midnight, and the frigate " Sabine " lay off the bar in nine fathoms of water, fifteen miles from the bar. Any man that feels disposed to look on the coast chart can see that nine fathoms of water must put the ship that distance off. I will here mention several facts in regard to the other ports: November 2, the " Preble " was lying off Berwick's Bay, twelve miles south by west from Shell Key Light, which leaves a space of twenty-six miles to get out or in to Berwick's Bay. Mobile has not been blockaded at all, when I have passed there five times in five months, and I never saw one of our ships in less than eleven fathoms of water, which would place them five miles from the bar. The schooner ——— came out on the 11th of October, 4·30 P.M., with a cargo of spirits of turpentine. The " South Carolina " blockading off Pass à l'Outre, caught her, as the wind and current set her in that direction. The steamer " Mohawk " lay of St. Mark's, seven miles from the bar. On the 14th of November saw the " Savannah " off Savannah at anchor, ten miles from the bar. Is it strange that the British steamer ——— entered that port and left without being seen ? On the 15th steamer " Alabama " lay at anchor nine miles south-east from the lighthouse off Charleston, and the steamer " Susquehanna " lay north by east from her ten miles. Any one can see how easily a ship could escape. I have yet to learn who saw the " Nashville " when she came out of Charleston ; she could not come out until four hours' flood, and they would never attempt to leave after one hour's ebb ; therefore you can see there is only six hours out of twenty-four that she would be able to escape, viz., two hours before high water and one hour after ; and, in fact, at certain times there is hardly sufficient at high water. I have known the " Columbia " to lie off the bar for forty-eight hours before she could get in, when her draft was only fourteen feet.

MORE ANON.

No. 113.

Mr. Elliot to Mr. Hammond.—(Received January 10.)

Sir,   *Downing Street, January 9, 1862.*

I AM directed by the Duke of Newcastle to transmit to you, for the information of Earl Russell, a copy of a despatch from the Lieutenant-Governor of New Brunswick, reporting the arrival of two vessels of the Confederate States at the port of St. John, having eluded the blockading squadron without any apparent difficulty.

I am, &c.
(Signed)   T. FREDK. ELLIOT.

Inclosure in No. 113.

The Lieutenant-Governor of New Brunswick to the Duke of Newcastle.

My Lord Duke,   *Fredericton, December* 16, 1861.
    I HAVE the honour to inform your Grace that within the last three weeks two vessels
have arrived in the harbour of St. John from ports situated in the so-called Confederate
States of America, having eluded, without any apparent difficulty, the vigilance of the
blockading squadron.
    One of these vessels belongs to the port of St. John, and sailed thence nominally
for Snowhill in Maryland on the 11th October last. On the 28th ultimo, however, she
returned to St. John, and was reported as from Cherrystone, in Virginia, a Confederate
port. The master stated that he experienced no difficulty whatever, either in running into
Cherrystone harbour or leaving it, and saw no signs of any blockading force or cruizers.
    The other vessel referred to arrived on the 13th instant from Georgetown, South
Carolina. She belongs to Charleston, and her master states that she sailed, without molestation or difficulty, from that port to Georgetown, and thence to St. John.
    I think it my duty to inform your Grace of these facts, and have, &c.
                          (Signed)   ARTHUR H. GORDON.

No. 114.

The Secretary to the Admiralty to Mr. Hammond.—(*Received January* 22.)

Sir,   *Admiralty, January* 20, 1862.
    I AM commanded by my Lords Commissioners of the Admiralty to transmit herewith,
for the information of Earl Russell, a copy of a letter dated the 1st instant from
Vice-Admiral Sir Alexander Milne, with its inclosure, from Commander Lyons of the
" Racer," reporting as to the state of efficiency of the blockade by the United States' forces
of the ports of Charleston, Wilmington, &c.
                                              I am, &c.
                          (Signed)   W. G. ROMAINE.

Inclosure 1 in No. 114.

Rear-Admiral Sir A. Milne to the Secretary to the Admiralty.

Sir,   *"Nile," at Bermuda, January* 1, 1862.
    REFERRING to my letter of the 9th ultimo I have now the honour to inclose for
their Lordships' information, an extract of a letter which I have just received from Commander Lyons, of Her Majesty's ship " Racer," dated the 19th ultimo, relative to the state
of efficiency in which he found the United States' blockade on his recent cruize as far
south as Port Royal, South Carolina, between the 1st and the 19th ultimo.
                                              I have, &c.
                          (Signed)   ALEXR. MILNE.

Inclosure 2 in No. 114.

Commander Lyons to Rear-Admiral Sir A. Milne.

(Extract.)   *December* 19, 1861.
    WITH reference to the blockade by the forces of the United States of the several
ports off which I have lately called in Her Majesty's steam-sloop under my command, I
would observe, with regard to Charleston, that a squadron consisting of two powerful
steamers, such as the " Susquehanna " and "Florida," aided by the sailing-vessel
" Roebuck," should be quite sufficient to maintain effectively the blockade of the port.
Nevertheless I have learnt, that on the 5th instant, the day previous to my arrival off the
harbour, the American steamer ————, drawing fourteen and a-half feet of water, and
laden with cotton, had sailed from Charleston for Nassau and Havana. Again, three days prior
to that (2nd), the steamer ———— left with a like cargo, and for the same destination.
    As regards Wilmington, I had the honour of reporting to you in my letter of

proceedings of the 21st ultimo that the blockade of that port by the new inlet was open. Since then the United States' steamer "Monticello" has been stationed off here ; I learn, however, that on the 4th instant the English brig ——-——, and the schooner ———, both laden with naval stores, had left Wilmington, and also, that on the same day the English schooner ——— arrived at that place from Matanzas with a cargo of wool, lead, and tin.

It would thus appear that the blockade, either intentionally or through want of ordinary vigilance, is not effective.

No. 115.

Consul Archibald to Earl Russell.—(Received January 24.)

(Extract.) *New York, January 11, 1862.*
I HAVE the honour to transmit herewith inclosed, for your Lordship's information, a copy of my despatch of the 9th instant to Lord Lyons, transmitting a list of British vessels against which proceedings are still pending.

Inclosure in No. 115.

Consul Archibald to Lord Lyons.

(Extract.) *New York, January 9, 1862.*
THE British vessels brought into this port for alleged violation of blockade, and against which proceedings are still pending, are the following :—

Schooner "Joseph H. Toone," of Nassau, New Providence, belonging to William H. Aymar, of St. Andrew's, New Brunswick, but latterly carrying on business at New Orleans.

Schooner "Ezelda," of Nassau, New Providence, belonging to the same owner.

Schooner "Louisa Agnes," of Halifax, Nova Scotia, belonging to H. Slanghenweight, of Lunenburg, Nova Scotia.

Ship "Cheshire," of Liverpool.

Ship "Express " of Hull.

Brig "Delta," of Liverpool.

Schooner "Jane Campbell," of Liverpool.

Schooner "Edward H. Bernard," of Nassau, New Providence.

Schooner "William H. Northrop," brought into this port two days since, port of registry unknown.

No. 116.

Earl Russell to Lord Lyons.

My Lord, *Foreign Office, February 15, 1862.*
HER Majesty's Government have had under their consideration the state of the blockade of the ports of Charleston and Wilmington.

It appears from the reports received from Her Majesty's naval officers that although a sufficient blockading force is stationed off those ports, various ships have successfully eluded the blockade ; a question might therefore be raised as to whether such a blockade should be considered as effective.

Her Majesty's Government, however, are of opinion that, assuming that the blockade is duly notified, and also that a number of ships is stationed and remains at the entrance of a port, sufficient really to prevent access to it or to create an evident danger of entering or leaving it, and that these ships do not voluntarily permit ingress or egress, the fact that various ships may have successfully escaped through it (as in the particular instances here referred to) will not of itself prevent the blockade from being an effective one by international law.

The adequacy of the force to maintain a blockade being always, and necessarily, a matter of fact and evidence, and one as to which different opinions may be entertained, a neutral State ought to exercise the greatest caution with reference to the disregard of a *de facto* and notified blockade ; and ought not to disregard it, except when it entertains a conviction, which is shared by neutrals generally having an interest in the matter, that the power of blockade is abused by a State either unable to institute or maintain it, or unwilling, from some motive or other, to do so.

I am, &c.
(Signed)   RUSSELL.

No. 117.

The Secretary to the Admiralty to Mr. Hammond.—(*Received February* 15.)

(Extract.)   *Admiralty, February* 12, 1862.

COPY of a letter from Commander Ross, of the "Desperate," received from Vice Admiral Sir Alexander Milne, relating to the efficiency of the blockade by the United States' forces of the ports in the Gulf of Mexico, is sent herewith for the information of Earl Russell.

Inclosure 1 in No. 117.

Commander Ross to Commodore Dunlop.

(Extract.)   *"Desperate," Havana, December* 28, 1861.

I HAVE the honour to acquaint you that, in obedience to an order from Captain Vansittart, of Her Majesty's ship "Ariadne," dated November 30, I immediately proceeded to sea, and herewith forward a report of my proceedings, accompanied by a list of the vessels actually seen by me.

1. On reaching Galveston on the night of December 5th I anchored in 9 fathoms, latitude 29° 12' north, longitude 94° 36' west, keeping a light up all night, and weighing on the morning of the 6th. Stood so close in as to see every object on shore distinctly, and anchored in latitude 29° 13' north, longitude 94° 47' west, in 5¼ fathoms, off the town ; the beach being, in my opinion, only about two miles distant, and nearly the entire length of Galveston Island being visible. The weather was partially foggy, but not so much so as to prevent our obtaining sights and meridian altitude. We cruized for about six hours in the neighbourhood without seeing any blockading ships, and I am of opinion that any vessel might easily escape from Galveston or St. Louis' Pass, and that the blockade there was not effective.

2. Touching at the remaining ports the blockade appeared to be generally actively maintained, and the number of vessels by no means decreased from what it was when I last visited the blockaded ports in August. At Tampa the vessel seen was at anchor inside Egmont Islands, and consequently could not be closed by us.

3. Standing close in-shore off St. Andrew's and St. Joseph's Bay (north of Port Blas) I was surprised that an anchorage affording such facilities for throwing supplies into Florida should remain apparently unnoticed, as I saw no signs of any blockading vessels in the neighbourhood.

4. Approaching close up to South-west Cape Appalachee (being as far as seemed practicable to take this ship, the Directory giving notice of various shoals which could not be traced on the General Chart, West Indies, sheet 4, and the plan supplied being upwards of 50' wrong in its longitude, and consequently useless), I was surprised to see only the "St. Louis" sailing corvette stationed off St. George's Sound, although it is possible that light draught steamers may have been stationed among the shoals.

Inclosure 2 in No. 117.

LIST of United States' Vessels blockading the Ports in the Gulf of Mexico, fallen in with by Her Majesty's ship "Desperate," since November 30, 1861.

Place.	Date.	Name of Vessel.	Guns.	Crew.	Tonnage.	Horse-Power.	Description of Vessel.	Commanded by	Remarks.
Galveston	1861 Dec. 6								"Santee," 50 guns, sailing-ship; said to be stationed there.
Atchafalaya	10	Montgomery	5	91	800	250	Three-masted screw-steamer	Commander D. Shaw	Boarded us off Ship Island shoal.
South-west Pass, Mississippi	13	Colorado	40	550	3,400		Screw-ship	Captain Bailey	Described as commanding the blockading squadron off Texas.
Ditto	13	De Soto	9	140	1,650		Paddle-brig	Commander W. Walker	Did not know their horse-power.
Ditto	13	A small tender					Schooner		
North-east Pass	14	Vincennes	20	160	700		Sailing-ship	Lieutenant Marcey	Armed merchant-vessel.
Pass à l'Outre	14	Mississippi	11	400	1,692		Paddle-barque	Captain Selfridge	Cruizing at the entrance.
Ditto	14	Kingfisher	9	70	500		Sailing-barque		Cruizing.
Off Naso Sound	16	Aruel schooner					Schooner		Did not know their horse-power.
Horn Island	17	Two armed schooners	3	20			Ditto		Going from Mobile towards Chandeleurs.
Off Mobile	17	Hunkville	50	400	1,000		Three-masted screw-schooner	Commander Price	Hoisted no colours.
Ditto	17	A steamer			1,726		Sailing-frigate	Captain Powell	Similar to De Soto; hoisted United States' colours.
Ditto	17	Potomac	12				Screw-schooner		
Pensacola	18	Niagara	9	700	4,500		Screw-ship	Captain McKean	
Ditto	18	A steamer					Paddle-brig		Apparently a tender.
Ditto	18	Schooner launch					Two masts		Looked like a small river-boat.
St. George's Sound	23	(Supposed) St. Louis	20				Sailing-ship		Recognized as the St. Louis seen last August.
Tampa Bay	24	A large barque					Sailing-barque		Hoisted United States' colours, and appeared to be an armed store-ship.
Off Tampa Bay	24	A steamer					Steamer		Seen to south-eastward, and appeared to be steering for the Tortugas.

The steamer seen going from Mobile towards Chandeleurs I believe to have been the "New London," of four 32-pounders, 80 men, and 400 tons, described to me as being stationed among these islands; the one seen at Pensacola answered the description of the "Coyler," similar in all respects to the "De Soto." Besides these actually seen, I had information of the "Massachusetts" being in Chandeleurs, she being the vessel that boarded us in August; also of the "South Carolina" (formerly seen at Galveston) being now in Batavia Day.‡

Her Majesty's ship "Desperate," at Havana, December 28, 1861.

(Signed)   J. F. ROSS, Commander.

Mr. Mason to Earl Russell.—(Received February 17.)

My Lord,   109, *Piccadilly, February* 17, 1862.

I HAVE the honour to transmit to your Lordship herewith (by permission) returns of vessels entered and cleared at the blockaded ports of the Confederate States of America at the respective dates to which they refer.

Your Lordship will observe that the Returns from the ports of Charleston and Savannah only are up to the 31st of October last ;

From New Orleans, Mobile, Pensacola, and Lavaca, to the dates given, in August;

And from Wilmington till 10th September.

Your Lordship will further observe, that in the list from New Orleans a large number were inland by the River Mississippi, and therefore involved no question of a breach of blockade.

Wishing to be perfectly frank it may be proper to remark also, that others from some of the ports may have been *quasi* inland ; that is to say, through the estuaries and sounds along the coast. I state as an example, from New Orleans to Mobile, where the route for small vessels may or may not have been through the inland sounds. But in regard to the latter, I do not see why the obligations of a blockade do not extend as fully to them as by access to the port from the open sea.

These estuaries or sounds are accessible by inlets from the sea, and, if not guarded, the ports to which they lead may be reached as successfully by sea-going vessels of light draft through those channels as by a direct sea route.

That the Government of the United States so considered, is proved by the fact that the inland sea communication between New Orleans and Mobile, Charleston and Savannah, and perhaps other places, is claimed to be blockaded by naval forces of that Government.

The transcripts herewith were those furnished to me by my Government, to be communicated to your Lordship. Although purporting to be copies of the original Returns, they were copies made at the proper Department at Richmond from those Returns, and are therefore authentic.

I ask permission also to include herewith a printed list of vessels entered and cleared at ports in Cuba from and to the blockaded ports of the Confederate States. Thse, for the most part, are enumerated in September; and all for the months of November and December are, of course, not included in the transcripts from my Government. This paper, sent to me from Havana, was taken from official documents there by a gentleman of intelligence and integrity, well known to me, and worthy of entire reliance. The marginal notes are of course unofficial. The fact (assumed) of the arrival of the vessels cleared (at their ports of destination) was matter of notoriety, from the almost daily intercourse between Havana and those ports.

I have no official Returns from my Government for the months of November, December, and January, to be accounted for in the fact that until very recently it could not be known when I might reach London. But, as your Lordship is doubtless aware, breaches of the blockade at most if not all of these ports by vessels of large as well as of small tonnage, both inward and outward-bound, have been during the last three months, and yet are, constantly reported.

I have, &c.
(Signed)   J. M. MASON.

Inclosure in No. 118.

Lists of Vessels which have run the Blockade of Southern Ports.

[The greater part of the Lists inclosed in this letter are printed as No. 96. The following are the further Lists.]

(1.)—LIST of Vessels entered and cleared at Port Lavaca, Texas, from April 19 to August 7, 1861.

Date of Arrival.	Class.	Name.	Where from.	Date of Clearance.	Where bound.
April 29	..	..	Boloxi, Mississippi	April 27	Hansboro, Mississippi.
,, 29	Steam-ship .	..	New Orleans ..	,, 27	New Orleans.
May 1	ditto	..	ditto ..	May 2	ditto.
,, 2	Schooner ..	..	Pensacola ..	,, 6	Pensacola.
,, 7	Steam-ship .	..	New Orleans ..		
,, 20	Schooner ..	..	Galveston ..		
June 13	ditto ..	..	ditto ..		
July 4	ditto ..	..	ditto ..		
	Steam-ship .	..	.. ..	May 15	New Orleans.

(Signed)   J. H. DAVIS, *Surveyor.*

(2.)—LIST of Vessels arrived and cleared at the Port ot Wilmington, N. C., from August 10 to September 10, 1861.

Date of Arrival.	Class.	Name.	Port where from.	Date of Clearances.	Port bound for.
Aug. 15	Schooner ..	..	Beaufort, N. C. ..	Aug. 16	Georgetown, S. C.
,, 15	do. ..	..	do. ..	,, 21	Washington, N. C.
,, 15	do. ..	..	Newbern ..	,, 22	Newbern, N. C.
,, 15	do. ..	..	Beaufort, N. C. ..	,, 26	Beaufort, N. C.
,, 15	do. ..	..	Hyde County ..	,, 27	Hyde County.
,, 17	Steamer ..	..	Beaufort ..	Privateer	In Port.
,, 20	Schooner ..	..	Shallotte, N. C. ..	Aug. 22	Shallotte, N. C.
,, 23	do. ..	..	Elizabeth City ..	,, 23	Georgetown, S. C.
,, 25	do. ..	..	Beaufort ..	,, 29	Hertford, N. C.
,, 26	do. ..	..	do. ..	,, 30	Beaufort.
,, 27	do. ..	..	Havana ..	..	In Port.
,, 28	Steamer ..	..	Beaufort ..	,, 29	Charleston, S. C., Privateer.
Sept. 7	Schooner ..	..	Nassau ..	..	In Port.
,, 5	do. ..	..	Beaufort, N. C. ..	Sept. 5	Georgetown, S. C.
,, 6	do. ..	..	Nassau ..		In Port.

Collector's Office, Wilmington, N. C.

(Signed)   JAMES T. MILLER, *Collector.*

(3.)—LIST of Vessels entered and cleared at the Port of Charleston, South Carolina, from 17th to 30th September, 1861.

Date of Entry.	Class.	Name.	Whence arrived.	Date of Clearance.	Port of destination.
Sept. 18	Schooner ..	..	Combahee River, S.C.		
,, 19	Steamer ..	..	Fernandina, Fla.		
,, 20	Schooner ..	..	Georgetown, S.C.		
,, 23	Schooner ..	..	Santa River. S.C. ..		
,, 30	Sloop ..	..	Pon-Pon River		
,, 30	Steamer ..	..	ditto ..	Sept. 24	Fernandina. Fla.

(Signed)   W. F. COLCOCK, *Collector.*
Collector's Office, Charleston, South Carolina,
September 30, 1861.

List of Vessels Entered and Cleared at the Port of Charleston, South Carolina, during the month of October 1861.

Date of Entry.	Class.	Name.	Port where from.	Date of Clearance.	Port of Destination.	Flag.	Remarks.
October 1	Steamer	...	Fernandina, Florida	October 2	Fernandina	Confederate States of America.	
„ 2	Schooner	...	Georgetown, S.C.	„ 2	Ditto	Ditto.	
„ 7	Ditto	...	Ditto	„ 2	Ditto	Ditto.	
„ 7	Sloop	...	Ditto	„ 7	Matanzas...	British.	
„ 9	Steamer	...	Fernandina, Florida	„ 9	Fernandina	Confederate States of America.	
„ 11	Sloop	...	Santee River	„ 9	Ditto	Ditto.	
„ 11	Steamer	...	...	„ 11	Havana	Ditto.	
„ 14	Ditto	...	Savannah, Georgia	„ 11	Ditto	Ditto.	
„ 16	Ditto	...	Fernandina	„ 19	Fernandina	Ditto.	
„ 16	Schooner	...	Santee River, S.C.	„ 19	Ditto	Ditto.	
„ 21	Ditto	...	Ditto	„ 19	Ditto	Ditto.	
„ 21	Steamer	...	Georgetown, S.C.	„ 19	Ditto	Ditto.	
„ 22	Schooner	...	Darien, Georgia	„ 19	Ditto	Ditto.	
„ 22	Ditto	...	Ditto	„ 19	Ditto	Ditto.	
„ 22	Sloop	...	Santee River, S.C.	„ 19	Ditto	Ditto.	
„ 22	Barque	...	Ditto	„ 23	Liverpool ...	Ditto	Still in port.
„ 22	Brig	...	Ditto	„ 23	Savannah, Georgia	Ditto.	
„ 28	Steamer	...	Fernandina, Florida	„ 28	Fernandina	Ditto.	
„ 28	Schooner	...	Nassau, New Providence	„ 28	Ditto	British	With cargo.
„ 28	Ditto	...	Nuevitas, Cuba	„ 28	Ditto	Ditto	Ditto.
„ 28	Ditto	...	Ditto	„ 29	Cuba	Confederate States of America.	
„ 28	Ditto	...	Ditto	„ 30	Georgetown, S.C.	Ditto.	
„ 28	Ditto	...	Ditto	„ 31	Savannah, Georgia	Ditto.	
„ 31	Steamer	...	Havana	„ 31	Ditto	Ditto	Ditto.

(Signed)   WM. F. COLCOCK, *Collector.*

Collector's Office, Charleston, South Carolina, October 31, 1861.

(4.)—A List of Vessels entered at and cleared from the Port of Savannah, Georgia, during the month ending October 31, 1861.

Date.	Class.	Name.	From what Port.	To what Port.	Character of Cargo.
1861.					
Oct. 5	British schooner		Havana	..	Coffee, &c.
„ 7	Confederate States' schooner		..	Havana	Rice.
„ 10	do.		..	St. Thomas	do.
„ 14	British brig		Halifax	..	Fish, sat ,
„ 15	do.		Havana	..	Coffee, &c.
„ 24	British schooner		..	Havana	Rice.
„ 25	Confederate States' schooner		..	Nassau	Turpentine, &c.
„ 25	do.		..	do.	do.
„ 25	do.		..	do.	Rice.
„ 26	do.		..	do.	do.
„ 26	do.		..	Havana	do.
„ 28	British brig		..	Halifax	Turpentine, &c.
„ 28	Confederate States' sloop		..	Havana	Rice,
„ 29	British steamer		..	Havre	Cotton.

Attest,   Z. N. WINKLER, *Clerk.*
(Signed)   JOHN BOSTON, *Collector.*

(5.)—Mercantile Weekly Report.—Extra.   List of Vessels that have run the Blockade.

HAVANA.

	Nationality.	Class.	Name.	Cargo.	Port.	
1861						
May 26	Spanish	Brig	.. ..	Lumber	Fernandina.	
„ 28	American	Schooner	.. ..	Ballast	Galveston.	
June 6	British	ditto	.. ..	Assorted	New Orleans.	
„ 8	Spanish	Barque	.. ..	ditto	ditto.	
„ 13	ditto	ditto	.. ..	ditto	ditto.	
„ 16	British	Schooner	.. ..	ditto	ditto.	
„ 20	ditto	ditto	.. ..	ditto	ditto.	
„ 28	Spanish	Barque	.. ..	Lumber	St. Mary's.	
Aug. 3	British	Schooner	.. ..	Rice	Savannah.	
„ 8	ditto	ditto	.. ..	Cotton.	New Orleans.	
„ 11	ditto	ditto	.. ..	Rice	Newbern.	
„ 30	ditto	ditto	.. ..	ditto	ditto.	
Sept. 9	ditto	ditto	.. ..	Resin ‚	New Orleans.	
„ 15	ditto	ditto	.. ..	Rice	Savannah.	
„ 26	ditto	ditto	.. ..	ditto	Beaufort.	
Oct. 1	ditto	ditto	.. ..	Assorted	New Orleans	Captured in Gulf; taken to Key West; released.
„ 16	ditto	Ketch	.. ..	Turpentine	ditto.	
	Confederate	Steamer	.. ..	Passengers	Charleston	Via Cardenas.
„ 28	British	Schooner	.. ..	Turpentine	New Orleans	
	ditto	ditto	.. ..	Cotton.	ditto.	
„ 30	ditto	ditto	.. ..	Rice	Charleston	Viâ Nassau.
Nov. 4	ditto	ditto	.. ..	ditto	Savannah	ditto.
	ditto	ditto	.. ..	ditto	Charleston.	ditto.
„ 8	Mexican	ditto	.. ..	Turpentine	New Orleans.	
„ 10	British	ditto	.. ..	Rice	Savannah.	
„ 11	ditto	ditto	.. ..	ditto	ditto	Viâ Nassau.
„ 13	ditto	ditto	.. ..	ditto	ditto	ditto.
„ 20	ditto	ditto	.. ..	ditto	Wilmington	ditto.
	ditto	ditto	.. ..	ditto	Savannah.	
„ 26	Confederate	ditto	.. ..	Turpentine	New Orleans.	
Dec. 3	ditto	Steamer	.. ..	Cotton	ditto.	
„ 5	ditto	Schooner	.. ..	Turpentice	Mobile.	
„ 11	ditto	ditto	.. ..	ditto	Apalachicola.	
„ 21	ditto	ditto	.. ..	ditto	New Orleans.	
„ 24	British	ditto	.. ..	Cotton	ditto.	
„ 25	Confederate	ditto	.. ..	Turpentine	ditto.	
„ 26	ditto	ditto	.. ..	ditto	Apalachicola.	
„ 27	Mexican	ditto	.. ..	Cargo	Brazos Santiago.	
„ 31	Confederate	Schooner	.. ..	Turpentine	Mobile.	

MATANZAS.

	Nationality.	Class.	Name.	Cargo.	Port.	
1861						
May 31	American	Brig	.. ..	Rice	Savannah.	
June 23	ditto	Schooner	.. ..	Ballast	Galveston.	
Aug. 12	British	ditto	.. ..	Rice	Newbern.	
„ 21	Confederate	Ketch	.. ..	ditto	Charleston	First vessel that entered under Confederate flag.
Nov. 10	ditto	Schooner	.. ..	ditto	ditto.	
	British	ditto	.. ..	ditto	Savannah	Viâ Nassau.
„ 11	ditto	ditto	.. ..	ditto	Charleston.	

CARDENAS.

	Nationality.	Class.	Name.	Cargo.	Port.	
1861						
Oct. 28	Confederate	Steamer	.. ..	Passengers	Charleston.	
„ 22	ditto	Schooner	.. ..	Rice	ditto.	

LIST of Vessels that sailed from Cuban Ports and ran the Blockade.

HAVANA.

	Nationality.	Class.	Name.	Cargo.	Port.	
1861						
May 28	British	Steamer	..	Assorted	Mobile.	
June 3	do.	Schooner	..	Sugar	Georgia coast	Supposed to be Savannah.
,, 8	do.	do.	.. ..	Cigars	Berwick Bay.	
	Spanish	Barque	.. ..	Ballast	St. Mary's river.	
,, 28	British	Schooner	.. ..	Assorted	Barataria.	
Aug. 8	do.	do.	.. ..	Lead and coffee	Savannah.	
,, 19	do.	do.	.. ..	Coffee	Beaufort.	
,, 20	do.	do.	.. ..	Assorted	Barataria.	
Sept. 19	do.	do.	.. ..	Coffee	Savannah.	
	do.	do.	.. ..	Assorted	. . .	Captured off Berwick's Bay.
,, 24	do.	do.	. . ..	Coffee	Savannah.	
,, 26	do.	do.	.. ..	. .	. . .	Ditto.
Oct. 12	do.	Steamer	.. ..	Coffee	. . .	Captured off Key West.
	do.	Schooner	.. ..	do.	Savannah.	
,, 23	do.	Ketch	.. ..	do.	Mobile.	
,, 28	do.	Schooner	.. ..	Rum, sugar, coffee	. . .	Captured off Fernandina.
,, 29	Confederate	Steamer	.. ..	Coffee	Fernandina.	
Nov. 8	British	Schooner	.. ..	. .	Barataria.	
,, 9	do.	do.	.. ..	Coffee	Brazos Santiago.	
	do.	do.	.. ..	Fruit	. . .	Captured off Stone Inlet.
	do.	do.	.. ..	Coffee	. . .	Captured off Cape Canaveral, 40 miles E.
,, 12	do.	do.	.. ..	Assorted	Brazos Santiago.	
	do.	do.	.. ..	do.	do.	
	Mexican	do.	.. ..	do.	do.	
,, 23	British	Ketch	.. ..	Coffee	Savannah.	
	do.	Schooner	.. ..	do.	do.	
	do.	do.	.. ..	do.	do.	
	do.	do.	.. ..	do.	do.	
Dec. 1	do.	do.	.. ..	do.	Wilmington.	
,, 9	do.	do.	.. ..	do.	Savannah.	
,, 14	do.	do.	.. ..	do.	do.	
,, 22	do.	do.	.. ..	do.	Mobile.	
,, 24	do.	Steamer	.. ..	. .	Barataria.	
	do.	Schooner	.. ..	Coffee	Savannah.	
	Confederate	do.	.. ..	Sundries	Mobile.	
,, 27	British	Steamer	.. ..	European	Texas.	
,, 31	do.	Schooner	.. ..	Sundries	Mobile.	
	do.	do.	.. ..	Coffee	Savannah.	

MATANZAS.

	Nationality.	Class.	Name.	Cargo.	Port.	
1861						
June 4	American	Brig	.. ..	Molasses	Savannah.	
	do.	Schooner	.. ..	do.	do.	
July 6	do.	do.	.. ..	do.	do.	
	British	Brig	.. ..	do.	do.	
Aug. 23	do.	Schooner	.. ..	Coffee	Charleston.	
,, 31	do.	Ketch	.. ..	do.	do.	

CARDENAS.

	Nationality.	Class.	Name.	Cargo.	Port.	
1861						
June 8	British	Schooner	.. ..	Sugar	Savannah.	
Aug. 1	do.	do.	.. ..	Molasses	Charleston.	
,, 13	do.	do.	.. ..	do.	Savannah.	
Nov. 1	do.	do.	.. ..	. .	. . .	Captured off Charleston.

N.B.—Since the above was put in type, one steamer and four schooners have arrived, with cotton and naval stores, at Havana and Matanzas from Confederate ports.

www.ingramcontent.com/pod-product-compliance
Lightning Source LLC
Chambersburg PA
CBHW060245030726
47493CB00025B/2322